The
Spaghetti Afterlife

A Novel by
L.J. Zinkand

Silverlining Press
Talent, Oregon

The Spaghetti Afterlife

© L.J. Zinkand 2012

ISBN-13: 978-0615605760
ISBN-10: 0615605761

Library of Congress Control Number: 2012905186

Cover Art by L.J. Zinkand

Silverlining Press
PO Box 1346
Talent, Oregon 97540
www.ljzinkand.com

ACKNOWLEDGMENTS

I am lucky to have had these people, all excellent writers themselves, be so helpful in the shaping of this book: Ruth Wire, Cynthia Rogan, Darlene Ensor, Phil Loveless, Kris Heywood, Sarah Cornett-Hagen, Carol SeCoy, Heidi Silva and Linda Waller, plus Lyda Woods and Cassandra Wass. A boatload of thanks to Mary McLean and Lily Stephen for their sage advice in matters of life, love and publishing.

And of course, many thanks to my husband Wayne, who found me again after thirty-six years and shed all sorts of light on the finishing touches.

For my family

ONE

1995

JULIA LLOYD SAT IN THE FUNERAL HOME with her brothers and her father's wife Rose, choosing hymns and a suit while the rain drizzled outside on a gray spring day in the Poconos.

"Could we use a tie with a little mustard on it?" she asked, attempting to smooth the wrinkles out of her crumpled black satin shirt. "He always seemed to have a tiny bit of food stuck somewhere on the front of his clothing."

Her brothers, Teddy and Nate, burst out laughing in spite of the setting. Even Rose managed a tiny squeak of a giggle. Julia felt her father, Ed, chuckling from a distant realm. He would have appreciated that jab, too. She drew her small frame forward and rested her elbows on the table in a feeble attempt to stay awake after traveling for twenty-two hours.

Julia's father had lay submerged, deep in a coma for the past six weeks. At first, she and Teddy had flown in from California to join the rest of the family in pleading, aching, bargaining, even teasing their father into waking up. After a few weeks they moved him to a hospice facility and agreed to let him slip away on his own. Julia and Teddy went back to their lives in Northern California to wait.

"He's not even *in* there anymore," Nate lamented, when they'd disconnected all the tubes. "Every time I visit, I whisper in his ear, 'What's keeping you here? Is there anything else you need us to do?'"

"Bring him his cat," Julia suggested.

So the next day Nate and Rose brought in Kinkster the Siamese, who curled up on Ed's stomach and took a nap. When visiting hours were over, their father passed away. Teddy called Julia to tell her the news. "It looks like we'll have to fly to New York, hook up with Nate and Uda, then drive the rest of the way up there... but I haven't been able to find a bereavement fare that isn't astronomical."

Julia gulped back a sob. "Let me get myself together and take a look. I'll call you back in a few minutes." She sat down on her bed and wept, releasing a tangled web of hope, misery and relief. Her own two cats, Joey and Bee, quickly jumped on the bed beside her, plying her with tiny licks and head butts in an effort to comfort her. Erin, her housemate, was still at work, so Julia rocked back and forth with her head in her hands, waiting for the gut-clattering wave of grief to pass. Then she blew her nose, lit a beeswax candle and whispered a Tibetan prayer. Pushing a swag of curly blonde hair away from her face, she got up and turned on her computer.

Scrolling through Compuserve's primitive online ticketing system, she noticed a round trip fare from San Francisco to New York for $441. She blinked. It was still there. "Dad?" she whispered. Hearing nothing but the low buzz of her computer, she clicked on the fare, booked tickets for herself and Teddy, and called the airline to see if it was real.

"Did you do this from home?" the agent asked.

"Yeah I, uh, did it on Compuserve." Feeling like a hacker caught red-handed, she added, "What's the bereavement fare for this flight?"

"That would have been $1,200. Honey, you did good."

The next night Julia and her brother Teddy sat in the San Francisco airport, snacking on popcorn and beer. A brief wave of giddiness interrupted Julia's gloom when the bartender paused and gave her a wink. "You're old enough, right?"

"Working for his tips," she muttered to Teddy. Matching light hair and a relaxed demeanor seemed to belie the brother and sister's ages; Julia freshly forty, and Teddy two years older. "You're looking a little gaunt," she added.

"Yeah, lots of overtime. We're putting in a new mainframe."

An episode of *Seaquest* played on the bar TV as the brother and sister sipped their beers in the numbing vacuum that surrounds recent death.

"Dad really liked that show," Teddy said.

Julia glanced at the television just as the underside of a boat appeared on the screen. Images of foundering ships rolling over and sliding down into murky oblivion quickly flooded her mind and she shuddered. "I guess he never lost his fascination with undersea stuff."

An hour later they waited for a rare San Francisco thunderstorm to finish pounding the outside of the plane until the flight attendants finally closed the doors. By the time they reached cruising altitude Julia had dipped into an eerie half-sleep as a baby howled somewhere in the back. She woke to warm morning sunlight streaming through the windows as the pilot announced their descent. Then they dropped through a thick cloud cover, emerging over Manhattan Island. The Statue of Liberty stood graciously in the harbor as the plane banked for a panoramic view of all the sites Julia remembered—Yankee Stadium, the Twin Towers, the Chrysler Building, the Empire State Building... everything in full view as if it were a board game of itself, surrounded by a curtain of fog and low clouds.

"Always picture perfect," Teddy remarked, when Nate and his wife Uda came into focus at the airport in long, carefully tended ponytails and stylish black trench coats. After they'd taken turns squeezing each other silently, Julia moaned, "I *have* to have some coffee."

"Over here," Nate said, pointing her toward a kiosk where a stout, middle-aged woman stacked paper cups.

After the woman poured her coffee, Julia called across the counter, "I'm sorry—I'm allergic to non-dairy creamer. Do you have any regular milk?"

"Can't you see it over there in the cooler?" the woman snapped on her way to the cash register.

Nate put his hand on Julia's shoulder and whispered in her ear, "Can I have some cream, or should I just go fuck myself?"

Fog had settled over the airline terminal when they pulled away in a rented car, laughing helplessly to Howard Stern as he railed all the way to Pennsylvania about some kind of filled-crust pizza. "It's *satanic!*" he yelled out over the Tri-State area.

Rose stood at the front door in jeans and one of Ed's t-shirts, her deep blue eyes wiped plain and swollen by grief.

"Kinkster brought in a chipmunk last night. It's still alive somewhere in the house."

Julia nodded numbly and stepped in the door. After she dropped her rolling suitcase in one of the extra bedrooms, she joined her brothers at the kitchen table in muffled disbelief. Just beyond the sliding glass door, several squirrels milled around on the patio, glancing toward the door. Teddy opened it and tossed out a few peanuts from a nearby canister.

"No, like this," Nate interrupted, kneeling on the threshold. He held out a peanut and one of the squirrels edged up to his hand. It gingerly opened its mouth, took the nut and scampered off the patio.

"Dad trained them. The big one's braver."

The town of Nanticoke was coated with a dreary grey wash that afternoon when the pastor came by to take them down to the funeral home. "Even the flowers are hiding," remarked Rose, as they rode past spring-drenched suburban lawns.

Julia took a deep breath and stepped into the mortuary. The funeral director appeared in the hallway and introduced himself as Charles, ushering them into sitting room. Charles was so fair-skinned and soft-spoken that Julia could hardly imagine him in the business of brokering caskets and pickling cadavers. New-age harp music tinkled softly in the background while he went over the costs with Rose. In a gentle voice, he explained crematory issues.

"Couldn't we rent something for the viewing?" Nate asked. "They're just going to burn it."

But there was built-in liability about transporting a body to and from church that required something wooden, and you had to buy it. There would be no getting around that; Ed loved his church and his choir, and Rose was making the final decisions.

They entered the showroom of caskets. On display were ostentatious $22,000 coffins made with copper and steel, and varying degrees of wooden boxes. "Can you *believe* this?" Julia whispered, slightly horrified that anyone would want to keep their spirit entombed and decaying for all time in one of the metal monstrosities.

"Reminds me of my house, with all the knotty pine," Teddy remarked, pointing to a plain one.

"How did we even *get* here?" Rose wondered out loud.

They nodded back at her in bewildered agreement.

"A lot of his patients and colleagues are going to show up to say goodbye," Nate said. "We can't just stick him in a plain one."

"But these..." Julia mused, tapping the side of an absurdly ornate oak box with one knuckle, "...are a bit much."

Rose settled on a modest "Newport Poplar" with beveled edges.

"Julia, are you going to play something for the service?" Teddy asked.

"No... I don't think I can do it without crying. Besides, I need to focus on staying vertical." Feeling dizzy and slightly nauseous, she climbed the stairs back up to the sitting room.

Back at the house, Nate's wife Uda took charge of organizing the food arriving on a steady basis. Large casseroles and lasagnas packed the tables and counter tops. Friends and neighbors moved between the rooms in a haze, and Julia stayed as cordial as possible in her caffeine-filtered twilight. In an act of selfless hospitality, Rose had stopped to pick up some beer for Ed's kids and one of her friends from AA spotted her coming out of the bar, brown bag in hand, so the guests were in the kitchen having a good laugh over that. Julia heard a small kerfuffle in the living room and turned just in time to see the chipmunk scurry past the piano, unusually large and surreal. It disappeared behind the couch, hounded by Teddy and Nate.

Two

1948

IN THE OPERATING ROOM at Bellevue Hospital in New York City, Dr. Ed Lloyd sat at the head of the table with his hand on a sleeping patient's forehead, monitoring the dials of his anesthesia tanks. New to her shift, the petite Nurse Clarisse Buckman stood on the other side of the table with a tray of instruments. Now and then Dr. Lloyd and Miss Buckman's eyes would meet and pause. His were deep and stormy ocean blue while hers were a soothing shade of hazel. Anonymous except for their eyes, they worked as a group to remove a gallstone, then sewed the patient back together.

Nurse Buckman went back to the apartment she shared with several other nurses that evening and considered Dr. Lloyd's eyes. She combed out her curly brown hair and thought about Nathan, her favorite older brother, killed in a coal mining accident three years before. He'd had those same deep stormy ocean eyes, often sad and red when he came home from the war.

A wave of grief threatened and she thought, "Oh no! I didn't come all the way to New York to be depressed." She put her roommate's new Dinah Shore album on the phonograph player and drew herself a hot bath, singing along to "Buttons and Bows" as she sat soaking in the tub.

On a subsequent shift Miss Buckman's and Dr. Lloyd's eyes played hide and seek once more, meeting, pausing, then darting back to the patient. Outside the operating room she'd noticed that Dr. Lloyd knew a lot of the nurses' names by heart. From then on, she made an effort to be seen more often in the hallways of the hospital, making sure he recognized her.

Late one evening Dr. Lloyd and his friend Bill Quinn left a severed hand pinching a memo in the nurse's station during Clarisse Buckman's and her friend, Nurse Winifred Hause's shifts. Winnie shrieked when she saw it. "Need a helping hand?" it read.

"That's disgusting!" Clarisse exclaimed. "I know who did this." She used a towel to pick up the hand with the memo in it and stalked out of the nurse's station. She already suspected it was the flamboyant Dr. Quinn, who was just emerging from the dressing room, and drew a breath of reproach. The door to the dressing room opened once more, and Dr. Lloyd stepped out in his street clothes.

"Hello, Miss Buckman. Nice to see you."

"Oh—hello, Dr. Lloyd. I was just... wondering about this... note," she stammered, handing him the severed body part.

Winnie ducked her head out from the nurse's station and saw the three of them standing together in the hallway. Her thick auburn hair billowed from beneath her nurse's cap as she watched with timid green eyes.

"We were just having a little fun, right Miss Hause?" Dr. Lloyd called down the hallway. "I assume you know Miss Buckman. This is Bill Quinn, my cohort in crime." He winked at Clarisse, who blanched, then headed back to the nurse's station. The doctors followed until they all stood together, each one blinking nervously until Bill said, "Why don't we all just go over to The Automat? After I return this," he added, taking the hand from Ed.

Later, Ed and Clarisse sat together watching Bill and Winnie drop nickels into the glass wall of sandwiches, soups and pies. Clarisse thought Ed was cute and slightly puckish, with wavy brown hair that he combed back over his head, Mickey Rooney style. Plus he made her laugh. "See those people over there?" he whispered, tipping his head toward a couple seated at a table in the corner. The man looked uncomfortable. "He played one of the flying monkeys in *The Wizard of Oz*, and he can't decide whether to tell his new girlfriend or not."

The following year, Ed and Clarisse were married and headed west in their Studebaker. "We'll be pioneers!" Ed exclaimed, as they crossed the border of Pennsylvania into Ohio. A colleague of his had convinced him he'd be living a real western life if he came to work in Iowa, and offered Ed a position as an anesthesiologist at the Wahatchee Hospital. They bought a modest house with a giant TV antenna and a wet bar. On Saturday nights Ed and Clarisse jitterbugged at the Wahatchee Country Club. Then Teddy was born, and his sister Julia two years later. Her skin was so porcelain-light that Ed often called her "my little pearl."

When Clarisse bought Ed an eight-millimeter movie camera for his thirtieth birthday he began recording their lives. He spent hours in a makeshift closet in the garage, editing his homemade films. Easter for instance, with the family headed down the front walk in their new Sunday clothes, cutting to an operating room scene with masked nurses waving and vamping at the camera. Then, the close-up of a beating heart! Cutting to Julia and Teddy in their tiny cowpoke outfits atop their new spring-powered rocking horse—to a Charades game where the adults all hoisted their highball glasses toward the camera and took turns jumping up from the couch faster than life.

Then daylight saving time ended and it was dark by five o'clock, with spent leaves strewn about like last summer's hangover. Ed wandered glumly around the house on his days off until the Christmas season revived him. He went out and bought the biggest tree that would fit in the living room. He cruised the hardware store for the latest technology in Christmas lights, adding to his collection of bulbs and spinners and nutcrackers. Eggnog and bourbon flowed freely in the basement's wet bar when they had company, and Mitch Miller's orchestra ruled the hi-fi set, along with Ed's favorite Christmas hymns.

After New Year's, the tree was thrown out, the outdoor lights taken down, the stencils wiped clean from the windows.

Ed sat on the South Seas wicker couch with its tropical upholstery, staring out beyond the backyard. A thin layer of fog wove through the stalks of the neighbors' tattered cornfield. It was a gray Januarythaw day, the clouds heavy and dour, the snow old and worn out by the holiday season. Ed's wavy brown hair drooped over his ears as he sipped a beer and gazed into the distance. Three-year-old Julia sat in her musical rocking chair wearing her red and white fringed cowgirl outfit, rocking "Home On The Range" to him. She'd been there for half an hour, hoping to stir him from his listlessness. Ed had spent the morning giving anesthesia while the surgeon sewed part of someone's cheek back on, then later calming the recipient of rectal buckshot before putting him into a deep, ether-induced sleep. "Just count backwards from 100..." he told them in his soft, operating room voice.

"There's nothing to look at," Ed complained, when Clarisse passed through the family room with her feather duster. He gestured out the window. "Everything's so flat. It doesn't provide any inspiration."

"Put a fire in the fireplace," Clarisse sighed. "That ought to cheer the place up."

Julia got off her rocking chair and helped Ed crunch up newspaper. When the fire was crackling, she climbed into his lap and handed him a tattered copy of *The Little Red Hen*. They both dozed off before he got to the end of the story.

"I'm claustrophobic!" Ed blurted out during dinner that evening. "I have to see the same people in the grocery store that I see at the club, *and* at the hardware store, *and* at the movie theatre."

"Isn't it comforting to see so many familiar faces?" Clarisse asked, wiping a dribble of marinara sauce from Julia's chin.

"No, it's not," he answered, smoothing his hair back over his head. "I want to be someplace where people don't care about what I'm going to watch on television that night. I miss Bill and Winnie, too."

"Do you want to go back to New York then?" Clarisse asked. "Just say so."

The next Christmas they celebrated with the Quinns on Long Island like never before, grateful to have their two young families close together. At Bill and Winnie's sprawling Victorian home in Garden Park, they toasted Ed's new job at the local hospital. Blender upon blenderful of whiskey sours were whipped up while Bill pretended to smoke cigarettes out of his ears and played piano wearing the shoulder strap pistol holster he kept for late night emergency calls. Bill and Ed mustached and bearded each other in a gregarious Redi-Whip fight, and soon Ed's bright camera lights flooded the place. Clarisse and Winnie became animated and theatrical, putting on the brightest of bright red lipstick and singing at the camera. It frightened Julia. She thought they were wearing too much make-up on purpose so they could look like scary clowns.

Riding home in the car that night, she dozed in her mother's lap when there was a sudden crash. Clarisse abruptly tumbled out of the car onto the ground, still clutching Julia in her arms. Julia turned and looked into her mother's unconscious face and began to whimper as Ed came around from the other side of the car. He pried her out of Clarisse's arms, picked her up and set her in the back seat next to Teddy, then went back to wake up Clarisse. Julia stared at the fuzzy squirrel on her red felt skirt, rubbing the half-walnut shell that was glued on just beyond the squirrel's paws until she heard her father say, *"Thank God."*

THREE

JULIA SAT IN HER FIRST GRADE CLASS on Long Island trying to draw the Tin Woodman on the lined notebook paper where she was supposed to be practicing her vowels. A siren pierced the chalky air, growing louder as it approached.

"Drill!" cried the teacher. She herded the children into the crowded hallway and Julia sat in a line against the wall, hugging her knees as the siren drew closer. Even the teachers crouched down. The principal appeared between the rows of silent children, turning the crank of his black siren box solemnly. You were supposed to tuck your head when he passed, but Julia peeked through her fingers to watch the principal stride by in a dark three-piece suit, his eyebrows furrowed under a steep shiny forehead. The siren wailed louder and louder until she felt like screaming when he turned down the next hallway, his alarm fading in the distance.

That evening Julia was perched happily on Ed's shoulders as he moved from room to room while Teddy stalked in front of them with a toy rifle.

"Hold on, Pearlie, we're headed deep into the African jungle!" Ed shouted, passing beneath the ivy Clarisse had trained over the doorway to the dining room. Tchaikovsky's *1812 Overture* blared from Ed's hi-fi stereo.

"Watch out for the skeletons!" Teddy yelled.

"Now we're headed up to the North Pole!" Ed continued, entering the kitchen with its sparkly blue Formica counters. "Here's where the Eskimos store their polar bear meat!" He opened the freezer door and a cloud of frosty air billowed out.

"Everybody duck!" he yelled when the cannons went off. "The

British are shooting at us!" They ran to the kitchen table and scrambled underneath.

"The baby-sitter will be here any minute," Clarisse's voice cut through the clatter.

"Oh, no, not Mrs. *Hogford!*" Teddy groaned, referring to Mrs. Halford, the frumpy, middle-aged baby-sitter who watched TV the whole time and asked them to bring her something to eat every ten minutes.

"No, we're trying somebody new."

A much younger baby-sitter arrived wearing light blue pedal pushers with a matching blouse and white sneakers. Her hair was set in huge wiry curlers, covered with a red polka-dotted scarf.

"Say hello to Debbie," Clarisse said to Teddy and Julia. "Be polite and do what she says, okay?"

They nodded and Clarisse took Debbie upstairs to see Nate, the baby. Julia cringed, taking Teddy's hand. *"She looks like a monster from outer space!"*

When Ed and Clarisse finally pulled out of the driveway, Debbie snapped her gum at Teddy and Julia. "You're *going* to behave." She turned on her heel and traipsed into the kitchen.

"She's worse than Mrs. Hogford!" Teddy whispered. They went back down to the TV room.

A few moments later Debbie appeared with a sandwich and a bottle of root beer. Julia was seated in the big green easy chair in front of the TV, rocking back and forth.

Debbie sat on the South Seas wicker couch, eyeing the easy chair. She finished her sandwich and stood up. "Okay, that's where *I'm* sitting."

Julia got out of the chair and Debbie flounced into it.

"Let me give it a spin for you," Teddy offered.

"Oh, it rocks *and* spins?"

"Yeah!" Teddy spun the chair around in a circle slowly, its springs twanging.

"Pretend you're at Disneyland!" he said, spinning the chair faster.

"On the Teacups ride!" Julia chimed in.

The chair spun faster and Debbie clutched its arms. "Whoaa... Nelly! It's time to stop!" she cried, as a curler flew from her head.

"Just a few more spins and you'll be back on Earth!"

"Now! Stop!" Debbie shouted. Julia thought her face matched the color of the chair's green upholstery as she got up and hurried toward the bathroom.

"I think we got her," said Teddy.

A few minutes later they heard water flushing. Debbie emerged from the bathroom and went into Ed's den. Teddy tip-toed to the door. "She's on the phone with her boyfriend," he reported, coming back and flopping into the easy chair.

Julia sat down in front of the fireplace watching the last of the fire Ed had stoked earlier, letting her eyes go in and out of focus. She imagined it was a burning city where thousands of tiny people lived inside the flaming buildings, fulfilling their destinies in a matter-of-fact way even though everything was on fire. Then she was living in it. She had a lavish penthouse in a tall apartment building with windows all the way around. She was as doomed as anyone else. But then, just as she leaned out the window to see the fire escape crumble away, the Tin Woodman himself crashed through the front door of her penthouse with his ax and carried her down through the burning building to safety. She married the Tin Man, he built a tin suit for her and they lived happily ever after.

The next evening, Ed sat in the TV room sipping a Manhattan and watching *A Night To Remember* on the Million Dollar Movie, while Clarisse was at her ceramics class. Nate slept in his playpen, and Teddy pitted green plastic army men against each other on the tile floor, tossing ice cubes in the air so they'd land and explode around the troops. Julia had grown too big to fit in the seat of her Home On The Range chair, but Ed looked so gloomy that she stood in it, rocking to try and cheer him up.

"Do that stuff during the commercial," he grumbled, settling back into the movie.

On the decks of *Titanic* people sang, "Nearer My God To Thee," and Julia thought surely God would rescue them if they sang loud enough. Then, right in the middle of a verse, there was an explosion and everyone tumbled to the floor as the ship tilted vertically and began to sink. People in nearby lifeboats watched in helpless horror as the gigantic ocean liner foundered and slipped beneath the surface.

"My first ceramic creation!" Clarisse announced later that night, unwrapping a rendition of Santa and His Eight Tiny Reindeer in white porcelain, with gold highlights. She held up a reindeer for Ed to see.

"It's… beautiful," Ed breathed, charmed by the sight of something Christmas. "Unwrap the rest. Let's put them on the mantle right now!"

When the whole set was in place, he nodded and said, "Why not leave it up all year?"

In the spring Clarisse decorated around the reindeers' hooves with Easter basket grass and filled the sleigh with jellybeans.

"I got the lead!" she shouted one evening, slamming the front door shut behind her. "I'm Mrs. Anna Leonowens!" From then on, she practiced the songs of Garden Park Little Theatre's production of *The King and I* during the day while she was cleaning, and in the bathtub at night. Ed bought the record album so she could sing along with Deborah Kerr. Sometimes Clarisse coaxed Ed off the couch and made him dance the polka, singing, "Shall we *dahnce!*" at the top of her lungs while Teddy and Julia rolled their eyes and pulled themselves closer to the TV.

As the play progressed, the theatre group bonded and sang the songs together on their way out after each rehearsal, often gathering at the Hamburger Express Coffee Shop. When costumes began appearing, Clarisse was thrilled with the wide hoop skirts of Mrs. Anna. When she polka-ed with The King, she did her best to ignore how well developed his chest was, and how deftly he twirled her around the stage. "The play's the thing," she reminded herself, eager to present a theatrical masterpiece to her family and friends.

Clarisse returned home from a rehearsal one night, closing the door quietly. "Why are you so late?" Ed demanded. Nate wailed from his crib upstairs.

"We went out for coffee afterwards, like we usually do."

"You could have let me know. I would have told you that there's a sick baby here."

"Oh, and I suppose a baby with a cold is beyond the realm of your medical abilities?"

"That's not the point!" he shouted.

Clarisse noticed a warm blast of alcohol on his breath and lowered her voice. "I'm sorry. I should have called. Just lie down and let me take care of this," she said, and hurried upstairs with the retort, *"But you told me to get out and do things more often"* stuck firmly to the roof of her mouth.

Opening night of *The King and I* finally arrived. Julia, Teddy and Nate sat with Mrs. Halford in the front row, surrounded by the Quinn family, while Ed moved around the auditorium during the performance, snapping dozens of pictures. Clarisse sang and danced her heart out and the show was a smashing success. Teddy and Julia thought their mother looked just like a movie star. Even Nate was so taken that he sat still until he fell asleep.

Later at the cast party, Clarisse and The King started things off by waltzing together, until Clarisse spotted Ed leaning against the bar with a highball glass in hand, chatting with the bartender.

"Come and dance with me," she said, dragging him off toward the polished wooden floor.

A few rounds of the Bunny Hop later they headed home, Clarisse feeling a little too tired to keep a watchful eye over how many highballs Ed had.

Standing on a hot sidewalk in downtown Garden Park a few months later, Clarisse adjusted the shopping bags in her arms while she kept hold of the harness attached to Nate. The leaves of the maple trees had grown to their fullest, oozing with late August heat. Locusts buzzed, cutting through the still air like a teeming, inter-dimensional choir. A wooden tent sign sat outside a brick storefront with the words "Air-Conditioned" painted in snow-capped water and ice.

"You promised, Mom," Teddy reminded her.

"Then be a gentleman and open the door for us," she answered. Teddy grasped the heavy wooden door of The Hamburger Express and they entered, pulling themselves onto stools at the counter. Setting down her bags, she lifted two-year-old Nate onto her lap. A toy train trundled around the inside of the counter with silver passenger cars, a flatcar between each one and a red caboose. It pulled up in front of the kitchen window and whistled. The short order cook leaned out and deftly set a plate with a hamburger onto one of the flatcars. It inched forward and he placed an order of French fries onto the next flatcar. Then the train gave another whistle and pulled out of the loading station, chugging around the inside of the counter until it reached a stocky man in a t-shirt, where it stopped with a toot. Car by car, the waitress unloaded his lunch.

They ordered the same thing all around; burgers and fries and milkshakes except for Nate, who shared some fries with Clarisse.

A few minutes later their order chugged up and the waitress unloaded their lunches. They settled into an earnest munch, glancing back at the train.

"Who are you looking at?" Teddy asked suddenly. Their mother was smiling at a tall man who had just walked in. The man approached them and Clarisse stood up blushing, as she set Nate back onto the stool. He took Clarisse's hand and kissed it.

Clarisse turned to Teddy and Julia and said, "This is Mr. Frank, the man who played The King in the play. Remember?"

"Why isn't he bald?" Julia whispered to Teddy, noticing his full head of sandy brown hair.

"Maybe he shaved his head and it grew back again, or he wore a wig like Bozo," he shrugged, sucking the last of his milkshake noisily through the straw.

"Nice to see you, Clarisse," said The King. "How have you been?"

"Busy as usual," she answered. "Shopping for school clothes."

They gazed at each other for a few seconds.

"Are you still hot, Mom?" Teddy asked, noticing her red cheeks.

"Moo-*Cow!*" Nate chortled, perched on the stool. He held a plastic cow creamer upside down, watching it spit up its contents onto the counter, splattering the windows of the passenger cars.

Horrified, Clarisse whisked him up in one arm, apologizing to the waitress. She turned back to speak with The King, but he was already across the room, shaking hands and sitting down at a table with friends.

Julia stood in the doorway of her empty dance class. Her father should have been there a half hour ago, after his shift at the hospital. Today was Scarf Day and their teacher Miss Violet brought a boxful of large, colorful scarves. Instead of doing those sissy little ballerina steps where you had to get everything perfect and act like a poof, Miss Violet told everyone to take as many scarves as they liked and encouraged them to move about the stage freely. *Swan Lake* blared on the Motorola as the girls pranced around, pirouetting and twirling their scarves. Some of them knelt on the floor flicking them when the music became soft. Several girls played leapfrog over them, Julia included. Some of the parents had arrived early, and watched from the hallway. Julia kept checking the doorway to see if her father had come to witness this amazing spectacle of moving art, but the music ended and Miss Violet told everyone to put their scarves back into the box. The rest of the class left with their parents until Julia was alone with her teacher.

"Did you have fun today?" Miss Violet asked, packing up her record albums.

"I really liked the scarf dance," Julia answered. "I... I think my father will be here any minute," she added, trying to close the embarrassing space between everyone else's parents and hers.

Ed finally arrived. Relieved, Julia glanced at his face, but he looked like he was somewhere else and still smelled like the hospital. "Let's go!" he said, putting a shaky hand on Julia's shoulder. They got into the car and he asked, "How was class?"

"It was... fun... I guess... Everybody else's parents were there..." she trailed off, looking out the window.

"Hey, I got here as fast as I could, so don't bawl me out for being late!"

Julia whimpered and began to cry.

"What are you *yammering* about?"

She shook her head and wept quietly. When they arrived home, she ran past Clarisse and upstairs into Teddy and Nate's room. She was about to slam the door when Teddy shushed her and pointed to Nate sleeping in his crib.

Julia squatted on the floor watching Teddy build a windmill with his Erector set while an argument escalated downstairs.

"Why was she crying?" Clarisse asked.

"I don't know. She wouldn't tell me," Ed answered, taking off his overcoat and dropping it onto the couch. Clarisse picked it up and opened the closet door, reaching for a hanger. She could smell alcohol on his breath, mixed with residual ether fumes from the operating room on his clothes.

"Make any stops on the way home before you picked up our daughter?" she asked.

"Leave it alone!" Ed shouted. "It was a really difficult day and I don't see any problem with having a drink on the way home from a job where two people died!"

"Shhh! That's no excuse!" Clarisse lowered her voice. "That happens on lots of days and you don't need to get bombed before picking up one of our children."

"I'm not bombed!" he answered, swaying.

"I can smell it."

Ed took a deep breath and hissed, "Maybe some people don't mind when their wives are out getting their hand kissed by strange men but I don't happen to be one of them."

"He's not a strange man," Clarisse continued. "He was The King from the play. It was just a theatrical gesture."

"Theatrical, schmeatrical! Don't tell me what my schedule should be, or what I can eat, drink or do after work, etcetera, *etcetera, ETCETERA!*" he roared, sweeping Santa & His Eight Tiny Reindeer off the mantle with one arm. They crashed in a heap onto the floor and he charged past Clarisse down the steps into his den, slamming the door.

One tiny reindeer survived. Clarisse bent to pick it up and turned around to find Julia standing behind her. "Did someone try to drop a bomb on Daddy?"

"No... he's just in a bad mood," her mother whispered.

The next morning, Ed sat hunched in a chair in the living room with his head resting in one hand, staring out the front window while Nate pushed a wooden duck toy back and forth on the floor. Julia crept downstairs with her Home On The Range chair and tried to put Nate into the seat to rock him, but he fought and cried out. Clarisse rushed into the room, shushing them. She led Julia into the kitchen by her elbow and told her in a hushed tone, "Don't upset your father. He's very sick. Do you want to make him worse?"

A few minutes later Bill Quinn arrived with some other men Julia didn't recognize. They spoke quietly just inside the front door and she could hear them whispering, "A good rest," and "some dry time," until Clarisse appeared with a suitcase and told her to go upstairs. Teddy stood watching the scene from the top of the landing. "I think they're taking him to a hospital somewhere," he whispered.

"Is he… going to be okay?" Julia asked, her lips quivering.

"I don't know."

Bill's wife Winnie appeared with their children, who quickly blended into the downstairs TV room with Julia and her brothers. Clarisse and Winnie went into the kitchen to make coffee and closed the door behind them.

"Aunt Ginger will be here any minute!" Clarisse announced a few days later, clearing the breakfast dishes.

"With Cousin Randy?"

"Of course with Cousin Randy!"

Julia and Teddy danced around the kitchen with their dishtowels while Nate jumped up and down inside his playpen.

A weathered Oldsmobile pulled into the driveway with a honk.

"They're here!" yelled Teddy.

Their stocky thirteen-year-old cousin jumped out of the passenger side, with a crew cut and glasses.

Clarisse picked up Nate and they all raced outside.

"Look how much you kids have grown!" Aunt Ginger exclaimed. She wore a light blue, flowered dress, and looked like an older, wiser version of their mother.

They piled into the house and sat at the kitchen table drinking lemonade and munching oatmeal cookies until Aunt Ginger announced, "We brought you kids a present! Randy, go out to the car and get it."

Randy went outside and returned with a large, colorful cardboard box.

"Looks like a beach toy," Teddy said.

"No, it's a Slip n' Slide!" Aunt Ginger exclaimed proudly. "You hook your hose up to it and shoot across through the water!"

Bright yellow vinyl twinkled from the inside.

"Sounds like fun!" Clarisse said. "Go and get your bathing suits on and we'll see how this thing works." Teddy, Randy and Julia thundered upstairs to change.

"How's he doing?" Ginger asked her sister.

"Bill says he's doing all right, but I have to wait a few more days to visit until he finishes detox," Clarisse said, trying to keep the lump in her throat from exploding.

Out in the backyard, they unraveled the Slip n' Slide and hooked it up to the garden hose. In a few minutes it lay on the ground in all of its vinyl glory, a long, watery yellow corridor.

"Randy, show them how to do it!" called Aunt Ginger.

Their cousin stood at one end of the yard and took a running start. Just before reaching the edge, he launched himself forward and dove headlong onto the slide, skidding through the water like a rocket.

"Neat!" yelled Teddy, bounding toward the other end of the slide. Teddy and Julia took turns as Clarisse and her sister watched. Finally Julia yelled, "Come on Aunt Ginger, it's your turn!"

"Aw, let me go back inside and change into my suit!"

She emerged a few minutes later in a one-piece bathing suit with a skirt. Then Clarisse went inside to change and returned, setting Nate in his springy chair. Curious about the new attraction, half a dozen neighborhood kids were now launching themselves onto the slippery slide.

"Aunt Ginger! You go!" yelled Teddy. Their aunt geared herself up at the runway, took a running jump and slid over the wet plastic yelling, "Whoo! Whoo! I'm a torpedo!" to the delight of the children.

"Now it's Mom's turn!" yelled Julia.

"If I can do it, so can you!" added Ginger.

Clarisse hesitated, then trotted toward the runway. "Here I go!" she shouted from the other end of the yard.

Julia watched as her mother ran a few steps and dove forward onto the mat, speeding over the surface like an otter.

"Keep him busy," the psychiatrist told Clarisse upon Ed's release from the hospital. "Don't let him get bored."

Clarisse went out and bought him a wood-carving kit.

"I'm not doing any of that old fart crap!" Ed said angrily, tossing the box aside and heading out the door. Later that afternoon, Clarisse and the kids and Bill Quinn's family all stood around a brand new red and white Ford Fairlane hardtop convertible in the driveway. Ed sat in the driver's seat, showing them how the roof majestically detached itself from the top of the windshield and then sank with the push of a button, folding down into the open maw of a flap over the trunk. Then in reverse. The maw opened and the shiny roof emerged from the trunk, raising itself to its full height before gracefully settling onto the tops of the windows.

FOUR

THE SMALL OUTBOARD CRUISER pulled out of Pattituck Cove Marina early one morning, plying through the dark green canal water. Cattail marshes swayed on the embankment, giving way to corrugated metal retaining walls on either side of the channel that kept the sand from sliding into the water. People fished over the edges of the walls in yellow raingear, shrouded in early morning fog.

"What do they think they're going to catch in here?" Teddy asked. "The water looks yucky."

"It must be something, or they wouldn't keep coming back," Ed replied from the pilot's seat.

Harbor buoys clanged in the mist—a black can first and then a red nun, their tops sprinkled with white bird droppings. Ed eased the throttle forward and the little boat nosed its way into Oyster Bay. A foghorn moaned in the distance. The water shifted from dark green to blue and the air became moist and fishy. Snuggled inside of his orange life preserver, Nate sat on the bench in the stern next to Clarisse. Teddy was at the kitchen table inside the cabin, practicing his knots while eight-year-old Julia stood on the potty seat cover in the bow with the hatch cover open. Her life preserver straps and braided hair flapped in the breeze as the boat bounced over choppy waves. Motoring out past Matinecock Point, she watched the sun gently burn its way through the fog as her father steered the boat in toward Gregory Beach. When he took the engine out of gear, Julia could smell suntan lotion and hamburgers from the shore.

Ed knocked on the windshield from the pilot's chair. "Let Teddy in there—he needs to drop the anchor."

She climbed back down into the cabin and soon heard the jingling of chains knocking against the bow of the boat as Teddy got the anchor ready. They drifted closer to land, just outside of the public beach rights.

"Now!" he shouted to Teddy, who threw the anchor out. It hit the water with a splash and rope rasped against the edge of the boat as the anchor sank.

"Make sure you have that rope in the cleat!" Ed shifted the engine into reverse and the anchor dug into the sand. Teddy tied it down and climbed back through the hatch.

"Swimming tests!" Ed called, slipping off his t-shirt. Clarisse picked up the marine ladder and hung it over the side of the boat. Ed stood on the small wooden gangplank and dove off, landing in the water with a thud and an echoing splash. He came up and wiped his hair back over his head.

"Take off your lifejackets and jump in!" he called. "Twice around the boat and then tread water for five minutes."

Julia hesitated, peering over the side of the boat into the fathomless water. Ed had taught Teddy and Julia to swim at the Garden Park Pool, where you could see lines painted on the bottom. Teddy jumped in feet first and paddled around as Julia climbed down the ladder cautiously.

"Chicken," Teddy laughed, and began swimming toward the bow. Julia let go of the ladder and followed him.

"Come on, Julia," Clarisse called from the boat where she held Nate by his lifejacket. "Do something besides the dog paddle!"

Twice around the boat they circled, Julia struggling to keep up with Teddy until she finally gave in and did the crawl.

"Now tread water for five minutes," Ed ordered.

Several minutes passed before Julia began to imagine a sunken ship lying beneath them on the floor of Long Island Sound. Somehow it had dislodged itself from the sand and was now slowly rising to the surface, its funnel belching sea water and smoke while skeletons drifted free, coming up right under her. A piece of lettuce seaweed brushed past her and she screamed, kicking and paddling in a frenzy toward the ladder.

"Where are you going?" Ed called.

She grabbed the ladder and clung to it, shivering.

"What's the matter with you?" Teddy shouted. She shook her

head and climbed into the boat.

"What were you afraid of?" Clarisse asked, wrapping Julia in a beach towel.

"Old sunken boats," was all Julia could think of. "Coming back to life."

"Oh, that's silly," her mother laughed, giving her a hug. "They can't do that."

A few weeks later they were anchored in the small cove by Matinecock Point after dark. Julia, Teddy and Nate each lay in small camp cots next to each other on the deck, zipped up in their sleeping bags. Ed snored softly from the cabin, on the kitchen table-turned-bed next to Clarisse. It was their first overnight on the little boat. Gentle waves lapped at the hull, and Julia stared at the trees on the end of the point, silhouetted against the moonlit sky. A motorboat buzzed in the distance.

Moments later, its wake rocked their boat. "Feel that?" Teddy whispered. "It's the Sea Monster of Matinecock Point. He comes up at night to look around when he thinks no one's watching."

"Stop scaring me!" Nate called from inside his sleeping bag.

Me too, thought Julia. "There's no monster," she said to Nate with a shiver. Pulling her sleeping bag over her head, she hoped the monster wouldn't be able see her if it climbed on board.

The next morning they woke to the smell of bacon and fresh coffee. Julia peeked from her sleeping bag to see her parents seated at the dual-purpose kitchen table bed, now returned to its upright position with a Coleman stove on top. Long Island Sound glistened in the early morning light, a gentle aquamarine blanket that sparkled with the movement of the water. *The Pearl*, a name Ed had chosen for their new motorboat, christening it with a bottle of root beer, rocked on the tiny waves.

"Come on—get up and have some eggs!" Clarisse called from the cabin.

They fished in the early morning, waiting for the sun to warm the air. Teddy sat in a deck chair with his feet propped up on the side of the boat, fiddling with the reel. Julia was on the bench in the stern holding a pole of her own when she saw the end of Teddy's pole bend way over and jerk several times.

"You've got a bite!" Ed called from inside of the cabin. "Give him a little line," he added, hurrying out to the deck.

Teddy let the reel spin as the fish pulled away with the bait and then he yanked the rod back. "He's still there!"

"See if you can reel him in," Ed coached.

Teddy wound the crank until a fish broke the surface of the water, flapping furiously at the end of the line. Ed bent over the side with a fishing net, scooped it up and hauled it into the boat.

"It's flat," Teddy said.

"It's a flounder."

Julia stared at the gasping fish that lay flopping on the deck. Two eyes were set close together on the dark side of the fish, and when they turned it over the other side was white and featureless except for a gill. "Eew! Do we have to keep it?" she asked.

Several hours and flounder later, they chugged over to The Sandbar, an off-shore beach spot Ed had found near Matinecock Point. When it was low tide they could pull *The Pearl* right up to the shore. They spent that afternoon swimming and digging for clams. Ed teased everyone by kicking on the surface with his hands clapped together over his head like a shark's fin.

Julia stood in shallow water watching Ed chase Nate. She'd completed her swimming test the week before by treading water right next to Teddy, and was now free of the cumbersome orange lifejacket. Feeling an unfamiliar presence, she looked down and saw a dark shape moving toward her on the sandy bottom. Then two more. Suddenly her feet were surrounded by a group of sinister creatures. She screamed and flopped into the water, swimming away frantically.

"Don't touch the bottom!" she cried, pointing to the spot where she'd been standing.

Teddy swam over and looked down. He reached into the water, pulling up a large dark brown crab by its spiny tail, and dragged it onto the beach. Julia followed him. It was a prehistoric looking thing, with a dome-shaped shell and then another segment with spikes coming out the back of it. Teddy turned it over and pegged its tail into the sand, trapping it. Six sets of armored legs flailed helplessly in the air.

"The tail's probably a stinger," he said. "You're lucky you got away in time!"

He began to pour sand into the body of the huge crab.

"No!" Ed ran up the beach shouting, "You'll kill it!" He grabbed the crab by its dome-shell and rinsed the sand out, setting it back down in the shallow water. "That's a horseshoe crab. Just don't step on them and they won't bother you. You're too big for them to eat anyway."

"There's supposed to be a sunken ship out near The Sandbar," Ed told Clarisse one evening. "Bill knows a few guys who go skin diving there."

Clarisse hesitated. "Sounds kind of dangerous—"

"No," Ed interrupted. "You take classes in skin diving so you can go down with air-filled tanks and breathe underwater. It's called 'SCUBA—Self Contained Underwater Breathing Ap-par-a-tus,'" he said, pronouncing each syllable with importance.

"Oh... well then, maybe you should give it a try," Clarisse replied. "Count me out, though."

"The Glen Island, a side-wheel steamer that ferried well-to-do passengers from New York City to the North Shore of Long Island, caught fire and sank..." Clarisse read from the microfilm of an old newspaper at the Garden Park Library, *"...off the shore at Matinecock Point. Ten persons were burned to death..."* A hand touched her shoulder and she straightened up to see The King standing beside her.

"Don Frank!" she exclaimed and, remembering the Moo-Cow incident, quickly covered her mouth and glanced around the library.

"It has been awhile, hasn't it? You're looking beautiful as always," Don whispered, starting to take her hand. She pulled away and fiddled with a knob on the microfilm projector.

"What are you researching?" he asked, leaning over to look into the screen. A lock of wavy brown hair fell from behind his ear and framed his cheek. The legs of her chair shrieked against the tile floor as Clarisse pushed herself back.

"My husband is joining a skin diver's group. He wants to explore a shipwreck," she said.

"Shhhhh!" hissed the librarian, from the desk across the room.

Clarisse scanned the library for other patrons and seeing none, she turned back to Don and told him in a low voice, "I have to go and get dinner started." She rewound the film and collected her things, dropping the reel into a return basket. Don followed her out. A light drizzle had begun outside and she hurried toward her station wagon.

"You know, we really ought to have coffee and catch up," he suggested.

Clarisse stared straight ahead. "I'm very busy with my family."

"Sometime in the near future then," he persisted, holding the car door open for her.

"Maybe, sometime," she answered, climbing in. She closed the door and waved to him from inside.

"There's the unofficial markers to The Wreck," Ed pointed, as he slowed *The Pearl* down just inside the cove of Matinecock Point. "Between that last tree on the Point and that piling of rocks on the beach where the mansion is, about thirty feet down. It's loaded with blackfish and bass!"

A few minutes later, Ed and Bill, newly certified as SCUBA divers, stood at the stern in their matching Bluefins club jackets, assembling their dive gear. Clarisse fitted the swim ladder onto the side of the boat and Teddy, Julia and Nate stood cautiously nearby, watching their father.

"Why don't you monkeys go and put your bathing suits on?" he ordered.

They clamored down into the cabin. Julia shut herself in the tiny bathroom in the bow while Nate and Teddy suited up in the galley. When she emerged in her little red two-piece suit, her father and Bill were dressed in full scuba diving gear, with dark blue wetsuits and silver tanks strapped to their backs. They sat on the edge of the boat with their backs to the water. Ed held the top of his mask with one hand, tipped himself backward and rolled over the side of the boat, landing in the water with a loud splash. Bill followed. Julia looked over the side to see them sink in a fury of bubbles and pop back to the surface again. The frogmen tested the mouthpieces of their regulators and nodded to each other. Then they dropped underwater and Julia watched in fear as they sank slowly. They disappeared into the murkiness, leaving two small trails of bubbles in the hazy blue water.

"Go ahead, jump in," Clarisse said. "You can wear your masks and snorkels and tell us when they come back up." Nate clung to her hand. Julia headed down the ladder backwards, careful not to disturb the sets of bubbles left by Ed and Bill, when Teddy climbed stood on the edge of the boat in his flippers and jumped in, making a loud splash. "Teddy!" she cried, "how're we supposed to know where they are?"

Clarisse eyed the water nervously. "Put your mask on and you'll be able to see the bubbles again." She leaned over the side of the boat and helped Julia adjust her mask and snorkel, and handed Teddy her little yellow flippers. "Here, Mister Smarty Pants. Help your sister put them on."

They floated on the surface, staring down at the two sets of bubbles leading into the dark mist. Julia stayed close to her brother while she listened to the hollow sound of her breath through the plastic tube of the snorkel. Teddy honked through his snorkel, trying to coax her into swimming underneath the boat to the other side, but she wouldn't dare. She was afraid the propeller might start itself on a whim and chop them to pieces. Besides, she needed to stay focused on those bubbles. Clarisse and Nate kept vigil from inside the boat.

Twenty minutes later, two large figures emerged from the underwater darkness, their silver air tanks flashing in the distance. Julia watched until they finally broke the surface, their heads covered with lettuce seaweed. Teddy took the snorkel out of his mouth and yelled, "They're back up again!"

"What's down there anyway?" Julia asked as the divers took their regulators out of their mouths.

"The Sea Monster... of Matinecock?" Nate called out.

"An old junker of a ferry that's fallen apart," Bill answered, "and lots of muck."

"It's an old side wheel steamer," Ed told them, when they'd climbed aboard and taken off their dive gear. "A party boat. People used to ride over from the city to relax out here."

"Why did it sink?" Julia asked.

"Maybe it hit a rock or something," Teddy suggested.

"Or crashed into the Sea Monster!" Nate exclaimed.

"Or had an explosion in the kitchen and burned," Clarisse said.

"Were there any skeletons down there?"

"Oh yeah, some of them were still sitting in chairs around a table with scarves and pearl necklaces," Bill teased, "with playing cards in their hands!"

"And fancy hats!" Ed added.

"And baby blackfish swimming through their ears and out their eyes!" Teddy cackled.

"No, not really," Clarisse said, noticing the horror that crept onto Nate's face.

"There's an old ferry down there, keeled over on its side and rotting in the sand," Ed explained. "It still has part of its paddle-wheel, but most of the stern is missing."

"Can it float back up to the surface?" Julia asked.

"Ha! That would be a real laugh," Teddy said.

"It's down there for good," Ed chuckled.

"Did you try to go inside?"

"No, we just shined our underwater lights in there and chased out the fish."

At home that night, Julia dreamt she was aboard the ferryboat during an evening soirée. Colorful Chinese lanterns lit the entire outside of the boat and an orchestra played "The Merry Widow" on the deck where couples waltzed. The women's skirts bustled and twirled in the breeze. Julia sat on a wooden bench in the cabin oiling the mouth of her date, the Tin Woodman. Suddenly there was an explosion down below and the cabin burst into fire. Smoke spewed from the funnel up above as the engines blew off steam, creating a thick fog on the deck. The boat pitched back and forth wildly, sending the Tin Man head first into the black water. A giant finned head popped up, grabbed him in its jaws and dove back under the surface. A choir stood in the back of the boat singing, "Nearer My God To Thee" as the boat began to sink. Julia awoke with the sound of gurgling in her ears and cried, *"Mommmm!"*

Ed and Clarisse sat on the edge of Julia's bed trying to convince her that their boat was still safe.

"It was just a bad dream," Clarisse said.

Julia sniffled, pressing herself closer to her father. "Don't go down there anymore."

"Why not?"

"There might be... a monster or something!" She buried her head in his shoulder and sobbed.

"There's no such thing as a sea monster," he said, chuckling softly.

Clarisse ran her hand over Julia's hair and added, "Maybe they really did have a fire on that ferry boat. But it was a long time ago, before fire extinguishers were invented. We have a fire extinguisher *and* a ship-to-shore radio, so we can always call for help."

During the next few weeks Julia drifted in and out of sleep with an ear infection. Sometimes her dreams flowed together, one picking up again where the other had left off. She dreamt that she and her brothers were scuba divers on a mission to discover hidden treasures that had gone down with The Wreck. They followed their father into the burned back end of the boat and watched as he held onto the crooked door to the cabin and pulled himself through, kicking his fins to propel himself inside. Bits of old clothes and pearls still attached to the boat waved in the current, along with some Christmas lights that blinked on and off. Curls of smoke wafted impossibly from the funnel of the old ferry, tilted in the sand with blackfish darting in and out of its broken windows. They watched as their father scanned the cabin with his underwater flashlight. The school principal paced the gangplanks sternly, winding his portable siren box.

"Looks like a squall coming up," Ed said, glancing out the window of *The Pearl's* galley a few weeks later. "We should head home."

Menacing thunderheads gathered around them as Clarisse washed the last of the dinner dishes in the tiny sink. The tide had come in and submerged The Sandbar, making the shore look even further away. The air turned green, and wind whipped the surface of the water, flinging the rubber bumpers off their roosting places to dangle furiously over the side. Rain began to pelt the roof, mixed with the crackling of small craft warnings on the ship-to-shore radio. The waves swelled, and it looked to Julia as if they had become tall white-tipped yawns, coaxing the little boat to pass beneath the surface.

"It's too late to make it back," Ed decided. "We'll have to ride it out here."

They motored closer to shore and Teddy dropped an anchor off the bow while Ed threw one off the stern, pegging the boat in place. Unrolling the canvas cover, they buttoned themselves inside the cabin as *The Pearl* shuddered in the wind.

"Everyone put on a lifejacket," Ed ordered. "On a cheerful note, if anything bad happens we can always swim for it!"

They huddled in the small galley as rain spattered for a half hour and then let up. Ed unbuttoned a corner of the canvas cover. The air had become still and heavy.

"I think we're in the eye of the storm," whispered Teddy.

"Better than the mouth," answered Ed.

"What's the eye?" asked Nate.

"The middle, where it can't get you," answered Teddy. "Can we stay inside of the eye and move at the same time as it does?" he asked, turning to his father.

"Maybe. Let's wait and see. Watch the flag."

The flag on the radio antenna was still for a moment and then fluttered toward the inside of Pattituck Cove Harbor.

Ed squinted up at the sky. "I think we can make a run for it. We're not that far from the harbor and the storm may be coming after us." They rolled up the back of the canvas cover and Ed started the engine. Teddy hauled the anchors up and they motored toward the harbor, picking up speed. The storm clouds loomed behind them, ominous and dark.

"You kids get underneath the kitchen table," Ed ordered.

They sat huddled together on the floor, elf-like in their hooded sweatshirts and bulbous lifejackets.

"Faster Daddy!!" Nate yelled.

There was a loud snap. The steering wheel spun out of Ed's hands as the boat pitched from side to side. Julia saw frothing water just below the gangplank and gasped.

Ed grabbed the throttle and took the engine out of gear, coaxing the wheel back and forth.

"The steering mechanism is shot!" he shouted to Clarisse. "I need you to steer the boat by the engine while I drive."

With Nate wedged between them, Julia and Teddy clung to each other's lifejacket straps, their eyes fixed on the whitecaps. The gravity of the situation was heightened by the rare sight of Clarisse in a lifejacket, her curly brown hair soaked and dripping from her rain hat as she gripped the giant outboard engine by its handle. Riding over the tops of the waves, the boat seemed to pause in mid-air, as if deciding whether to continue or just slide backward again. It crested each wave and slammed down into the trough, accompanied by the hysterical ringing of the ship's bell. Water sprayed over the top of the boat, drenching the deck and Clarisse. Julia shivered under the table, wondering if the boat would break into pieces with each slam.

"Right!" Ed shouted, abandoning the nautical terms for desperation's sake.

"No, left!" he yelled, remembering that the boat turned in the opposite direction.

Clarisse pulled the engine to one side by the handle, glancing out over the water to get her own bearings.

"If we tip," said Teddy, "then we'll have to swim for the back of the boat so we don't get stuck inside."

"Won't the propeller get us?" Julia asked.

"Dad'll turn it off in time," he guessed.

"How, if we're busy tipping over?"

Nate wailed.

"We're coming to the breakwater!" Ed shouted, as waves exploded over the bow.

"We'll be home free in a minute," said Teddy.

Julia felt the sea softening, each slam over the crests more forgiving than the last. Her mother looked haggard in the stern, still steering the boat manually. Climbing out from under the table, Julia saw the rock wall of the breakwater move past them as they chugged into the harbor breathing sighs of relief. Foghorns mooed to each other from around the bay. The storm had become a benign, light rain. People still fished in raincoats from the corrugated metal sides of the canal, unaffected by the crisis the Lloyds had just survived. Ed nosed *The Pearl* into its slip and turned off the engine. "Let's get this thing washed up and go home," he said.

Filling buckets with soapy water, they washed the salt off the boat and buttoned up the canvas before heading up the wooden ramp to the car.

"Look what we missed!" Teddy exclaimed, as they drove through Garden Park. Trees lay in the streets, blown down by the storm. Garbage was strewn everywhere. Julia noticed the whites of Ed's knuckles on the steering wheel as the road crew waved them through a clogged intersection where the traffic signal had stopped working.

"I'll just drop you guys off. I have to run some errands," Ed said, turning into their street.

"Are they something that can be done in the morning—?" Clarisse began, fearful of an imminent side trip to the liquor store.

"Dammit," he muttered. A maple tree lay across their driveway. He parked at the curb and they went inside, Ed heading for the phone while Teddy went upstairs and returned with his Brownie camera. Teddy and Ed stayed outside taking turns snapping pictures of the downed tree until twilight, when a tree crew pulled up.

"Busy day, huh?" Ed asked.

"We'll probably be up past midnight," one of them grumbled, lighting flares and sticking them in the ground in front of the tree. "Got five more calls lined up after this."

Sitting at the front window, Julia and Nate watched the crew use chainsaws to dismantle the maple tree as Teddy snapped pictures outside. Limb by limb in the glow of the flares, they loaded the branches into the back of the truck.

Ed sipped a cup of coffee at the kitchen table and sighed.

"Feeling better?" Clarisse asked.

"Yeah... I think I'll take a shower and go to bed."

FIVE

"IT'LL BE JUST US AND THE KIDS for awhile until we get settled," Julia overheard Ed say to Clarisse, as they unpacked in their new Pattituck Cove home. "Maybe I'll even be able to have a drink someday… maybe at Julia's wedding."

In her bedroom across the hallway, Julia fiddled with the aquamarine-blue gravel at the bottom of her new aquarium, moving the pink ceramic castle around until it looked perfect. She imagined stately schools of angelfish swimming through its windows in military formation.

Ed had begun to feel isolated at the Garden Park Hospital after Bill Quinn left to start a general practitioner's office in his own home. He complained about the staff constantly until Clarisse spoke up one night. "If it's so bad, then why don't you do something else?" she demanded.

Spirited away to Pattituck Cove by some of the local Bluefin divers, Ed joined the anesthesia department at the local hospital. He liked the relaxed pace of the North Shore with its rambling old Victorian houses and quiet streets, and they would be much closer to the boat.

Their new house was an older, 1940s Tudor-style home surrounded by a stone wall. A mound of granite boulders and bushes further concealed the front of the house, and a half-circular gravel driveway ducked in and out opposite sides of the wall. The backyard had tall pine trees and a wooden swing; paradise compared to the development they'd moved from. They were finally able to set up the baby grand piano Ed's mother had left them, and Clarisse wasted no time in starting Julia with piano lessons.

Ceddie, who lived two doors down, was Julia's age. She walked over one day in early November to appoint herself as Julia's new friend and fourth grade mentor.

"I'll be taking you to your first day at school," she announced. Her straight black bangs were cropped short and taut above glasses with pink frames. She told Julia she'd gone to a Catholic school for one year, where the nuns hit kids' knuckles with a ruler when they were bad. Her chin jutted out making her look angry, so Julia figured she was probably still thinking about all those nuns.

In the school library, Julia quietly slid *A History of Sunken Ships* out of its place on the shelf. It fell open to a chilling old photograph of the *General Slocum*, a ferry half-submerged in the East River, her side wheel and funnel still visible above the water line. Julia cringed and began to read. On the opposite page was a picture of the ferry in happier times, her decks loaded with passengers on their way to a church picnic on Long Island in 1904. When the boat caught fire, a thousand people drowned trying to escape from the burning ferry, all within full view of the shore. Mesmerized, she continued, feeling powerless to resist the horror. The decaying cork lifejackets fell apart in peoples' hands when they tried to put them on, or became waterlogged and pulled them beneath the surface with their weight. The ancient fire hose burst when it was turned on, and the flaming steamer pounded toward North Brother Island in search of a safe place to run aground.

"*Eeewww!* Why are you reading that?" Ceddie demanded, leaning over her shoulder. "It looks scary!"

Julia slammed the book shut and headed for the front desk, hoping for a quick, covert check-out.

"Don't you think she's too young to be reading that?" Ceddie whined to the librarian, who frowned at the book and said, "You could pick out something closer to your age group. How about the Jenny Linsky stories?"

"I read all those last year."

"*Henry and Ribsy?*" Ceddie asked, waving her copy in the air.

"I'm…doing a report on sunken ships," Julia stammered.

"We don't have any reports due," Ceddie snapped. "We don't

even *get* reports until fifth grade."

Julia gave the librarian a pleading look, and the woman stamped the inside of the cover.

"Due back in three weeks," she said. "Ask your parents to help you with this."

Outside, Julia turned to Ceddie and asked, "What's the matter with you? Why do you care what I read?"

Ceddie's lower lip drooped. "You don't want people to think you're a book-worm, do you?"

Later that afternoon, Julia sat cross-legged in the cavernous leather chair in Ed's den, fully absorbed in the book of ill-fated nautical journeys. Nate lay on the sofa, riveted to the TV as Soupy Sales argued with a giant white paw. Outside, the sky had shifted to dark blue, leaving a faint pink glow over the silhouettes of bare trees and houses across the street. The smell of pot roast wafted in from the kitchen when the lights flickered and went out.

"Hey!" Nate yelled.

"Hey!" Clarisse yelled back from the kitchen.

Julia stared at the dull gray spot that faded from the TV. "Did we blow a fuse?" she called.

"I don't know," her mother replied. "Wait till I go downstairs and check."

The kitchen was faintly lit by the blue flame on top of the stove where peas still bubbled. Clarisse fumbled around in the junk drawer until she found a flashlight and pointed the beam down the basement steps. Drawing a deep breath, she went to check the circuit breaker box. She flipped the switches one by one, but there was no change. Mystified, she came back upstairs and found some camp candles in the pantry.

With their arms hooked, Julia and Nate felt their way out of the den and down the silent hallway toward the kitchen. Clarisse had lit several candles, and the yellow flames danced over the dishes she'd dripped wax on to hold them in place.

"Listen," Nate whispered. "You can't hear anything."

"None of the neighbors' lights are on either," Clarisse said, staring out the window.

"Or the streetlights," Julia added.

Footsteps crunched in the gravel driveway, and a wave of dread passed over Julia. She drew close to Clarisse as the front door swung open. It was Teddy, returning from football practice.

"You should see it out there," he said. "All the houses are dark. I think the whole town went out."

"Do we have any more candles?" Julia asked.

"We'll have to use the fancy ones from the dining room," Clarisse answered. "You guys go find some more flashlights," she added, handing them hers.

Huddled together, they searched from room to room upstairs. Julia found the little Barnum and Bailey Circus flashlight that was still hanging on a corner of her dresser mirror. They continued on, until they found more flashlights. From the bottom of the stairs, Julia could see out the front window, where a few lights moved about in the street.

"Let's go out there. We might be able to find out what's going on—"

"No!" Clarisse shouted, hurrying out from the kitchen.

"There's people out there," Teddy insisted. "They might know what happened."

"Okay, just you and Julia. Stick together and stay right in front of the house where I can see you."

"Ma!" Nate cried. "Why can't we all go?"

"Because I want to be here in case your father calls. He's supposed to be coming home from work any minute."

Slipping their jackets on, Teddy and Julia stepped out into the chilly darkness. The scent of burned leaves mingled with the smell of a dozen half-cooked dinners floating out the front doors of confounded neighbors. Faint candlelight flickered from the windows of the houses across the street. People were beginning to come outside where they huddled together talking, their breath rising in frosty wisps above the glow of their lanterns.

Julia twirled her flashlight in a circle in front of her and in an instant, a pair of lights from down the street twirled in response. They crept toward each other until the faces of Ceddie and her older brother Winston came into view.

"Those circus flashlights sure came in handy, didn't they?" Winston chuckled.

"Sabotage!" a nasal voice called from an upstairs window. "The Commies are coming! Khrushchev is on his way!"

"Tch," said Ceddie. "Morty... he never misses the chance to scream something stupid out his window."

"This is it!" the boy continued, "Start learning Russian!"

"Start learning how to bottle your own gas, Morty! Khrushchev was overthrown, you dummy!" Winston shouted back.

"Teddy! Julia!" Clarisse's voice cut through the darkness.

"We're here!" Teddy called back.

They heard the front door close, and Clarisse and Nate's footsteps on the gravel. Julia twirled her flashlight again. Clarisse arrived at the group and Julia saw her shiver in spite of her heavy overcoat.

"Ceddie! Winston!" Julia heard Ceddie's mother cry nervously through the darkness.

"Over here!"

Just then a pair of headlights appeared at the end of the road. The car slowed next to the group and the driver's window slid down. It was Ed, in his new Buick.

"I had to take it slow," he said. "All the traffic lights are out, but I picked up a station from Jersey in here," he continued, pointing to the radio on the dashboard. Clarisse leaned into the car window and inhaled deeply, searching for the scent of alcohol. Noticing only the faint touch of anesthesia ether, she breathed a sigh of relief.

"They think it happened at Niagara Falls. Should be awhile, though."

Ceddie's mother appeared looking uncomfortable, and Julia noticed the tiniest hint of an upturned nose when she offered a perfunctory hello and began shepherding her children back toward their house. "Hope the lights come on soon," Winston called back over his shoulder.

"Let's go inside," Clarisse said, still shivering.

Ed went around checking all the doors and windows to make sure they were locked, then they ate pot roast in front of the fire in the living room, listening to bits of static-broken news on

Teddy's transistor radio until the batteries went dead. Julia placed a candelabra on the piano and fumbled her way through the Mozart piece she'd been learning while the rest of the family played Hangman in the light of a kerosene lantern.

Everyone was asleep when the lights blinked back on at 9:15.

"Finally," Ed sighed, stretching on the couch. They sat stunned by the light of the blazing lamps until Clarisse got up and took Nate to bed. Then Julia went into the den and brought back her library book. She held the picture of the *General Slocum* open for Ed to see.

"Is this The Wreck?"

Ed studied her for a moment. "No, that one's a little older. Besides, it looks it sank right after it got through Hell Gate," he answered, referring to the turbulent channel where the East River meets Long Island Sound.

"How many wrecks are under the water around here?"

"Oh, I hear the bottom's littered with them."

Julia shuddered, imagining the floor of the Sound strewn with wreck after wreck, each one lying in wait for the perfect time when gravity would loose it from its resting place, raising a ghostly carcass to the surface.

"But sometimes they haul them up and float them again," he added, chuckling. "Hey, why are you so interested in all this morbid stuff?"

Julia shrugged. "I don't know..."

"You should concentrate more on your piano. You've got some real talent there."

Lighting two of the leftover candles on her night table, Julia climbed into bed with her book. Spellbound, she read about the sinking of the *Titanic* before drifting off.

SIX

JULIA DARTED BETWEEN STREAMS OF WATER flying in every direction in an attempt to reach math class without getting soaked. Several boys were locked in battle on both sides of the hallway, oblivious to the throngs of seventh and eighth graders ducking and scrambling to get to their classes.

"It's the Age of Squirt Guns," Teddy had warned her at the beginning of the school year. "Everybody has one."

"It sounds like the age of a big pain in the ass," she'd remarked. The year had already started out horribly when Ceddie had publicly broken off their friendship to join the pubescent snob culture, stomping on Julia's burgeoning sense of eccentric fashion on her way out. "Desert boots with striped knee socks?" she'd laughed out loud in the hallway, pointing at Julia's feet and crinkling her nose.

Julia quickly changed her mind about squirt guns when she saw a rich opportunity for revenge. She showed up at school the next day with one of Teddy's retro-rocket models. After lunch she took a shot at Ceddie, who turned out to have her own little pink designer squirt gun tucked in her purse. They dueled fiercely in the hallway before the bell rang, leaving Julia splattered, with a craving to come back and finish the battle.

That night she went into her father's black doctor's bag and found what she was looking for. A huge 60cc plastic syringe, the kind she'd seen Ed and Uncle Bill playing squirt guns with once before. She carefully broke the needle off into a paper towel. Filling it with water, she took the syringe out to the backyard and pumped. It shot a hearty stream of water twenty feet, better than any squirt gun she'd ever heard of. She couldn't wait to bring it to school the next day and try it out on Ceddie. Victory would be hers!

The next day was St. Patrick's Day. Ceddie and Julia both sat in math class and although they now ignored each other, they joined in the fun of getting the old codger Mr. Clark to go off on a tangent. He was much more passionate about his stamp collection than eighth grade math, and often they could get him to waste an entire class talking about it. Ceddie sat in the front row, tossing back her long, shiny black hair as she egged Mr. Clark on about his Irish stamps. Her obnoxious green shamrock sweater and matching Villager skirt tantalized Julia for the entire hour. She couldn't wait to give them a proper soaking. She'd filled the syringe at a water fountain just before class and it sat on one end in her bag, ready for duty. When the class was over Julia ran out first, taking position across the hallway. Ceddie emerged from the classroom and seeing Julia, reached for the squirt gun in her shoulder bag. But Julia pumped the entire syringe of water at her first, hitting her right in the forehead and knocking her back into a row of lockers. A girl with green streaks in her hair yelled, "Wow—you got her!"

"What a stream!" someone else shouted.

Gripping her elbow, a heated voice growled, "This isn't what the halls are for." Mr. Grumman, the science teacher, redirected Julia toward the principal's office. They waded silently through the crowds rushing from one class to another, although it felt to Julia as if every single person knew she'd been caught, pretending not to notice. Mr. Clark dragged Ceddie along, who acted embarrassed to be seen with Julia. The girl with green streaks in her hair also wound up in the office because of her hair. The three of them sat quietly waiting to be seen by the principal, Mr. March. The school secretary ushered them into his office one at a time, closing the door behind them. Ceddie went first, and when she came out she scurried past Julia, ignoring her.

Then it was Julia's turn. Everyone called Mr. March "The Frog," and it was the first time she'd had the chance to see him close enough to view the details of his frogginess. He had unusually large lips, his eyes were buggy, and the skin underneath his lower eyelids drooped in soft pink bags. His neck was thick, under a double chin that looked as if it might bulge out any second with an involuntary *ribbit!* A fly buzzed around his office as he spoke, and Julia drew a deep breath.

"I'm not sure you understand what a serious situation this is," said The Frog. "Bringing drug paraphernalia onto school grounds is illegal."

"Huh? Drug parafin... *what?*" Julia didn't even know what that meant.

"Where did you get this?" he asked, holding up the syringe Mr. Grumman had confiscated.

"From home. My father's a doctor. He has all sorts of things like that."

"What happened to the needle?"

"I broke it off last night."

"Why did you bring it to school in the first place?" he asked.

Blinking her eyes, Julia began in her most earnest voice, "I was tired of Ceddie bothering me and I just thought if I got her once really good, then she'd leave me alone," The fly zipped back and forth across the room, bouncing off the window.

"Sounds like a case of Charlie Brown's 'Why's Everybody Always Picking On Me.'" The Frog smiled faintly, sending tiny quivers through the pink bags under his eyes.

Ugh! He probably thinks he's the coolest thing, quoting a Coasters song, thought Julia.

"We'll be contacting your parents about this. You may go back to class now."

Julia nodded and got up to leave. The fly landed on his desk and she paused.

"Anything else I can help you with?" he asked.

"No... " She shook her head and hurried out of the room.

Leaving school that day, she ran into the girl with the green hair on the front steps.

"You looked a little scared coming out of the principal's office," the girl remarked. "Was that your first audience with The Frog?"

"Yeah, but I was more worried about the fly in his office... I like what you did to your hair. Is that what you were in trouble for?"

"Yeah. Turns out green food coloring is a breach of fashion

etiquette... I'm Erin. I see you a lot but we never talk. Where did you get that amazing squirt gun?"

"My father's a doctor," Julia shrugged. "He always has them around."

She walked partway home with Erin, who noticed the copy of *20,000 Leagues Under the Sea* Julia had tucked under her arm along with her textbooks.

"Have you seen the movie?" she asked, nudging the book with her elbow.

"No, I'm holding out until I finish the book. I don't want the story to get spoiled by Hollywood the way they wrecked Mary Poppins."

"Yeah, they really messed that one up," Erin agreed. "If I didn't have such a crush on Dick van Dyke I'd write a letter of complaint to the movie studio. *20,000 Leagues* is pretty good, though. I saw it last weekend."

Just after they split up at the Four Corners, Julia felt an embarrassing dampness between her legs and hurried the rest of the way home.

"What's for dinner?" she asked Clarisse, feeling faint as she closed the kitchen door behind her.

"Meatloaf," her mother answered. Julia winced at the thought of the fatty, putrid-looking flesh, mixed together with onions and squeezed into a giant ketchupy turd of a meal. She lurched toward the bathroom and closed the door, panting heavily while her heart raced. Her lower back ached, and when she pulled down her tights, her underpants were stained red.

Clarisse pounded on the bathroom door. "We have something to discuss," she announced sternly.

"Yeah, as a matter of fact."

"The school called about the squirt gun you were using. How could you *do* such a thing? Ceddie's mother called, absolutely fuming! She wants us to pay for the sweater she says you ruined. That'll come out of your allowance."

"Mom...I think I started that bleeding thing..."

Clarisse paused. "Well then," her voice softened. "Open up this door. We'll have to get you the necessary *accouterments*."

Later on, after Julia had been initiated into official womanhood, outfitted with pads, Clarisse lectured her about keeping up appearances because their father was an important community figure. They had to reflect his level of integrity in public. "Acting up could cause your father a lot of trouble," she warned.

That evening when Ed came home, Julia thought she heard Clarisse imitating Ceddie's mother in the kitchen, and both parents snickering. But when she came in to add her impression of Mr. March, Ed fumed, "Never, *ever* go into my bag and take anything again!" Horrified at his anger, she slunk back upstairs and took another aspirin.

"Get a load of this," Julia said, reading from *The Perils of Long Island Sound*. "Execution Rock Light was so named because in Colonial times, a murderer would be shackled and chained to the rocks at low tide. Then, when the tide came in..." She looked up and drew her fingers across the front of her neck and made a choking sound.

"Eeeww," said Erin, setting up an ironing board in her bedroom.

Erin and Julia had developed their friendship by passing notes back and forth in class with snide comments about Ceddie and her snob club. "Her real name is Mercedes," Erin told her. "Can you believe that? She was supposed to go to private school but it fell through. Then she went to a Catholic school for a while before she came here. Now she's mad because she has to go to school with us *plebes*."

"Plebes?"

"Commoners."

"Oh."

Julia thought Erin was especially cool because her family lived in one of those big old Victorian houses close to the water in Sound Bluff and her mother was a junk sculptor. Don Quixote's horse stood on the landing of the stairs, made from an old water heater and some car parts. Junkyard beetles and samurais peeked out from various pockets in the backyard and besides that, Erin had an older brother who was a hippie in Greenwich Village. Her parents talked about books and music and art, and they put their salt into clay dishes, using tiny wooden spoons to sprinkle it over their food at dinner.

"Come on, the iron's hot," Erin said. They were ironing Julia's hair today, since everyone's hair was supposed to be long and straight, with big sulking bangs like Cher. Julia's hair did neither of those things. Her naturally wavy hair had a mind of its own, different on every day. Having to get glasses at the beginning of seventh grade didn't help things, either.

Julia laid her head sideways on the ironing board with a towel covering her hair. Erin drew the iron over her hair and sighed, "Now that you've officially entered 'womanhood,' you'll want to look the brooding part."

"It doesn't seem that great so far. Everybody acts so... I don't know... *anxious* about the whole thing."

"You mean, hanging out with boys?"

"Uh-huh," Julia groaned from the surface ironing board. "They're no fun anymore. They're different. Kind of mean."

"My mom says they're 'infused' with a new set of chemicals."

"Oh, is that what that smell is?"

"Ha! You're a funny one. Switch sides, now."

"Wait, I have to look first." Julia stood up and looked in the mirror. One side of her hair was its naturally wavy self, while the other hung ominously straight, as if waiting for the first opportunity to spring back to into eccentric curls.

"Come on, let's do the other side," Erin coaxed. Her own hair brushed just below her shoulders, straight and strawberry red.

"Okay, but those creeps like Ceddie are going to find out and make fun of me even more. I heard them calling me 'Goldilocks' behind my back in gym yesterday."

"Just tell them to shut up. Besides, Ceddie's pissed off because her father ran away with another woman."

"When?" asked Julia. She took a gulp from her soda and belched.

"A long time ago, when she was a little kid. My mom told me. That's why she says she doesn't have a father. They just pretend he never existed."

"Wow. I bet that's why her mother's such a bitch!" Julia exclaimed, blushing as she heard herself use that word out loud for the first time.

"No, I bet that's why the father left," Erin answered. "She's a bitch-and-a-half!"

"A real bitchasaurus! Ha!" yelled Julia, flopping back onto the bed.

Erin snorted, spraying cola through her nose onto the ironing board, and rolled onto the floor laughing. Julia imagined Ceddie's mother as a Tyrannosaurus rex lumbering around in an evening gown and keeled over onto the floor where they both squealed hysterically.

Erin got up and sponged soda off the ironing board, then set the iron back on. The dampness disappeared with a sharp hiss. "Hmmm. I wonder if we wet your hair, whether it would cook more straightness into it?"

"Why not? Maybe you're supposed to do that anyway."

"How am I supposed to get my bangs straight?"

"Tape 'em flat at night, I guess," Erin shrugged.

SEVEN

JULIA SAT IN THE BACK SEAT OF ED'S NEW CAR with her nose
buried in *A Night To Remember*. Twirling one of her long, curly
pigtails around an index finger, she cringed when she read about the
wireless operator of nearby ship, the *Californian*, who had turned
in for the night while *Titanic* was sinking. And how officers noticed
flares coming from *Titanic's* direction and dismissed them as party
fireworks as the giant ship foundered with hundreds of screaming
people lining her decks.

"It's official—I'm the new boss!" Ed had announced the week
before, slamming the front door on his way in after work. Julia, Teddy
and Nate thundered downstairs when they heard the commotion
and clamored around their father, who went straight out the next
day and traded in his Buick for a silver Cadillac.

Now Julia and her family were on their way home from the
south shore of Long Island, tired and coated with a thin film of salt
from the chilly Atlantic air. They'd driven from marina to boathouse
and climbed on and off a variety of cabin cruisers with showers, full
kitchens, deep sea fishing chairs and flying bridges. Julia thought
each one was better than the last, and enjoyed clamoring up and
down marina steps like a kid in her new bell-bottoms until she
noticed more than one boat salesman eyeing her fledgling breasts.
The sun had made numerous attempts to break through the sullen
March clouds but the day stayed overcast just the same. Patches
of ice lay scattered across the sandy beach outside Freeport while
seagulls hunted in the receding tide. The family paid little attention
to the fatigued waves of late afternoon.

"Just a minute—slow down." Clarisse said suddenly. She pointed
to a group of frenzied swans on the shore. One in the center was

tipped over with its wing frozen in a patch of ice. Ed pulled over and got out of the car. The kids began to follow, but he waved them back. Hurrying down the beach, he approached the gaggle and they took off in a group, leaving the stuck one to fend for itself. It pecked and honked furiously at him. Undaunted, he knelt down with his overcoat dragging in the icy sand and gently scraped the ice around the swan's wing with his foot. The bird went mad with fear, flapping its one free wing and pecking at Ed. He stayed just out of reach and continued to scrape the ice around the frozen wing with the tip of his shoe as his family stared through the car windows. The other birds squawked from a distance but he kept scraping until the swan freed its wing. Ed tumbled backwards as the bird rose in one clumsy jump, attempting to lunge at him. It flew for several yards, then landed on the beach and honked, puffing out its chest. The other swans gathered around it as Ed stood up and walked back to the car.

"I think that's all we can do for now," he said, closing the door.

Later that spring, Ed found a cabin cruiser within the budget of his dreams. A used 32' Pacemaker with twin engines, a flying bridge, and a stand-up bathroom and shower.

"It's a sea-going vessel with a real keel, he chortled when he got home that evening. "'Seventy-five hundred?' the insurance agent asks me; 'You stole this boat at seventy-five hundred!'"

He bought it from an older couple on the south shore and one warm Saturday he, Teddy, Bill Quinn and several other Bluefins helped drive it around the Hamptons into Long Island Sound. They named it The Pearl II, painted in gold leaf script on the wooden transom.

Julia and Erin sat around the far side of the horseback-riding ring behind some bushes, sharing a joint Erin had gotten from her older brother. Julia, having taken up riding with Erin the previous fall, now had a summer job as a junior instructor in exchange for free riding and whatever tips she could muster from pleased parents. Ed and Clarisse were just happy that it provided a distraction from her continuing obsession with sunken ships.

"Is that the one your parents gave you for your birthday?" Erin asked, touching the pearl bracelet Julia wore.

"Yeah. I think it was my father's idea. He still calls me his 'pearl' sometimes... it's kind of embarrassing."

"I think it's cute," Erin said.

"Hmpf," Julia snorted. "I guess." Still, she felt obligated to humor Erin, who'd been diagnosed with diabetes earlier that spring and had to miss Julia's fourteenth birthday dinner while the doctors got her blood regulated. She stayed at home and made art, eventually presenting Julia with a watercolor portrait of the two of them laughing, which she'd painted from a picture Ed had taken. Now that she was well enough to come riding, Julia felt a little more comfortable prodding for information about her disease.

"So... does that mean you'll die if you accidentally eat anything with sugar in it?" Julia asked, still worried that Erin might suddenly vanish from her life.

"No!" Erin said, tossing her long red hair over one shoulder. Several strands caught in her black riding cap as she shook her head. "Julia, it's not all that bad. I just have to be careful. My mother has it, too. We hoped it would skip a generation or at least me, but it didn't. See? I even have a little emergency kit I carry around, just in case." She opened a small brown leather pack on her belt and showed Julia a Milky Way bar and her insulin kit.

"Just don't let The Frog catch you with that thing," Julia warned.

Through an opening in the bushes, they watched a young girl steer her horse through the field nearby, carefully avoiding the jumps.

"Danielle has leukemia, you know," Erin said softly, exhaling a cloud of smoke and nodding toward the girl. "Her parents bought her that horse when she got out of the hospital, but she's not expected to live for very long."

Julia took a drag and held her breath. A deep chasm of mortality rolled over her. "Does she know?"

"I don't think so. She's only ten. Maybe they don't want to tell her. Still, I feel terrible for even thinking this, but it sure puts things into perspective for me—wait! Don't move your foot one inch!" Erin exclaimed suddenly.

"Wha...what?"

"Just... look... down at your left heel..."

Julia looked down to see a nest of pinkies—five tiny newborn mice right next to the heel of her riding boot. "How did they get here?"

"I don't know! Maybe the mother abandoned them."

"Well, somebody has to take care of them!"

"Julia, try to make a little sense. We'll just have to move it back under the bushes and hope the mother comes back. You don't want a litter of dead mice on your hands, do you?"

Julia sighed. *She's right, as usual. It's not like I'm God or anything.*

A maple leaf lay nearby and Julia slid it under the tiny writhing litter with one hand while she steadied them with the other. "It's so dusty here—I bet they could use a little water."

"I'll go get some," Erin said, getting up and heading toward the stable. Julia heard the steady clomp of a horse approaching and looked up. It was Danielle, astride her palomino mare Ariel, wearing a modest outfit of jeans and a football jersey. Her riding helmet covered the top of her peach fuzz head.

"Hi Danielle," Julia said, quickly stubbing out the joint. "How r'you?"

"Pretty good for an old lady!" the girl joked, coughing. "What are you guys doing over here anyway?"

"We thought we heard a weird noise and we came over to check it out," Julia fibbed, hoping the pungent smoke had dispersed. "The minute we got here a bird flew away, and it turns out there's a litter of mice here."

"I bet the bird was trying to eat them," Danielle said. "You probably saved their lives."

"I don't know about that. Erin went to get some water, but I don't expect they'll live long without their mother."

"Maybe she'll come back in a little while."

Julia stared up at Danielle. Her face seemed to be aging as she spoke. She had puffy cheeks and dark circles around her eyes. "How's Ariel doing?" she asked.

"She's doing very well... for a captive *houyhnhnm*," she nodded.

"A whone-what?"

"A *houyhnhnm...* from *Gulliver's Travels.* Haven't you read it? They're a race of horses that are superior to humans. That's why I like to treat Ariel with respect," she said, patting the side of her mare's long neck.

Erin came back with a paper cup of water and they sprinkled some of it around the edges of the maple leaf while Danielle watched from atop Ariel.

"Don't drown them now," she warned, as they nudged the maple leaf nursery underneath the bush. "Me and Ariel are going for a ride. See you later." Danielle gave the reins a tug and the horse turned and clopped off, leaving small puffs of dust in her wake.

The Pearl II bobbed on the water off Matinecock Point a few days later, anchored over The Wreck. A thick fog had rolled in just after breakfast, leaving a heavy layer of wet salty film on the windows. Teddy, Julia and Nate fished off the bow, hoping the fog would burn off in time for a swim. Teddy had cracked open the leftover clams they'd dug up the day before at the Sandbar, for bait to catch the blackfish that lived in the sunken ship. The ship-to-shore radio crackled weather reports from the Port Jefferson Coast Guard station while Ed and his friend Bill sat in deck chairs in the cockpit, each smoking a Belair.

"Looks like we'll be socked in for awhile," Ed remarked.

"Yeah, we might as well go down," Bill answered. "I'd like to bring home a couple of bass for dinner."

As they suited up in their dive gear, Julia watched the giant sycamore trees on the shore of a nearby estate fade in and out of view as the thick mist rolled by. The Sound was calm except for the occasional ripple from a boat wake. Ed and Bill jumped off the stern, each splashing into the water with their heavy gear and popping back up to adjust their masks. Then they dropped beneath the surface and sank into the murky blue-green water. Julia was used to it now; she'd seen them come back up dozens of times.

Without the sun, the underwater visibility was only about fifteen feet, so they turned on their dive lights and aimed them toward the bottom. A few seconds later, The Wreck began to appear through the underwater mist. It lay on its side, the faded hull partly buried in the silt and sand. The side wheel was skeletal from sea-salt disintegration over the years. Parts of it had dropped off and floated away but the metal frame still remained, covered with seaweed, barnacles and mussels. The funnel lay in many pieces in the sand, rotted away by salt and time, and the stern had all but disappeared. A school of blackfish appeared out of the misty darkness and swam into the boat toward the half-buried cabin. Ed reached for his spear gun and swam after them. A wide open space was all that remained of the galley, and some ancient, decaying wood from tables that had once seated New York City's affluent vacationers. The sides of the cabin were encrusted with more mussels and barnacles, with tiny crabs snacking their way over the tops of them. Ed watched as several flounder darted past his mask, followed by a large, slow-moving shadow. *What the...? It must be huge!* Ed turned quickly, expecting a group of bass, and bumped his head on the wall of the cabin, knocking the regulator out of his mouth. It danced in a frenzy of bubbles, animated by the force of air rushing out the mouthpiece. Panic stricken, Ed saw nothing but bubbles all around him as he waved his arms to try and catch his regulator. Then Bill came up behind him, putting a hand on Ed's shoulder. He took hold of the rogue mouthpiece and handed it to Ed, who put the regulator back in his mouth and inhaled deeply, nearly choking on the water in the mouthpiece. He took several retching breaths before he was able to breathe steadily again. Bill peered into his mask to make eye contact and Ed put his thumb and forefinger into the "okay" signal and nodded. The water was now a murky brown, the silt from the bottom stirred up from the flailing of Ed's regulator and his fins. They headed for the surface.

Ed looked up and felt relieved to see the bottom of *The Pearl II*, then Teddy, Julia and Nate looking horrified through the water, their faces rippling over a sky background.

"What was going on down there?" Clarisse called, when they popped up. "It looked like an underwater volcano! I was ready to call the Coast Guard!"

Ed and Bill set their masks on their foreheads and exchanged glances. "Shit," Ed whispered through his mouthpiece. Bill rolled his eyes toward the boat and shrugged. Ed pulled out his regulator and yelled, "Just practicing our underwater skills!"

They tossed their fins up to the cockpit. Teddy caught them one by one, and Ed climbed up the ladder first.

"How was the fishing?" Clarisse asked.

"Not much luck," Ed answered.

"Well, there's these," Bill said, slinging a chain with two large blackfish into the boat. "Bagged 'em while you were sightseeing in the cabin."

"You dog!" Ed laughed.

A few weeks later Julia and Erin were seated on a hay bale in the stable.

"Danielle died last night," Erin whispered. "I just heard Andy on the phone with her parents."

Julia was stunned. She couldn't feel much except for a big empty space when she thought about Danielle. She went over to Ariel's stall and rubbed the mare's neck.

"There's a group of four beginners coming at one o'clock," barked Andy, the stable manager. Leaning against the wall, he tapped his unlit cigarette on the side of a stall to pack the tobacco. He would have been handsome if it weren't for his greasy hair and thirty-five-year-old paunch. "Do you want to teach that class?"

"Okay," Julia nodded, trying to avoid his eyes.

"Up-down, up-down" she cried out like a mantra to the four children on trotting horses. The air was heavy, soaked with the bewildering mystery of death.

"Heels down, sweetheart—you're doing fine!" one of the mothers called out to her eight year-old.

Julia sighed from the center of the corral. *Why don't they just shut up and let me teach the class?*

Afterwards, Julia and Erin took their favorite horses out for a ride in the jumping field. Julia's mare was an energetic older one named Bella, with a light tan coat, black mane and tail. She was gentle, and still loved to run fast. She took the three-foot jumps easily, and sped up between them in her exuberance. She headed for another fence and in mid jump Julia heard a loud crack, then both she and Bella were lying on the ground staring at each another. The mare looked dazed, and Julia was filled with horror that she had ridden her too hard and ruined her. Then Bella staggered to her feet and shook herself off, dust flying from her black mane. Andy appeared, taking the horse by her reins and patting her while Erin helped Julia to her feet.

"Is she okay?" Julia asked, her voice quivering.

He led Bella around for a few steps. One of her front legs was bleeding a little, but she pawed the ground and snorted.

"She just looks a little shaky. Don't worry. You didn't maim her."

Julia was trembling all over, filthy from falling in the dusty field. She looked at her wrist and panicked when she didn't see her pearl bracelet.

"Here it is," Erin said, reading her thoughts as she stooped over to pick it up. They walked back to the stable and Erin took her horse to its stall while Andy tended to Bella. When he returned, he looked straight at Julia and asked, "Are you sure you're all right?"

Julia burst into tears. Andy put his arm around her and hugged her while she cried. Then he pressed himself closer to her and she felt his eerie hardness prod her, ever so gently. Horrified, she pushed him away and ran down the ramp just as Ed drove up.

"Julia—wait!" Erin called, running after her.

"What happened to you?" her father asked, when she flopped into the car shaking and out of breath. Erin climbed into the back seat.

"I fell off…" she answered, too embarrassed to say anything else. "Nothing serious… it just scared me." She fiddled with the radio dial until it landed on "Penny Lane" and turned up the volume.

After they dropped off Erin, Julia went upstairs to the shower and scrubbed herself deeply, trying to remove every trace of what happened with Andy. It just needed to go down the drain and be forgotten.

"You're awfully quiet tonight," remarked Clarisse during dinner. Julia set down her fork and started to cry. Nate stared at her with an open mouthful of mashed potatoes and Ed said, "She took a spill today." Clarisse looked at Ed, who nodded and rested a forefinger on his lips.

Everyone sat quietly as Julia wept.

"This kid died... a little girl who owned a horse there who had leukemia and she died last night..." she said between sobs. "Then my horse Bella tripped over a fence and fell down..." In spite of her tears, she was careful to leave out the part about Andy.

"Is she okay?" Clarisse asked.

"Yeah..."

"How awful... that little girl's parents must be in agony," Clarisse sighed.

"*Gulliver's Travels* is a great allegory," Ed told Julia later that evening, when she was calm enough to explain what had happened to Danielle. "You should read it yourself."

She read it during the next week and never returned to her job at the stable. She told Erin she couldn't face going back, using the *houyhnhnms* as an excuse. "Fine by me," Erin answered. "Don't worry," she added, noticing Julia's bereft expression. "There's a million other things we can do. Besides, we never really fit into that horsey crowd anyway. Sooner or later we would've run into Ceddie and her snot club, so now's as good a time to quit as any."

A dinosaur in riding breeches and a hat cantered through Julia's mind and she laughed.

"Could I take organ lessons instead?' Julia asked her parents at dinner that evening.

"Sure!" Ed was pleased. "Your great-grandfather was a church organist at a Lutheran church in Ohio. You'd be carrying on a family tradition."

"You'll be just like Lurch!" Teddy added, sending the family into a hearty dinner table laugh.

"No, she won't!" Clarisse scolded.

Julia nodded, thinking instead about Captain Nemo and his undersea pipe organ.

EIGHT

SWEAT RAN DOWN JULIA'S TEMPLES as she sat at the organ console in the Good Shepherd Lutheran Church in Pattituck Cove, trying to force her feet to play the pedals. Toe, heel, toe heel… gripping the wooden bench, she walked her feet up and down the pedal board, glancing at the row of silver pipes in the apse, as if she might see a tangible result of her work. Before her were two sets of keyboards and a wall of round wooden knobs, each one controlling a different sound.

"Just take it slow," Mr. Sidney, the church organist, had told her. "Practice the scales with your hands first and we'll add the feet when you're a little taller."

She stood on the farthest pedal to the left and it emitted a rich, low bass note that resonated through the church and vibrated a place deep inside of her she hadn't known was there.

Meanwhile, Ed dropped over the side of *The Pearl II* by himself, with his spear gun. Since his children had become teenagers, or close enough in Nate's case, he'd begun taking the boat out alone when there wasn't another member of the Bluefins available. Bill and his family were on a camping trip to the Catskills for the weekend, and Ed was hoping to outdo his friend's previous haul of blackfish. The tide was out, making the depth of the sunken ferry less than thirty feet, so he figured he could surface safely if there were any equipment malfunctions.

The water was filtered with sun that morning as Ed made his way down to the ferry. He finned around it slowly, peering through the crumbled window casements for schools of blackfish when he thought he saw something large and dark coming out of the cabin.

Thinking it might be an illusion created by his mask or some drifting lettuce seaweed, he kept going. A moment later he saw it again. This time it slithered around the side of the paddle wheel and back into the cabin. In the misty water, Ed thought it looked like an eel with an enlarged, ridged head. *It must be six feet long! Bill would have a hard time topping that.*

The current was stronger than usual, and there was a layer of murkiness two feet deep along the bottom. When Ed tried to position himself to get a closer look at the creature, the current drew him away from the ferry. He swam back and grabbed one of the old window casements, hanging vertically upside down. Mud and algae that had grown on the casings loosened, and a cloud of underwater dust burst in front of him. Something moved beneath the layer of murk, leaving a dust trail as it went. He thought he saw a dorsal fin three feet long and his stomach tightened with fear. Ed aimed his spear gun in the direction of the fish and discharged it into empty space. His heart beat wildly as he glanced upward, relieved to see the bottom of his own boat in the distance. He spun around slowly, looking for evidence of the creature. Seeing nothing but bits of seaweed and empty clam shells strewn around the ferry, he hurried to the surface. *I'll come back with Bill and we'll bag this monster together.*

Julia walked home from the church after practicing. She smelled rain in the air tinted green by humidity, and thunder rumbled in the distance. The wind had picked up, exposing the light undersides of the maple leaves as they danced in the breeze. Lightning flashed, then the clouds opened and began pelting rain. She ducked into Fred's Luncheonette to avoid getting soaked. Inside, Ceddie was seated at a booth with her friend Lorraine. Julia nodded and said, "Hi."

"Hi, yourself," Ceddie answered. "Looks like you're melting. Sit down and have a soda with us."

Julia slid into the booth, wondering why Ceddie would even bother inviting her to join them, now that she was so firmly entrenched in the popular, fashion-conscious crowd. She'd even traded in her old glasses for those new hard contact lenses. Both the girls' hair was teased up and they wore heavy mascara. They looked like a pair of adolescent Agent 99s from *Get Smart.*

"What were you doing out there in the rain?" Ceddie asked.

"I was on my way back from organ practice at the church."

"Church organist?" Ceddie said. "I didn't figure you for that."

Lorraine snickered and Julia looked at her sharply.

"Oh, don't listen to her," Ceddie said. "She's just mad because Davy broke up with her last night."

"I keep telling you—he didn't break up with me. *I* broke up with *him.*"

"Yeah, like about five seconds after he broke up with you. So, Julia, who are you going out with these days?" asked Ceddie, teasing one of her hoop earrings.

"Uh, nobody right now."

"So what's the problem?"

"There's no problem," Julia shrugged. "Nothing appeals to me right now."

"Well, maybe if you weren't spending so much time with that weirdo Erin, the boys would pay more attention to you."

"She's not a weirdo. She's my best friend."

Lorraine snorted. "Okay, if you wanna call it that."

"What are you saying?"

"I'm just saying, maybe you shouldn't be spending so much time together. Boys might get the wrong idea."

A clap of thunder ripped through the sky just then, rolling overhead for a few seconds. The lights in the soda fountain flickered.

"I gotta go," Julia said, gathering up her music books.

"But it's still raining out there—you'll get soaked!" Ceddie protested.

Julia headed for the door. She thought she heard Ceddie and Lorraine giggling as she stepped out into the rain. Stuffing her music books under her shirt, she ran the two blocks home.

Clarisse stood in the kitchen, clinging to the phone. Her nose was swollen and red as she glanced up at Julia, dripping with rain. She nodded and hung up.

"Mom—?"

Clarisse looked cold, as if there were a layer of empty space around her. "That was Winnie. Bill just... died," she said, finishing the sentence with a choking sob.

"Where... how?" Julia asked, moving awkwardly toward her mother and putting her arms around her.

"The Catskills... camping... he had a sudden heart attack... only forty-two years old," she sputtered.

Julia went numb as she listened to Clarisse cry on her shoulder. She'd never seen her mother so upset, and couldn't seem to find a response that felt right.

The church in Garden Park had been transformed into an ornate display of flowers surrounding Bill's polished, dark brown casket gleaming in the front. Bill's wife and three children sat in the first row, crying through the service. The Lloyds sat directly behind them, Julia and her brothers too stunned to show any emotion. Julia felt a pang of guilt that she and her brothers had slowly drifted away from close friendship with Bill's kids once they'd moved to Pattituck Cove. Clarisse wept, holding a handkerchief to her face through most of the service, and when Julia thought she saw Ed's shoulders shaking, she broke down and cried. When the service ended and the choir sang "Amazing Grace," Ed and nine other men, including several Bluefins, helped carry the casket down the aisle and out the door to the waiting hearse. Julia stared at Ed when he passed their row. He walked stiffly, stone-faced, like he was holding his body together by sheer will.

After the funeral, Ed became despondent, spending hours in the black leather chair in his den watching TV. Clarisse knew if he isolated himself, he'd eventually want to drink, so she began a series of tactical diversions. "How about a movie with Dad?" she would ask Nate, who'd grumble when he was set on playing baseball with friends, but he usually went along, especially if Teddy was going. Once she even suggested that Ed accompany Julia on a shopping trip to Roosevelt Field, but Julia turned it down. Sitting across from Ed at the kitchen table, she could see the fragility in his eyes. A trip to the mall, passing through store after store trying on shoes could push him right over the edge.

Finally George from the Bluefins, who'd just bought his own boat, convinced Ed to join the Coast Guard Auxiliary. Following several weeks of night classes, they became official members of the Auxiliary, so Ed added that flag to the masthead along with the American flag they flew when they took the boat out. It was Julia's job to pin these flags on in the right order. At the marina store, she picked out a little pirate flag for Ed's birthday, which he agreed to include in the line-up. There turned out to be a flag for nearly every boating situation a person could think of, even one with a martini glass that indicated drinks being served on board. Clarisse shuddered when she saw it and bought Ed a captain's cap instead, which he proudly wore whenever they took the boat out.

"Careful," Ed told Julia one morning, holding the Chinese go-box of nightcrawlers open. She stood in the cockpit of *The Pearl II* and pulled one out with its dozens of tiny legs wriggling, gently so as not to rip it in half. Two black pinchers instantly appeared from inside the head and bit the end of her thumb. "Ouch!" she shrieked.

"Told 'ya," Ed chuckled.

Julia swallowed the pain, happy that she'd managed to get a laugh out of her father.

They fished a lot during the rest of that summer, trolling for hours in the morning with the engines puttering at one or two knots, lolling peacefully in the middle of the Sound between Long Island and Connecticut. Sometimes Ed turned off the motor and they drift-trolled. It was hypnotic, the gentle rocking of the boat in the early morning, with the occasional motorboat passing in the distance. They'd listen to Mets games or just leave the ship-to-shore radio on and eavesdrop on the crackled conversations of other boaters.

"This is the *Joe-Barb*, Whiskey Delta 4545, calling the *Lazy Susan*. Come in Lazy Susan," a man's voice mewled over the radio.

"This is the 'Schmoe-Bawb calling the Lazy Nuisance," Nate mimicked through his nose, fiddling with his fishing reel.

"This is the *Lazy Susan*... Weeeeeah, uhhhhhh," *(crackle-crackle),* "ova heah fishing at Sand's Point without a bite but we got a few steaks and beehs on the ice, f'lata. Ova."

"This is the *Joe-Barb* to the *Lazy Susan*: Weeeeeeah...ova heah, too... can you see us?"

"Uhhhhhh... this is the *Lazy Susan*. I don't think so... Suzie, can you see 'em? No, she can't...ova."

"What a doofus," Teddy groaned.

"Yahoos...they're not supposed to do that," Ed reminded them.

Julia giggled at the *Gulliver's Travels* reference.

"The radio is for emergencies and weather reports," her father continued. "Not to gab on."

"Can you teach me how to dive now?" Julia asked. "I'm fourteen now. Big enough to wear the tank."

"The water's become too murky" Ed shrugged. "There's nothing to see anymore."

NINE

"JULIA."

Hunched over her desk, absorbed in writing a fifteen-minute essay about a rip-tide, her mind was far away on a beach, watching the breaking waves. The spot she stood on was being steadily eaten away by churning foam and sand.

"Julia?"

She looked up. Mr. Ohlman, her ninth grade English teacher, was squatting next to her desk, staring at her with deep, watery blue eyes.

Struggling to return from her seaside adventure, she stared back at him. He held a short story she'd written the week before called "The Wreck," about a shy deckhand framed for starting the fire that sank the ferry. The paper had an A+ circled in red at the top. Mr. Ohlman's dark curly hair swirled zestfully around his head, and this morning's close shave was already challenged by a new wave of forthcoming stubble. His interest seemed like an invasion. Her pulse quickened, and she ran her tongue around the inside of her mouth, trying to decide if her breath was okay.

"Do you like stories about the sea?" he asked.

"I like… shipwrecks…" she stammered, hoping he didn't hear her heart thumping in her throat.

"If you'd like to read an interesting story about a shipwreck, try *Collision Course* by Alvin Moscow. It's an account of the sinking of the *Andrea Doria*, written by a well-known journalist of the 1950s."

Julia hesitated. She'd already read it a year ago, but didn't want to insult her teacher. "I-I'll look for it in the library." Ears burning, she stared down into her notebook until Mr. Ohlman stood up walked away. He was by far the cutest teacher at school, but she couldn't summon up a grain of courage to return his gaze. She scribbled *Collision Course* in the margin and felt a little thump as Erin tossed an eraser at her back and gave a tiny snort. Mr. Ohlman spoke again, from the front of the room. He'd moved on to a different subject by then, and Julia straightened up when she heard him say, "*The Wizard of Oz* has a few poignant lines in it."

Some of the boys snickered.

"Really. Pay attention next time you see it. For instance, when the Scarecrow says, 'Some people without brains do an awful lot of talking.'"

Morty, her loud, window-narrating neighbor from up the street was seated in front of Julia. He turned around to her as if to make a wisecrack. He was winking emphatically, and she thought he was making fun of Mr. Ohlman. He kept on winking at her, and then she saw that his whole body was twitching harder and harder until his mouth dropped open and his eyes rolled up into his head. His straight blonde hair slapped his damp forehead in time to each twitch, and then his books fell from his desk as he slid off his chair and crumpled onto the floor.

"Somebody get the nurse!" Mr. Ohlman shouted, and Julia was out in the hall instantly, hurrying to the nurse's office with Erin right behind her. "Help!" she yelled into the office. "Somebody fainted!" "He might be dying!" Erin added. The nurse emerged at a full run. Julia watched from the doorway as her teacher knelt on the floor over Morty. "Is he dead?" she whispered, wondering if she might miss his caustic window-side observations if he were gone. "No," Erin answered. "Mr. Ohlman was using a pen to keep him from choking on his tongue."

Mr. Ohlman and the nurse helped Morty into a wheelchair and rolled him into the hallway past Julia. He was barely conscious, and looked like he might throw up. Julia ducked back into the classroom. The pen was still lying on the floor. "Ugh," Ceddie said, picking it up and tossing it into the trash can.

The Bluefins, in their autumn guise, arrived home that evening from a hunting trip in the Catskills with a dead deer tied over the trunk of

Ed's silver Cadillac. Teddy went out to look while Julia stayed inside and shuddered. She couldn't bear the thought of looking into the deer's vacant eyes.

"Did Dad do it?" she whispered, when Teddy came back in.

"No. George, the lawyer guy did."

They took the deer to a butcher in Pattituck Cove who dressed it out. George kept the head, and several days later some of the venison was returned in small parcels of white butcher paper, where it remained in the freezer for many years to come, after the first tasting. Teddy got the tail, and Ed kept the heart. He used it to demonstrate all the working parts of a heart to his children and then stored it in the freezer with the rest of the meat.

Several days later Julia decided it was time to impress her biology teacher on her own terms. She took the frozen heart out of the freezer one morning and placed it in a lunchbox, storing it in her locker at school until class that afternoon.

She came to class early, which she loathed for personal reasons; she hated Mr. Drummling, with his callous temper and impatience for anyone under the age of twenty. He had an olive complexion, fierce black hair graying at his temples, and a large, angry brow. She could see the veins pulsing in his forehead, and wondered if they were secretly planning a coup amongst themselves.

Julia showed him the heart, which he was clearly impressed by, suggesting she make a short presentation to the class.

"*Eeeeewwww!* How could you bring such a gross thing here?" Ceddie and her friends wailed at Julia later, as she demonstrated the operation of the ventricles just as her father had done, by sticking her fingers up the freshly defrosted, squishy tubes of the main arteries.

"Try to be strong for Mother Nature," Erin quipped from her seat.

There was a loud crash and Julia looked over to see Mr. Drummling slump over his desk and roll onto the floor, knocking the green wastepaper basket on its side.

A class full of shaky students watched from the windows as their science teacher was carried from the school on a stretcher and loaded onto an ambulance. He lay still, his arms resting at his sides, with a white sheet pulled up to his chin. His olive skin was several shades lighter, and Julia could see that the veins on his forehead were at rest, their mission accomplished.

A school of neon fish traveled around her aquarium together, turning as a group to keep clear of a gang of hatchet fish. Julia's old sparkly blue eyeglasses from seventh grade lay on the gravel at the bottom of the tank next to some marbles, loose change, and a sunken ship with a little plastic skeleton that sat up and bubbled air when it popped in and out of the hatch.

"He shouldn't have been teaching children in the tenth grade," she heard Clarisse say from her parents' bedroom across the hall. "He just didn't have the right disposition."

"He had a minor stroke, not a nervous breakdown," Ed answered. "He'll be all right as long as he retires from teaching and finds a more suitable job."

Yeah, like prison warden or something. Julia breathed a sigh of relief. She'd spent most of the day feeling guilty for Mr. Drummling's collapse, especially when Ceddie blamed her for trying to murder him. "Just because your father is supposed to be some hot-shot doctor doesn't mean you should be bringing gross stuff to school to kill the teachers."

"Yeah, bitch," hissed Lorraine as they followed Julia down the hallway.

"Just because you're an obnoxious half-wit doesn't mean you should go around accusing people of preposterous things," Erin's retort cut through the stream of students.

"Sooo... two tragedies in one week," Teddy remarked at dinner that night. "And Julia was lucky enough to be on hand for both."

"Shush!" Clarisse said.

"What was the matter with Morty?" Julia asked. "He was twitching all over and then he passed out."

"Besides being mad at the world, he had a seizure," Ed answered. Pattituck Cove was such a small town that he'd seen most everyone who was ill-fated enough to land in the one-hundred bed hospital.

"Will he do it again?"

"It's possible."

"Maybe you should think about getting your seat changed in that class," Teddy said.

"Now that's enough," Clarisse said sharply.

"What about Mr. Drummling?"

"His brain exploded," Teddy said.

"Ugh!" Nate gasped.

Ed put down his fork and glared at Teddy and Nate. "He had a stroke. A blood vessel burst in his brain. So I'd appreciate it if you didn't go spreading inaccurate rumors around town."

"That's right," Clarisse added. "People's medical issues are private. No one is to discuss anything they hear at this table from the hospital with their friends at school. Understood?"

"What if we hear someone saying something really dumb about a person in the hospital?" Julia asked. "For example, 'his brain exploded.'" She glanced at Teddy, who sent a pea flying toward her from the end of his spoon. Ducking, she continued, "Should we just say nothing?"

"Just say, 'I don't think that's true.'" Clarisse said. "And please don't boast about your father's position at the hospital."

Ed chuckled softly and whispered. "That's your mother's Pennsylvania Dutch ancestry poking through."

Everyone laughed, then Clarisse said, "Alright. Now let's change the subject."

"Here's your *cherces*: You can tell me who you are and where you live now, or we can take you down to the station and call your parents from there."

Teddy sat in the back of the squad car as it crept through the darkened streets of Pattituck Cove. His friend Ernie had already been dropped off at his house although Teddy, knowing that Ed and Clarisse had company for the first time in ages, would not tell the police officer where he lived. Teddy and Ernie had been caught in the headlights of the police cruiser while wandering around the neighborhood with Ernie's pellet gun.

Teddy shrugged, figuring if the police couldn't find his parents from here, then they probably wouldn't find them from the station either. The cruiser drove around town for another half hour.

"Any of this look familiar to you?" Officer Henley sipped on coffee from Stockard's Deli and stifled a belch as they turned onto another street. Teddy was silent for another few blocks.

"Okay," he decided. "I'll tell you as long as you drop me off a block away. My parents have company."

"Nope. Have to bring you home myself."

"But I'm not the one who had the gun!"

Teddy cringed, imagining a humiliating meeting with his father and Bluefin George the lawyer in a dark somber office with the freshly killed deer presiding from over the mantelpiece. Then he remembered the snippet from a phone conversation he'd overheard earlier that week between Clarisse and her sister Ginger. "Ed's doing great. He loves this area and seems to be handling the loss of Bill pretty well. I've been keeping a close watch on him, though."

I can't wind up at the police station!

Teddy gave in with a gulp. "It's this street...here. Second house down."

The patrol car came to a stop and Officer Henley turned around to look at him, his features suddenly clear in the overhead light of the cruiser. "You're Dr. Lloyd's kid, huh?" Teddy realized it was one of the Bluefins. He'd known who Teddy was all along.

"Yes, sir."

He passed the house and then stopped a few doors down. "If I ever catch you messing around with guns or anything else, I'll take you down to the station and book you."

Teddy got out and skulked back to the house as the police car pulled away.

"Promise me that you'll take care of this and return it immediately when you're finished reading it," Mr. Ohlman said, pressing a vintage copy of *Life Magazine* encased in plastic, into Julia's hands. "There are some great pictures, and stories about the survivors."

"Uh...okay, I promise," she stammered, blushing.

On the cover was the ill-fated Italian luxury liner *Andrea Doria,* mortally wounded and listing to her starboard side with an expanse of sea around her. A lifeboat with the captain and the last few officers bobbed in the water nearby.

TEN

EARLY THE NEXT SUMMER, Julia lay curled up in the forward bunk of *The Pearl II* while waves thumped against the bow. Her family was crossing Long Island Sound on their way to Connecticut. In spite of the sunny, warm day she stayed down below, re-reading by incandescent light the story of Linda Morgan, the "miracle child" in *Collision Course*. She figured if Mr. Ohlman was so keen on her reading the story, she ought to give it another go in case she'd missed something. On impact, the bow of *The Stockholm* had swept beneath Linda's bed on the *Andrea Doria*, catapulting her from cabin 52 onto a sea breaker wall eighty feet behind the tip of *The Stockholm's* bow. "Whew..." Julia mused, beginning to feel sleepy. "Some rescue story. I guess they could've done worse..."

The drone of *The Pearl II's* engines finally won out, lulling her to sleep. When she awoke, they were pulling into a marina on the Connecticut side of the Sound as the sun began to set. She climbed up the ladder to the flying bridge and watched the shore pass by as they cruised through the inlet. It looked softer, greener, and more exotic than their Long Island side, as if they'd traveled much further, to a different country. "Stonington, CT," a weathered sign read.

As they neared the dock, Ed took the boat out of gear. Teddy threw a line to a dockhand from the bow. Nate tossed the man a line from the stern, and they tied the boat to the dock for the evening. Ed shut the engines off and the air was still.

"Let's go for a walk and see what's around before it gets dark," Clarisse called out.

As they sauntered through the cobblestone streets past old ivy-covered stone buildings, Julia noticed a forty-ish couple holding hands as they paused to look in the windows of the shops. She glanced at her parents, feeling a little dismayed that they walked several feet apart from each other. She realized that she probably hadn't ever seen them hold hands like that. Sure, they hugged now and then, but hand-holding warmth seemed to be missing. In fact, she noticed a slightly strained look on her mother's face that seemed out of place for a vacation. On the way back to the boat, Ed bought some live lobsters from a street vendor. Julia hurried to the forward bunk with her book to avoid the lobsters' descent into boiling water.

The next day they got up and wandered through Mystic Seaport, climbing on a preserved schooner that smelled like whale oil and salt and sampling homemade ginger cookies baked by women in 17th century costumes. It was mildly interesting to Julia, who couldn't get Mr. Ohlman out of her mind. *Why did he seem so interested in my writing? And the sunken ships?* Even though the thought of her former English teacher evoked an inner musky stirring she couldn't deny, she still recalled the forward moves of Andy, the stable manager, with disgust. She'd finally confided this to Erin, who remarked, "Andy was a decrepit old dirt ball. I think Paul is just being a really cool teacher."

"Paul..." Julia echoed. She loved that Erin referred to all her teachers by their first names.

Standing at the curb, Ed joked and cajoled everyone into posing in front of one nautical curio after another. "Closer together," he ordered, waving his camera at them.

"Again?" Nate complained. "How much old boat crap can we stand in front of?"

"Your father needs a peaceful vacation," Clarisse hissed, as they gathered before a giant anchor.

She glanced back at her father, standing there in his Bermuda shorts and boat sneakers. He seemed fidgety and impatient underneath his jovial veneer.

Julia was glad when the sky began to cloud up, sending them back to Stonington in a water taxi. "What time are we taking off tomorrow?" she asked.

"Bright and early," Ed answered, perking up at the notion of getting back in the boat and moving on. "We'll cruise out past Watch Hill Point and then cross over to Block Island from there."

"And the rains, came, dowwwwnnn...!" Ed sang after dinner, as raindrops splattered the boat. They'd made it to the marina just before the downpour began in earnest and now, as daylight faded, they sat on the covered part of the deck watching the streetlights of Stonington come on. Rain teemed on surface of the water around them, creating an extra layer of bouncing mist. The evening air was warm and mushy.

"You look bored," a woman's voice called. A man and woman stood next to the boat in dripping yellow rain gear. "We thought you might want to play with this," she continued, handing a narrow box to Teddy, who took it and answered, "Uh, thanks." The couple waved and continued down the dock.

"Thank you," Clarisse echoed. "What a nice thing to do," she added, turning back to Teddy.

"What is it?" Julia asked.

"Or-ig-am-i..." Teddy answered slowly, reading from the cover of the box.

They brought it into the galley and spent the rest of the evening folding colored bits of paper, laughing at each other's attempts to create exotic birds and fish. Outside, the rain downgraded itself to a mild drizzle.

"Now hear this," Ed's voice crackled through the megaphone. "Time to get up... rise and shine!"

Julia stirred as the smell of bacon and eggs wafted from the galley. She sat up and rubbed her eyes, knocking a red paper crane from the ledge over her bunk. Pushing up the hatch cover, she squinted at the sunlit harbor with a feeling of odd comfort in being far from anything familiar.

A morning haze hung over the water when they chugged out of Stonington. A flock of seagulls escorted them from the marina, flying over the wake of the boat as a foghorn called in the distance. Julia and Nate sat on the bridge with their father, listening to the jumble of voices crackling on the marine radio. Ed pointed to a lighthouse on the eastern shore. "Once we get there, we'll change course and head south, over to Block Island."

They motored up the Connecticut coast and turned south when they reached the lighthouse. The ocean lay in front of them, sparkling with tiny diamonds of morning sunlight. "Feel the way the waves roll, now?" Ed asked. "We're officially at sea." He puffed his chest out as the boat surged forward through, up one watery trough and down another.

"It feels like a giant rocking chair," Nate remarked.

"Next stop, Europe!" Teddy called from the deck.

"Or Africa, depending on the wind," Ed chuckled.

"How long will it take to get there?" Julia asked, peering through a set of binoculars as she searched for Block Island. The fact that the *Andrea Doria* had gone down a little more than a hundred miles east of them hadn't escaped her.

"Two, maybe two and a half hours," Ed answered.

Seeing nothing but a vast, open sea, she looked backward. A bank of fog had crept up the shore, covering Stonington. "Good thing we're leaving. Look at that," she said.

Glancing over his shoulder, Ed frowned when he saw the growing fog.

"Wow!" Teddy yelled. "That stuff's coming in really quick!"

"Should we try to outrun it?" Nate asked. As they chugged further out, another fog bank swelled in from the north until it joined the first one, churning up a giant miasma of white air. Ed looked at the compass and edged the throttle forward. Seeing the speed of the burgeoning clouds, he changed his mind and took the boat out of gear as the ominous mist engulfed *The Pearl II*.

Julia glanced at the depth finder, then at her father. *It's too deep to even drop an anchor,* she realized.

They bobbed on the water as wet, cottony air began to surround them.

"How did this happen so fast?" Clarisse called from below.

"I don't know," Ed answered, his proud sea captain spirit beginning to deflate. "I didn't see anything in the weather forecast."

A foghorn pierced the air, joined by the floating bell markers from the harbor behind them.

"Why do they sound so close?" Julia asked, shivering.

"Because we slowed down, dummy," Nate said.

"Maybe the heavy mist is amplifying the sound," Teddy guessed, climbing halfway up the ladder to the bridge.

"No really, it sounds closer!" Clarisse called.

Ed took the boat out of gear and listened. Over the low putter of the engines, they heard the unbelievable sound of waves breaking on a beach. Seagull cries sliced through the haze as the family froze. Ed glanced at the compass again and shook his head. "This shouldn't be happening," he muttered under his breath.

"What the hell is going on?!?" Clarisse shouted.

"I don't know, there must be a strong current!" Ed called back.

Just then the bow of a large sailboat loomed through the mist with its sails down, traveling on motor power. Julia, along with the rest of the Lloyds, cringed in silent horror as the boat approached, sounding its horn. She recognized one of the crew as the woman who'd given them the origami set the night before. The families stared helplessly at each other as the white hull of the sailboat careened past the stern, missing *The Pearl II* by less than twenty feet. They were headed in the direction of the beach, and Ed waved frantically for them to turn around. He pushed the throttle forward, driving the boat away from the sound of the breakers. Then he picked up the radio transmitter and shouted, "Mayday! Mayday! This is *The Pearl II*, Whiskey Charlie 7745. We have a vessel in distress, repeat, a vessel in distress near Watch Hill Point!"

"You kids come down here!" Clarisse called.

Julia and Nate scrambled down the ladder. Standing on the deck, they heard a thump in the distance, then a splintering crash. Julia covered her ears. The fog had begun to lift, revealing the sailboat pitched to one side, lodged between an outcropping of rocks just below the lighthouse with its mast broken off. Waves pummeled the hull as the crew clung to the side rails in bright orange life jackets. Julia sighed with relief when she saw that they were still alive. A Coast Guard cutter sped toward them from the harbor, and another came racing from the north. Ed stood poised on the bridge with his radio transmitter in hand.

"Thanks for your assistance, *Pearl II*," an official voice crackled over the radio. "We'll take it from here. Over and out."

"Roger that. *Pearl II* out."

"Some fog," he whistled, climbing down the ladder. "How about some coffee?" His face was two shades lighter, but he looked heroic. Julia leaned over the side and dropped a green origami fish in the water and watched as it floated toward the lighthouse.

The fog finally burned off, and sun sparkled on the early afternoon water as they set a course for Block Island. Haunted by the memory of the miracle girl, Julia decided to forego reading the rest of *Collision Course*. She stayed on the flying bridge next to her father until the shape of the island began to appear on the horizon.

ELEVEN

JULIA WAS INSTANTLY SMITTEN by the cozy remoteness of Block Island. According to the dockhand, a person could bicycle from one end to the other in an hour, past sun-bleached farms and weather-worn houses, and still see the ocean lapping on all sides.

"Feels like camp, doesn't it?" Ed asked, as they all peddled past the town on rented bikes. He still wore his captain's cap perched jauntily on the side of his head.

"No, not really," Julia cringed, recalling a short stint at Girl Scout Camp, where the counselors hid those tiny cereal boxes in the woods and made the girls hunt for them in the morning. "I could live here, though," she added.

"When the season ends and all the tourists go home, you'd have to get used to seeing the same fifteen people all the time," Ed said, scowling.

"What's wrong with that?' Julia asked.

"You'd get tired of them."

"Let's hope the astronauts don't get tired of each other, crammed in that giant tin can," Teddy piped up. Freshly back from his first year of college, the Apollo 11 was all he could talk about. Even though the first moon landing was imminent, Julia was still more interested in the island. The water was so clear you could see down to the bottom from the dock. While Teddy stayed glued to the radio, Julia and Nate fished for hermit crabs with a homemade trap made from a perforated coffee can. Later on, they set them loose in the women's shower at the marina and hid in the bushes outside to listen for the screams.

That evening, the Lloyds were squeezed into a booth in the packed bar of Deadeye Dick's Restaurant, watching the landing of *The Eagle*, along with everyone else on Block Island. As Neil Armstrong took one giant step for mankind, the crowd broke into a cheer.

"How do you like that?" Ed mused. "They're standing on a whole other world."

"Just think: *anything* could come popping out from behind a hill," Teddy added.

"Like a flying saucer?" Nate whispered.

"Or a Russian spy ship," Teddy whispered back.

When the newscast was over, Clarisse noticed Ed staring wistfully at the frosty glasses of beer that sailed by on the trays of cocktail waitresses. She quickly herded the family out to the street, where the sound of ships' horns and bells coming from the harbor created a din lasting well into the night.

They left Block Island the next morning and headed home, this time hugging the coast of Long Island.

Anchored in Milton's Neck Cove a few weeks later, *The Pearl II* was tied together side by side with several other boatfuls of families. A favorite spot for weekenders, the cove was protected by a curved arm of sand. At high tide you could see the lights from Connecticut at night, and at low tide it was dotted with horseshoe crabs, a steep dune cutting off the view to the Sound. Erin was the guest of the outing, as the boat would only fit one extra friend per overnight trip.

A greased watermelon hit the water with a dull thud and sank in slow motion before popping up to the surface. Everyone raced toward it. Ten pairs of hands grappled for a hold, while the players kicked and splashed around to position themselves. The dads shouted the loudest, making combined efforts to lift the watermelon and throw it into the opposing team's dinghy, but it was mostly a free-for-all. Julia saw an opening in the fracas and raced toward the melon, but several other swimmers clawed right over her and she was pushed beneath the surface. She opened her eyes underwater and looked up. Through the green-filtered sunlight, she could see kicking and flailing bodies surrounding the dinghy. Then a foot caught her shoulder and pushed her further down. Frantic and out of breath, Julia fought for an opening when a hand grabbed her by the hair and dragged her up. She gasped, staring at Erin's freckled face and blue eyes. Erin stared back. "You okay? Jeez. Some people are taking this game a little too seriously." Her long red hair billowed in the water as she floated next to Julia.

"You... you saved me," Julia sputtered.

"Let's get outta here. This game is stupid anyway," Erin said, pushing her toward the boat ladder.

"But no one ever seems to *be* there," Nate complained later, gazing at the beach through binoculars. Four large white signs with black and red letters strictly advised, NO LANDING ON BEACH.

"They're probably afraid all the yahoos will crap it up like they did to Eaton's Neck." Teddy said.

"Besides, it's private property," Clarisse added.

Just then a couple landed a dinghy on the beach and jumped out with their Springer spaniel. Within minutes, a jeep sped from the neck of the peninsula with a loud megaphone, chasing the couple and their dog back to their dinghy. People from the boats shouted nasty comments to the driver of the jeep. Some of them honked their boat horns in disgust.

"Hey, why don't you arrest the dog!" yelled Nate.

"Shush!" said Clarisse. "Don't be smart-alecky!"

"I'd like to go and chop those signs down," Julia said.

"Ha!" Ed laughed. "You'd never do anything like that."

"Hmph," Julia replied. Erin leaned over and elbowed her.

Later on, Ed and Nate were attempting to install the little dinghy motor to the stern of the lifeboat when it slipped off the back and sank, leaving a trail of bubbles.

"Dammit!" Ed yelled, "I thought you were ready!" An uncomfortable silence fell over the group.

"There's one motor you'll never see again," remarked Freddie on the boat next door, gesturing with his beer can.

Ed refused to call it a lost cause, and a few minutes later he was pulling on his old wet suit and tank he kept in reserve for emergencies. Sticking his regulator into his mouth, he waved and tumbled backward over the side of the boat. He bobbed up to the surface and said, "If I'm not back in five minutes, send out a search party." Julia peered over the edge of the boat, tracking Ed's bubbles as he sank. The minutes oozed by as she took deep, long breaths in an attempt to stay connected to her father's breathing. The bubbles moved away from the boat.

Clarisse frowned under her sun hat and sighed loudly. "We should have attached a rope to him."

"It's not that deep," Teddy answered. "He can probably see the surface from under there."

By now everyone on the bound flotilla watched from flying bridges, decks and sailboat riggings, focusing on the set of bubbles moving in a circle.

"Here he comes!" exclaimed Nate, and Ed popped up to the surface with the motor, removing his regulator with one hand. The audience cheered as he handed the motor to Teddy, and Julia noticed that her teeth had been clenched in anxiety. She waggled her jaw back and forth a few times.

"I had to drop my weight belt down there," he said, climbing into the boat. "It was so murky I practically gave up, and then at the last minute I kicked something hard and grabbed hold, and it turned out to be the motor!"

After dinner Julia and Erin climbed up to the flying bridge. The cove had mellowed out for the evening, and the afternoon noise of water play was being replaced by quiet laughter and the clinking of ice in cocktail glasses. Julia glanced down and saw her parents and brothers deep in a game of gin rummy on the boat next door, each one nursing a can of 7-Up. "Hurdy-Gurdy Man" wafted from a radio somewhere in the cove, sprinkled with a set of muffled groans.

"Your father's really brave," Erin said, surveying the cove with binoculars. "I mean, when he said he felt something and turned around and grabbed it… it could have been something really creepy!"

"Yeah, I know. It scares me when I think about it, so I try not to.

What do you see?"

"Mostly people resting like beached seals... a couple of onboard TVs going... wait, look at this! Coming to you live, from Eye on New York!" She handed the binoculars to Julia.

"On the boat with the blue hull. Feast your eyes."

Julia latched onto a naked couple rolling around together on the floor of a cockpit in a motorboat anchored across the cove. The woman had her legs wrapped around the man's waist and they were humping furiously.

"Wow...I never saw it before..." she trailed off, secretly wondering whether there ought to be a flag on the masthead for this occasion.

"I walked in on my parents once," Erin said. "It was weird."

Julia felt another musky stir and thought about what it would be like with Mr. Ohlman. A heat wave passed through her and she sighed, handing the binoculars back to Erin, not quite ready to share what she was feeling about a school teacher. "I guess you just have to be there yourself to really appreciate it."

"Yeah, I know. I'm just not in that much of a hurry," Erin said. "I want to find somebody really good."

"Do you ever... at least...imagine it?" Julia asked.

"Sure! Like with Donovan," she said, gesturing toward the boat with the radio. Or John Lennon."

"Come on, let's go," Erin whispered, tapping Julia's shoulder. "Everyone's asleep. Time to prove the old man wrong."

Julia groaned and rolled over. She and Erin had opted to spend the night on the deck in sleeping bags, and she would have been perfectly fine with forgetting the whole idea, but Erin needled her softly until she finally got up. Already dressed in a halter top and cutoff jeans, Julia tucked a keyhole saw into her back pocket. They snuck down the swim ladder into the warm, black water while light from a half moon flooded the beach. Julia stayed close to Erin, secretly wary of what might lie beneath them.

"Isn't this cool?" Erin whispered, moving water with her hand. Green plankton sparkled all around them and Julia focused on carving slow, silent breaststrokes through the glittery water. Fifty yards later she felt the sand under her feet and scrambled out of the water, trying not to step on any horseshoe crabs. They crept up the beach with the saw and knelt next to a NO LANDING sign.

"It's much bigger up close," Erin remarked.

Heavy four-by-four wooden posts anchored it in the sand. Erin cleared a small ditch around one pole with a clam shell and Julia began to saw gently, so as not to wake anyone on the boats. Waves from the Sound side of the peninsula created a distraction, and a slight breeze blew over the crest of the sandbar. She got halfway through one post, handed the saw to Erin, and sat back to rest. Lit by moonlight, tiny whitecaps riffled on the Sound. Connecticut twinkled from the other side.

"We're through this one," Erin said, handing the saw back to Julia.

After sawing for a few minutes, the sign began to wobble.

"Hold on to it!" Julia said. "I think we can push it over now."

"Quietly!" Erin said, trying to keep the wood from creaking as it splintered.

They carried the sign down to the shore and eased it into the water, guiding it back to the boat like a raft. Julia climbed up the ladder to get some rope. Then they hoisted it onto the deck. Leaning it on its side like a hunter's bounty, they peeled off wet clothes and climbed into their sleeping bags. Julia shivered, breathless in the excitement of pulling off such a stunt.

"I can't believe they did it," Ed remarked the next morning, standing out on the deck.

"Yeah, that thing's as big as she is." Their boat neighbor Freddie added, pointing to Julia, who pretended to be asleep.

"Cover it up before anyone important sees it," Clarisse snapped, storming onto the deck with a blanket.

"What were you *thinking?*" her mother demanded, when Julia and Erin finally emerged from their sleeping bags.

"Oh, it's just a sign," Ed said. "Still, we probably ought to get out of here."

Passing Matinecock Point on their way home, Ed slowed the

boat down and they anchored over The Wreck to try and catch some blackfish for dinner.

Erin and Julia stayed on the flying bridge out of Clarisse's way to avoid any further scolding over the sign-stealing. Julia was explaining to Erin about The Wreck that lay submerged beneath them when they heard Teddy yell, "This one's huge!" His fishing rod bent over in a deep arc.

"Stay with him," Ed said. "Don't let the line go slack!"

Teddy let the fish swim away with the hook for a few seconds, then yanked the rod back. When the line became taut, he reeled as hard as he could. To Julia, watching from above, it began to look as if he were reeling in Matinecock Point. The harder he reeled, the more the entire peninsula seemed to curve toward the boat.

Ed ran back with the net and held it next to the fishing line as it danced up and down over the water. Clarisse and Nate joined them, and they stood anxiously at the stern watching Teddy play tug of war with his fishing rod. Then they saw it coming up behind the boat. First a large, dark shadow, then a ghastly figure began to appear. It loomed up, fins flapping, with pointed ridges all over its face. A spiky dorsal fin and bulbous grey lips broke the surface of the water. With ancient yellow eyes, it gave them a warning look. Then the fishing line broke and it disappeared.

Everyone groaned.

"Good grief!" Erin yelled.

"What the hell was that?" Nate exclaimed.

"Watch your language, mister!" Clarisse barked.

"Maybe a giant blowfish," Teddy said, looking wistfully over the side.

"No, it was the Monster of Matinecock Point!" Julia called from the bridge.

"Oh, that's silly," Clarisse snapped back, clearly still angry over the sign-stealing.

"What's the matter with her?" Erin whispered to Julia. "She's really uptight."

"I don't know... she's been acting kind of anxious lately."

Ed stared intently at the place where the creature had sunk beneath the waves.

They chugged into the harbor with the NO LANDING sign in the back of the boat and, covering it with blankets, carried it up the dock and brought it home in the Cadillac, with its sawed off posts sticking partway out of the trunk.

TWELVE

O N THE HOCKEY FIELD behind the high school, Julia, Erin and several other friends clung to the edges of an Air Force parachute Erin had brought from home. It was a warm, breezy fall day during lunch break, and wind filled the parachute enough for the girls to be pulled along, letting the force of the air stream swirl them around the field.

"It's better when you hold on tight!" Erin shouted.

Just then a big gust of wind filled the chute. The girls shrieked and giggled as they flew over the grass, clinging to the nylon. It spun them in a circle, and then off toward the basketball courts. The door of the cafeteria opened and Mr. Ohlman stepped out. He surveyed the scene for a moment, then trotted over to join them, grabbing an edge. Julia muffled her girlish shrieks and tried not to blush as the billowing parachute whooshed them over the grassy field.

When the break came to a close, he helped them fold up the parachute before heading back inside. Julia and her friends lingered outside until the new, electronic blip echoed over the outdoor P.A. system signaling the end of lunch period.

"Whooaa. Here comes 'Phantom of the Opera' and her butch friends," sneered Ceddie, echoed by her henchwomen, who'd formed their customary insulting gauntlet inside the door.

"Gee, Ceddie, you better take the rest of the day off. It looks like you chipped your nail polish," Erin shot back.

"Don't forget to tell your parents to vote for the library," Mr. Ohlman called from the door of his classroom, oblivious to the girl-banter.

After school, Erin and Julia walked home together as far as the Four Corners. Julia snuggled in Clarisse's old woolen nursing cape that her mother had allowed her to wear if she promised to behave like an adult, following the beach sign affair. "You always know what to say when Ceddie makes fun of us. I wish I could do that. I always think of stuff later. Why did she keep calling us butch?"

"Because she's a snot-sicle," Erin answered.

"I mean, sure, we do lots of cool stuff but..." Julia gasped, suddenly realizing the magnitude of Ceddie's accusation. "Do we act like we're... too *close* or something?"

"Maybe."

"Are we?" Julia asked carefully.

Erin stopped in her tracks. "Alright. Let's find out for once and for all." She led Julia through a break in the bushes, into a thick hedge row. Setting her books down in the dirt, she said, "Okay. Let's do it."

"Do what?!?" Julia whispered.

"Kiss, you dummy. We have to find out if it means anything. Come on," Erin said.

Julia hung back for a few seconds until her bewilderment cleared. "Oh... okay." She leaned in toward her best friend's face still clutching her books under one arm, and closed her eyes.

They met, brushed lips softly and backed off.

"That wasn't a real kiss," Erin said.

"I... don't know what a real one's supposed to feel like... I just don't feel very...*mushy,*" Julia answered.

"Me neither, actually."

There was an awkward silence, then Erin threw her arms around Julia and exclaimed, "Best friends' kiss!" kissing her hard on one cheek, then the other.

"Best friends forever!" Julia agreed, dropping her books and kissing Erin on both of her cheeks. They stood with their arms wrapped around each other for a few seconds more, and then stepped back, letting go of each other gently.

"So we're not butch and now we know it," Erin shrugged. They peered out of the bushes, checking for any possible witnesses, and stepped back onto the sidewalk. "Forget about anything Ceddie or anyone else says, okay?" Erin continued. "Sooner or later, boys will show up who don't trigger the gag reflex."

"Yeah, maybe like Mr. Ohlman," Julia sighed.

"I knew it! You have such a crush on him!"

"Yeah, but he's just so... perfect, so... *together*. He probably has a gorgeous girlfriend anyway."

"Who lives in a penthouse in New York City," Erin added.

"Yeah, probably a model."

"No, he's too smart for that. She's probably some brainiac scientist who ties her long blonde hair up in a bun and wears horn-rimmed glasses and a white lab coat during the day. Then she lets her hair down at night and wears tight, sexy dresses."

Julia arrived home from school and headed to the kitchen, where a pot of meat sauce was bubbling on the stove. She lifted the metal lid and sampled it before she heard Clarisse yell, "Stay out of there!" from the laundry room. It was Friday night, their traditional spaghetti night. Julia opened the refrigerator door and saw the odd sight of a bottle of Chianti in a straw cask. Following the monster fishing incident, Ed had convinced Clarisse that a glass of wine with dinner once a week was something he could handle. "I'm the Chief of Staff. I've worked very hard for this. It's my due," he'd insisted. Clarisse finally relented, although she went out and bought a set of apéritif glasses because they would hold less wine.

As they ate dinner, Julia told them about Erin's parachute.

"Where would she get something like that?" Nate asked.

"From an Army surplus store. Erin has a cousin in Viet Nam right now."

"We got a letter from Teddy today," Clarisse said. "He decided to join the ROTC program at college. He's worried about the draft when he graduates, and thought he might want some officer training just in case."

"We'll be done over there long before that," Ed said, taking a long sip of wine.

"How was school today, Nate?" Clarisse asked, drawing the attention away from her husband.

"We had this nerdy old substitute in music. She made us listen to a record by someone named Edith Piaf and she sang along with it, like this." He stood up and leaned against the side table on one arm, singing in a fake French accent and batting his eyes. Everyone erupted with laughter.

"I heard a funny one in the operating room this morning," Ed said, finishing the wine from his aperitif glass with a quick gulp. "A man shows up at a house of ill repute in Alaska during a storm one night—"

"Ed!" Clarisse protested.

"And engages the services of one of the women. They go upstairs and get into bed, but suddenly, a fierce wind blows the window open and the couple freezes together instantly! Another gust of wind whips them out the window and down into the street. "Uh!" Clarisse harrumphed, giggling at the same time. He continued, "So a passing hobo stops and knocks at the front door. The Madame opens it and he drawls, 'Hey lady, your sign fell down.'"

Julia laughed so hard she wheezed. Clarisse tried to restrain herself, but ended up laughing uncontrollably anyway.

Nate laughed along with everyone until he asked, "What's ill repute?"

"I'll tell you later," Ed chuckled, filling up his wine glass.

"Mr. Ohlman says to remind you guys to vote for the library," Julia said. "Are they building one in Pattituck Cove?"

"Some of us would like to, although others would rather have a new tennis club," Ed answered.

"But there's already a tennis court at the beach," Nate said.

"Well, I guess they want a fresh one. Indoors."

Julia looked forward to Friday dinner after that. Everyone seemed funnier that night, and it quickly became the party night at the Lloyd household. Ed liked the Chianti, Julia and Nate got a kick out of seeing him become more animated, and Clarisse seemed to lighten up and enjoy the humor, in a guarded sort of way.

A few weeks later Julia and Mr. Sidney, her organ teacher, were headed up Route 95 in his old Rambler station wagon. Julia, who'd now been playing the organ for almost two years, was starting to show real promise. Clarisse and Ed were delighted that Mr. Sidney, the talented organist at their own Lutheran church, had offered to take their daughter on a field trip.

"This won't be your ordinary place of worship," Mr. Sidney said proudly. He wore a cardigan sweater with patches on the sleeves, a style which had clearly run its course by the time he'd graduated from high school in the 1950s. Julia sported a brand new pair of lime green corduroy bell-bottoms and a peasant shirt. They were on their way to Connecticut, to a church where he'd helped to install a new organ.

Edging through the clogged traffic in Stamford, Julia mused, "I've never been to Connecticut in a car. We always came by boat. It seemed so much more exotic."

They pulled over to the curb and she sat straight up in astonishment, squinting through her blue-tinted aviator glasses. The church was built in the shape of a fish, with multi-colored stained glass windows all around it. "Amazing!" she gasped.

"Yep," Mr. Sidney nodded. "We'll be spending the afternoon in the belly of a whale."

He let them into the empty church with his own key and they went straight to the organ console. It had five tiers of keyboards, knobs everywhere, and a full set of wooden pedals.

"Listen to the trumpets...we installed them up in the balcony!" Mr. Sidney exclaimed, flicking a lever and playing a few notes. The sound of a trumpet ripped through the air from the rear of the church and echoed for a few seconds afterwards.

They took turns playing the huge organ for the entire afternoon. Outside, fat puffy clouds passed in front of the sun, causing all the colors in the church to shift from dazzling to muted, then back again. Julia felt as if she were inside a giant kaleidoscope someone was holding up to the light. The bass notes of the organ rumbled through her body as she watched Mr. Sidney play a Bach fugue, while shades of yellow and green light passed over his face.

"Play your Purvis piece while I do the trumpet solo on the keyboard!" he chortled.

Organ music filled the church again, thrilling Julia that such a massive sound could be coming from her small hands and feet. The trumpet solo pealed across the sky from the balcony.

"It felt like I was driving a giant spaceship," she told Mr. Sidney, when the music stopped echoing.

"Yes, it really is amazing, isn't it?" he said, diving into Bach's Passacaglia in C Minor, while the leviathan rumbled and glowed. Julia relaxed, basking in the beauty of the rolling colors and sounds.

That night she dreamt she was riding inside a nuclear whale with Teddy and Nate, driven by her father. They stood together in the forehead, looking out the front window. The ocean bottom flew past them, with an occasional posh sandcastle sparkling through the dark water.

"Can we stop and go inside one of them?" Julia asked.

"No, they're private. We have to keep going," Ed answered.

"I think we're in range," Teddy said.

Suddenly the whale split open and Julia floated out by herself, somersaulting through the water until she came to a stop. A shark swam toward her. *That figures.* She remembered reading something about going straight to the bottom when you see a shark because they feed from underneath. She let herself sink. As she landed on the ocean floor, the shark came up and nuzzled her with a cold nose. *Just a few minutes more, and I'll go back up.* Then she realized she had no breathing apparatus. Feeling the iciness of dread, she decided it would be best to head for the surface, shark or no shark. She kicked off the bottom and felt the patient, cold nose of the fish on her neck again. She took a deep breath and woke up, curious about her dreaming ability to breathe underwater.

"Schmucks. Total schmucks," Erin lamented, sitting at a table in the courtyard of the high school during lunch.

"I can't believe it," Julia groaned. "They have a chance for a new library and they vote for a *tennis court*? What *is* this?"

"I agree. I wish it had gone differently," Mr. Ohlman said, flipping through a *Village Voice*. His hair had grown out since he was their ninth grade English teacher, with dark curls that teased the tops of his wire-rimmed sunglasses. Since teachers and students had begun mingling in the courtyard due to the recent Open Campus policy, it was Erin who'd finally convinced Mr. Ohlman to join them at their table.

"So," Mr. Ohlman said, changing the subject, "Are you starting to look at colleges, Julia?"

Erin gave her a subtle, sideways glance which Julia tried to ignore, thinking, *he even cares?*

"Yeah. I mean yes. My parents want me to go to a liberal arts school. They say I should have something to fall back on in case I don't become a famous organist."

Erin elbowed her.

"And a-also..." Julia stammered, "Would you be able to write a recommendation for me?"

"Absolutely. Just tell me the schools you're applying to."

The intercom blipped over the courtyard. Mr. Ohlman folded his paper, stood up and excused himself from their table.

"I miss having him as a teacher," Julia said, after he left. "I didn't appreciate him enough back then. Now all we get of him is homeroom for ten minutes in the morning."

"Yeah. I heard he played "Strawberry Fields" for his class the other day and got them to discuss the lyrics. But relax—you're still jail-bait anyway," Erin laughed.

Thirteen

"That's the Philosophy Building," said the student guide, pointing to a turreted white Victorian on a wide street in Saratoga Springs. "Diamond Jim Brady built that house for his girlfriend, Lillian Russell. You can still see bullet holes in some of the floors."

Visiting the campus of Skidmore College in the late fall of 1970, Julia followed the guide from building to building in her fake fur waist-length jacket, mini skirt and high leather boots. This was rapidly becoming her first choice for college, as Teddy was already at Rensselaer Polytechnic, fifty miles south of Saratoga, and Erin had just gotten a full scholarship to Bennington College, an hour to the east in Vermont. Clarisse trailed behind with Ed, who slowly panned the Lillian Russell building with his new Super-8 movie camera. Half of the school was located in town, a collection of rambling Victorian houses and dormitories sprinkled around the south end of the city. In the center of all the quaint houses with their wrap-around porches on the Old Campus stood a faded pink six-story cement building.

"Ugh. What's that doing there?" Julia asked.

"Oh, the Pink Palace?" the guide answered. "It's a dorm they built before they began the New Campus. Isn't it ugly? The good thing is, it has the campus cafeteria on the first floor, so you don't have to go out to get breakfast."

"And you don't have to look at it if you're already inside," Ed added.

"Still... I hope I never have to live there."

"Eventually," her guide continued, "everything will be up on the New Campus. Probably in about eight years. For now, we take the bus back and forth."

They walked around the Old Campus peering into the buildings, one of which housed an old, rarely used pipe organ, and then drove up to the newer section in Ed's silver Cadillac. The other half of the Skidmore campus lay on the far north end of Broadway in crisp brick buildings, all connected with fresh new cement walkways. Julia peeked in the windows inside the music building and appreciated the solitude of the students practicing in their small, insulated rehearsal rooms, each with its own piano or console organ. Even the sterile forthrightness of the science labs, the library with its window seats, and the dormitory suites zipped into a neat brick package impressed her in an odd sort of way. But the Old Campus had an air of mystery with its antique buildings, a casual sloppy art department and the natural springs that flowed beneath the whole town.

Back in Pattituck Cove, Julia and Erin sat cross-legged in the bushes outside the Lutheran Church with their friends, Charlie and Jeff from the drama department at school, taking sips from a bottle of Bali Hai. Clarisse, Ed and Nate were already seated inside at the "Covered Dish Supper and Variety Show," where Julia and her high school youth group were the main attraction. Julia felt the wine begin to calm her swelling stage fright. This would be her first non-musical performance since she and Erin had gained the attention of Charlie and Jeff, the funniest guys in their class.

A car door slammed and they heard several pairs of footsteps on the sidewalk. Over the shrubbery, Julia saw Ceddie, bowl in hand, marching up the path with her mother. To Julia's dismay, Ceddie's mother had remarried a Lutheran and they'd become church members. Julia sucked back an angry snort and held her breath, but Ceddie trotted over and peered through the bushes.

"What are you doing in there?" she demanded. Her old Agent 99 look had been replaced with a peach, bell-bottomed pants suit, and her dark hair seemed to have petrified into a flip. She glared at them through the hedge like a curious crow.

"Hey! What'ja bring?" Jeff asked, while Charlie quickly stuffed the bottle of wine inside his suede, fringed jacket.

"Ambrosia," Ceddie snapped. She caught a glimpse of the bottle disappearing into Charlie's jacket and frowned. "*You* better not be drinking any of that, Julia." She backed out, nearly knocking the top off her covered dish. She smoothed out her pants suit and stalked into the church.

"What if she tells?" Julia whispered.

"She wouldn't... would she?" Jeff asked, peering over the top of his rectangular wire-rimmed glasses.

"I wouldn't put it past her," Erin muttered. "Ever since she began to lose her position in the snob society she's become an even worse pain."

"How did she do that?" Jeff wondered out loud.

"Her mother married for love instead of money this time," Erin answered.

"Well that's a step in the right direction, huh?" Julia shrugged, feeling the warmth of the wine.

"Let's just rehearse one more time. I'm hungry," Charlie said.

Long tables were set up in the church basement, with white tablecloths and a bowl of flowers on each one. Once the cheerful Lutheran flock had all sampled each other's covered dishes and were savoring their last dollops of ice cream, the lights went down and everyone hushed each other. The stage curtains opened on the high school group, and they burst into a spirited rendition of "Hair." The audience gave a hearty applause as the stage went dark. Then Julia appeared in a single spotlight, dressed as the telephone operator from *Laugh-In*, seated in front of a makeshift board of electronic plugs.

"One ringy-dingy... two ringy-dingies... A gracious good evening. Is this the party to whom I am speaking?" she asked, teasing her cleavage with one finger and adding a quick snort.

The audience burst out laughing and continued to chuckle on and off through Julia's Lily Tomlin sketch. More comedy followed, including Mr. Sidney doing an imitation of Jonathan Winters as the granny from the Hefty Bag commercial, and Charlie and Jeff's "Interview With A Clairvoyant." Even Ceddie stunned everyone by singing a jazzy version of "Onward Christian Soldiers."

When the show was over and they'd taken their last bows, the curtain opened and the fluorescent lights of the church basement flickered on. People mingled, shaking hands and patting their kids on their backs. From the stage, Julia spotted Ed and Clarisse talking to Ceddie's mother.

"Where did you get the wine?" Ed demanded on the way home.

Julia and Erin both cringed and exchanged glances.

"I...*I* didn't get it," Julia stammered.

"Charlie brought it," Erin said.

"I just tried a sip. It tasted gross," Julia added.

The minute they dropped off Erin, Clarisse lit into her. "How could you do such a thing?" she cried. "What do you want people to think about this family?"

Ed cleared his throat and added, "You're grounded for the next month. If I hear about you drinking before you're eighteen again, you can forget about using the car. *Ever.*"

Later, Ed climbed into bed next to Clarisse, who glanced at him over the top of *Newsday.* He sighed and said, "I'm tired. Let's just drop it for now." He began to drift off to sleep when he remembered standing at the window of his family's third floor apartment in Washington Heights one summer. It was a hot July day, and he'd been grounded for smoking. His father lumbered around the living room growling, "Only ten years old. It's disgusting!"

"Well, if you were present more often, maybe you could participate in raising him," his mother Eleanor hissed.

Ed heard a stickball game down in the courtyard and decided fifteen minutes of atonement was enough. The bedroom door opened and his younger brother Rob barged in. "You're still grounded," he announced.

"If you keep quiet and help me, then we'll let you play with us," Ed told him. He pulled the sheets from the beds and began tying them together.

"We'll just tie one end to the back of the fire escape and I'll climb down. You go outside the regular way." Ed tugged at the knots to make sure they held. He climbed out the window and threw the knotted sheet over the edge of the metal stairs. Clinging to the sheet ladder, he slid down. The fire escape creaked with each step. One hand at a time, he climbed lower until he passed the second floor balcony. Suddenly the sheets tore and he landed in the courtyard below with a dull thud. He howled and the neighbors came running. Eleanor and Ed's sister Margaret flew from the back door as a crowd gathered around him.

Several days later Ed sat in the window seat with his broken ankle in a plaster cast, luring the neighborhood squirrels up the fire escape with peanuts. Eleanor appeared in the doorway and announced, "I'm going grocery shopping. Can you be alone for an hour without getting into trouble?"

When he heard the front door close, Ed hobbled out to the living room on crutches, dragging his throbbing ankle in its cast. He reached into the liquor cabinet and brought out a bottle of scotch. Pouring it into a highball glass like he'd seen his mother do hundreds of times, he took a long swallow.

"Criminey!" he yelled out loud, when it burned all the way down his throat. He took a much smaller sip and felt the alcohol's warmth seep into his bloodstream. He finished the glass with several small sips, and then rinsed it before returning everything to the cabinet. Then he slid onto the piano bench and played "Clementine" with one hand. He played it again, singing along in a boisterous voice until he became dizzy and hobbled back to his room where he slept for hours.

Ed sat up and turned to Clarisse. "Maybe we should teach her to drink—let her have a glass of wine at dinner with us, so it doesn't seem rebellious or mysterious."

"I don't know," Clarisse sighed. "What if she enjoys it too much?"

"We'll monitor it, so it won't be something she has to sneak around and do with her friends."

"I don't think it's a good idea. I'm not sure I want people knowing we let our underage daughter drink. A month of being grounded ought to teach her to stay away from it. In the meantime, you should be monitoring yourself."

"I'm fine. Just as long as I stay away from the harder stuff. Besides, it relaxes me, and I *know* you like that," he said, caressing Clarisse's thigh.

Julia spent the next few weeks of reprimand playing the organ after school, even though the church secretary eyed her suspiciously. She squashed an army of snails who were taking over her aquarium and read a story she'd found in the school library about the *HMS Hussar*, an English frigate that struck a rock in the Hell Gate channel and sank in 1780.

"It was believed to be carrying two to four million dollars worth of gold and silver on board. Back then, a pyramid-shaped rock stood in the center of the channel. The river current swept the Hussar off course and over Pot Rock, tearing a gash in her side. She sank near Port Morris, opposite Astoria in Queens. The tops of her three masts showed above the water through the following winter, until she finally disappeared underwater. Numerous attempts were made to salvage her over the next 150 years, including one time in 1823 when they tried to raise her, but she broke in two. The Hussar now lies under New York City traffic somewhere in the South Bronx, with millions of dollars worth of treasure buried for all time, under an array of metal and concrete."

While Julia did her penance, Jeff and Charlie broke into Ceddie's locker at school and left her a jar with a fetal piglet soaking in formaldehyde.

Erin came over for dinner on Spaghetti Night later that spring to celebrate Julia's acceptance to Skidmore, and also her eighteenth birthday. Four apéritif glasses graced the table; two for Ed and Clarisse, and another pair for Erin and Julia. Erin charmed Ed with her wit and humor when she noticed Julia dabbing her mouth with a napkin the exact same way that Clarisse did.

"It's her *momecules*," Erin said. "The molecules you inherit from your mother. They influence you to behave like her, no matter how hard you try not to." Everyone laughed, including Clarisse. Ed was finishing his third glass of Chianti when an argument erupted over Viet Nam.

"We should get out of there now," Erin said.

"We can't just leave. It's our job to keep Communism from spreading," Ed answered. "Otherwise we'll all be speaking Russian in a few years."

"The odds are stacked against us. They're fighting in a jungle. Casualties are over twenty-five thousand!"

"Sometimes that's what it takes to prove a point," Ed said, gesturing and knocking his empty wine glass over. A few drops landed on the white tablecloth and Clarisse put a hand to her forehead and sighed.

"But we're not winning," Erin told him. "American soldiers who aren't even old enough to vote are getting killed over there!"

"You have a relative over there, don't you, Erin?" Clarisse asked, giving Ed a stern look.

"Yes, my cousin Jerry. Luckily he's been assigned to a radio station in Saigon. But it's still dangerous all over," she added with a shiver.

"That's certainly true," Clarisse nodded.

Ed looked over at Clarisse and said, "Well, I wouldn't believe much of what I read in that foofy liberal *Newsday* paper if I were you."

"You're starting to sound like Archie Bunker, dear," Clarisse warned. She got up and whisked away the Chianti.

"As a matter of fact, I *am* Archie Bunker!" Ed hollered, banging the table with his fist.

"Those—were—the—*daaaaaaays!*" Nate screeched, raising his glass of milk. The table erupted into laughter again.

On a spring day, Ed, Clarisse, Julia, and Nate were at the marina preparing the boat for another summer. Julia had finished painting the trim and was cleaning up to leave when she heard Emerson, Lake and Palmer blaring from a new 45-foot sailboat in the slip behind them. She looked over to see a long-haired man squatting on the dock in short cut-offs, scrubbing the hull.

"Hey, I just heard this on the radio the other night," she called over to him.

"Oh yeah? What station?"

"102.7-FM, of course," she said, coming across the dock.

"Oh. I ought to be able to find that."

Julia glanced at his curly Robert Plant hair and bare muscular chest, guessing he was in his early twenties. "How come you don't know that? Where are you from?"

"Ohio. I'm helping my uncle get his boat together. But lately I've been feeling more like a castaway," he said, nodding at Julia with deep blue eyes.

Julia looked down at her own paint-spattered clothes and said, "You're in good company." Across the dock, Ed and Nate were zipping up the canvas cover.

"I'm Damian, by the way," he said, setting down his sponge and offering a hand.

"Julia," she said, shaking it.

"Come on—you'll be late for your organ lesson!" Clarisse called, heading up the ramp to the car.

Julia rolled her eyes and stood up. "I gotta go... nice meeting you."

Toward the end of their senior year, Julia, Erin, Jeff and Charlie had started sneaking down to the Pattituck Cove Marina on days Julia was sure her father was working at the hospital. They climbed onto the boat and locked the cabin door, smoking cigarettes and marijuana in the galley while they acted out comedy sketches. One such afternoon, Jeff and Charlie were midway through an improvisational commercial about the nautical chart placemats when there was a soft knock at the galley door. Julia froze, imagining her father had decided to take the afternoon off.

"Hey, Julia," a voice called from outside. "It's Damian. Can I come in?"

Julia glanced at her friends. "It's just the guy from the boat next door," she whispered. "Yeah, okay!" she called with a shaky voice, getting up and unlocking the door.

He stepped down into the cabin and sat at the table. "Smells pretty good in here," he remarked. Erin stayed aloof, watching him carefully.

"Oooo, is this the older man?" Jeff whispered to Julia, nodding at Damian.

"No!" she hissed back. She and Jeff had made out a few times but hadn't officially declared themselves to be an item. She was looking forward to college and didn't want to be tied down, but she did have her date for the senior prom to consider.

"Have a puff?" Charlie asked, holding up a glass water pipe he'd made from science lab parts.

"Don't mind if I do," he answered.

"How is it that you're living here, on a boat?" Erin asked him.

Damian glanced around. "Just... taking a break for the summer and deciding what to do next."

"After what?" Erin asked.

What could be better than living on a boat? Julia wondered. *Away from your parents.*

Jeff spat out a mouthful of marijuana smoke, stifling a guffaw.

Damian sat back and calmly explained that he was living on his uncle's sailboat as its caretaker for the summer. He described being arrested for selling marijuana in Ohio several years ago as if it were a rite of passage, and was the first man Julia had ever met who obviously didn't wear any underwear. This one detail kept her from falling in love with him on the spot.

When Moving Up Day finally arrived at school, Erin and Julia marched in the outdoor ceremony and then snuck off into the woods for a quick joint. They came back just as the awards presentation was starting in the gymnasium.

"Typing sixty-five words per minute is.... Mercedes Sheeley!" Her former friend and nemesis was stepping up to the stage in a white sun dress and sandals, her shoulders slightly rounded.

"God, what happened to her? She looks prematurely secretarial," remarked Julia.

"She clearly has fallen from grace with the snot club. Must've bought the wrong shoes or something." They both stifled guffaws.

Cheerleaders were chosen, math nerds awarded, and then Mr. Ohlman took the stage in a Nehru jacket and jeans to make his speech as Teacher of the Year. He began by praising the seniors for their curiosity and strength, adding that the town could have supported them even more with a real library. Some of the parents booed from the bleachers, and Mr. Ohlman responded, "You had your day at the polls. Now I'll have mine here!" The seniors stood up and applauded, nodding at each other, while parents continued booing and jeering at the stage.

"Kick him out!" a mother yelled from the bleachers right above Julia. She turned to see a handsome woman dressed to the teeth, her face twisted in a horrible grimace as she cupped her hands and continued to shriek at Mr. Ohlman. Then Julia felt a wave of gratitude when she glanced over to see her parents, looking uncomfortable as they clapped along with the students.

"This community has a responsibility to both its children and adults to provide a library!" he shouted into the microphone. The entire student body rose, cheering and clapping. Mr. Ohlman was sweating in the hot gymnasium, his dark curly hair matted against his forehead.

"Knowledge is power!" he yelled, raising a fist in the air. The students went wild, drowning out the parents. Mr. Ohlman smiled and waved to the crowd and left the stage, clutching his award plaque. Julia felt an impulse to follow him. Over the din, she shouted to Erin, "I have to get out of here. I need some air."

"But my parents are still up in the bleachers faking normalcy. Let's just stay for the Senior's 'Last Will and Testicle.' Maybe one of us will get roasted."

"I'll be back in a few minutes." Julia hurried out the back of the gymnasium, just in time to see Mr. Ohlman getting into the passenger seat of a red Mustang. Her heart sank as he leaned over and kissed the blonde woman who was driving. Then they sped away.

"What is that hideous thing you're wearing?" Julia asked, when Erin appeared at the Lloyd's front door a week later in a fringed skirt, white boots and a cowboy hat.

"I just had to come by and show you or you wouldn't have

believed me. Can you take a picture of me for 'Children From Better Broken Homes and Gardens?'"

"You're working at *Roy Rogers?*"

"I need the money for school."

"Hey, Julia had an outfit just like that when she was little!" Ed piped up from his study. "She loved it! We could barely get it off her!"

Julia went to get her camera. "I'm going to the movies with Damian tonight," she told Erin, snapping pictures on the patio.

"That basket case?"

"He hardly knows anyone around here. Can you get Charlie or somebody and come with us?"

"No, I actually have to be at work at seven in the morning. It's brutal. What does Jeff have to say about this?"

"He and Charlie are getting an apartment in the Village," Julia shrugged. "They want to do stand-up comedy. Besides, neither of us wants to be exclusive anyway."

"Oh well… maybe they'll let us stay with them when we go into the city," Erin said.

Julia spent the next few hours grooming herself for her date with an "older man," settling on culottes and a tank top.

Later that night, parked at the Syosset Drive-In in his uncle's BMW, Julia tried to watch *Fritz the Cat* while Damian tried to push her hands down his pants. She wouldn't have minded just making out. She still missed Jeff's long, slow kisses on the beach, especially the ones on prom night. She'd even considered going all the way that night, but changed her mind when it started to rain.

Damian was getting impatient.

"I want to watch the movie," Julia said, edging away from him. He got out and opened the trunk of the car, coming back with a bottle of scotch. Taking a long swallow, he belched softly and then handed the bottle to Julia while he unzipped his jeans. He fondled himself for a moment as she stared in disbelief, holding the bottle like it was a dirty diaper. He took the scotch back and tried to coax Julia's head into his lap.

She slid over to the window in disgust. "Take me home or I'll scream!"

Damian sat up. "Uh, okay. You're not much fun, are you?"

Julia cringed. *If this is what it means to be fun, then I guess I'm not.*

He started the car and drove her home with his zipper still down. After Julia got out, he floored the accelerator and sped out of the driveway, scattering gravel onto Clarisse's roses. Julia went upstairs and drew herself a warm bath, where she soaked until she stopped shivering, ashamed of her first venture into adult dating.

Several days later in a surprise coup, Ceddie, who'd also gotten a job at the Roy Rogers Family Restaurant, had worked her way up to "Ranch Hand of the Month." Erin promptly quit and got a job at Gregory Beach, handing out color-coded rubber bracelets to people who rented clothes baskets. Julia subbed on and off all summer for the church organist, Mr. Sidney.

"Ugh!" Erin exclaimed, when Julia told her about her night with Damian. "He brought out his wanger right there in the car? What a freak! Just tell your Dad and he'll kill the guy. Then you won't have to worry about seeing him at the marina anymore."

"Yeah, and I'd never be allowed to leave the house again, either. God, I can't wait to get out of here and start school."

FOURTEEN

JULIA STARED UP AT THE PINK PALACE and sighed. "I can't believe they put me here. It said plainly on my application that I was a *music* major," she said, as Ed and Clarisse helped her unpack the car. Attempts to change her dorm assignment from home had been unsuccessful and she'd been placed on a waiting list.

"Be patient. They'll come up with something soon," Ed said, handing her a box of clothes. "Besides, they've got that great little pipe organ down here in College Hall."

People walked up and down the sidewalk lugging pillows, cartons of records, stuffed animals, and books. A faint scent of patchouli drifted through the air, and Cat Stevens' *Tea For The Tillerman* played from an upstairs window. Julia and her parents rode the elevator to the fifth floor and stepped off, into a foyer with spartan, pale yellow couches and chairs. Several young women sat at a table in the corner, smoking cigarettes and playing cards.

"Looks like the hospital," she muttered, heading down a hallway.

"Yeah, it's kind of fifties, isn't it?" A young woman in front of her wearing a backpack and overalls turned around and smiled. "Which room are you?" she asked.

"Five-o-five," Julia answered.

"Hey, we're roommates! I'm Sophie!"

"Julia," she said, extending a hand.

"Where are your parents?" Clarisse asked.

"Still on vacation in Europe," she shrugged. "I took the bus here and had the rest of my stuff shipped."

"All right now, *who can name a composer?*" the professor asked, clasping his hands together.

Julia slumped back in her seat and rolled her eyes. *'Who can name a composer?'* She doodled a cartoon of her music theory teacher with an extra large chin in the margin of her notebook.

The next few days were a whirl of mixers and orientation meetings, with freshmen scrambling around trying to fit themselves in. Her roommate Sophie turned out to be a theatre major who'd lived at a boarding school, so she was already adjusted to dormitory life. She took Julia under her wing and began a campaign to keep her on the Old Campus.

Julia's organ professor had given her the key to College Hall, once a chapel and now home to the theatre department. It had a working old pipe organ which not only thrilled Julia, but also cut down on her commutes to the New Campus. She locked herself in there to practice when the theatre department wasn't using it, which was often late at night.

At Thanksgiving, Teddy and his girlfriend Sandy drove to Saratoga Springs and picked up Julia for the trip down to Long Island. Teddy had recently "pinned" Sandy to him and his fraternity, and wanted to introduce her to the family. Julia climbed into the back seat of the car in a borrowed pair of Sophie's overalls, with braided hair, dragging a knapsack behind her.

"So you're a hippie now?" Teddy asked her.

"Not exactly. But I'm trying to be sympathetic."

"This is Sandy," he said. The woman in the front seat turned around and gave Julia a wide, synthetic smile, offering her hand with long, pink fingernails. Julia could see that she was smartly dressed in a wool pants suit, with her light brown hair pulled back in a tight ponytail.

"Hi," Julia said, shaking her hand. "Nice to finally meet you."

"Still stuck here, huh," Teddy said, nodding at the Pink Palace. "Classes going okay?"

"Yeah. They say something might open up on the New Campus after Christmas."

Sandy slid over next to Teddy on the front seat and snuggled close to him as he put his arm around her shoulder. They drove up Union Avenue past the racetrack and Teddy pushed an 8-track Santana tape into the stereo.

"Not so loud!" Sandy snapped, quickly turning down the volume.

"It's okay back here," Julia said

One silent hour later on the Thruway, Teddy asked, "Does anyone need to make a pit stop?"

"I don't know, Ted, what do you think?" Sandy said.

'What does Ted think?' Julia thought to herself. *Jeez, lady, it's your bladder!* "I could use a break," she piped up from the back seat. As she was climbing out of the car, she overheard Sandy hiss, "She's so weird!" Julia spent her pit stop feeling slightly grimy, trying to figure out what college could have possibly done to her brother's mind to make him to select Sandy.

Julia slept in until eleven the next morning. She sat up and rubbed her eyes, wondering where her aquarium had gone until she remembered giving it to Nate. She padded downstairs in her bathrobe to find Nate glued to a football game on TV, while Sandy nuzzled Teddy on the couch. Ed was in the basement in his movie editing room with the door locked. She got dressed and helped Clarisse in the kitchen.

"Dad's been down there almost all day," she said later, nodding toward the basement door. "What's he doing?"

"He's getting some movies ready to show after dinner," Clarisse answered, mixing up the mashed potatoes. "Would you set the table please?"

Julia fingered the silverware, an ornate French design Ed's mother had given them for their wedding. Tension filled the house like a packed elevator stuck between floors. Nate was distant, as if he were counting the minutes until he could get away and hang out with his friends. Erin was spending the holiday with relatives in Westchester while her parents sorted out their divorce, so Julia resigned herself to being stuck at the house over the long weekend.

"Anyone want a whiskey sour?" Ed called, coming up the basement stairs.

"I'll have one," Julia said, wondering to herself why a whiskey sour was called a sour when it actually tasted sweet, like a sugary portal into the world of adult drinking.

"Yeah, us, too," Teddy called from the living room.

Ice jumbled in the blender as Julia finished setting the table.

Ed served the tray of whiskey sours and went back to the kitchen to carve the turkey. Almost everyone showed up for the meal in clean, casual clothes except Clarisse, who wore a flared skirt and silk top with a gold pendant. When they sat down to eat, Julia noticed that Ed's highball glass was full again, and two bottles of Chianti had appeared on the table, along with the little apéritif wine glasses.

"I thought these were just for Spaghetti Night," Julia said.

Nate snorted.

"Well, we figured this was a special occasion," Ed said, opening a bottle. They toasted Teddy and Sandy, and began passing dishes of food around.

"Oops—forgot the music!" Ed said, popping up. He scurried down to the basement and put an Art Tatum record on the stereo. Piano music came tinkling through the remote speakers. "Think you could ever do this, Julia?" he asked, sitting down again.

"I don't know…"

"Just some practice and the desire is all you need," Ed prodded cheerfully.

Clarisse noted the exhaustion in Julia's face and changed the subject, turning to Sandy. "So Sandy, what do you do to keep busy?"

"I'm a legal secretary."

"Can somebody pass the potatoes?" Nate mumbled.

Sandy nudged Teddy and nodded toward the Chianti. He poured her another glass and said, "Anybody else?"

"Down here." Ed pointed to his empty glass.

"Let's all try and take it easy, "Clarisse said. "There's lots of food and dessert on the way. Nate, why don't you tell everybody about your latest achievement?"

He paused. "Uh, I got on the Varsity Soccer Team."

"Wow, that's great!" Teddy said. "Hardly anyone does that their freshman year."

Despite Clarisse's efforts, the conversation seemed to fall flat between sentences. Nate shrugged off Julia's attempts to coax him into some of his old funny routines, while Sandy and Ed guzzled more wine than anyone.

After dessert, they piled into the living room to watch home movies featuring Julia and Jeff waving at the camera in their prom outfits, Teddy heading off to his summer job at the local light bulb factory, lunchbox in hand, and a shot of Erin in her Roy Rogers uniform. There were scenes of Nate's soccer team running up and down the field, cutting to a pumpkin patch with steam rising from the ground in the morning sun. Then the camera panned *The Pearl II* at its slip in the marina, moving to a shot of Damian standing in the stern of his uncle's sailboat. He tipped a can of beer toward the camera, causing Julia to squirm in her seat. White dots appeared on the screen and the film ran out. The reel continued to spin until Nate got up and switched it off. Ed snored in a corner of the couch.

It rained hard the next the day. Ed had gone to work, and Nate disappeared early. Clarisse sent Teddy, Sandy and Julia off to a matinee of *The French Connection* so she could set the house to rights after the holiday dinner.

"Did you notice how much Dad was drinking?" Julia asked Teddy, on the way home from the movie.

"Yeah. When did that start?"

"Remember Spaghetti Night?"

"I only remember a couple with wine last summer. He seems to have graduated to whiskey."

"I thought he was cute," Sandy said.

Julia bit her tongue.

That night they had hot, open-faced turkey sandwiches and soup. There was no wine at the table when they got into a discussion about the draft. Teddy had pulled number fifty-one in the lottery. Julia remembered the night they'd shown the numbers on TV, and the way Clarisse had muffled a shriek when Teddy's birthday appeared on the screen.

"They'll be after me the second I graduate," he said. "I fully plan on moving to Canada when that happens."

Julia glanced at Sandy, who barely hid a shudder.

"What about ROTC?" Ed asked.

"I quit after freshman year, remember? It was idiotic."

Good to know he still keeps part of his brain somewhere safe from Sandy, thought Julia.

"You can't just run away," Ed continued.

"Maybe we could all move to Canada," Julia suggested.

"Hey, my friends are here!" Nate exclaimed.

"Don't panic," Ed said. "We aren't moving anywhere. Teddy has another year to think about it and maybe things will calm down by then."

Driving out to the mall at Roosevelt Field the next day, Julia asked, "Mom, when did Dad start drinking whiskey?"

"Oh, that was just a special occasion. He thought it might be nice for Teddy and Sandy at Thanksgiving," her mother answered, pulling into a parking space. Julia noticed a tightness around her mother's mouth she hadn't seen before. Only one holiday in, and Clarisse was showing signs of wear. Julia couldn't decide whether is was something she just hadn't noticed before, or her time away at school had brought a new sense of reality that her mother was clearly entrenched in her late forties. Plus her friend Winnie had recently moved out west to be with her sister's family, taking the children with her, and ending one more haven in Clarisse's life outside the home.

They wandered from store to Christmas-lit store, past Santa's Workshop, manned by a handful of ill-tempered elves, until Julia decided on a pair of platform boots. Walking back out to the car, she ventured, "Sandy's kind of boring. I don't know what Teddy sees in her."

"She seems nice..." Clarisse said.

"But she has talons for fingernails."

Clarisse burst out laughing and said, "I'm hoping Teddy will keep his options open for a while longer, too."

Back at school, Julia puffed on a joint as she tromped through a fresh blanket of snow toward College Hall late one evening. Entering the old building, she turned on one small light that illuminated the massive organ console. She walked through the darkened chapel and flipped on the organ's blower switch, which seemed to inflate the entire building with a long, deep hiss. Then she pulled out all the stops and laid her hands and feet into the biggest, brightest chord she could reach, held it for a few seconds, and let go. The chapel echoed, and she heard the rumble of snow sliding down the steep roof, landing in clumps on the sidewalk below. She began playing her favorite, a Bach Fugue in G Minor. She knew it by heart, and played it only because she felt like it; the piece she was supposed to be working on, a Mendolssohn sonata, seemed boring and dry.

"Miss Lloyd," her teacher had announced during her lesson, "*Zees* is a piece *vee alvays reqvuire* of our students." She was a humorless German immigrant with a complexion that reminded Julia of bologna, clearly lacking the passion with which Mr. Sidney attacked the keyboards.

Julia played the fugue that night with vigor, knowing the building was far from the dormitories and wouldn't bother anyone. When she finished, she lifted her hands from the keyboards and the chapel echoed deeply for nearly half a minute.

"Pity this place isn't available more often," a man's voice called from one of the church pews.

Julia froze. She must have forgotten to lock herself in that night, and reached into her pocketbook for the two-pronged French bottle opener Erin had given her as a going-away present last fall.

"You don't have to draw a weapon. I promise I'm not a twisted townie."

"Holy shit!" she exclaimed, continuing to clutch the bottle opener. "You scared the hell out of me."

"Then this would be the appropriate setting for such a thing," the voice answered.

She slid across the wooden bench and saw a man with his hair drawn back in a long ponytail. He rose and walked up the aisle toward her.

"Have you been here the whole time?" she asked, shivering in spite of the long johns she wore underneath her jeans.

"No, the snow you played off the roof landed on my head while

I was walking by. I came in to dry off."

Julia stared at him for a moment and then giggled softly. "Well, what do you do when you're not walking under churches getting pelted by snowdrifts?" she asked.

"I'm a person in college still trying to decide why I'm here. I suppose I'm wasting time in a misdirected course of study."

"Such as..."

"Art, theatre, philosophy... and a great desire to stay off the Ho Chi Minh Trail."

Julia took off her wire-rimmed glasses and began gathering up her music.

"Don't stop on account of me. I enjoyed it."

Julia paused. "Okay. Tell me your name and I'll play one more."

"I'm born Michael, although my alter-ego is known as Professor Xavier."

Julia gave him a puzzled look so he continued. "When I'm not fumbling through college I teach at a school for mutant, super-human teenagers." He gazed at Julia, waiting for a reply.

"G-Goldilocks, reformed Play-Doh eater," she stammered, hoping that sounded clever as she turned back to the console. Michael burst into a deep, comfortable laugh as she rearranged a few of the organ stops. She played a short Bach chorale, letting the church echo once more when she finished.

"Ahhh..." Michael sighed from the front pew.

"Okay, that's it." Julia was beginning to feel uncomfortable, wondering what her next move ought to be.

"Well then, are you up for a beer?" Michael asked. "I know this great little place downtown, only a few blocks from here."

No longer in the mood for practicing, Julia said, "Sure, I'll go for little while." She put on her maxi-coat and locked up the old chapel. They picked their way down the icy sidewalks to a little restaurant on Phila Street called The Executive. By the time they got there, they had discovered that they both came from Long Island and had parents in the medical profession.

"This place has the best French fries," Michael assured her, as they slipped into a booth near an old Wurlitzer jukebox with red and yellow tubes that bubbled around the edges. A few men sat at the bar still wearing their lumberjack coats. *Wow... thought Julia. This is the real thing.* So far, she'd only been to a few mixers and a preppie bar with her sophomore "mentor" and friends, who drank Chablis and talked about their engagements and their weddings planned for one week after graduation. Julia would nod politely at this kind of prattle. It sounded like a series of lukewarm, family-arranged business deals.

"So," Michael said, smiling at her, "Do you actually have any classes down here, or are you a nightly apparition?"

Julia sighed. "I've been struggling to get off the Old Campus since the day I got here. They put me in a dorm over here by mistake, so I have to be really creative about practice time."

"Which dorm?"

"The Pink Palace," she groaned. "The one place I didn't want to live."

"Yeah, I heard that place was an insane asylum before it became a dormitory."

"Great. Just what I need. Where do you live?"

Michael told her he lived a few doors down in Furness House, one of the huge old Victorian dorms with a wrap-around porch. He was a sophomore who'd transferred from Colgate. He had bright blue eyes, long dark hair and a matching moustache and beard, which he stroked sometimes when he spoke.

Another group of students came in and filled a large table near them. When they saw Michael, they invited him and Julia to join them. They shared a few pitchers of beer and more French fries, and danced to fifties music coming from the Wurlitzer. One woman had a unique talent of being able to stretch her lips into opposing diagonal directions which sent Julia into writhing laughter.

Later, they left together in a pack, all headed back to various dorms on the Old Campus. It was snowing again, and the road glittered as they crunched their way back up Phila Street. Then, *whack!* A snowball exploded against Michael's arm, and he jumped behind a snow bank, pulling Julia with him. They quickly packed and tossed snowballs in the direction of other snow banks, which returned fire. "Don't worry," Michael told her, "It's just another bunch of guys from school." Slowly, the group moved up the hill toward the Old Campus, a volley of frozen ammo soaring back and forth amid loud, raucous laughter. Occasionally someone would defect from their group and cross the street, getting pounded with a barrage of snowballs. Reaching the Pink Palace, Julia, who was mindful of an early Ear Training class, went up to her dorm room to bed.

The next morning she shuffled down to breakfast in a haze. She recognized some of the people from the bar last night at a table and shyly sat down with them, successfully avoiding the group of Chablis drinkers who waved to her from across the room. The lady who could twist her lips was there and when she saw Julia, obliged her by twisting them once again. Julia chuckled, a little tired and slightly hung-over.

"Oh yeah, the 'Torn-Pocket Mouth,'" remarked another woman who had been there the night before. "Are you the one who plays the organ late at night in College Hall?" she asked Julia.

"Yeah... I'm a misplaced music major living on the wrong campus... but I really like my writing class," she added, careful not to insult the art denizens of the Old Campus.

"That New Campus is so sterile, with all that brick and everything. I get lost every time I visit someone up there."

"You get lost in your own room, Kristin."

They all laughed and stirred their coffee, smoked cigarettes and made wisecracks about the food until one by one, they left for classes. Julia liked the way they dressed casually in paint-splattered workman's pants.

The next day on her way back from English Comp she ran into Michael, who had just finished a class in Diamond Jim Brady's House of Philosophy.

"Playing the snow off the roof again tonight?" he asked.

"No. I've got to wait until another layer builds up."

"Well, would you like to go and see a movie with me? We could have an adventure in Glens Falls!"

"Uh, okay," Julia stammered. This was serious. He evidently liked her, prompting her to feel nervous.

Michael came by her dorm room later to pick her up and once they started over the mountain toward Glens Falls he pulled out a joint and lit it.

"Why I'm shocked—just shocked!" Julia teased, taking a puff.

After watching *Bullet*, Michael felt inspired to drive his old Triumph at terrifying speeds over East Mountain Road. "I'm fast, but good!" he shouted over the roar of the engine. He invited Julia to his dorm room in Furness House. Once inside, he showed her his collection of X-Men comic books, lit some candles and put on a Joni Mitchell album. They sat on his bed and smoked another joint, kissing as they slowly removed each other's clothes. Michael was gentle, attentive, and whispered to her each step of the way, "Is this okay?" as he slipped his fingers up her thighs. "Yes..." Julia moaned, arching her back. A barrage of thoughts flooded her mind. *He'll know I'm a virgin! Will he care?* She melted toward him. He even had a rubber, and slipped it on when he was hard. "Ready?" he asked. Julia nodded, breathless and fully charged for the long-awaited initiation.

He entered her in careful stages, each one pounding a little deeper and hurting less.

"Relax," he said. "You're so small."

This is it... this is really it! She began to rock in motion with Michael as he coursed through her, faster and faster. "Is it okay?" he asked between gasps.

"Yes... okay!" she gasped as her excitement rose, and she felt a wave beginning to surge over her. Then Michael let out a long, *"Ahhhhh!!"* and kissed her tenderly, rolling onto his side.

"So what did you think?" he asked a few minutes later. "Was it good?"

"Yes..." she breathed, wondering what happened to the wave.

FIFTEEN

A T HOME THE YARD TWINKLED with Christmas lights wrapped around the evergreens and over the front doorway. Julia climbed out of Teddy's old Chevy Impala after the trip down from school to a tinny choir singing "We Three Kings." On the porch stood a group of life-sized illuminated plastic carolers with a speaker behind them. "Oh boy, backup singers," Teddy remarked, pulling duffle bags from the trunk. Julia squeezed the front door handle and pushed.

"Wait now, you have to meet Sarge!" her father called from the other side. A tan and white terrier-mix rushed the door as Julia tried to step in. It lunged forward and bit her on the hand before Ed had the chance to restrain it.

"No!" he shouted, yanking the dog back by its collar. "Sarge, sit! This is Julia. She's friendly. We love her," he said, putting an arm around her.

Tears rushed to her eyes from the sharp bite.

"Are you alright?" Ed asked, picking up Julia's hand. "Looks like he got a little piece of you. Better go up and wash it with warm soapy water."

Clarisse appeared and cried, "Merry Christmas!" flinging her arms open. She hugged Julia and then Teddy. Turning to Ed, she snapped, "Get that dog out of here!"

"This is Sarge," Ed said calmly. "I found him wandering around the parking lot of the hospital a few weeks ago and almost ran over him, so I brought him home and Nate named him. He's had his shots," he added, hauling the reluctant dog off toward the basement.

"You're bleeding!" Clarisse said, taking Julia's hand. "Let's get it cleaned up."

Julia saw a few drops of blood dripping from her fingers and shivered. "I can do it myself. I don't think it's too bad—it startled me more than anything."

She went upstairs and cried as she washed the small puncture wounds, wrapping bandages around two of her fingers. In the bathroom mirror her swollen-red eyes were accented with dark circles. Between bussing back and forth from one campus to the other to complete her finals, and nursing a relationship she hadn't felt ready to tell her family about, she was exhausted. She'd stopped trying to keep her hair from curling altogether, leaving it free to explode in a hundred eccentric, honey-colored corkscrews. Michael liked it, and the women painters and sculptors on the Old Campus approved.

Downstairs, Ed had sedated Sarge, who lay on the living room floor near the fireplace with his eyes glazed over, growling faintly whenever Teddy or Julia walked past.

Nate arrived fresh from a high school rehearsal of *You Can't Take It With You,* dressed in a cardigan varsity sweater with garishly huge plaid bell-bottoms. "Letting your hair grow out, huh?" he teased Teddy. He did a noticeable double-take at Julia's wild hair and gave her a quick hug.

They gathered in the living room for appetizers and cocktails, putting the final touches on the Christmas tree. Ed climbed up the ladder in his slippers to put the tiniest, most delicate bulbs near the top. The ladder swayed, and Nate and Teddy stood close-by until he descended with shaky steps, clearing his throat. He'd begun leaving his cigarettes burning in odd places and Julia noticed Clarisse and Nate performing a number of mine-sweeping operations behind him in case a cigarette found its way into the upholstery or a rug. Clarisse looked as if she'd paid to have her hair done in a cotton candy machine, and her smile appeared to be painted on. Once his sedative wore off, the criminally insane Sarge kept a watchful eye on everyone at dinner.

Later, Teddy and Julia stood behind a group of holly bushes in the backyard, sharing a joint.

"I don't know how much more of this I can take," Teddy said. "I brought my laundry to the basement and Mom was down there smoking a cigarette in one of those plastic filters and pretending she wasn't crying. I didn't even know what to say. As if I haven't had enough whining for one holiday season."

"What? You mean Sandy?" Julia asked.

"Yeah. We split up after Thanksgiving. She didn't have much depth. I think she went to Russell Sage to get her MRS. degree. She thought *you* were a Martian," he added.

"I'm starting to get that a lot," she said. Tossing back a wad of feral curls. "So much for keeping up appearances in our small town. This Christmas stinks. I've never seen Dad this out of it and I'm afraid if I say anything, everything will just fall apart."

Teddy exhaled a cloud of smoke. "Did I ever tell you I got picked up by a cop once, about six years ago? Me and Ernie were shooting at Coke cans with his pellet gun when old Henley drove by in his squad car and saw us. Mom and Dad had company for the first time in ages since Uncle Bill died, so I was afraid to tell him who I was."

"You rode around in a cop car all night?"

"No, he threatened to book me unless I told him where I lived. I tried to get him to drop me off a few houses away. Then he asked me if I was Dr. Lloyd's kid. It turns out his son got hit by a car a few months before that. Dad kept him alive all night while they put him back together."

The Lloyds all went to the Christmas Eve Candle-Lighting Service that evening and keeping with tradition, they left a plate of cookies and some eggnog out for Santa. Clarisse and Julia sat together, quietly blubbering their way through Nate's solo performance of "O Holy Night." He looked so grown up, singing in front of the huge church Christmas tree in a dark suit and tie. Since Julia had always been amused with Nate's hilarious imitations of other people, she hadn't realized how beautiful his singing voice was. She noticed Ceddie and her mother a few pews back in the glow of their hand-held candles and decided to ignore them. When the service was over, they all moved out to the front steps to wait for Nate.

Mr. Sidney appeared in the doorway. "How's school going, Julia?"

"Okay," she answered. She wanted to tell him how much she

missed him, but held up her bandaged fingers instead. "I might take a break from practicing for a few weeks."

"You can still use your feet and one hand," he reminded her.

"I know, I know," she answered, as the rest of her family herded Ed toward the car.

"Uh, say hi to everyone for me, will you?" Mr. Sidney said, looking after them with concern.

When they returned home, the cookies and eggnog had been polished off by Sarge, who lay on his side panting, his eyes lolling in their sockets. Ed was furious, and headed to the kitchen to make a fresh batch of eggnog.

"We're out of whiskey," Clarisse called after him.

"We'll use something else then," he answered.

"We can all have a plain one, right?" she asked.

Teddy, Nate and Julia quickly filled the void.

"Yes!"

"Okay with me!"

"Sounds good!"

"You're having a plain one anyway," she reminded Nate.

Ed paused, looking at his family, and sighed deeply. "Okay."

The next morning, Julia woke up early and tiptoed downstairs with the gifts she'd brought when she heard a low growl from the living room. "Shit," she hissed between her teeth.

Clarisse appeared on the steps and whispered, "He just needs some attention. I'll show you how I get him to play." She padded downstairs in her slippers and bathrobe and picked up a toy bunny. Sarge trotted over to her and chomped on it. Clarisse held on. "Come on, Sarge. Dance with the bunny!" She began hopping up and down. Sarge clung to the bunny, hopping up and down with Clarisse, who sang, "Dancie-dancie-dancie-dance-dance!" He growled through his teeth and wagged his tail, as they jumped together in front of the gift-laden tree. Julia stared in groggy disbelief until Clarisse stopped and turned to her. "Want to give it a try? I need to get breakfast started." She handed the bunny to Julia, with Sarge still attached.

"Hey, Sarge..." Julia shook the toy. The dog gave a snort and snatched it away. He circled in place a few times and flopped onto the rug next to the fireplace, gnawing on the bunny.

On New Year's Eve, Michael drove over from his parents' house in Valley Stream and took Julia to a party on the South Shore. She didn't know anyone although they all seemed impressed with her, being Michael's girlfriend and a musician. She felt content in smiling and nodding agreeably, and relaxed into a comfortable façade of success and happiness.

"Nice job simulating a good time," Michael remarked later, pulling into the Lloyd's driveway. "I could tell, you know."

Julia sighed. "My dad is trying to fake being straight when he's obviously bombed, my mother's trying to smooth everything over and freaking out at the same time, and my brother Nate is completely weird. We hardly even know each other anymore. Plus you and I have to sneak around like we're back in high school. I wish I could invite you in, but we seem to have a new, psychotic watchdog."

Michael sighed. "I would whisk you away and marry you in a second, just to rescue you from all this."

A bolt of excitement passed through Julia. "I dare you to," she whispered.

He threw the car into first gear and sped out of the driveway through Pattituck Cove toward Long Island Expressway. As they skirted around Manhattan heading north, Julia began to feel uneasy. She tried to smoke one of Michael's cigarettes but it tasted awful and made her dizzy. They got as far as Poughkeepsie, where Michael used a credit card to check them into a motel off the Thruway.

Once inside, Julia looked around and sniffed. Chintz curtains and a Magic Fingers machine failed to cheer the room, which smelled faintly of men's cologne and old sweat. Drawing her to the edge of the bed, Michael sat down tried to kiss her. She turned her head.

"I can't help you feel better if you keep pushing me away," he said.

"I'm not... I don't feel like doing anything..." After the getaway ride, she suddenly felt empty.

"All of this is about them, not you," Michael said.

"I know, I just don't... know what I want right now..." she stammered. "Maybe this was a bad idea... I don't even have any clothes or toothpaste or anything..."

Michael sat back. "I just drove for an hour through half a dozen toll booths. Don't tell me this was a bad idea."

"Well maybe I should just hitchhike home by myself," Julia snapped, getting up off the bed.

Michael stared at her. "Hey fine, maybe that's a great idea."

Julia grabbed her coat and pocketbook and stormed outside, slamming the door behind her. Feeling a peculiar sense of freedom, she headed for the Thruway entrance ramp and stuck her thumb out when Michael's weathered Triumph pulled up. He rolled down the window.

"Come on, sweetie, get in. We'll go home and you can get some of your stuff."

She stared back at him and a shimmer of reluctance passed through her.

Michael got out. "Julia, will you just get in the car? It's the middle of the night and we're standing on the fucking Thruway!"

"I don't care! I just can't..." An icy rain had begun to fall, and she stood on the entrance ramp with tears running down her face, thinking about her warm bed at home. She got back in the car, sitting numbly in the passenger seat as they drove down to Long Island.

Michael let go of the gearshift and found her hand. "Talk to me."

"I'm sorry I panicked," she said. "When we got to that room, it felt like we were playing marriage and it scared me." She paused. "I'm afraid of turning into a cliché. .. falling into a cookie-cutter life. I remember watching some of the people in my high school scrambling around during senior year trying to get engaged, like it was an automatic part of growing up... something you did without thinking much about it."

"Maybe they had growing up confused with moving out of their parents' houses."

Julia laughed. "You always know how to take the piss out of a rotten mood."

"Then you won't be insulted if I agree that this was a bad idea?" he asked.

"Not a bit. It was worth seeing you tear out of our driveway, though."

Michael chuckled. "Maybe I'll try it again when the timing is better."

"Besides, I can't just split—there's too much going on with my family," Julia added. "I think my father's getting really depressed. Maybe all the sickness and death at the hospital is starting to get to him."

They pulled back into the circular driveway quietly, in the pale onset of another cold, winter day. Michael kissed Julia softly before she got out of the car and let herself into the house. In the living room, tinsel from the Christmas tree shimmered in the low light as Sarge growled from behind the basement door.

Back at school in late February, Erin got a ride over from Vermont for the weekend. Julia gave her the tour of both campuses, stopping for a quick lunch at The Executive, and then thundered her way through a Caesar Franck piece on the organ in the chapel.

"You really are something," Erin remarked, as the old church echoed.

"Keeps me off the streets at night," Julia shrugged. "Sort of."

"No, seriously," Erin continued. "It's like you've created a whole mystique for yourself—like Captain Nemo."

"Minus the submarine."

"Yeah, but remember, you've got to keep your head above water, especially now that your parents are in trouble. You can't let them drag you under."

Julia nodded. Erin was right. She'd been navigating the divorce of her own parents for more than a year, and had entrenched herself in psychology and anthropology courses at Bennington in an effort to stay buoyant.

They wound up at one of the art buildings, where Julia was enrolled in Painting 101 instead of the Music History class she should have been taking. The studio was deserted, so they walked from canvas to canvas, critique-ing the works in progress.

"Gee, let's see… this guy misses his mother, right?" Erin pointed to an abstract *pieta* in browns and grays.

"I guess. He acts like he's God's gift to painting, too."

They passed a canvas lying flat on a table, with the imprints of a woman's naked body stamped onto it. "That's pretty cool," Erin remarked. "But this is drivel," she said, pointing to a flat, uninspired landscape.

"Yeah. I heard she's headed for an arranged marriage with somebody else in the class. So, what do you think of Michael?" she asked. They'd met up with him for dinner the night before, and now he was tactfully giving them some free time together.

"I like him a lot. He's whip-smart, and very kind to you. Do you think it's going anywhere?"

"I don't know. It sort of scared me when I couldn't run away with him at Christmas."

"Is this yours?" Erin asked, when they arrived at a painting of a pair of platform oxford shoes barking at each other in a storm of flying nuts and bolts.

"Figures you would guess."

"It's coming along. Really," she said, rubbing one eye.

"You've been doing that a lot," Julia remarked.

"What?"

"Rubbing your eye."

"Yeah, I know. It's been blurring up a lot lately. I have an appointment to see a specialist next month."

Julia had wanted to tell Erin about her father's drinking, and how Spaghetti Night at the Lloyd's had turned into something dreadful since she'd left for school. But what scared her more was the idea of Erin beginning to lose body parts. She stayed silent, in an attempt to protect her friend from unnecessary stress.

Seated in a booth at the Spa City Diner several weeks later, Julia fiddled with her fortune from the coin-operated Madame X machine. "Your dearest wish will come true," it read. Ed sat across from her, sipping from a cup of coffee as they finished breakfast.

"It would probably be best if you didn't discuss the details of this weekend with your mother," he said.

He'd spent the last few days visiting Julia for "Happy Pappy Chummy Mummy Weekend," an annual gala celebration with the parent of your opposite sex, which Michael referred to as the Oedipus-Electra Complex Weekend. Although Clarisse had been reluctant to let him go, Ed arrived early Friday evening. After he was settled in his hotel, they met Michael for a late dinner at D'Andrea's.

The next evening Ed picked up Julia and Michael and they drove out to an Italian restaurant near Ballston Lake. Ed was in a jovial mood, and he and Julia entertained Michael with adventure stories from the boat. They shared several bottles of cabernet at dinner before heading over to the big dance at the Hall of Springs in Saratoga. Michael bowed out then, since his mother hadn't come. Julia and Ed shared a table inside with her roommate Sophie and her father, and some other friends from her dorm. Ed charmed everyone with his dancing, and Sophie fell in love with his jokes. There was an open bar, and they drank and danced until Julia saw the room begin to spin. Ed took her out to the balcony and told her, "Breathe... just take long, deep breaths..." Her heart was racing and she prepared for the worst, but seconds later she began to feel better. Ed drove her back to her dorm, where she went up to her room and fell asleep in her clothes.

When the waitress finished clearing their breakfast dishes, Julia asked, "How are things going at the hospital?" She searched his face for evidence of wear and tear.

"Oh, same old grind," he answered.

"Do you ever wish you could do something else?"

"Sure. I'd like to get a bigger boat and sail to the Caribbean! Maybe after you monkeys finish school."

Julia could tell that Ed wasn't in the mood for a deep conversation, and her own hangover headache throbbed. "Do you like Michael?" she asked.

"He seems like quite the gentleman," Ed answered. "But you still have a long life ahead of you, so try not to get tied down too early."

"Your father was a little out of control last night," Michael told her later, after Ed headed back to Long Island.

"What do you mean? We didn't go through any red lights or anything, did we?"

"No, but he was starting to weave on the way back from Ballston Lake," Michael said.

"Why didn't you say something?"

"Because I thought you were going to."

Julia sat back in her chair as a nauseating wave of guilt began to wash over her.

"I'm leaving Skidmore," Michael said.

"What? To go where?"

"I'm not sure. I just have to get away from this place. My parents are pressuring me to come up with some kind of decision about my life and I'm stumped. If I quit school, I'll probably have to go up to Canada for awhile until this ridiculous war is over."

Julia was dazed. Michael had said it so matter-of-factly. When she found her voice she asked, "Have you been planning this for awhile, or did you just decide? What happened to whisking me away and marrying me?"

"Julia, please understand that I feel stupid taking classes here. I don't really fit in, my professors are tedious at best, and I'm afraid I might go crazy if I try to stay."

"Can I come with you?" she asked, wiping tears from her eyes.

"Let me figure out what I'm doing first. Find a place to stay. Besides, you need to finish out the semester. You have an actual sense of direction here."

There was a long pause where Julia teetered on crying and begging, but her hangover eclipsed any desire to argue.

"Well, can I at least come and visit you?"

"When I get settled," he said, enveloping her with a warm hug and kissing the top of her head.

SIXTEEN

O NE EVENING LATE IN MARCH, Julia and Sophie were on the Skidmore bus headed to the New Campus for a private party at the Field House, planned for thirty women and thirty men from a fraternity at Colgate. In a bacchanalian dispatch, the hostess, someone named Avril who lived on their dorm floor, planned on using the occasion to officially break up with her boyfriend. Sophie had convinced Julia to go, telling her, "We'll look really great in saris and kohl eye shadow, plus have a good time flirting."

Julia relented, in spite of feeling bereft over Michael's departure. He'd recently sent her a postcard from Calgary saying, "Better or worse, the jury is still out on this place," signing it, "xoxoxo."

When they arrived at the party, the other women were dripping with expensive jewelry, drinking their flying buttresses off in their formal gowns and long gloves. Potted ficus trees decorated with tiny Italian white lights had been placed around the Field House, and loud voices mingled with a Jim Croce tune.

"Why did she even invite us?" Julia wondered out loud, as they removed their coats and left them on a pile with the others.

"She probably doesn't have that many friends, or had two spaces to fill. Or maybe her imminent-ex has a couple of freaks in his fraternity."

Sophie and Julia wheedled their way up to the bar, operated by cheerful fraternity men in suits, ties, and top hats. Sophie ordered two banana daiquiris and handed one to Julia.

Glancing around the huge knotty pine room, Julia watched women fiercely in pursuit of men as she sipped her drink. "This isn't a party, it's a horror movie," she whispered.

The hostess, Avril, stood flanked by several friends near the large windows, looking furtive and deadly in a tight black gown and pearls.

"Yeah… and she even *looks* like Morticia," Sophie said.

"Who's the lucky loser?" Julia asked.

"The guy over there with the blonde hair and wire rims. Come on, let's mingle for a while. It'll be good for a few laughs." Sophie drifted into the crowd.

A flushed, chubby man surfaced in front of Julia. "Oh, great, some counterculture!" he exclaimed, licking his lips. "Know where we can find some weed?"

"I thought this was a more sedate affair."

"Maybe for some," he said, loosening his necktie.

"I meant, as in sedatives," Julia muttered to herself.

Skirting the periphery of the party, she drank two more daiquiris, listening politely to snatches of conversations about "Tricky Dick" Nixon's trip to China. Across the room she saw Sophie waving her arms around, acting out a funny story to a captive audience. A cavern of loneliness opened in Julia's stomach, and she ached for Michael's warm arms. He would have been able to clarify this boring debacle in one hilariously sarcastic phrase. She felt an overwhelming desire to disappear, and knew she wouldn't be able to convince her roommate to leave any time soon. Standing by the huge stone fireplace that was roaring for the occasion, she flashed on a childhood dream of people living and dying in flames. She retrieved her overcoat from the coat check and slipped away.

Outside, there was a full moon so bright the snow sparkled. Bare trees etched themselves vampirically against a pale grey sky. She waited for the campus bus for a few minutes, and then decided to walk downtown by herself. Reaching into her pocketbook, she drew out a pack of cigarettes. She'd tried enough of Michael's to finally develop a taste for them, and enjoyed using them as a prop to her creative process. Besides, she'd come to enjoy smoking cigarettes by herself and dwelling on the lives of tragic artists.

Everything at that stupid party was a cliché. Most of those people have already grown into predictable molds cast by their parents. She lit a cigarette and tromped over the hard snow where she guessed the sidewalk might be. *I'm even a cliché of myself.*

A campus police car pulled up next to her. Julia stopped and heard the officer call out, "It's a little late to be wandering out here by yourself. Are you a student?"

She nodded. "I'm just headed back to the Old Campus from a really dumb party."

He opened the passenger door from the inside. "Get in, young lady. I'll give you a lift."

She slid in, hoping the officer wouldn't notice how loaded she was.

"What kind of shoes are those?" he asked, eyeing her open-toed platforms. "Aren't your feet cold?"

"Yeah. I was supposed to be getting a ride."

The officer drove her back to the Old Campus and dropped her off at the Pink Palace. Feeling claustrophobic and overheated, she went upstairs, where her room began to whirl. She knew she had to get back outside. Changing into jeans, a sweatshirt, thermal coat and hiking boots, she slipped the French bottle opener into her pocket along with some cigarettes and a joint, and rode back down the elevator. Breathing deeply, she stepped into the moonlit night.

She passed College Hall and thought about going in to play the organ, but dismissed the idea for the sake of staying outside in the fresh air. Besides, she'd been turning down the music theory classes she should have been taking in favor of drawing and painting since Christmas, hoping the music department wouldn't notice. The pedantry of music theory bored her, and she spent many a class in her first semester mulling over the condition of her family instead of paying attention, and earned a C in the class. On better days, the thought of Captain Nemo playing his undersea pipe organ conjured vague optimism for her at this land-locked college she'd chosen, which the structure of a Bach chorale could not. Pushing away a festering cloud of misgivings and guilt, she paused at the top of Phila Street and lit a cigarette. Exhaling, the smoke merged with the frosty air, surrounding her in a brief cocoon of mist. She could see people leaving The Executive. Withered piles of snow still lined the streets, sprinkled with dirt from the sanding trucks. "Crumb-cake mines," Sophie liked to call them.

Julia walked on, turning her thoughts to her new favorite artist,

Caravaggio, whom they'd studied in art history that week. She'd sat in the front row at class, mesmerized by a floor-to-ceiling slide of *The Calling of Saint Matthew*. You could almost see the muscles moving under the skin of the models. Caravaggio's characters looked so painfully real it's no wonder his work created an uproar, she thought. Back then, even painted clouds were supposed to have the shimmer of mysticism, mandated by the Counter Reformation. As she learned more, she'd felt her fragile sense of faith eroding into religious propaganda. Churches, those places that housed her beloved pipe organs, were beginning to lose their charm.

Caravaggio painted the real story instead of selling a neat package of promises, and ended up dying in misery. Meanwhile, I'm surrounded by flamboyant trust-funders filling the world with dull, flat landscapes and fraternity mixers. Michael was right. It's hard to be here. Even the business majors are starting to wear those white painter's pants, all smart and spiffy with their preppie sweaters. They're bastardizing the identity of the true artists!

Julia walked on until she reached Caroline Street. It dipped down sharply before her, into the geological fault that ran through town to create the famous carbonated springs. She descended into the trough, passing a number of rooming houses and abandoned buildings. Then the street rose again just as steeply, on the block before Broadway. She climbed up and paused in front of the Tin and Lint, a bar run by east coast cowboys. Glancing in the window, she saw that the crowd had thinned, although an Elton John song was still blaring on the jukebox. She edged down the stone steps in the basement pub and headed for the bar, where the bartender, in full-faced beard and cowboy hat winked at her. "What's a pretty little thing like yerself doin' here all alone?"

He reminded her of a Sesame Street Muppet, and she fought the urge to snicker.

"Just sightseeing," she winked back, taking her fifty-cent beer over to a pinball machine called Rodeo Roundup. She studied it first, just as her father had taught her, testing the flippers. Ed was a sucker for pinball and had made sure his kids were skilled players, too, on the Houdini machine at Cannucci's Pizzeria back in Pattituck Cove. Up above, behind the glass, there was a horse with its hindquarters attached by a spindle, and a cowboy bent over with his butt facing the horse. Julia dropped a quarter in, pulled the spring-loaded knob and shot a ball into play. It pummeled the bumpers in a frenzy, flashing islands of colored light, then dropped past the flippers and disappeared. *Sheesh. Dad would have laughed at that.* She shot again. This time she kept the ball alive until there was a loud knock, and the machine went insane with bells and lights. The horse kicked the cowboy's butt again and again. She exhausted all her free plays and finished her beer. A few people were still bouncing around the dance floor, and now an older man had joined them. He wore a tattered suit and was clearly drunk, a vacant smile showing one missing tooth behind a scraggly moustache. The dancers jostled him around, pushing him from one person to another. Julia frowned, putting her jacket back on. *He looks pathetic, dancing out there with a bunch of twenty-year-olds.* She pulled up her fuzzy hood and hurried outside.

Feeling fortified by the beer, she passed the darkened shops up on Broadway. There were a few stragglers from the bar scene, but no one even looked at Julia in her androgynous jeans and winter coat. *Hey, this is great—I'm invisible! I can just wander around thinking about great heroes in art and nobody's going to bother me. Yeah! Walking Tours in the Spaghetti Afterlife with the Invisible Girl. My own personal commentary. I just wish Erin were here.*

Reaching the corner of Spring Street, she could turn left and walk down the steep hill, back up, and over to her dorm. Or she could keep going straight, past the wrought iron fence surrounding Congress Park, through the main entrance—something she'd been warned never to do. It was far too dangerous. But the gateway on Broadway was tantalizing and she felt invincible. Gripping the French bottle opener in her pocket, she passed beneath the ornate iron arch and entered Congress Park.

Ha! The Invisible Girl makes her way through the forbidden park! On your left, the old Canfield Casino, once so snobby it was actually closed to women and locals. Julia reached into her pocket and brought out a joint. Lighting it, she took a long drag and blew a cloud of smoke at the front door. "Here's what I think of that!" she said, laughing out loud. Then like a poison dart, the image of her father dancing in the same tattered suit as the old man in the bar pierced her mind. Her breathing sped up, and she realized she was so parched with thirst she could barely swallow. Shaking her head to try and clear the image from her mind, she headed to a natural spring she remembered. *Right near the reflecting pool with the two guys spitting water through conch shells at each other.* The crouching white statues began to emerge from the darkness and Julia hurried toward them. She walked straight into the figure of a satyr, bumping her head on the hard stone. Stumbling back, she took off her glove and felt her forehead. *Good. No blood.* Feeling dizzy, she knelt to put her head between her legs and fell backwards onto the snow. The world spun.

The satyr sighed and gave her a nudge with one cloven hoof. "Come on, get up. You'll freeze to death down there."

Julia sat up and nodded toward his bare chest. "You should be the one to talk."

"I'm stone and not obligated to feel anything," he answered with a huff.

Julia thought she must be either dreaming or dead, yet felt compelled to speak to the granite man. "I'm a little envious," she said. "Sometimes I wish I could just turn my feelings off and on at will. Give 'em a little gas when I'm painting or playing music, then turn 'em off when I have to deal with people."

"Good luck with that. I'm solid rock and I still have a problem standing here for all eternity watching Spit and Spat get all the attention over in the fountain," he said, adjusting his loincloth.

One of the crouching statues grunted, stretching himself. "Complain all you want. At least you get to stand up."

"And you don't have to preside over a pool where people toss their wishes," said the other. "Then watch while the vagabonds come and fish them out later. People place far too many expectations on us, and then lose heart when the myth fails them."

"Well, at least the fountain's turned off for the winter," Julia offered, trying to be helpful.

"Now we just hang around bleaching in the sun and touting perfection all day," said the satyr, flexing his muscles. "But we're not much of an influence, really."

Julia regarded his sculpted muscles. He reminded her vaguely of Michael. "I know what you mean," she said. "People watch ridiculous parodies of themselves on TV every day and still don't get it. Seems like most of them would rather emulate the crazies than the heroes—in fact," she said, beginning to warm up, "we're probably so lost in shallow, commercial crap that the Second Coming could've come and gone without anyone even noticing!"

"Which one? Oh... there've been a number of those already, depending on your point of view," the satyr chuckled. "Highly overrated, like your lighted home theatre-in-a-box."

All three statues rocked with laughter, their stone chests heaving up and down in the moonlight. Julia joined in, hoping the absurdity of the situation would purge the image of her father as the drunken old man in the bar, which had crept back into her mind unnoticed until now. *Dammit—I can't seem to get away from it! And how do they know about TV anyway? Do they go around peeking in peoples' windows at night?* "Hey, there's still some good stuff on TV!" she giggled, recalling the telephone operator from *Laugh-In*.

"Change of heart?" The satyr turned to Julia, his horns flashing in the light of the moon.

Julia cringed, fearful that he might be able to read her thoughts. She stood up and shook her head. If she could turn this conversation into a discussion about tragic heroes and art, then she'd be able to hide the nagging image of her father from them. She lit a cigarette and began pacing up and down by the fountain. "My favorite artist, Caravaggio, was a real hero. He painted the truth about people. He expressed beauty in what was genuine and natural nearly four hundred years ago, and look what happened to him. His paintings frightened people and he died unappreciated. Martyred, practically—"

"That's not entirely true," the satyr interrupted. "Back in the day we modeled for Bernini's studio, so we occasionally mingled with some of those people. Although Caravaggio shocked the public with his realism, he was well compensated and respected for a while. But he couldn't help sabotaging himself."

"You mean he was a tragic hero?"

Spat guffawed.

"A screw-up, in contemporary terms," Spit snorted.

The satyr continued. "In between commissions, he was a drinker and carouser, jailed for fighting and even a murder once. He collapsed while running up and down the beach trying to flag down a boat that had taken off with his luggage. You're the one painting him as a tragic hero."

"And you'd do well to extinguish that stinking tar stick," Spit interjected. "It's highly unattractive."

Julia sighed and rubbed out her cigarette on the bottom of her boot, stuffing the remains into her coat pocket. "Well, at least Caravaggio ruffled the feathers of the church for awhile," she said, yawning. "*And* made a great contribution to art."

"I suppose so." The satyr put a set of pipes to his lips and blew a few sweet notes as Julia sat down and drifted off to sleep.

She woke to a faint, melodic tune and turned just in time to see the scruffy old man from the bar trudging up the walkway, whistling his way through the park and out the Circular Street gate. Glancing up at the lifeless stone satyr, she put a hand to her sore forehead. *God. I must have passed out.* She waited until the man was gone and hurried back up the hill to the Pink Palace with a soaking frozen butt, feeling as if she owed death a favor for letting her out of the park. Dawn tinted the edges of the sky pale blue, and all traces of drunkenness had been chilled out of her. She stopped to toss her half-full pack of cigarettes into a trash can outside the building with a hiss of disgust. *Stinking tar sticks.*

The early morning aroma of bacon and eggs wafted from the cafeteria as she drank deeply from the water fountain and waited for the elevator. Upstairs in the hallway, she saw the door to her room open. A blonde man with wire-rimmed glasses tip-toed out and closed the door softly. She pulled the hood of her coat up and slipped past him.

"Oh my God, what the hell happened to you?" Sophie demanded, sitting up in bed. "I thought you took off with one of those fraternity guys."

"Looks like *you* got lucky," Julia said, nodding toward the hallway.

"He was a little needy once Avril was through with him. Where did you go?"

"I got too loaded at the party and couldn't stay inside, so I went for a walk."

"In the middle of the night, you idiot? Where?"

"Just around town." Getting bonked on the head and conversing with several statues in Congress Park seemed a little ridiculous to bring up just now.

"It was freezing! You could have died out there!" Sophie exclaimed.

Julia rubbed the small lump on her forehead, thankful that the room was dark. "I'm okay. Really. Just a little cold." Changing into her terry cloth bathrobe and slippers, she padded down the hall to the showers and stood under the hot water until her teeth stopped chattering.

SEVENTEEN

STANDING IN FRONT OF THE CHURCH in Pattituck Cove the following summer, Mr. Sidney handed Julia the key and said, "Just be creative. The congregation won't mind." He was taking his family on a vacation to Europe, leaving Julia in charge. Getting to practice the organ every day in the cool, quiet church seemed like a great idea, although she winced when Mr. Sidney told her about the choir.

"It's slow during the summer, so you can get by with the old standards. Mrs. Sorensen will help you out. Oh, and by the way, Ceddie has been begging to do a solo, and I promised you'd work with her on something she picked. Good luck," he said with a wink. Even vacation bound in his Bermuda shorts and sandals, Julia still felt a lot of warmth and respect for her high school organ teacher, so she bit her tongue rather than suggesting he give up the black socks.

The week after he left, Ceddie appeared at choir practice with sheet music for "A Mighty Fortress Is Our God." Showing it to Julia, she said, "I hope you can handle the accompaniment."

Julia looked over the pages, stifling a sigh. She'd played the hymn a number of times before, even modulating to the next key up between the third and fourth verses like Mr. Sidney had shown her. It always whipped the congregation into a frenzy for that last verse. "I think I can manage. We'll get started on it next time, okay?"

A week later, it was clear Ceddie was struggling. The choir fidgeted as she tried again and again to sing all the notes in the right places. She frowned at the organ console as if it were Julia's fault. Exasperated, Julia suggested she rehearse at home before the next practice. Working hard to keep a straight face, she thought, *Why doesn't she just air out her old "Onward Christian Soldiers" routine? That was a real hit.*

"Mr. Sidney would've spent more time with me," Ceddie pouted, gathering up her music. "But if Miss High and Mighty doesn't think we have enough time for a proper rehearsal—"

"That's not what I said. I just think it might help to listen to yourself. Do you have a tape recorder?"

Ceddie snorted. "Oh yes, and a ten-speed bike and a boat."

The church was silent until Mrs. Sorensen cleared her throat. "Ceddie, I have some time this week to work with you on the piano at my house. Meanwhile, I think we should show Julia some respect. After all, she's agreed to cover for Mr. Sidney this summer."

"Mrs. Sorensen always comes up with the right thing to say. She's a true Christian," Julia told Erin later on, as they clumped along in their new suede clogs. "The kind Jesus probably had in mind before all the control freaks began manipulating everything," She was introducing Erin to her Walking Tours concept, adapted for Pattituck Cove. They could do an intellectually satisfying loop from the Four Corners to Sound Bluffs, the beach, and back before midnight.

"Bear in mind," Erin reminded her. "There was a long line of control freaks before that." Now an anthropology major at Bennington, Erin was preparing to launch into a soliloquy about pre-Christian history when a sharp laugh erupted from one of the houses.

"You guys sound like a couple of horses!" Morty yelled from his upstairs window. "I thought it was the Canadian Mounted Police!"

"Some things never change," Julia mumbled.

"Hey, Morty, how's it going at Columbia?" Erin called, as they moved closer to his house.

"Not too shabby," he answered. "My parents are letting me sleep it off for the summer. Did you hear about the sea serpent sighting near Matinecock Point?"

"Sea serpent?" Julia gasped. "In Long Island Sound? You're full of it."

"Did anyone get a picture?" Erin asked.

"I don't know. We'll have to wait and see if it comes out in the paper. They said it was about twenty feet long."

"You mean, the one that got away?" Erin teased.

"I swear, it was this big!" Julia joked, opening her arms wide.

"Yeah, right," Morty laughed along with them.

"How could they see anything?" Julia asked. "My dad stopped diving there because he said the water was too murky. But we saw something pretty freaky a while back when we were fishing near there, remember?" she asked, turning to Erin.

"Ugh, that thing was prehistoric," Erin said. "I thought it had horns."

"Really?" Morty said. "Good thing your dad stopped poking around in there."

"Did they see this serpent from a boat?" Julia persisted.

"No, somebody spotted it from the bluff. I bet it was an oarfish. It's the only thing that seems possible, really."

"What's an oarfish?" Erin asked.

"An eel sort of thing," Morty said. "But it's unusual for them to come into the Sound this far."

Erin elbowed Julia and nodded for them to move on. "Letting your hair grow out?" she called up to Morty.

"Yeah," he answered, running a self-conscious hand over his hair.

"Looks good. See ya later."

They clopped on. "Sea serpent," Erin laughed. "What a goof."

"Still... that thing Teddy tried to reel in was creepy," Julia said remembering the ghoulish, spiny monster fish with a shiver. They arrived back at the Four Corners and she hesitated.

"How's it going over there?" Erin asked, nodding in the direction of Julia's house.

"Weird. Definitely weird. Invasion of the Body Snatchers weird."

"Let's go back to my house. You can call your parents from there."

"Call my parents..." Julia mused, after spending a year at college. "I keep forgetting to do that."

"Are you guys still doing Spaghetti Night?"

"Yeah, but it's not much fun anymore. Mostly my father gets loaded and lectures everyone. We just end up arguing a lot."

"Damn those assholes for not building a library," Julia muttered the next day, desperate to get somewhere and read about the oarfish. She'd tagged along with her mother to Hofstra University, where Clarisse had begun taking courses in philosophy, and spent the entire morning in the library. Pictures were scarce, although most books agreed it had a red dorsal fin along its entire length, and grew as long as fifty feet, but no horns. *What about that hideous thing Teddy reeled in? The one with the bony head that got away? No one's talked about it since.* She brought home a copy of *The Case for Sea Serpents,* and flopped onto the living room couch, opening it.

A while later, Clarisse appeared. "I've got to go down to the boat and pick up your father," she announced, fluffing up a couch pillow.

"Why?" Julia asked.

"Because his car's in the shop. Will you come along and keep me company?"

On the way down to the marina, Julia asked, "Remember that time we were fishing last summer and Teddy pulled in that really weird looking fish?"

Clarisse frowned and said, "Vaguely. Why?"

"Do you think that's the sea serpent they're talking about in the paper?"

"Oh, that's silly. It was probably a blowfish Teddy hooked that day. Sea serpent..." Clarisse trailed off. "How ridiculous."

Julia breathed a sigh of relief when she saw that Damian's sailboat was gone. She remembered he'd taken it down the coast last September to winter in Florida and hadn't returned. Ed sat on the edge of the engine well in an oil-stained t-shirt and baggy plaid shorts, finishing a can of beer. He pushed the throttle lever and the engine roared, billowing blue smoke.

"Is something the matter with it?" Julia asked.

"Just puttering, that's all," Ed answered.

"Sounds okay to me," Clarisse said. "It's time to get cleaned up and go. Nate's show starts in three hours."

Ed grunted. Lifting himself out of the engine well, he knocked over the empty beer can, which dropped into cavernous hull and bounced several times. As Ed bent down to retrieve it, Julia heard a faint groan coming from Clarisse and turned in time to see her mother rolling her eyes in disgust.

Following a stiff dinner where Ed pontificated about the importance of keeping boat engines in tune, they went over to the high school to see Nate play Tevye in *Fiddler On The Roof*. Ed moved around the auditorium with his camera, snapping picture after picture. At intermission, Julia followed the crowd into the large foyer in front of the auditorium, drifting away from her parents. An electric jolt passed through her when she saw Mr. Ohlman coming toward her. Trembling, she glanced around for the blonde woman she remembered from Moving Up Day. So far, he seemed to be by himself. His dark curly hair had grown out even more since high school, and he was beginning to look more like a rock star than a teacher.

"How was your first year of school?" he asked, his eyes gently searching hers. She wanted to tell him all about her art history class, the pipe organ in College Hall, maybe even her Walking Tours.

"It's been fun," was all she could stammer. "L-lots of hard work. How about you?"

"I've just finished my last year here. I'm helping out with set design for the summer theatre, and then I'm off to the Galapagos Islands to crew on a schooner and write for a year."

"Wow... that's amazing," Julia said. Tromping through the icy streets of Saratoga Springs smoking cigarettes in the middle of the night suddenly seemed trivial.

"Your brother Nate is doing a great job," Mr. Ohlman offered. "They haven't seen a Tevye that good in many years, so I hear. Talented family."

Julia looked at her feet, hoping her parents were far away. Drawing together any stray particles of courage she could find in herself, she looked back up just as the lights blinked off and on, signaling the end of intermission. Mr. Ohlman shrugged and smiled at her. "Nice to see you again," he said putting a hand on her shoulder, as the crowd moved them along toward their seats in the muggy auditorium. Fanning herself with her program, Clarisse turned to

Julia. "That was Mr. Ohlman, your homeroom teacher, right?" Julia nodded, fanning herself extra hard. The lights went down for the second act and Nate outdid himself as the charismatic dairy farmer.

"Coast Gawd! Coast Gawd! This is the *Del-Char*, Whiskey Kilo 2328!" a man's voice whined over the static of the marine radio. "I'm just off Sand's Point and this small motor boat full of teenagers keeps circling and harassing me! I request assistance immediately!" *Crackle-crackle.*

"*Del-Char*, this is the Coast Guard. Please repeat your location," a voice answered.

"This is *Del-Char*. I'm just off Sand's Point, being harassed!"

"I'm being *haraaaaassed!*" Ed mimicked from the bridge.

"*Immeeeeeediately!*" Julia chimed in from the deck.

"We'll send some assistance, *Del-Char*. Coast Guard out."

"*Del-Char* out."

"Keep a stiff upper lip," another voice crackled.

Ed laughed. "That's enough of that," he said, turning off the marine radio.

"Are we supposed to go over there and rescue them?" Julia asked.

"No, it's too far away. Someone else can handle it."

Julia reached over and switched on her transistor radio. A Crosby, Stills, Nash and Young song burbled out. Abandoned by Clarisse who was at her philosophy class, and Nate, a fledgling golf caddy, Julia and her father were on the boat by themselves, drift-trolling in the middle of Long Island Sound as *The Pearl II* rocked in a gentle breeze.

"Hey Julia, keep an eye out for a second, will you?" Ed called. He climbed down the ladder and swayed slightly when he reached the bottom. Steadying himself on the deck, he ducked into the cabin. Julia glanced out over the Sound. She could barely make out Rye Beach on one side, and Matinecock Point through the haze on the other.

She thought about Erin, who'd gone to an eye specialist during spring break. The doctor had given her the bad news that, due to her advanced diabetic retinopathy, she would continue losing vision in her right eye.

"Another one of the exciting features of this stupid disease," Erin said.

"Can't you get an eye transplant or something?" Julia asked, trying not to cry.

"Maybe. I don't know. They mostly do cornea transplants. Just stop worrying for now, okay? It's creepy enough without you crying about it."

Julia wondered whether Erin was telling her everything she knew. *What happens if her diabetes starts taking one organ after another?*

Ed interrupted her thoughts when he came back up from the cabin and climbed the ladder to the bridge. "Not too much happening out here. What do you say we head back in?"

He started the engines while Julia reeled in her line, and the boat lurched forward. She took a few quick steps to regain her balance. The sun had baked her, so she stretched out in the shade, letting the rumble of the engines lull her to sleep. She woke with a start when she felt the boat take a sharp turn, and tumbled off the couch onto the deck. Over the gunwale, the breakwater flew by.

"Hey!" she yelled up to Ed. Looking out over the water, she could see the harbor was crowded with sailboats and motorboats. Ed slowed the engines down to a mild chug. *Probably some yahoo was about to crash into us.*

When they got back to the marina, Julia hosed off the boat while Ed packed some things in the cabin. He was quiet on the way up the ramp to the car. As they pulled out of the parking lot, Julia noticed for the first time what a mess his hair was. He'd always kept it combed straight back, but now it was sticking out in a wavy jumble. The car crawled up the street, past the Bait & Tackle Shop, and the engine seemed louder than usual.

"What's that noise?" Julia asked.

"I think there's a hole in the exhaust pipe."

Wasn't the car just in the shop? "Dad, are you alright?"

"I'm fine," he told her, belching softly as the car wavered in its lane. "Everything's okay..."

They turned onto Pattituck Cove Avenue, and Ed sped up. Julia watched wide-eyed as the car drifted into the other lane. Horrified, she grabbed the steering wheel and pulled the car back over as an oncoming car blasted its horn. Ceddie's blue Chevy Nova swerved to avoid them. Ed pulled over and drew a few deep breaths. "That was close. But I'm okay now," he said, straightening up in his seat.

"Dad ...!" *Shit!* He smelled like Damian the night they'd gone to the drive-in. "Can I please drive?"

"No, everything's okay," he repeated softly, pulling back out. "We're practically there."

Julia fixed her eyes on the road for the entire minute it took to get home, ready to grab the steering wheel again. Her heart was pounding when Ed pulled into the circular driveway, and she was relieved to see Clarisse's Camaro parked in the garage. Sarge, the over-zealous watchdog, was behind the chain link fence patrolling the backyard. He'd calmed down since last Christmas but Julia still didn't trust him. She got out and followed Ed into the kitchen.

"Hey Sarge," he called, clinging to the screen door as he swayed back and forth. Julia could not stand this bewildering sight any longer. Seeing people get too loaded was supposed to happen at school; not at home with a parent. She headed upstairs to find Clarisse.

"Go check out Dad in the kitchen," she wept to her mother on the landing. Then she went up to her room and fell asleep.

Later, Clarisse woke her to say there were leftovers from dinner. "He's asleep," she whispered, nodding toward their bedroom.

Julia climbed out of bed and tip-toed downstairs. Clarisse made some chamomile tea while Julia lit a mushroom-shaped candle she'd bought at a head shop in Roslyn. They sat on the patio watching the lightning bugs.

"What's going on? How did Dad get this weird?" she asked.

Clarisse looked uneasy. "He's been taking Percodan for a tooth infection. When he has something to drink, it just hits him much harder."

"We almost *crashed* on the way home."

"I know. I got an earful from Ceddie. She called while you were asleep. Honestly, she thinks we're trying to bump her off or something."

"That wouldn't be such a bad idea, come to think of it. She's such a little twit-face."

"Now, now..." Clarisse went inside and found a pack of cigarettes in a kitchen drawer. She came back out and lit one, setting the pack on the table. Julia began to pull one out but the phrase "stinking tar sticks" stopped her. She wanted to scold her mother, but Clarisse looked as if she needed something to calm her nerves. "Did you just start this at Christmas?" Julia asked instead.

"No, I smoked in nursing school and then gave it up once I got pregnant."

"I had to grab the steering wheel," Julia whispered.

"I don't think he realizes how bad it can get when he takes his medication."

"What are you going to do?"

Clarisse looked down at her teacup and sighed. "I don't know... he said he could handle it."

"What did you tell Ceddie?"

"That he had something in his eye."

The tiny *Pattituck Cove Crow's Nest* newspaper came out the following day with a photo on the front page, of what looked like a large dorsal fin cresting the surface of the water. The caption read, *"Our own Nessie? This photo, taken by C.L. Nuston on Matinecock Point last Thursday, shows the apparent dorsal fin of an unusual visitor to our waters. Marine biologists from the Woods Hole Oceanographic Institution in Massachusetts have been invited to pay us a visit."*

"What a *podunk* waste of time," Ed snorted, sipping a Manhattan at the dinner table. "They'll come all the way down here to find out it's a hoax."

"How could someone fake something like that?" Clarisse asked.

"Oh, a couple of divers could just swim underneath a piece of rubber or something," he said impatiently, setting his glass down hard. The ice cubes clattered, jockeying for position.

"Well, that's true," Clarisse agreed.

"What if it's not a hoax?" Julia asked. "Remember that huge, hideous thing Teddy caught near there? What if there really is a Monster of Matinecock Point?"

"There's no monster," Ed insisted. "It's probably something from the ocean that got caught in a tide and floated into the Sound. They ought to just leave it alone."

"Or use it as a mascot for the new baseball team," Nate suggested.

"Well, if they find anything weird, you can be sure the government will come in and cover it up, just like they're trying to do with the war we're losing," said Julia.

"We're not losing. That's just the spiel from a bunch of kooky liberals who don't understand the threat of Communism," Ed answered gruffly. Unattended, his cigarette burned helplessly in the ashtray nearby.

"That's not true. It's been proven that the government faked the Gulf of Tonkin attacks."

"How do you know that?"

"The Pentagon Papers, remember? By continuing this charade of American imperialism, our government is merely breeding more contempt for itself!"

"What?" Ed shook his head in disgust. "Where did you get that crap? Dammit, you don't know what you're talking about!"

"You can't pretend you don't see it," Julia argued. "Just look around. Haven't you noticed the moratoriums, the rioting, the bomb scares? I can't stand it when people deny what's happening. It really turns me off—"

"Turns you off?" Ed shouted, slamming both hands down on the table and standing up. "You turn *me* off! You're a real horse's ass!"

"Me?" Recoiling from the sting of her father's attack, Julia stood up to meet her father's glare. "I'm not the one who's drunk every night!"

The floor seemed to open up underneath her, leaving a gaping hole where the unsaid had been festering. Nate sat wide-eyed while Clarisse got up and began clearing the dishes. Sarge stood at attention.

"LEAVE THIS TABLE!" Ed roared, pointing toward the kitchen door.

Julia threw her napkin onto the table and stomped out of the kitchen. "Asshole!" she cried. She thought she heard a chair scraping and darted out the front door.

Julia called Teddy from Erin's house later that night. After his graduation, he'd stayed up in Troy, lying low at his fraternity house until he got word about his draft classification. Due to a hockey game last winter where he'd torn a ligament in his knee, he finally received a 4F, or "Get Out of War Free" ticket, as he called it.

"Dad spends a lot of time puttering with the boat engines when he's not working," Julia told him.

"There's nothing wrong with those engines," Teddy said. "He just goes down there to get bombed."

"Yeah, he got totally loaded when we were out on the boat last week. It's weird—I don't remember seeing him drinking much— he must have tied one on secretly. I get chills thinking about what could've happened. Besides, Nate barely speaks to anyone anymore, and that psychotic dog is still here. Can't you come down?" That last part bordered on a whine and Julia immediately felt a sense of weakness that embarrassed her.

"I'll be down for Labor Day Weekend. Meanwhile, you guys have to keep your eye on him. Mom needs to get serious about it, too. It's not cute anymore."

The following Sunday, Julia played *Thus Spake Zarathustra* from *2001* as the prelude to the church service. Mr. Sidney would have been proud; he'd played it for her at the fish-shaped church the day they went up to Connecticut. Ceddie's solo went smoothly, but when the service was over and everyone had filed out, Julia saw her pounding back up the aisle with her cheeks blown out like a puffer fish.

"You just had to hog all the attention and turn the service into one of your little freak shows, didn't you?" she sputtered. "You think just because your family's got a bunch of money that you can be the center of everything? How about if I tell everyone your father was schnockered the other day when he practically crashed into me!"

Julia stared at her, scratching one ear in an attempt to draw attention away from the dread she felt. *Was she bluffing?* Ceddie turned and stormed back down the aisle and out of the church.

EIGHTEEN

Two YEARS LATER, Julia sat in her weathered green Volkswagen Squareback on a stormy afternoon between Christmas and New Year's. Unable to spend one more minute in the house, she'd driven out to Gregory Beach and parked in the lot overlooking the sandbar and Wreck site. Whitecaps danced crazily on the water while the trees on Matinecock Point swayed in the wind. Julia didn't care; anywhere would have been better than home. Emotions were now at critical mass, packed so tightly Julia was afraid the house might explode if she said the wrong thing.

The wind picked up on the beach and Julia pulled the latch underneath the driver's seat, letting the chair glide backward. She took a joint from her pocket and lit it, inhaling deeply. The tide had come in and covered most of the sandbar, causing it to surge up and down like the crest of a dorsal fin. Julia exhaled and shook her head. The people from the Oceanographic Institute had sent someone to follow up on the "Matinecock Sea Monster" just after the sighting a few years ago, but nothing had come of it. Most of the town had chalked it up as a hoax.

The following Christmas, Julia and Teddy had come home to an Ed-less house. Clarisse had discovered that he was seeing another woman on the side and thrown him out. He'd moved into the hospital dormitory. The day Teddy, Julia and Nate went to visit him, they'd squeezed around a small round table in his room while he served cookies and milk using plates and coffee mugs he'd managed to sneak out of the house. Like their father, the dishes looked chipped and forlorn to Julia, as if they'd survived a storm on their way over.

"Everything will be okay," Ed assured them. He'd given up drinking, and this new woman turned out to be a "platonic buddy" who worked at the hospital. Although the scene was surreal and affected, Julia was still willing to give him the benefit of the doubt. *Whatever it takes to keep him sober, I guess.*

On the way home, Nate began weeping from the back seat.

"Stop driving, just park somewhere," Julia whispered to Teddy, but he kept going, his eyes pasted to the road in front the car. They drove on through Pattituck Cove until Julia made an attempt to cut through the icy silence. "You know, this whole thing is just temporary—"

"Oh, you guys are so fucked up!" Nate exploded. "You don't even know what it's like to live here!"

"We can't help that we're away at school—" Julia began, but Nate cut her off. "You just come down here for a few days and then leave! YOU'RE PROBABLY STONED THE WHOLE TIME, TOO!" He collapsed into hysterical tears.

Teddy and Julia didn't dare glance at each other. Teddy just continued on, with Nate sobbing in the back seat the rest of the way. When they reached the gravel driveway, Nate jumped out and ran across the yard, down the street.

Ed had made a special appearance on Christmas Day, to exchange gifts with the kids. Clarisse's presents were quality things she knew they wanted; beautiful art history books for Julia, preppie clothes for Nate, and big, warm sweaters for Teddy. Ed gave everyone fun gadgets like mechanical card dealers and counter-top pinball games. The whole event was stiff at best, and Nate disappeared again as soon as Ed left.

Afterwards, Teddy began to pack up his car.

"Please don't leave!" Clarisse cried out.

"This is your problem, not ours," he answered. "You guys need to work this out yourselves."

Julia wanted to go too, and spend the rest of the holiday in her dorm, but Ed had helped her buy the used Volkswagen under the condition that she would stay with Clarisse for the rest of Christmas break.

Julia and Clarisse sat at the kitchen table later that evening, finishing a plate of cookies. Sarge was table-side, and Julia fed him gingerbread men to gain his trust.

"Dad watches all those people die in the operating room," she offered. "Maybe it's just too intense to do that day after day, long-term."

"That's not the point," Clarisse answered. "Lots of people have high-pressure jobs. Did he tell you about his lady-friend?"

"A little. It sounded like she was more of a friend than a lover."

"Well, I don't really give a hoot..."

Julia glanced at her mother's face and felt pity for her feigned bravery that masked complete bewilderment.

On the beach the wind had picked up, creating tiny, short-lived tornadoes. Gusts rocked the little station wagon in its spot on the cement, and sand began to pepper the windows. Julia stretched out her legs and winced, remembering the events that led up to her father's breakdown. He'd begged Clarisse to let him move back into the house that winter. Clarisse finally relented, although selling *The Pearl II* had been a contingency. Like Ed, Julia had pleaded over the phone with Clarisse to let him keep it, but she'd stayed firm. Even with the boat gone, Ed had fallen off the wagon a few weeks after he'd returned home, dashing once again, the hope Julia and her brothers had held for a sober father. When she'd come home for spring break and played "Jesu, Joy of Man's Desiring" on the piano one day, Ed staggered into the living room in a scotchy haze. "That's so beautiful," he gushed. "Would you promise to play that at my funeral?" Julia kept playing and curdled inside, nodding silently, unwilling to open a dialogue with him.

Julia stayed up in Saratoga the following summer, waiting tables at Caffé Lena. She turned raw for a week when Michael had written to her that he was exploring a relationship with another man in Toronto, pleading with her to keep their friendship alive. Erin listened to Julia rant and cry for half an hour on the phone, and said, "He's being honest with you. Don't go up there in a fit of rage like a woman scorned," she advised. "Friends like that are hard to come by. Try to calm down before you say something you might not be able to take back."

Then Julia gathered herself, sent Michael a postcard of a giant rabbit wearing a saddle and signed it, "Your friend, as always."

The next day she started seeing a mandolin player with an affection for vodka.

Saratoga was hot and sticky. She'd gotten a tiny apartment on Caroline Street, cooled by a rickety fan. She missed the salty air of Pattituck Cove and swimming in the Sound at night, swishing the glittery plankton around in the water. Frequenting the Tin and Lint with friends, she tried to avoid the sight of the tattered, older man she'd first seen a few winters before, since he still flailed around on the dance floor with the college kids and townies. In late July, Ed wrote to her to tell her that he'd given up drinking, this time for good. She'd re-folded the letter with a snort, not even bothering to show it to Teddy when he came up from Troy to visit. The merchants of Saratoga enjoyed their busy season when the New York City Ballet came up for the summer and the racetrack was in full swing. Restaurants were packed every night and the streets were filled with tourists, college professors, musicians, gamblers, panhandlers, and religious zealots. Julia suspended her Walking Tours in the Spaghetti Afterlife when a Lincoln with a red and purple fringe around its windows pulled over and offered her money if she'd get in. Toward the end of summer, Ed had called to tell her he'd left his job at the hospital.

"I'm done with that place," he said flatly.

Relieved, she stammered, "At least you'll be getting away from all the stress of the operating room." She knew she'd sounded frail and slightly phony, and changed the subject.

"Where's Mom?"

"At school," Ed answered.

He'd taken a job in the city as a toxicologist for a drug company that also produced bug spray, but he couldn't seem to adjust to the steady, nine-to-five schedule. Commuting into New York by train, he often dozed off and slept past his stop on the way home, calling Clarisse from the Glen Cove station to come and pick him up.

Julia got out of her car and stood on the sandy cement. She adjusted the rainbow scarf Erin had knitted when she was in the hospital. By then, Erin's health forced her to take time off from Bennington, and then she transferred to Columbia and started seeing Morty. The following semester, they'd moved off-campus to an apartment on the Upper West Side.

"Don't worry. I'll never be one of those ninnies who gets into a relationship and forgets about their friends, I *promise*," she told Julia. True to her word, she was almost always available when Julia called, and Julia was relieved that someone was around to take care of Erin, now that her right eye was beginning to fail.

In spite of the wind, Julia headed down to the shore, carrying her clear, plastic umbrella. Rain spattered against it, and the wind formed long, horizontal columns of sand that blew over the surface of the beach. Her mind swirled as she walked on, rehashing details of the previous fall.

At Thanksgiving break, she'd been the only one who agreed to accompany Ed when he bought a new car. His Cadillac had been in decline for quite some time, stalling and losing power. An inside door handle had fallen off in Nate's hand a few months back, and Clarisse disclosed that Ed had once thrown a scotch bottle at the window, smashing it. When Teddy looked under the hood, he noticed that Ed had tried to use surgical tubing to repair the air conditioning system. On the curb outside the Mercury dealer sat the forlorn silver coach that chauffeured them through the demise of the upper middle class family. Julia looked down at the salesman's white patent leather shoes as she heard him offer Ed a $200 trade-in for the Cadillac, locking in the deal for a foam-green Comet.

A few weeks later, Teddy called Julia at her apartment in Saratoga.

"I have some bad news."

She immediately assumed the worst, that their father had died.

"Mom checked Dad checked into a hospital to dry out."

"What? *Where?*" She gave a shiver of relief, partly due to an ongoing struggle with her landlord over the lack of heat.

"Somewhere down south."

"S-should we go down there?" Julia stammered, feeling her heart beating somewhere near her mouth.

"No. Let's wait for Christmas, like we planned."

That night she'd dreamt she was lying on an air mattress just off the shore of Nantucket, watching the *Andrea Doria* sink beneath her. "This is it!" someone called from the nearby lifeboat. "She's going down!" Back paddling with her arms to avoid being dragged down by the suction, Julia watched helplessly as the ship went down, issuing streams of spiraling bubbles from its windows as the deck lights flickered on and off.

By the time Teddy and Julia arrived home for Christmas, Clarisse looked deflated and too worn-out to try and raise their spirits. Nate still wore his garish plaid bell-bottoms. He was in the preppie crowd, the high school star of everything, but at home he remained aloof and wouldn't talk about Ed. Clarisse finally coaxed him to stay in one evening with some of his friends and watch TV. She made popcorn in one of those new hot air poppers that spewed melted butter from a module on the top. Teddy and Julia attempted to join the group and watch *The Carol Burnett Show*. Nate sat on the couch, buffered by his group of over-achieving friends. During the commercials, the girls eyed Julia suspiciously. By this time her wavy hair had grown out, achieving full feral-hood, and she wore overalls and wire-rimmed glasses.

"Well, you're not supposed to plug up your pores with goo," Julia remarked to a TV model who was complaining about irritating underarm antiperspirant.

"Oh, why don't you just go outside and get stoned?" Nate scoffed.

Julia blanched, looking at her feet.

"Because we already did," Teddy answered.

Toothy, green gnomes ran around the hospital room, leaping over the table where Ed lay tied. They leered nastily at him as they flew over his body in the rehab center. He was furious. He writhed and swore at them, attempting to tear off the restraints. They grouped themselves into a corner, whispering to each other. Then, from underneath the table, a dark, horny-headed serpent emerged and slithered upright over the bed, looking down at Ed. Fins fluttered on both sides of its head and its eyes burned bright yellow.

It opened its mouth and hissed, "Do you want to live or die?"
Ed screamed and the monster repeated itself.

The next evening Clarisse and her children gathered at phone extensions around the house and called Ed.

"He's not supposed to have any visitors, but we're allowed to call him," she said.

Julia picked up the phone in the kitchen and stood listening. Her father's voice was small and fragile.

"They said I could have visitors, so it would be great if you guys could come down and keep me company."

He's lying. Julia felt faint as she held the button down and quietly hung up her extension.

"Well, that was feeble," Nate said when they regrouped in the kitchen.

"Yeah, it sounds like he's gone about as low as he can go," Teddy offered.

"He woke up one morning and couldn't get out of bed," Clarisse said, choking back sobs. "Someone from work called and asked him why he wasn't there. He said, 'Because I'm drunk,' and burst into tears. They referred him to the hospital in Maryland. I was told to let him have one drink on the way down there."

"Why?" Julia asked.

"To keep him from going crazy in the car."

As Clarisse broke down, her children gathered around in a clumsy attempt to console her.

Standing on the beach with the breeze whipping around her, Julia opened her umbrella. She turned into the wind and stood firm, bracing the bowl of the umbrella against an oncoming tunnel of flying sand. It blasted the front and exploded over her as the wind howled. In her small bubble of air on the beach she wept, letting the angry weather tear past her.

NINETEEN

THE FOLLOWING EASTER, Julia made a cautious trip down to Long Island. Ed, having completed his recovery program, had moved up to a halfway house in New Jersey.

"He comes back on most weekends," Clarisse told her, when she arrived. Julia paused, and her mother added, "He's blessing us with a visit *this* weekend, just for you and Teddy."

Oooh.. sarcasm. This can't be good.

She dragged her knapsack up the stairs. Even the house seemed to have an air of stiffness, as if it were slightly wary of Julia and her curiosity about her parents' relationship. Nate was spending most of his time with his new girlfriend, and Teddy wasn't due from his apartment in the Bronx until Saturday, which left Julia and Clarisse by themselves in the house. Polishing the silverware in the dining room, Julia glanced out the window and saw Nate's dog Sarge patrolling the backyard. She sighed, picking up a tarnished soup spoon. She wanted to asked her mother more about Ed's recovery, but sensed her fragility, and feared further digging might make her burst into tears. Weighing the delicate balance of calmness against knowing more details, she finally spoke up. "It's been three months. Why does Dad have to stay there so long?"

Her mother's response felt like a garage door slamming down between them. "He says it's a way to regain sobriety on his own, without having to deal with exterior circumstances... so I support him."

Yeah right, thought Julia. She could feel him slipping away, and her mother's denial of it.

They laid the silver out on the table, dusted the wrought iron chandelier and replaced the candles. Julia was turning to leave when she noticed Sarge out in the backyard, working his way paw over paw to the top of the chain link fence.

"Mom! Quick! Come look at this!" she whispered, beckoning Clarisse to the dining room window. The dog reached the top of the fence and perched briefly on all fours, then leapt over the other side and scampered off. Clarisse ran to the front door and flung it open, yelling, "Sarge! Come here!" When he didn't respond, she turned to Julia and exclaimed, "We have to try and find him. Nate will be furious!"

They drove around the neighborhood for an hour, calling Sarge's name out the car windows, with no success. When Nate came home for dinner and heard the news, he slammed back out without a word, to search for the dog.

"A friend from my theosophy class invited me to this event," Clarisse said, standing in the doorway of Julia's bedroom the next afternoon. "It's some kind of self-awareness thing from California that's catching on around here. It sounds a little silly, but I told her I would go. Would you come and keep me company? I'll take us out to dinner at Cast-A-Ways first," she coaxed.

Julia started to groan and complain about her final projects at school, then changed her mind when she noticed the loneliness in her mother's face, like part of her was adrift. That and the thought of steamed clams prompted her to say, "Okay. I need a break anyway. You have to have a beer with me, though."

Julia was happy not to run into anyone she knew at Cast-A-Ways in Sound Bluffs. She wasn't in a public sort of mood, given the splintered state of her family. The fishnet-strung, South Sea Island décor of the small restaurant was goofy enough to distract them into making fun of the place, and Julia watched her mother's face begin to relax. She saw her opportunity to ask the nagging question. "So Mom, what do you think is going to happen?"

Clarisse shook her head and took a tiny sip from her beer. "I don't know... I said I'd stick with him."

"I'm glad you're at least taking some courses," Julia said, secretly wondering how theosophy and philosophy would get her on her feet if Ed stopped coming home on the weekends. Clarisse's face had grown dark again. Sensing the urgency to shift the course of her mother's mood, Julia turned to the thatched-roof bar. "Look!" she whispered, pointing toward the bar. "How about a nice Hawaiian Punch?"

Clarisse looked over to see the chubby bartender in a tattered straw hat, gazing vacantly at a basketball game on the bar TV. She bubbled with laughter and whispered, "Maybe he needs a nice *diet* Hawaiian Punch."

Afterwards, they drove over to the Marriott in Manhasset. The entrance to the banquet room was clogged with clean cut men in leisure suits and women in flowery pastel dresses, all wearing "Hello, My Name Is..." tags.

"I have a bad feeling about this..." Julia muttered.

"There's Naomi," Clarisse said.

A woman approached, smiling broadly, and shook their hands. "You've got to put on a name tag first," she said, herding them over to a long table. Julia sighed and wrote Alice B. Toklas on hers. Inside the banquet room, there was a podium with large bouquets on each side. A man in a light blue suit got up and introduced himself, embarking on a slick, fifteen-minute motivational lecture about The Program, and how everyone in the room should make the commitment to take control of their lives today—right now!

Julia began to nod off, until Clarisse nudged her. "You're snoring," she whispered. The sound of clapping brought her back into the room just in time for audience testimonials.

"My life was a mess," one woman said. "I couldn't even maintain eye-contact with people before I found The Program. Now I have a wonderful new job, and I've starting dating. I think I *got it!*" Huge round of applause. Someone else stood up, and the voice reached Julia like fingernails on a blackboard. "I'm learning how to take responsibility for myself..." Ceddie squawked from a few rows back. Clarisse and Julia exchanged glances and covered their mouths to hold the snickering in.

When the talk was over, they got up and headed for the doors as fast as they could, but Naomi caught up with them. "So, are you ready to sign up?" she asked breathlessly.

"Well, I'd like to think about it," Clarisse said politely.

"What's to think about? It's the most fantastic thing I've even done!" Naomi exclaimed, planting herself in front of the exit. "How about you, Julia?"

"I'm finishing college."

"It's a little expensive right now," Clarisse added. "Besides, we have a graduation gift to consider."

"Oh, the gifts The Program offers far outweigh anything material," Naomi said. "When I took the seminar last fall, I just made cookies for everyone that Christmas."

"What a surprise!" a familiar voice chafed from behind Julia. Standing on a pair of platform shoes shrouded by flared trousers, Ceddie now wore her dark hair long, pulled back in a neat ponytail. Julia braced herself for an insult when Ceddie chortled, "Wasn't that the greatest talk? Are you going to take the seminar? It would do you a world of good. Especially *now*."

A white-hot flash of anger ripped through Julia. She clasped her hands together to keep from punching her childhood friend.

"We've got to get going," Clarisse said, taking Julia by the arm and charging past Naomi.

"Wow, Mom, that was brave," Julia remarked, as they got into the car. "I'm glad you reacted so fast. Otherwise I might have lost it with Ceddie." She figured any praise of her mother's courage would be helpful.

"I'm sorry. I didn't think it would be that bad," Clarisse said, starting the engine.

"Est-holes," Julia shuddered. "They're starting to infiltrate Saratoga, too... worse than the Jesus freaks who keep trying to get everyone to sing in the snack bar."

Clarisse laughed. "Can you believe she suggested making cookies for everyone at Christmas? I could've just slapped her."

"Well, at least we escaped before they could brainwash us. Did you know Ceddie was going to be there?"

"Heavens, no. But she did us a favor by showing up. It got us out the door faster."

"How much do you think she knows about Dad?"

"I don't know. I haven't discussed it with anyone except Aunt Ginger and the pastor. Your father says we should be going to Al-Anon Meetings. I've tried, but the people there were all… still living with alcoholics and crying a lot, and I feel like I'm past that. It just wasn't me."

When Ed came home for the weekend, Julia felt like she'd stepped onto the set of a soap opera. Teddy had arrived, and everyone moved around the house warily, each one in their own private force-field of insulation. "We're the Wooden Family," she reported to Erin over the phone. "Living in a house made of fragile matchsticks."

Ed sat in his black leather chair in the den most of the time, reading from his *Book of Devotions*. He looked sheepishly defiant, clinging to the book as if it were a lifeline to his support system in New Jersey, deflecting conversation of any kind. At dinner though, he asked about Sarge.

"He's gone," Nate said, shaking his head and blinking back tears.

"We tried to look for him right when he got out," Clarisse said. "Then Julia put some Lost Dog signs up around the neighborhood, but no one's called. We even checked the animal shelter."

"Maybe he didn't want to be here anymore," Julia said quietly.

Nate stood up, picked up his water glass and tossed its contents across the table, splashing her in the face. "The hell with you!"

"Hey!" Clarisse yelled. "That's enough of that!"

Julia got up and left the table quickly, wiping her eyes as hot tears began to replace the thrown water.

"You can leave, too," she heard Ed growl, as she climbed the stairs to her bedroom.

Nate's chair scraped and he answered, "I have rehearsal anyway."

Later, Teddy and Julia sat in the Sarge-free backyard. "What an asshole," Teddy said, referring to Nate. "I can't believe he did that."

"He's really pissed off," Julia said. "It's true though, isn't it? That dog was reacting to all the angst around this place."

"Yeah probably, but I think he knew what he was doing: 'Gimme a cookie or I'll bite the crap outta ya!'"

"Yeah, I bet he went and joined a group of militant dogs

somewhere." Julia added. She shook with laughter, imagining their erstwhile terrier marching around in army fatigues.

The following June, Julia stood on the lawn of the Saratoga Performing Arts Center in her cap and gown freshly graduated from college. Ed moved around, snapping pictures of her with friends, by herself, with Clarisse. He insisted on using his time-delay function to photograph all three of them rather than asking someone else to take the picture. A few moments ago she'd had the great privilege of walking across the stage and shaking hands with Carl Sagan, the guest speaker. Now she watched Ed and Clarisse make the very thinnest attempts at congeniality for her benefit. *Great. I'm graduating college the same year my father graduates from rehab.* While that comment might have broken the tension a few years ago, no one in her family would have laughed today. Neither of her brothers had been able or willing to make the trip. It didn't much matter to Julia, as she'd been making plans to move out to San Francisco for several months. This event was a just a formality, a slightly awkward episode to be gotten through before her real life began, far away.

Later, Ed ordered some kind of spicy cake for dessert at Caffé Lena. When he took a bite, a horrified look appeared on his face, and he quickly spat it back onto the plate. Julia's heart began to pound.

"I tasted alcohol!" he exclaimed, wiping his mouth.

"Oh, I forgot to tell you it was made with rum," the waitress apologized. "Would you like something else?" Julia gave her a dirty look. "It'll be on the house," she added.

Ed leaned across the small, round table toward Julia and Clarisse. "I'm a recovering alcoholic. Don't even try to pretend that's not the case. If I have *anything* with alcohol in it, I could slide right back to where I was a year ago. I'm the real thing." Turning to the waitress, he added, "I'll have a slice of that chocolate cheesecake instead."

TWENTY

"HEAD, HEART, HEAD, HEART... how does that song go again?" Julia awoke to her father tapping his finger softly on her forehead. She was driving to California that day, and Ed had come into her room early in the morning to say goodbye before heading back to his counseling job at a recovery center in New Jersey. He'd been sober for more than eight months, and his gentle sense of humor was beginning to return. He was quieter now, deeply humbled. Much to Clarisse's bewilderment, he was coming home less and less, but he'd made a special trip to spend a few days with Julia and help with her garage sale before she left for the west coast.

"You'll be okay out there, right?" he asked.

Awkward thoughts rushed through her mind, though none seemed appropriate. *This could be the last time I ever see him.* Still wary of initiating the humor they once shared, she answered simply, "I'll be fine. I'll call you guys when I get to Michael's."

"Be careful on the road," he warned, kissing her forehead. "And watch out for those Moonies!" They both laughed, and then he was gone.

When Ed had left, she asked her mother, "What are you going to do?"

"I don't know... your father says I should act as if the old version of him were dead. It's so childish. But I promised, 'in sickness and in health,' so... I'm waiting to see what happens."

"If I were you, I'd think about getting a job," Julia said. "Then you'll have your own thing going on no matter what happens."

"I can't just leave Nate high and dry," she argued. "You and Teddy came home to dinner and fresh-baked cookies when you were his age, and I want him to have the same. At least until he goes away to school next year."

Julia finished packing up her little station wagon and drove to Queens to pick up Meg, a woman she'd met through the Skidmore ride board. Meg was headed for a residence hotel in downtown San Francisco, and a job at Levi's corporate office. She'd insisted on bringing her television set which struck Julia as funny since she'd given up on TV, meat, make-up, and anything remotely mainstream. Julia packed her oil paints, her new camera, a journal, some clothes, her bicycle, and the copy of Tom Robbins' *Even Cowgirls Get The Blues* Erin had given her for graduation.

Clarisse's attempts to keep her on the east coast had been in vain; when Michael read the long letter Julia had written about her father, he wrote back from San Francisco. "Sounds like a real dark-night-of-the-soul. Why don't you come out here after you graduate? You'd be better off watching that mess unfold from the other side of the continent." He and his new lover Monte shared a large Victorian flat in the Inner Sunset district, and they had a small guest room.

Meg was quiet at first. She looked a little startled to see Julia with her long, wavy hair and current favorite outfit, a pair of green overalls with a pink tank top leotard underneath. But when they pulled into a small town outside Toledo looking for a motel, they both groaned at the first thing they saw: a bar with a neon martini glass blinking on and off.

"Ugh," said Julia. "My family's just starting to get past that."

"Yeah, uh... that's sort of the problem at my house, too," Meg said.

"Really? Who?"

"My mother."

"Wow... I'm sorry... My Dad just got out of rehab last spring. It was a long haul before that." Julia sincerely hoped her father was past all the false starts with sobriety and the fender benders with the Comet and wanted to be proud of him, but she wasn't quite ready to dispense with the layer of psychic armor she'd worked so hard to create over the last few years. Plus she still shuddered when she thought about the drunken man from the bar in Saratoga.

"I just had to get away from all of it," Meg said.

"Yeah, me too," Julia nodded. "I was afraid the whole thing was going to break me, and I just couldn't let it."

While Meg jogged each morning, Julia found a quiet spot and did her Twelve Yoga Movements to the Rising Sun that she'd learned in Saratoga that summer. They took turns driving on Interstate 80 with the windows open and the car stereo blaring. When they passed the last toll booth in Indiana, the highway finally released them to the spaciousness of the Midwest.

"Freeway! Get it?" Julia exclaimed. "It means we're finally free!"

"Waa-*hoo!*" Meg yelled out the window.

Julia enjoyed the continuous travel more than reaching an actual destination. Stopping in Victor, Iowa, she tried to imagine a connection with the state where she'd lived her first two years, although it was a tiny town within earshot of the freeway. The waitresses all had big hair with beauty shop curls piled so high you could stick an entire finger through one of them and not touch their stiff walls. The only thing vegetarian was coleslaw and grilled cheese sandwiches. After dinner, she walked over to a pond across the street from the motel, took some pictures of the cows and whispered to them, "I'm a native, too."

The next day they drove through Nebraska until the hills reappeared, and the sky gradually became a giant bowl much larger than the land.

"San Francisco, 792 miles," Meg read from a sign, as they passed through Wyoming into Utah and headed down to the Great Salt Lake.

"Gee, we're practically there," Julia replied.

That night Julia dreamt that she was back inside the nuclear whale driven by her father. Teddy, Nate and Clarisse all sat on ribbed seats while Julia sat up front, looking out the left eye. Ed drove the whale from his pilot's seat in the forehead. He slowed the engines and they drifted. Clarisse laid out a buffet lunch on a picnic table, while Nate held the handle of an eggbeater to his forehead, winding it slowly. Julia turned to look at Ed, and saw that he was nonchalantly drinking a bottle of beer. The rest of the family acted unconcerned, so she screamed, *"How can you let this happen! He's not supposed to be doing that!"* and began throwing plates of food at Clarisse and her brothers.

She woke up sweating in the motel in Elko, Nevada. After showering, she went outside to do her yoga in the quiet courtyard, the dream still nagging her like an icy betrayal of her father's recovery.

The next day, when they crossed the Sierras, traffic picked up. After five days in the bucolic heartland, they quickly became bound in a mass metal force traveling eighty miles an hour toward the coast. Julia clung to the wheel for dear life, remembering what Ed had said once during a driving lesson. "Just try to blend with the movement of the traffic."

They tore through the Sacramento Valley and then crept over the Bay Bridge, arriving in downtown San Francisco at rush hour. The streets were packed and cable cars trundled past, with clumps of people hanging off of them in every direction. Most of them were smiling, Julia noticed. She stalled out the Volkswagen a few times on the steep hills before they found the Ansonia Residence Hotel and dropped Meg off along with her TV. Feeling overwhelmed, she called Michael from the lobby.

"Just stay where you are," he said. "I'll come and get you."

A few nights later they sat at the top of Corona Park sharing a joint. The lights of downtown San Francisco twinkled behind them, and they could see the tops of the trees in Golden Gate Park swaying below in the breeze. To the west, the ocean lay covered in a blanket of fog that was beginning to roll up through the Avenues. Foghorns moaning to each other in the distance were comfortably familiar to Julia. As they sat and talked, the blanket crept closer.

"It feels like I moved to another country," Julia said. "Everybody's so friendly."

"This is your chance to grow away from your family and become whomever you want. There's a bit of everything in this town—even Satan lives here. He has a black house."

"Eeeww!"

Michael laughed. His ponytail was longer, and he'd been taking psychology classes at San Francisco State. "I'm sorry I left you in the middle of all that," he said quietly. "You're so strong, I figured you'd be okay. Otherwise it might have been a double-drowning. You know I still love you though, right?"

Julia nodded. "It's weird to admit, but I felt so numb back then. Like everything was happening to someone else and I was just watching."

"You were compartmentalizing. People under a lot of stress tend to do that with their feelings, to keep everything from caving in at once."

"I think those psychology classes of yours are starting to kick in."

Fog now covered the Avenues and infiltrated Golden Gate Park, where it parted into soft, white tentacles that wound their way through the streets of Haight-Ashbury. Reaching the base of Twin Peaks it paused, extending creamy fingers of mist that circled around the bottom of Corona Park.

"How's your music?" Michael asked.

"Not really happening... everything just went down the drain a few years ago. I didn't want to be in a church anymore, and I couldn't even play the piano without crying. When Sarge, the psycho-dog bit my hand, I took it as a sign and began studying art instead."

"You were good, you know. I thought you might be having a *Five Easy Pieces* experience and became envious."

"I'm really getting into synthesizer music, though. Erin's been turning me on to all this incredible new stuff. Brian Eno, Kraftwerk, Tangerine Dream, Ultravox—"

"You know, there's an electronic music program at San Francisco State. Not that I think you should go right back to school. Just a thought."

Julia found a job as a hand painter at a ceramic studio called *Fragille!* on Third Street, as one of her art teachers at Skidmore had suggested. "Get something easy you don't have to think about so you can focus on your own work. Even René Magritte worked in a wallpaper factory for a little while."

Eager to get settled, she found a small, upstairs apartment on

6th Avenue not far from Michael's, with a back porch surrounded by pine trees. Golden Gate Park, in its fragrant expanse of eucalyptus and pine, was only three blocks away.

That Christmas Julia stayed in San Francisco. She was thrilled to be in a place where it didn't get cold in the winter. Especially after that last one in Saratoga, where the thermometer had dipped down to thirty below a few nights in a row.

Michael and Monte threw a holiday dinner party and invited her. "Look!" she exclaimed, standing at their front door with her date, Dennis, the glazier from *Fragille!* "It's December and I'm not wearing gloves!"

"Don't worry about her," Michael joked. "It takes about a year to stop comparing this place to the east coast."

Teddy had sent her a stiffly written postcard from New York saying, "We'll miss you, but your decision not to come east for the holidays was probably a wise one." She'd already heard about the official separation of her parents back in November and reacted with a sense of relief at first, knowing it would put an end to the cold uncertainty of the past few years. Then she felt guilty for not being more upset, and finally collapsed into tears for several hours before taking the N Judah out to the beach to watch the sunset.

Right before Christmas Day, Michael took her to an organ recital at St. Mary's of the Agitator Vane, as he called it, a white cement cathedral on Gough Street with swooping, hyperbolic architecture. "You've *got* to see this place," he insisted.

"Oh my God!" she exclaimed, stepping inside the church. Organ pipes were set on a massive pedestal near the front of the church, like a silver castle on a dessert tray. Julia secretly wondered how the Catholics could allow such an imaginative, fluid design, but quickly dismissed all prejudice once the organist took his place at the console. The music surged through her, awakening a segment of herself that she'd stuffed away since her late nights in College Hall. When she began to weep, Michael reached over and took her hand. "Just try and concentrate on the beauty," he whispered in her ear, causing her to sit up and replace her tears with awe for the remainder of the concert.

"No more school!" had been her mantra since she'd left Saratoga Springs, although Michael sensed her excitement. He plied her with Virgil Fox recordings whenever she visited their apartment until he finally convinced her to come with him to San Francisco State one day in February. "At least just ride out there with me and look," he pressed. "It's a nice campus."

Later, they stood at the front desk of the music department at SF State. When it was her turn, Julia explained to one of the administrators that she was interested in studying classical organ and electronic music.

"Would you like to see the practice rooms?" asked the administrator, whose named tag read "Constance."

"Sure," she answered.

"You guys have fun," Michael said. "I'll meet you outside after my class."

Once again, Julia walked up and down the halls of a music department, peering into the single, insular practice rooms with pianos, and one room with a Hammond B3 organ in it.

"Here's our electronic music room," Constance said, gently knocking on a large metal door at the end of a hallway. It opened, and a disheveled man with long blonde hair stood in the doorway.

"She's interested in studying here," Constance said. "Can she have a quick look?"

"Sure thing," the man said. He stood aside, revealing what looked like an entire wall of holes and knobs, several tape recorders, and strings of patch cords hanging on another wall.

Yikes. How will I ever make music in here?

"This is the real thing," the man said, as if reading her mind. "The teacher doesn't even allow a keyboard."

"We'll let you get back to work," Constance said, as they edged out of the room.

Down another hallway, Constance stopped at a solid wooden door. "We also have this," she said, opening the door with a key.

She switched on the overhead light and Julia nearly swooned. It was a small practice room with an entire pipe organ in it. The pipes stood against the back wall in a deliciously silver arc behind a two-manual console, with stops on either side. Julia could easily imagine spending long, happy hours in this room by herself, fugue after prelude tumbling from her fingers like syrup over a warm pancake.

It took a few weeks to petition the school into letting her study for another undergraduate degree until one day Constance handed her a key to the room with the pipe organ and said, "You'll probably want to practice to get ready for your audition. Just sign up on the sheet by the door when no one else is using it."

Astonished, Julia took the key and called Clarisse later on, asking her to send some of her old organ music books. When they arrived, she drove out to San Francisco State and gingerly opened the door to the pipe organ room. Sliding onto the wooden bench, she switched on the power and the instrument seemed to draw a deep breath. She opened her book of Bach fugues and laid into her comfortably familiar Bach Fugue in G Minor. Several bars in, she realized she was fighting back tears.

Where are these coming from? She stopped to wipe her tears with a sleeve. *I've got to get some control over this.* Remembering the yoga postures that she'd been neglecting lately, she tried breathing steadily as she returned to the piece.

Several weeks later she played it for the organ teacher and was cheerfully invited to join the music department, beginning with the summer semester. Ed was so thrilled that he sent her a check in an old envelope printed with The Lloyd Family and their Long Island address. He'd crossed out Family so it just read, "The Lloyd."

A few months later Clarisse was rolling her shopping cart up the dairy aisle of Bohack's Supermarket in Pattituck Cove. She'd just come from a job interview for a research assistant at Hofstra University, and was juggling the outcome around in her head, along with the idea of moving to a smaller house, and Nate's upcoming high school graduation. She felt faint. Passing a display of Easter egg coloring kits she blanched, recalling all the contests they'd had as a family, to come up with the best egg. Pushing her cart past the display, she hurried to the check-out in an effort to get out to her car before crying when she remembered she wanted to pick up an Easter ham. She chose one big enough for herself and Nate, plus a few days' worth of sandwiches, and sighed as she dropped it into her cart absently. It landed on a carton of orange juice which promptly exploded, sending its contents flying out the sides of her cart.

"Well, well. It's been a long time since I've gotten that kind of a reception!"

Clarisse looked up to see Don Frank a.k.a. The King standing next to her, dressed in a tweed sport coat and jeans, splattered with orange juice.

TWENTY-ONE

JULIA SAT ON THE EDGE of the examination table at the Haight-Ashbury Women's Clinic. The nurse practitioner entered with a swoosh, peering over the top of her half-glasses.

"Well, your test came out positive. You are definitely pregnant. How do you feel about that?"

"Like shit." *That prick.*

Julia and Dennis, the glazier from work, had struck up a relationship based on deep, beery conversations about art and music at a bar near the *Fragille!* studio. With his dark wavy hair and five o'clock shadow, Dennis reminded her of a struggling artist version of her old crush, Mr. Ohlman. When he wasn't spraying final coats of clear glaze onto ceramic dishware, Dennis poured paint directly onto horizontal canvases, letting the pools of color blend with each other at will. His paintings fascinated Julia, and when they slept together, he convinced her he'd been rendered sterile from a bad case of the mumps in high school. A few months into their relationship, he was fired from the ceramics studio when he started taking long lunch breaks at the bar and his glazing work deteriorated. Chicken-shaped gravy boats and Victorian cookie houses were exploding in the kilns, he argued with the owners, and he wore the same torn Sex Pistols t-shirt nearly every day. His tragically romantic artist image began to fade for Julia when he disappeared for a few weeks and didn't call. She finally reached him in the middle of a shouting match with his upstairs neighbors. He put the phone down and yelled, "Go ahead and call the cops, then—just leave me alone!"

"Want to get out of there and see a movie or something?" Julia asked when he picked the receiver back up.

"Uh… I don't know… I'll call ya later."

When he never did, Julia shed any lingering desire to rescue him.

"You're only about six or seven weeks along," the nurse practitioner told her.

"You have to tell him," Erin advised, from her and Morty's apartment in New York.

"Hell, no. I wouldn't give that pickled doofus the satisfaction of knowing he can breed," Julia said, finishing her eighth cup of pennyroyal tea. "When I imagine his foul offspring inside me it makes the morning sickness even worse."

"You *have* to," Erin insisted.

Michael agreed. "You have to let him know what he's capable of. Just in case he's ignorant."

They both snorted.

"Okay, but I'm waiting until afterwards. I don't want to get talked into something completely foolish."

A week later, Julia sat in a doctor's office downtown with her friend Jeanne, another painter from *Fragille!*, waiting for an abortion. She squirmed, hating herself for having been so stupid. *I have a college degree, for Christ's sake… I'm a doctor's daughter!*

"It can't be me, you slut," Dennis scoffed, when she called to tell him. She could feel his nasty sneer slithering through the telephone wires.

"But you were the only one!" Julia insisted.

"Yeah, right." Click.

> *She stood next to a giant redwood tree with an ear pressed against it, listening to its steady, ancient breath. Then she trotted down the beach trail to the water and climbed into a floating avocado half-shell. Down the river she went, through gentle ripples that flowed into large calm pools, then spilling into a group of rapids. Her boat bobbled over them and took*

on water as the foamy torrent became a speeding channel. Suddenly they were airborne, her and the avocado boat, bouncing from crest to crest, headed toward a waterfall. Fog rose from the chasm beneath it, and she clung to the sides of the fruit-skin as the boat was swallowed by a thundering rush of water. Just as the swirling froth began to consume her, she heard her brother Teddy yell, "I can see the lighthouse!" Tree branches reached out then, plucking her from the water and setting her back into the waiting avocado shell-boat...

Julia woke from a hazy dream on the deck of her second story apartment. She'd been cruising on painkillers and marijuana, dozing with her blue silk kimono open. The pine trees surrounding the deck still sported the Christmas bulbs she'd hung on them. Sutro Tower loomed in the distance and the sweet smell of star jasmine coming from Golden Gate Park made her feel as if she were living inside a giant bowl of incense. It was late morning, and the sunshine was already filtered by fog beginning to billow in from the ocean. She heard Jeanne coming up the back steps, and pulled her kimono shut.

"You're getting kind of pink," Jeanne remarked. "Didn't they tell you to stay out of the sun while you were on tetracycline?"

The phone rang. Julia considered letting it go, but it was right next to her chaise lounge, so she picked up.

"Hi," came Clarisse's voice from Long Island. Julia sighed inwardly. The last few months of phone calls from her mother had been tedious. When the divorce became final, Ed had immediately begun seeing another woman from his church choir in New Jersey, and Clarisse called Julia almost every night. "He hardly ever wanted to go to church when he was home!" she'd wailed.

"Hi, Mom. How's it going?" She rolled her eyes at Jeanne.

"You'll never guess who I ran into the other day."

"Ceddie?"

"No," Clarisse laughed. "Remember when I was in *The King and I?*"

"Sort of."

"Well, I ran into Don Frank, the man who played The King!"

"Where?"

"In Bohack's."

Julia vaguely remembered a tall, friendly man shaking hands with her mother in The Hamburger Express.

"Mom! Did he ask you out?"

"Yes... to the Swan Club!"

Julia paused, unsure how to react. She hadn't told anyone in the family about her recent "procedure." Besides being embarrassed and angry with Dennis, she was mystified by her deep sense of loss afterwards.

"You wouldn't be human if you didn't feel something," Jeanne told her the day before, driving Julia home from the doctor's office. When Julia had gone to bed that night, she woke up the next morning in a puddle of blood, sobbing uncontrollably. Stuffing a rolled-up towel between her legs, she'd made a frantic call to the clinic and they told her this sort of thing often happens the day after, to just stay home and rest. Now she wanted to warn her mother, beg her not to get involved with anyone too quickly, but she hadn't felt Clarisse smiling on the other end of the phone for a long time. "Okay, so what are you going to wear?"

Jeanne smiled and dropped off a bag of groceries and a box of Kotex pads. "See you at work," she mouthed, going back down the stairs.

Julia stood in a dark room lit by tiny multi-colored lights that winked on and off at different intervals. She'd been in the electronic music studio at school for hours, plugging wires into holes in the wall to get different combinations of beeps and boops. It was like being on a spaceship. Now that she knew her way around the system, she liked to switch off the overhead lights and let the soft glow of the LED lights illuminate the room. She turned the potentiometer knobs, bending sound waves, and rode on a sea of ambient music.

The student monitor knocked on the metal door, snapping her out of her trance. It was ten o'clock and the music building was closing for the night. *Damn. I've got to hurry.* She unplugged everything and shut down the studio, anxious to get out before she was the last one left. Leaving the building, she caught up with another group of students headed for the parking garage. Fear had been gripping her since the abortion; she was afraid of the streets, and stayed home most evenings when she wasn't at school. Her friends had started going to the Mabuhay Gardens nightclub to hear punk rock and new wave music, inviting Julia along, but she'd become claustrophobic and couldn't stay in crowded, smoky places for very long.

What a tragedy I've become, she thought, standing in front of the full length mirror at home. She'd lost ten pounds and was beginning to look waifish. *I'd love to see some of those bands. Especially the ones with synthesizers.* She finally agreed to meet Jeanne and Michael at the Deaf Club in the Mission to hear Tuxedo Moon. Toward the end of the performance, she began to get dizzy. The room shrank. Suddenly, getting outside to fresh air became a matter of life and death. She glanced around and saw everyone she knew enjoying themselves, mesmerized by the music, then darted down the stairs and outside. On the sidewalk, she breathed heavily, sweat running down her face as she clung to a No Parking sign. *This is so pathetic.*

"What's going on? Are you okay?" Michael asked, coming up behind her.

"I thought I was either going to faint, suffocate or throw up."

"Did you get too high?"

"No. I haven't even had a drink yet."

"You might be having a panic attack, dear. Just breathe." Michael stood with her on the sidewalk, rubbing her shoulders.

"I've just become scared of everything," Julia said, her voice quivering. "I hate this about myself. I feel trapped."

A few minutes later Jeanne joined them. "You know, if you're going to feel vulnerable, it might not be a bad idea to learn some kind of self defense," she offered. "You know, a double kick to the groin or something," she added, air-kicking at the No Parking sign.

"Oof," Julia shivered, glancing sideways at Michael. "Still, I've thought about doing a martial art."

"I've heard aikido is a really good one," Michael said. "A little more spiritual than the others."

A few weeks later Julia sat beside a canvas-covered mat in a large second story aikido dojo on Van Ness Avenue. A woman stood in front of the class wearing a Japanese *hakama* and training *gi.*

"Come from your heart center," the woman said, spiraling herself in a circle as she drew in her attacker, blended with his energy, and tossed him in another direction. He flew for a few feet, landed gracefully, then stood up again and smiled. When the class was over, Julia went straight to the front desk.

"How soon can I start?" she asked, pulling out her checkbook.

TWENTY-TWO

"I HAVE A JOB OFFER OUT YOUR WAY," Ed called from New Jersey. "I'm coming for a visit to see if I can handle living on the west coast."

"O-oh," Julia stammered. They hadn't seen each other since she'd left Long Island, so she wasn't sure if he'd become a Bible-thumping AA guy or had reclaimed some of his old personality.

"Can you pick out a nice place for me to stay in San Francisco?" he continued. "Just for a couple of nights." Through the phone, she thought she heard some of the old playfulness in his voice and was instantly certain he'd get a fresh perspective by changing coasts. She booked him a room at the Seal Rocks Inn at the tip of San Francisco's Ocean Beach, specifying a room that faced the sea. *That'll be the clincher,* she thought, using an old expression of his. *If he sees the west coast from this angle, he won't be able to resist.*

A few weeks later, Ed rode into town on an airport shuttle and Julia met him at the hotel. Except for a grey-tipped beard she'd never seen on him before, he looked more relaxed than she'd remembered, like an aged piece of furniture that had been sanded down to the bare wood, ready for refinishing. "Wow, a beard," Julia remarked.

"Yeah... it's part of the new me," her father said. He turned to push the sliding glass door open, and a breeze filled the curtain like a sail. "It's beautiful!" he exclaimed. The sun was beginning its descent, and Julia took it as a good omen that the fog had spared them this wintery afternoon. She'd made dinner reservations at the Cliff House and as they walked down the hill to the restaurant, they behaved like old school acquaintances who hadn't kept in touch.

"So... heard from your mother lately?" Ed asked.

"Just the other day... she's doing well. Has a new job at Hofstra University." Julia didn't mention her mother's new love interest, Don Frank. And of course she didn't feel comfortable asking about the mysterious woman in her father's church choir, since she'd heard about it from Clarisse. Standing at the entrance to the Cliff House, the hostess informed them their table wasn't ready yet.

"Would you like to wait in the bar?" she asked.

Gripped with embarrassment, Julia turned to Ed. He shrugged and said, "Okay with me."

"We'll find you a place by the windows," the hostess smiled.

Once they were seated at a corner table facing the sparkling, sun-lit ocean, Julia worked up the courage to ask him, "Does it bother you, sitting in a bar where people are drinking?"

"It would bother me more if we were sitting in a bar where *I* was drinking," he answered.

"Do you still... want to drink?" Julia asked.

"Yeah, sometimes. I don't think that part ever goes away. But I've got my camel," he added, pointing to a pewter pin on his lapel. "A present from my sponsor, when I turned 'one' a couple months ago. If a camel can go for days without a drink, then so can I."

The next day a representative from the hospital drove Ed down to San Jose for his interview while Julia was at school. He called from the hotel late that evening.

"So how did it go?" Julia asked.

"I think I did okay. I guess I'll have to 'let go and let God' for now. We use that a lot."

It was drizzling the next morning when she picked up her father in her old VW Squareback. The ocean was covered with a salty mist, but they could still hear the muffled barking of the seals between moaning foghorns.

"I hate to tell you this, Julia, but it's starting to look like a drunk's car," Ed joked, pointing to a dent on the rear fender.

"It happened in a parking lot," Julia protested.

"Yeah, that's what they all say," he answered, chuckling.

She drove him out to San Francisco State, where she played a

Bach fugue for him in the little pipe organ studio.

"You really do have a special talent, you know," Ed said.

Julia nodded, saying nothing. She was on a quest to impress Ed with her musical talent before attempting to bring up potentially volatile personal subjects.

Next, she showed him the electronic music studio.

"It's just a wall full of holes and some tape recorders. How do you make music?" he asked.

"That's what I thought when I first started. After a while things begin to make sense." She switched on a tape recorder and played a few minutes of a piece she'd been working on.

"Pretty strange," Ed said afterwards. "Like science fiction."

The rain had turned to a steady spatter as they drove back toward Golden Gate Park. Julia was beginning to relax, and wanted to show Ed all her favorite tourist spots. She parked in front of the Japanese Tea Garden. Huddled under Julia's umbrella, they walked through the gate, over the steep wooden bridge and past the giant bronze Buddha, shrouded in fog. They sat at a small table at the edge of the tearoom watching the rain drip over the roof. A middle-aged Japanese woman in a kimono set a pot of hot tea and a plate of rice crackers on the table, and several pigeons landed at the edge.

"They're always here," Julia said, holding out a cracker. One of the birds darted forward and nipped it out of her hand. Ed picked up another cracker and held it out. Soon they were hosting a small group of pigeons, gathered on the edge of the table. Julia studied their tiny orange eyes riveted to the plate of crackers, drew a breath, and said, "Dad, I've been having this recurring nightmare. We're always hanging out somewhere, the whole family, like at a picnic or on the boat, and then I turn around to see you nonchalantly having a drink. I end up screaming and throwing things at everybody for letting you do it while I wasn't looking, and then I wake up."

Ed cleared his throat. "It's really important for you kids to follow-up and find an Adult Children of Alcoholics meeting. I go to them myself. I've been uncovering a lot of submerged feelings about my mother."

"Really? I didn't know *she* was an alcoholic."

"Nobody told you. That's why it's so important to discover the patterns you might be repeating unconsciously."

"Sort of like peeling the layers off an onion?" Julia asked.

"Yes, exactly!" Ed looked impressed. "It's amazing," he continued, "but we turn out to be the classic alcoholic family. Teddy is the stereotypical quiet hermit, while you are the lost middle child. Nate is the entertainer, the class clown. Those Adult Children meetings are for meeting people like you."

"What do you mean, 'lost child?'" Julia asked.

"Not sure of your direction or personality, feeling left behind a lot... that sort of thing. But I'll let you figure that stuff out on your own—it's much better that way."

He reached into his wallet and pulled out a picture of a woman. "I want to show you my new friend, Rose. She's in our choir, and I started to notice she was coming to church drunk. We got her into recovery. This is her, three months sober—she's going on six, now."

"How old is she?"

"She'll be forty this December. I'm going to try and convince her to come out here with me if I get the job. She's going through a messy divorce right now and she's got three kids."

"Does Mom know?" Julia feigned.

"I haven't told her." Ed and Clarisse stopped speaking after the divorce was final. Julia had to be very careful what she said to one parent or the other over the phone, since they were still both ultra-sensitive and emotional when it came to each other's business.

"So, what's this job like?" Julia asked, changing the subject. Respectful of his new, sober life, she still wasn't in the mood to imagine her father with another woman, especially one so much younger.

"It's Medical Director of a small recovery hospital near San Jose," he answered. "Recovery and psychiatric treatment."

"Well, there'll be no shortage of customers, I'm sure."

"That's true. Ninety percent of the people in this country need psychiatric treatment, but only ten percent of them actually know it."

The rain was beginning to let up as they spoke. When the tea was gone and the pigeons had finished the last of the crackers, they got up and walked toward the band shell. Rays of sunlight permeated the fog, and steam rose in soft columns around them, as people began emerging from the mist. Someone was playing an accordion nearby, and several roller skaters appeared, gliding around the benches in front of the stage.

"My pals from San Jose recommend whale watching while I'm here," Ed spoke up.

"Really? Do you want to?" Julia asked carefully, ever fearful of being the one who might distress him into drinking again. *The water could be rough. He could have a relapse!*

The next morning they stood in the cockpit of a whale-watching boat motoring out of Bodega Bay. It was a chilly, partly gloomy day, as Julia was prone to call those fog-enshrouded days on the San Francisco coast, but the sun was still visible as a white dot behind the clouds.

"Still got my sea legs," Ed announced, when the boat sped up and he shifted, holding his ground. The captain's voice crackled over a loudspeaker, "We have a spray off the right side of the bow." Julia and Ed turned to look. A puff of water sprang from the surface of the ocean, and everyone ooo'ed.

They drove on for another ten minutes with their eyes riveted on the waves, not seeing anything.

"I guess you just have to get lucky," Ed said. "At least it's a nice boat ride. Different than the Atlantic."

"Yeah, the waves are wider, and much farther apart," Julia said, as the boat rode up one swell and down the other.

"Another spray, about fifty yards to your left," the captain announced. "We'll see if we can move in a little closer." The engines slowed and they waited until they saw another puff of spray, much larger. The captain shut off the engines and they drifted. "We're coming alongside," he spoke softly.

Then a huge mottled shape crested the surface of the gray water, right next to the boat. Julia gasped. It glistened as it rose and fell, blending with the movement of the waves.

"No wonder sailors used to think there were sea serpents," Ed whispered.

They drifted, mesmerized by the behemoth shape gliding through the water until it began to move off. Then Julia remembered she had a camera and reached for it, but the whale had already disappeared. She held it up anyway to check the light meter, and the lens went completely dark. As she glanced over the top of the camera, there was a group shout from the deck. The gigantic, sleek fluke of the whale appeared in the air fifty feet away, gave a weighty flick, and then dipped gracefully beneath the waves. The boat was silent for a few seconds, as everyone stared at the spot where the tail had been.

"That's... the biggest thing I have ever seen in my life," Ed murmured. "Did you get it?"

"No... I saw it, though. It was... *mystical*," Julia said, struggling for the right words.

"A spiritual experience," someone next to them remarked.

"Now do you want to move here?" Julia asked her father.

"Yeah, I think that did it."

Julia took Ed to the airport the next morning before school. As she watched him hand his boarding pass to the flight attendant, she wondered if she would ever shake the nagging feeling that she was about to lose him.

"There's a substitute job at a Methodist church on Balboa Street," her organ teacher told her when she got to school. "It has a nice, three-manual pipe organ and you don't have to direct the choir. Just get yourself familiar with the hymns. You can meet with the pastor and he'll give you a key."

"You probably know how everything works," the pastor said later, as they walked up the dark red, carpeted aisle toward the organ console. She noticed a few wax drippings on the rug near the altar.

"And just so you know," the pastor added, handing her a hymnal, "we like to sing 'em kind of fast."

Julia nodded politely. *Whatever gets them to Point B, I guess.*

When she turned on the blower fan the church seemed to inflate like a living, breathing entity. She played the pastor several verses from "Praise To The Lord, The Almighty." Afterwards he smiled, shook her hand and said, "See you around, then?"

"Okay," Julia nodded, sitting back and settling into a soft Bach Pastorale in F Major.

"There's a band here called *Andrea Doria!*" Julia shrieked into the phone to Erin, later that week. "Can you believe that?!?"

"What are they like?" Erin asked. "Are they sinking?"

"Ha! Funny. No, there are two Asian women singers who always wear Chinese silk dresses, and they've got blue lightning bolts dyed into the sides of their heads. You know, Andrea and Doria. Plus a guitar, bass and drums."

"Hmmm... no keyboards? What kind of music? Have you seen them?"

"Uh, well... cool new wave dance music." Julia hadn't seen them live. She was still struggling with the occasional panic attack in crowded places. She'd heard one of their songs on KUSF and seen band pictures in the Pink Section of the San Francisco Chronicle, but hadn't mustered up the courage to go to a live show. The name was still a little too coincidental for comfort.

"You've got to try and get into that band!" Erin squealed. "I mean, how often will the cosmos echo your deepest obsession in such a playful way? Show up at their next gig and offer your services."

"Oh... I don't know... I don't even have my own keyboards yet... okay!" Julia thought quickly. "I'll make you a deal: if I can get into that band, you have to promise to come and visit me."

"Deal," Erin agreed from her phone in New Jersey. Each time Julia suggested visiting, she could feel Erin yield a little more. She was consciously planting the idea of her friend actually migrating out to the west coast, and continued to nurture it whenever she got the chance. Besides, since Erin had recently moved out of Morty's apartment in New York for a fellowship at Rutgers, she was by herself, with only one eye that worked anymore.

Ed called the next night to tell Julia that he'd decided to take the job in San Jose.

"It'll be a great new beginning, moving away from an area with so many painful memories, now that you've recovered," she said.

"*In* recovery," he corrected her. "We're in a perpetual state of recovery. And remember what I said at that Japanese Tea Garden: don't just assume that you're okay because I've stopped drinking."

Julia furrowed her brow and said, "Okay," mentally filing away the notion of an Adult Children meeting for some undisclosed time in her future.

TWENTY-THREE

JULIA FINALLY SCRAPED ENOUGH MONEY TOGETHER from working at the *Fragille!* studio and substituting at the Methodist church to buy a synthesizer, an electronic keyboard and a keyboard amp. She set them up in her tiny living room and played for hours into the night with her headphones plugged into the amplifier. Michael and Monte began taking her to punk and new wave shows at Mabuhay Gardens and the Deaf Club in an attempt to help her over her panic attacks. Sometimes she even made herself go alone, standing at the back near the door, until the attacks started losing their potency. Her aikido classes also helped fuel a new sense of courage and well-being. She often came home from them slightly bruised, but happy.

Her final healing came on the day a rumor spread through San Francisco that The Clash would be doing an impromptu show that night at the old Temple Beautiful on Geary Street. Everybody went. The show was so spontaneous, so energetic, that Julia found herself out on the dance floor right in front of the stage, flailing alongside Jeanne and the rest of the hand-painters at *Fragille!*

Still too shy to actually infiltrate backstage after a show and offer her services to *Andrea Doria* as a keyboard player, she joined a fledgling techno-pop band with people from her electronic music class at San Francisco State and captured the attention of the new wave community during their first gig at the Savoy Tivoli in North Beach. Rodney, the bleached blonde guitar player from *Andrea Doria*, also happened to be there, and invited her to a whirlwind rehearsal at their South of Market studio the next night, after which he'd asked her to join the band. "This is like a *dream*," she told Erin later. "I mean, who could have predicted something like this? Now you *have* to come out here and visit."

Several weeks later, people milled around a South of Market loft at a multi-media show, drifting between the art installations and drinking bottled beer. The scent of clove cigarettes wafted through the air. Julia's band *Andrea Doria* had just finished playing, and they were taking down their equipment to make way for the next group, The Comparison Shoppers.

Andrea Doria's two Asian women singers, Monique and Beatrice a.k.a. Andrea and Doria, patted the sweat from the blue lightning bolts dyed into the sides of their shaved temples. Besides Rodney the guitar player, there was Greg the bass player, Steve the drummer, and now Julia on keyboards.

By the time Julia finished packing up her keyboards in the loft, The Comparison Shoppers had begun their set. She wandered around looking at the installations, still wearing her pink nylon flight suit from the performance, part of her new wave techno-industrial look, with the front unbuttoned revealing the top of a black lace camisole. She'd cut her hair short and darkened to nearly black with henna, and now wore soft contact lenses. The Shoppers, as everyone called them, had a French horn player whose microphone was patched into his synthesizer. It made an eerie wailing sound, as if the horn were some kind of extraterrestrial beast flying over the crowd. Crates were piled together around the loft and covered with fabric to create pedestals for artwork. One piece, a miniature landscaped hill under a clear plastic dome, caught Julia's attention. Plastic Barbie-sized doll's arms were lit from the inside and planted on the hill, interspersed with HO-train trees and half-melted telephone poles.

"You'll fog up the plexi if you stare at it too long," a voice behind her warned. Julia held still, trying to decide whether it was a snotty comment or not. She turned around to face a smiling man with short brown hair and a white tailored shirt with the sleeves rolled up. He wore tweed pants with cuffs, a black and white fake fur necktie, and glasses with blue lenses.

"What are they reaching for?" she asked, pointing to the doll's arms.

"They're not reaching, they're waiting," he answered.

One of Julia's aikido teachers was constantly telling her not to reach to intercept an attack. "Let them come down to your size, where your power is," he'd said. She considered complimenting the artist on his insight, but quickly remembered that her conversations with men about martial arts usually resulted in them looking for someone else to talk to.

"Well, what are they waiting for?"

"Post-apocalyptic rescue."

"Whew. For a second I was afraid you were going to say 'emotional rescue.'"

"Too trendy," he answered.

"Not like us." They both laughed.

"So you're Mark, the creator?" she asked, pointing to the name Mark Laughton, printed on a card under the plastic dome.

"I take partial responsibility. Some of it goes to varying plastic manufacturers of miniature train parts. Nice set, by the way. How come I haven't seen you before?"

"I just moved out of a convent," she answered.

"Really?"

"No, not really."

Mark let out a deep, ho-ho belly laugh which in turn, triggered Julia to laugh with him. Then the Shoppers burst into a lively song with the electronic French horn ricocheting over the tops of peoples' heads. Mark grabbed Julia's hand, dragging her onto the dance floor. He was a good dancer and attractive, with just enough geekiness to make him look interesting, Julia thought. A refreshing change from the scruffy starving artist look of creepy Dennis.

Later on, when they'd danced themselves out and the show had degenerated into spiky-haired men marching across the makeshift stage with plastic ray guns shouting, *"Rea-gun!"* Mark helped Julia load her equipment into her car. He followed her home to the Inner Sunset to help her unload, and then said, "Let's go down to Haight Street for a drink. I know a great little place that's still open."

"Okay, but you can't try to sleep with me tonight, okay?" Julia beamed inside, proud of herself for at least trying to protect her sense of virtue.

Mark laughed again, and said, "Okay... although sometime in the foreseeable future I may attempt to scheme my way into your panties as best I can."

"This is really out of place," Julia said, noting the odd Middle Eastern décor in the tiny pub on Haight Street. A stern, toad-like man in a black vest stood behind the bar until he noticed Mark and nodded faintly.

"You have to order a martini," Mark whispered. "He's a bit eccentric."

"Ugh," Julia whispered back. "I hate martinis."

"Okay then, I'll ordered one with a beer chaser and you can have the beer."

Julia was careful to maintain a safe distance using her brainy, synthesizer-savvy personae. She and Mark easily kept up with one another about new bands, books, the apocalypse, and a certain fondness for disaster movies, especially those involving sinking ships.

"No way!" Julia had exclaimed. "You liked *A Night To Remember?*" The bartender shot her a warning look.

"Be careful," Mark hissed. "If he suspects you're a hippie, he'll kick you out and tell you to go to a fern bar. Anyway, jeez, I mean, a sunken ship freak who stumbles into a band called *Andrea Doria?* How serendipitous is that?"

"Meant to be, I guess. You know, a teacher of mine actually lent me that *Life* magazine from the fifties with the *Andrea Doria* sinking on the cover, back in high school."

"Brave of him to lend something like that to a high school student," Mark said, and then touched his glass to hers, giving her a wink. "Of course, he had good judgment."

Despite her sincere attempts to preserve her aloof, nerdy-hipness, Mark wound up at her apartment that night. With a soft, two a.m. fanfare of foghorns and mist, they staggered up the stairs in a mish-mash of kisses. Inside, Mark began to undress her, but her entire history of sexual encounters quickly surfaced in her mind, attempting to corner her consciousness like oafish bores around the food table at a party. She shivered.

"Chilly?" he asked. "How about a hot shower?"

God, a hot shower! Julia tingled all over, glad that she'd taken the time to clean the bathroom earlier that week.

She marveled at Mark's size, massaging him soapily in the shower as he kissed the back of her neck. Then he carried her into the bedroom dripping wet. Her legs still wrapped around his torso, he set her down on the bed and she laid back quivering, heedless of the wet bedspread. *Don't be stupid again!* a voice cried from somewhere deep within her writhing body. She began to sit up, but Mark leaned back and reached for his pants, pulling out a rubber. Shaking her head in amused disbelief, Julia let herself melt into an ocean of carnal bliss, thrilled each time the waves swelled up and broke again and again. Once her thoughts surfaced, and she opened her eyes. Mark slowed down and gazed at her tenderly, then kissed her as he surged deeper. *Now I see what all the fuss is about!* Many hot, steamy strokes and sucking, fish-mouth kisses later, they spooned up and fell asleep together.

The next day, Julia still couldn't believe her good luck. Mark had taken her out for breakfast and followed up with roses, delivered later that day.

"He's almost *too* sweet," she gushed to Jeanne, when the roses arrived at her work table at *Fragille!*

TWENTY-FOUR

JULIA, MARK, ED AND HIS NEW SWEETIE, ROSE, stood inside a round yellow building on the stone terrace of the Cliff House, watching a panoramic view of their surroundings move slowly over a ten-foot dish. In the darkened room, the image in the huge saucer rolled over the ocean outside, past seals sunning themselves on the rocks, the Sutro Bath ruins, the restaurant, the sandy beach, and back over the water. The man who'd sold them tickets pulled the curtain aside and stepped into the small room wearing a worn top hat and tails.

Clearing his throat, he announced, "The Camera Obscura is an early precursor to photography, with its principles dating back to the time of Aristotle. Made of a rotating mirror, a large lens, and a parabolic dish, it uses the 'pinhole' camera logic, reflecting the image from outside..." he gestured toward the door, and then to the dish, "...onto this."

"Makes me feel a little god-like," Ed mused, staring into the bowl of ocean.

"Omnipotent," Rose added.

"Yeah... maybe we should give them some more money for the tickets," Mark said. Everyone chuckled quietly, still awed by the reflections in the dish. *Mark has regained a banter point*, thought Julia. He'd horrified her by ordering a beer at lunch, where Ed and Rose were picking up the tab, when Julia had been mindful of not drinking in front of either of them. Now she slipped her hand into Mark's and gave it a squeeze.

Ed had gotten settled at his new job in San Jose and Rose followed a few months later when her divorce was final. Today was Julia's first time meeting her. During lunch, both Rose and Ed were forthcoming, nearly rapturous about their recoveries. Rose seemed more like an older friend than a prospective authority figure. Her deep blue eyes and willingness to admit her mistakes impressed Julia the most.

Shore wind whistled around outside the little round building where they stood gazing into the parabolic dish, listening to electronic dream machine music that oozed softly from hidden speakers. The sea sparkled with afternoon sunlight in the huge saucer, and they stayed mesmerized for another twenty minutes before heading across the terrace to the *Musée Mécanique.*

"I bet you could make a soundtrack for this place," Mark whispered to Julia. It was his idea to take them to the Camera Obscura, but Julia was nearly bursting with excitement; she couldn't wait to show her father the arcade beneath the restaurant.

Inside, there was an exhibit of early coin-operated machines. Julia dropped a quarter into a box next to a miniature village made entirely of toothpicks. Ed stood spellbound, as everything in the town came to life and jittered around in time to calliope music. "Pretty nifty," he said. Then he moved over to some old-fashioned rifle boxes.

"Got 'im!" they heard him chortle now and then, as Mark wandered over to the high-tech electronic games in the next room, followed by Rose and Julia.

"These are the ones my kids would go for," Rose said.

Julia nodded, hesitant to add anything. Clarisse had been pointedly judgmental about Rose leaving her children behind after the divorce, although Ed's side of the story was more survival-oriented.

"People call us selfish," he'd said, "But we really have to learn how to look after ourselves first." She glanced back at her father at the old arcade game. He looked happy, popping off ducks and rabbits with the mounted rifle. *The way he used to look when he took us to Coney Island. Like one of us kids.*

Ed finished shooting and caught up with them in the modern end of the arcade.

"How did it go?" Rose asked.

"I still like the old machines, but I'd like to hit Ms. Pac-Man before we leave."

Later that week, Julia was practicing in the church after midnight. With the combination of her classes, the band and work, it was often the only time available. She'd locked the building from the inside and was stumbling her way through a Vierne suite. When she lifted her hands from the keys and the church echoed, she thought she heard a rustling sound. Peering over the console, she saw a man walking up the aisle, looking straight ahead. He was balding, dressed in a dark suit. Imagining it to be one of the church deacons who had a key, she called out, "Hello?"

Ignoring her, the man moved resolutely up the aisle.

Weird. Julia shivered as a puff of chilly air rolled over her. "Hello?" she repeated, wondering if he'd left a door open.

The man disappeared through a door on the other side of the altar.

Huh. Kinda snobby. She figured now would be a good time to leave anyway, especially if someone was around while she was locking up and getting into her car at this hour.

When she got home she called Mark to tell him about the silent man, waking him up. "Why would anyone come to the church so late?" she asked.

"I don't know. Ask the pastor."

Big help, she thought, undressing. Mark had invited her to move into his loft in the South of Market several times, but Julia was hesitant to give up her tiny apartment so close to Golden Gate Park. Still, she'd discovered she could roller skate around Mark's gigantic loft, and her knees weakened when she thought about the way he could churn her insides around. She just knew they belonged together. She drifted off to sleep, floating into a dream about the church.

> As her fingers trickled over a Bach chorale, she began to notice illuminated hands coming up through the altar floor. The congregation picked up speed, singing faster as Julia struggled to keep up with them. "Of course," she thought, "no wonder they like to sing 'em so fast. They just want to drop their sins and run." The hands reached higher, waving in the air. One by one,

people stepped up to the altar, carrying an assortment
of bags. "What is this? Reverse communion?"
Julia watched them empty brown paper bags, duffle
bags, popcorn bags and the occasional knapsack over
the luminous fingers.
"What are they doing?" she wondered out loud.
"They're recycling," Mark answered, appearing
behind her. "People bring their sorrows to church.
There must be a lot of pain floating around this place."
The man in the dark suit marched up the aisle,
winding a portable siren box. Then there was a crash,
and Julia turned to the back of the church to see the
prow of a massive steamship slicing through the wall.

She woke up panting, covered in cold sweat. It took several minutes of inner dialogue to convince herself that ships don't actually travel on land to crash into buildings.

The next day she gave notice to her landlord and began moving her things over to Mark's loft. Wistfully taking down the Christmas bulbs from the pine trees that surrounded her upstairs deck, she sighed, stroking a pine bough gently. *I'm tired of waking up after nightmares by myself. Besides, there's less fog in Mark's neighborhood.*

Ed called a few days later to invite her to an AA meeting down in Gilroy, a.k.a the Garlic Capital of the World. She could see their new place just outside San Jose and stay over in the spare bedroom.

"I'm the guest speaker," he told her. "It would be a great opportunity for you to hear my story."

"Bring back some fresh garlic," Mark said. He was busy working on a new sculpture and didn't want to be distracted.

Julia drove down to Ed and Rose's by herself, arriving at their rented townhouse in a newly built subdivision just before dinner. Stepping into their living room, the finality of her parents' divorce landed on her like a water balloon. Emptiness tried to take hold of her until she shrugged it off, thinking, *they just need more furniture.*

True to its reputation, the entire town of Gilroy had the distinct, ever-present smell of garlic. People stood around outside a Lutheran church, smoking and talking. Inside, Ed ushered them into the fluorescent-lit basement. On the table in the back were two large metal urns and several plates of pastries. The pungent garlic smell was quickly replaced by warm sugary treats and coffee.

"Your father likes to find the meetings with the best cookies," Rose whispered to Julia as they sat down. Julia counted at least forty people there, all treating each other with warmth that seemed genuine, all connected by a newly-found thread of humility. Someone read the whys and hows of the meeting and then introduced Ed. He got up and walked over to the podium.

"Hi, I'm Ed, I'm an alcoholic." Hot tears rushed to Julia's eyes.

"Hi, Ed," the audience answered.

"I'm also an Adult Child of an Alcoholic. I began drinking when I was about ten, and later drank my way through medical school. Then I got married and we moved out to the Midwest to practice there, hoping to escape booze and start a family." The audience chuckled, with a few men nodding. Julia thought her father looked quite comfortable up at the podium; a natural at public speaking. Ed continued, "We moved into a house with a wet bar in the basement and before I knew it, I was entertaining the hospital staff at the Wahatchee Community Hospital. We had two children and I had some bouts with depression, which I tried to drink my way out of, so we moved back to New York."

Julia flushed, fanning herself with a list of the Twelve Steps. *How come I don't know any of this?*

"We moved out to Long Island where I got a job at the local community hospital and faked my way through sanity for a while..." Ed explained, gesturing with his hands.

Soft chuckles rippled over the audience again, but Julia was feeling hot and dizzy. All this time she assumed her father started drinking when she was in high school, and she sat stunned by a history she'd never known. She began to fidget. *I could really use a beer right now.*

"We had another child, although the birth was a blur to me. I kept drinking and had a nervous breakdown, so my wife checked me into a hospital. Back in those days they gave electroshock therapy to drunks. It kept me sober for quite a few years..."

The room spun around Julia and she panicked, convinced that she had to get outside or she'd either pass out or throw up. As her father continued, she leaned over to Rose and said, "I promise I'm not mad—I just have to get some fresh air." Giving her father a hurried look of compassion, she got up and headed out the door, back to the garlic universe. She sat outside on the curb shaking, with her heart beating wildly. *Breathe... just breathe...*

Rose appeared, and sat down on the curb beside her. "The air was pretty stuffy in there... I had to get out for a while, too."

"I'm sorry if I scared you," Ed said on the drive back to the house.

"I wasn't scared. I guess it just surprised me and I started having one of those claustrophobic panic attack things I used to have—" She stopped short, remembering that they started after the abortion she hadn't told anyone in the family about. "I thought I was finished with those, but one just came up and slammed me. Dad, why didn't you tell us any of this stuff before?"

"Because you wouldn't have been able to stop me anyway. Besides, your mother ordered me not to."

"Who was that man that came into the church so late last Wednesday night?" Julia asked the pastor a few days later.

"Oh, you saw the ghost, Mr. Emerson."

"What? There's a ghost in here? W-why?" she stammered. The whole idea was so ridiculous she didn't know what else to say.

"He was a deacon back in the forties, when the church caught fire and was nearly destroyed. He ran inside to get some records and was killed in the blaze." Picking up on the horror in Julia's face, the pastor added with a smile, "He's harmless. He's never done anything but walk up the aisle now and then. You'll get used to it after awhile."

"I'm not going back there," Julia told Erin over the phone that night. "In fact, I'm going to *mail* the key back to the pastor."

"Are you *kidding?* What's the matter with you? If I were there, I'd try to talk to that ghost to find out why he keeps coming back."

"He died in the fire. Besides, he just ignored me when I called out to him."

"Yeah, but why would he keep coming around? Maybe there's something he still wants."

"Mark thinks he's just stuck between worlds."

"How's it going with him, by the way?" Erin asked.

"Great. He's busy with a lot of stuff. You ought to come out and visit us. Make good on that deal about me getting into *Andrea Doria*, remember? Take a break and see San Francisco. Now that you're single," Julia added.

"You mean now that I'm footloose?" Erin teased.

"Well, *yeah.* Do you ever see Morty?"

"We talk once a week or so. We're still good friends, but sometimes I think I just do better living by myself."

Julia gave a slight shudder. She'd been able to suspend worrying about Erin's health these last few years that Erin and Morty lived together in New York. The idea of her friend alone in a small apartment in New Jersey was still mildly alarming. Besides, Julia was secretly hoping that San Francisco would have the same effect on Erin as it did on her father, and she would decide to move out here.

"So meanwhile, I found out there's more to my family history than I thought," Julia said.

"Like what?"

"I went to hear my father speak at an AA meeting, and... it's kind of weird. It turns out he was an alcoholic when we were really little, and he got electro-shock in a mental institution! That's how he stayed sober all that time."

"Wow..." Erin was quiet for a moment. "Are you mad at them for not telling you?"

"I don't know. Maybe. It's like there's two versions of my childhood, now."

"Whew... a lot of unexpected feelings might start bubbling to the surface for you now. Maybe you should find a therapist who can help you deal with them."

"I talk to Michael sometimes."

"He's okay, but you need someone who knows about families and alcoholism. Board certified, and somebody you haven't slept with."

"Yeah. When I try to bring it up with Mark, he gets uncomfortable and changes the subject. So—what do you think about visiting? Are you going to come?"

There was a slight pause. "I think I will," Erin answered. "We'll go and check out that ghost together."

TWENTY-FIVE

JULIA, MARK AND STEVE, THE DRUMMER from *Andrea Doria*, huddled next to a video game in the I-Beam on Haight Street, watching Greg play Tempest. A DJ danced in a booth way above the stage, spinning new wave dance music through the ultra-modern nightclub as they sipped on bottled beer to calm their nerves before the show. Tonight was *Andrea Doria's* record release party for their 45-rpm demo. The club was packed, plus Rodney had invited reps from every record label in California, so the house glistened with the possibility of major record label interest.

Julia took a modest swig from her beer, dabbing at her lips with the back of her forefinger. She wished there was a pinball game with old-fashioned flippers available, as she'd gotten into the habit of sharpening her reflexes in the arcade at the student union before her classical organ lessons. Rodney appeared, flanked by Monique and Beatrice in their tight, red Chinese silk dresses.

"Come on. We have to get ready," he said, nodding toward the stage. A giant mirror ball hung over the dance floor, surrounded by high-tech disco lighting. Bodies ricocheted off each other to a B52s song. On the side wall, two huge screens played a rapid-fire mix of old movies, cartoons, music videos, and the people on the dance floor.

Backstage, a large bowl of fruit and cheese sat on a round table, with a pitcher of water. A smattering of punk and new wave posters covered the bare plywood walls, along with scrawled band graffiti.

"Siouxie and the Banshees are here!" Monique exclaimed, handing everyone copies of the set list. "We saw them over by the bar!" Beatrice added.

"Great... now I'm genuinely nervous," Julia muttered.

Mark rubbed her shoulders. "Just forget about who's here and get out there and have fun."

The thumping outside began to fade and the DJ's voice boomed through the club, "Okay, it's time to welcome… *Andrea Doria!*"

"All right, this is it. No prisoners," Rodney ordered.

The audience cheered and whistled as the band filed on stage. Julia looked up to see the skeletons from *Jason and the Argonauts* on one of the video screens, marching toward Jason with their swords raised. They charged as the band nodded to each other, turning purple in the glow of the stage lights. Steve tapped his drumsticks together four times, Rodney began a guitar riff, and Julia wove an electronic breeze around it as they surged into their first song, Beatrice and Monique crooning into separate microphones. Julia glanced down to see Mark in his usual spot on the dance floor, right below her keyboards. Michael was there too, with Monte. His ponytail was gone, and he now wore his hair cropped short, Everyone from *Fragille!* was there, and some friends from her old neighborhood in the Inner Sunset, all packed close to the stage and smiling. Even Meg from her cross-country drive had shown up.

The audience cheered and thrashed through the first set. When they began to play "Lifeboat," the A side of their record and their most popular song, the crowd went wild. The music seemed to have a life of its own, an electronic, cerebral sort of dance music, shifting with the lights and the energy of the audience, making sure that no song would ever be played the exact same way.

"Keep us afloat!" Beatrice called out afterwards. "Buy our record!"

They swept into Side B of the record, the "throwaway pop tune," Rodney called it. Dressed in a black jumpsuit with silver sneakers, Julia twisted the knobs on her synthesizer, bending the notes and sending the crowd into a bouncing frenzy while fleeting images of the band darted past on the video screens.

When they finished the set, the entire club cheered and stomped, bringing them back for an encore. They played one more song, bowed, and then left the stage.

"We *killed!*" Monique yelled.

"That was the best version of 'Lifeboat' we ever did!" said Rodney.

They gathered around the table and began picking at the food and jabbering. The muffled thumping from the DJ had resumed outside, and the backstage room flooded with people. A man with blue hair held a tiny line of cocaine out to Julia and she took a snort, quickly pinching her nose afterwards to keep from sneezing. *Ouch! I hated that! Why do I keep doing it when I hate it?* He began to babble about electronic music and synthesizers causing her to sigh inwardly. *Oh great, another techno-geek who wants to talk about computers.* Beatrice and Monique appeared quickly and the man offered them more nose candy. Then Mark showed up, and they became packed within a tight cluster of admirers.

"Did you see when they played a bunch of scenes from old shipwreck movies?" Mark asked. "It was so cool. When you guys were starting 'Lifeboat' they had the giant wave from *The Poseidon Adventure* coming toward the boat! Then it cut to the *Titanic* in *A Night to Remember!*"

"Then to *The Creature from the Black Lagoon!*" Steve exclaimed.

"And then *Steamboat Willie*," Mark added.

Could this be any more amazing? Julia wondered.

"Let's break down before we get too loaded," Greg suggested.

As Julia unplugged her keyboards and began packing them up, a familiar looking man called to her from the dance floor. She knelt down at the edge of the stage and he shouted, "I'm Joe from The Comparison Shoppers. I love what you're doing. Call me," he said, handing her a bar napkin with his phone number on it. "I'd like to talk to you about coming to the studio and laying down some tracks for us."

Later as they chugged down Fell Street to their loft in the South of Market in Julia's old green station wagon, Julia watched the road with great vigilance. Mark usually drove them home after shows, sensing her exhaustion, but he seemed a little more inebriated than usual.

"I saw Joe from The Shoppers giving you his phone number," Mark said. "What was that all about?"

Julia allowed her eyes to leave the road long enough to glance at Mark and see his jaw set at a disturbing angle. "He wants me to record with them! What? Did you think he was hitting on me or something?"

"I don't know." The car lurched forward as Mark drove through a ripe yellow light that turned red when they sped under it.

Julia gulped. "Take it easy."

"I'm okay. These timed lights are always a little off late at night." He continued to speed down the street, past the Panhandle.

"Are you too loaded to drive?" she asked.

"No, I'm fine."

Gripped with fear, she finally yelled, "Slow the fuck down!"

"Will you just chill?"

Julia burst into tears. Mark sighed and pulled over near Divisadero Street. Unbuckling his seatbelt, he leaned over and took her in his arms. "I'm sorry. I didn't mean to scare you."

"What the hell is wrong with you? Are you trying to kill us?"

"No—of course not! I was just feeling... I don't know... a little left out."

"About Joe from The Shoppers? Give me a break. Not only am I not attracted to him, he has a girlfriend anyway!" she shouted. "Besides, this is a good thing. I'm starting to get session work in an industry where there might possibly be other men working, so kindly don't get jealous and drive us to kingdom come before I even get a paycheck," she blurted, ending in a sob.

"I'm sorry... I'm sorry. Please say you'll forgive me and let me drive us home," Mark pleaded, kissing her softly around her head.

Julia drew a deep, shaky breath. "Okay. Just go slow, please?"

Mark pulled out and drove the rest of the way slowly as Julia stared at the road in front of them, silently preparing herself to unlatch her seatbelt and jump out, should the need arise.

TWENTY-SIX

"Ta-da!" Erin chortled, stepping into the airport terminal in San Francisco a week later. Julia hid her tears of joy in an embrace that lasted almost half a minute. Then Erin stood back and batted her eyes, one blue, and another green. "What do you think?"

"What did you do???" Julia stammered. "W-when did you do that?"

"Well, the right one was starting to look pretty bad, so I went ahead and had it taken out, and you know I couldn't just do something traditional."

"You didn't tell me."

"You had a lot on your mind and I wanted to surprise you."

"I'm... surprised. Is it real?"

"No, but it's removable. Watch." Erin put a hand toward her right eye and Julia practically shouted, "No!"

"Just kidding."

"You maniac!" Julia exclaimed, giving her another hug. "Let's go get your bags and get out of here."

The next day, Julia, Mark and Erin drifted around Stow Lake in Golden Gate Park in a rented rowboat. Mark sat in the middle, calmly rowing.

"I still can't believe I'm here," Erin sighed from the prow. "It's so beautiful!" They air-toasted each other with their champagne glasses. Julia and Mark's champagne picnics around the lake had become a weekly tradition when balmy San Francisco fall had set in, keeping the fog offshore all day. Dragonflies buzzed around them, while an armada of bugs skated on and off invisible runways on the lake's surface.

"So, tonight's the night we see the ghost," Erin said, letting her hand drag through the water.

"Uh-huh," Julia said. "Michael wants to come too, and Steve. I figure if we have a psychologist, an anthropologist, a filmmaker and a visionary," she paused, rubbing Mark's knee, "we'll be okay." Inwardly, Julia felt nothing but trepidation for the evening's plans. She would have been perfectly fine forgetting the whole thing and finding another church to practice in.

They napped in the afternoon and had a late Chinese take-out dinner before picking up Michael and heading over to the church. Steve from the band was waiting for them out front with his camera equipment when they arrived, in tight black pants and a knee length black dress jacket.

"He's cute," Erin whispered to Julia. "He looks like an intellectual undertaker from the 1890s."

"Hi Steve," Julia said. "This is Erin, my best friend on earth."

"Hey, Erin. Up for a little excitement? I'm not sure this'll work," he said, "but I have to at least try." He reached over and shook Erin's hand.

Julia noticed Erin perk up in a way she hadn't seen since they flew the parachute on the high school hockey field.

They went inside and huddled behind the organ console while Mark set up his tripod. Julia began playing the same Vierne piece from the last sighting. Nothing happened. She started into the next movement and then stopped and gave a shrug after a few minutes, covering her look of relief. "Maybe he only comes on certain nights."

"Or he's seasonal," Michael suggested.

"Just play one more and then let's get out of here and go have a drink," Mark said. "This place is starting to creep me out."

Julia nodded and began a soft, slow Brahms prelude. As she played, a chill crept over her, and she felt the skin on her arms tingle. The hair on them was sticking straight up, and she had the same feeling of spaciousness she'd had the last time she'd been there.

"*Oh—my—God,*" Michael whispered.

The man in the dark suit was walking up the aisle again, his eyes focused straight ahead. Julia stopped playing and froze, just as Erin slipped out from behind the organ bench and darted toward the front of the church. It happened so quickly no one had the chance to stop her. Erin stood in the center of the aisle with her hands at her sides, staring straight at the man as he approached her. Julia blanched, stupefied by the sight of not one but two bizarre things in a single frame of vision. The man passed right through her friend and kept walking, disappearing into the same door near the altar. Erin crumpled to the floor.

They all burst out from behind the organ console, scrambling toward her. She stirred and opened her eyes and everyone gave a sigh of relief.

"Are you okay—?"

"What happened—?"

"What the hell were you *thinking*—?" Julia asked. "Oops," she added, quickly covering her mouth.

"What a rush," Erin whispered. "It felt like... the past, present and future all moving through me at once." She sat up and shivered. "Now I'm freezing."

"Me too," Julia said. Her hands were so cold she could barely feel them.

"Can we get out of here now?" Mark asked.

Back at Mark and Julia's loft, Erin sat on the couch wrapped in a blanket, sipping a glass of red wine. "I didn't plan on doing that—it just came over me. Like some kind of cosmic wash or something."

"I felt kind of weird, too." Steve said, sitting close to her. "I can't even explain how. Mostly cold and spacey and... I don't know..."

"Don't worry, you've never experienced anything like it, so you don't have the vocabulary to explain it," Michael said.

"Are you going to calm down once you get your degree?" Mark snickered. "God. You can always tell when someone's a college student." He lifted his beer and knocked back half the bottle at once.

Cringing with embarrassment, Julia stared at him and frowned. He shrugged. "We saw a *ghost* tonight."

"No shit," Julia said. "What am I supposed to do? Call the police?"

"Ghostbusters?" Mark chortled.

"Goddammit, this is serious!" Julia shouted.

"No…" Erin's voice cut in softly. "I mean, not that it isn't serious. I mean we should just leave it alone."

"Why? It's a paranormal phenomenon!" Mark said. "We could sell a story to *The National Enquirer*."

"Please… let's just forget about it," Erin insisted. "It was weird enough."

Julia felt the underlying urgency in her friend's voice and waited to catch Michael's eye. He held her glance for a second and then spoke up.

"Erin's right. If the church were going to capitalize on the situation, they would have done it by now."

San Francisco Bay sparkled in the morning sun the next day as Julia and Erin crossed the Golden Gate Bridge. "Look," Julia pointed out the window toward the sea. "You can even see the Farallon Islands."

"Huh?" Erin asked, still a little groggy from the night before.

"They're like our tiny version of the Galapagos Islands."

Erin leaned forward to look out Julia's window. "It's so beautiful. Sorry. I keep repeating myself, over and over again." They both laughed. "I don't want to go back to New Jersey yet," Erin sighed, sitting back.

"Then just keep an open mind about this place," Julia insisted, referring to Sonoma State University near Santa Rosa, where Erin had heard about a job.

"It has a reputation as a basket-weaving school and the money's not as good," she'd told Julia, "but they have a great anthropology department and I think I could get my Ph.D. in less time. All I really need is a good hospital nearby. Just in case."

"I think Steve likes you," Julia said, changing the subject.

"Yeah, I know. He asked me out to dinner before I go back."

"Really? That's great! He's so sweet and thoughtful. I think he's actually more interested in filmmaking than playing the drums. I can't wait to see if he got anything at the church."

"Ugh," Erin shivered. "I don't feel like talking about that right now. It feels more creepy today than it seemed last night… like a stranger occupied my body for a second. So how come you didn't go for Steve anyway?"

"I don't know. Mark found me first."

"He seems a little distracted. I mean, he was quiet on the lake that day—before—you know, the *church incident.*"

"He's been kind of depressed lately. He hasn't had a show in a while and he sits around and watches TV a lot when he's not doing layouts for ad agencies."

"Have you found someone to talk to about your father?" Erin asked.

"Not yet... things have been going so well I kind of forgot. But hey, I'm going to do some recording with another band next week!"

Steve showed up at the loft that evening with the video from the church. "It's pretty sketchy," he apologized, setting up his equipment.

The scene opened to a shot of the altar, lit by a spotlight. Then it panned to the organ and Julia, whose face glowed softly in the light from the console. The faces of Michael and Erin were barely etched in the dark behind her. The camera returned to the aisle of the church, where Erin's outline suddenly lurched into view. The darkness seemed to ripple as she stood with her arms by her sides, and the air moved in front of her like heat-waves. Erin's face took on an eerie glow as the ripples passed through her. She crumpled and the screen faded to darkness.

Everyone sat in stunned silence until Mark spoke up. "You didn't really expect to get the actual ghost, did you?"

Julia shook her head, perceiving a faint snarl in his voice. "Not really... but you could always use it for something else, right, Steve?" Hoping to smooth over the animosity she felt between Mark and their guests, she added, "Like an art piece."

She'd noticed Mark's caustic comments cropping up with greater regularity during the past few weeks, and had begun mentally rehearsing scenarios to confront him about it.

TWENTY-SEVEN

O N A WARM SATURDAY MORNING several months later, Julia
and her brothers sped down 280 in a rented Buick Skylark on
their way to Ed and Rose's wedding in Gilroy. Julia sat in the front
giving Teddy directions, while Mark sat in the back with Nate and
his girlfriend, Uda.

"Nice ride," Mark said.

"I decided to splurge a little, since I was going to be driving all
over," Teddy answered.

"When is your job interview?" Nate asked from the back seat.

"Monday. I get to go way up north to Chico. I didn't go all out for
a wedding gift," he added. "It was kind of last minute."

"Don't worry—Dad said not to make a big deal about it," Julia
said. "As far as I know, they only decided to tie the knot a month or
so ago."

"I guess he just wanted us all to be here," Nate said, "This trip is
part of my college graduation present."

Julia winced; she hadn't gone back east for Nate's graduation.
In fact, she hadn't even spoken to him much in the last year or so,
except for a perfunctory hello during family holiday phone calls.
Ed and Rose went, and things had become tense enough when
Clarisse showed up with Don Frank. But Julia had decided to wait
and treat Nate and Uda to a good time when they came out to San
Francisco, hoping the city's charm and charisma would help heal
the painful memories between them. By a stroke of luck, Teddy had
simultaneously managed to score a job interview as a computer
systems analyst with a small start-up company in Northern
California.

It was a small wedding, about forty people at the same Lutheran
church in Gilroy that hosted the AA meeting Ed had spoken at.

The reception was dry; sparkling cider, meat and seafood platters, with a massive chocolate cheesecake. Rose was beautiful in her long, pink silk dress, and she looked genuinely happy. So did Ed, causing Julia to downplay the sadness she felt as she watched her father join a different family. After a short performance with his barbershop quartet, Ed introduced his children to everyone and entertained them with vivid stories about their boating adventures on Long Island Sound. Julia glanced at her brothers from time to time, hoping for some kind of facial expression to reveal how they felt, but they stayed neutral, punctuating the stories here and there with occasional chuckles.

An hour or so later, Julia noticed Mark dozing off in his chair. She put her hand on his thigh and gave it a gentle squeeze, bringing him back. "This is wearing a little thin," he whispered. "How soon can we leave? It's not like this is going to break out into a wild dance party or anything." His faux leopard-skin bow tie had gone off-kilter and Julia straightened it for him, looking around for her brothers. The confrontation she'd been mentally rehearsing over Mark's growing sarcasm surfaced for a second before she stuffed it deeply into the recesses of denial. Teddy and Nate were ready to go too, so they said their congratulations and goodbyes, and drove back up to San Francisco.

Sitting on the couch and chairs in the corner of Mark and Julia's loft designated as the living room, they drank beer and listened to the new *Andrea Doria* record. Nate was quiet, so Julia asked, "I hear you're starting at Circle in the Square Theatre School in the city."

"Yeah. We got a good deal on a place in midtown, so we're all set. Uda's been interning at NBC."

"Nice..." Julia said, turning to admire her brother's shy, leggy girlfriend. Uda smiled back, pulling her long blonde hair back behind her head and then letting it go again.

"Lift, anyone?" Mark stood at the edge of the living room, holding up a red Plexiglas bong.

Horrified, Julia braced herself for an explosion. Then Nate and Uda nodded at each other, and Nate spoke up. "Sure," he said. "We could probably use one about now."

Julia stared at her younger brother in mock shock. "What? When did you join this... den of iniquity?"

"Oh, last year sometime... it helped me give up regular smoking."

"Me too," Teddy added, moving his chair closer.

They passed around the bong, taking hits from the gurgling cylinder until everyone shifted into a relaxed buzz.

"Lots of crazy stuff, huh?" Nate said. "We are one screwed-up family."

Teddy burst out laughing, exhaling a cloud of marijuana smoke.

"At least no one's robbed a liquor store or hit anyone with a car," Julia said, quickly knocking on the side of the wooden coffee table. "Although I have to admit that I was blown away by Dad's electroshock therapy story."

"What?" Both brothers sat up and leaned forward.

"Dad had electroshock in the fifties to make him stop drinking," Julia said. "I found out when I went down to hear him speak at an AA meeting last year. I practically fainted."

"I think I remember that," Teddy said. "When Dad smashed the ceramic reindeer on the mantle and Uncle Bill came and took him away. Then he came home and slept a lot."

"Ugh," Nate said, holding his head with his hands.

"I have a vague memory of the broken reindeer," Julia continued. "After the AA meeting, I called Mom demanding to know why she never told us what was going on and she said she was protecting us. She was feeling pretty fragile back then, so I backed off."

"Yeah, she kept us in her own Bubble of Protection," Nate said, prompting everyone to burst out laughing again.

Julia spoke up. "I felt really bad about being away at college when you had to stay home and take the brunt of what was happening. Things were just too weird and we got... kind of alienated. I wouldn't blame you for being mad at me."

Nate sighed. "All that time I thought if I could win one more soccer championship or get one more leading role, it would keep my parents together."

"Yeah, but it was like the Cold War, right in our house." *It was almost a relief when they split up.* Relaxed as everyone seemed, she didn't dare say that out loud for fear of treading on thin emotional ice. She'd never spoken to her brothers with this kind of depth before. Remembering the disappearing Sarge incident back on Long Island, she thought it best to curb herself, considering Nate was still nursing a nearly full bottle of beer.

"Tension! Tension! Tension!" Nate exclaimed, bonking the top of his head with his fist, prompting another round of laughter.

Aha. He's using his humor to diffuse the situation. Very clever. That's what Dad meant about the class clown thing. "So what do you think of Don Frank?" Julia asked, changing the subject.

"He's a pretty cool guy," Nate shrugged. "Mom sure likes him. He teaches theatre at the high school now. He has a place over in Bayville, and I think she might end up moving in with him. Especially now that Dad's sober and remarried, and I'm done with school. She's been waiting very patiently."

Teddy and Julia laughed. Julia thought about Clarisse singing and dancing her way through a wedding ceremony in a giant hooped Mrs. Leonowens skirt.

"Should we tell them about the ghost in the church?" Mark piped up, tired of being left out.

"Ghost in a church?" Teddy repeated. Even Uda sat up and leaned forward, eager to hear more.

Julia rolled her eyes. She'd hoped the whole thing would just blow over. She'd been limiting her organ practice to daytime hours, when she knew the church secretary or the pastor was around. They didn't seem to mind the ghost at all.

"It was just this weird apparition we all saw in the church where I practice. The ghost of a dead guy walks up and down the aisle sometimes," she shrugged, trying to downplay the queasy feeling that came over her when she remembered that night.

"Has anyone ever caught him on film?" Uda asked.

"We tried, but nothing showed up except warm looking air." She left out the part about Erin trying to confront the ghost. "Besides, I don't think the pastor wants to make a big deal out of it anyway. I guess they just want to have a nice, modest place to worship and don't mind hosting the occasional specter." When no one was looking, she shot Mark a quick scowl and he chuckled back, blowing her a kiss.

On stage at The Berkeley Square several weeks later, Beatrice and Monique bobbed up and down to the music in green silk Chinese dresses, wailing into their microphones as Rodney turned up his amp. Julia leaned back and edged up the volume on hers, soaking the nightclub with the electronic swish of an incoming missile. Rodney grimaced and ripped a guitar solo out over the writhing dance floor.

Following their record release party they'd been playing all over the Bay Area, even down to Los Angeles several times. People in the audiences began to yell, "Louder keyboards!" prompting Julia to go out and buy a bigger, more powerful amplifier and monitor speakers which annoyed Rodney, as it threatened the hierarchy of sound in the band. After all, he was the songwriter and lead guitar player. They hadn't attracted any major music label interest yet, but Julia had branched out, adding tracks to The Comparison Shoppers' record in the studio, building a name for herself as a session musician.

Rodney's guitar screamed through the air when Beatrice and Monique took a break. Then Julia's deep celestial bass note bubbled up underneath everything like a breaking wave, ending the song in a soft hiss. The nightclub erupted with loud cheering and whistling. "Bitchin' synthesizer!" someone yelled from the audience.

When the show was over and they'd packed up their equipment, she paused when she saw Rodney sitting inside the manager's office with Beatrice and Monique. Beatrice was bent over a mirror with a rolled up dollar bill when Rodney noticed Julia, got up and slammed the door in her face.

Outside on the sidewalk, Erin and Steve, now a pair, waited until Julia climbed into Steve's van.

"Those assholes," Erin said, as they crossed the Bay Bridge back to San Francisco.

"It's okay, really. I can't stand that stuff anyway," Julia shrugged. "It really hurts my nose and I babble like an idiot when I do it. But I'm *sooo* glad you decided to move out here," Julia said for probably the hundredth time since Erin had jumped on that teaching job at Sonoma State.

"Yeah, but slamming the door to the coke room in your face.

It's so lame. They're just jealous. It's the only way they can feel superior anymore," Erin said. "Besides, you're the original sunken ship maven, not Rodney. Your keyboards have been adding a lot of depth to the situation, no pun intended."

"Yeah, I know," Julia laughed, along with Erin and Steve. "But I feel like I'm just in it for the exposure these days."

"I'm starting to get tired of them myself," Steve spoke up. "It was fun for awhile, but it's become their private blow party and we're not really going anywhere. I'd rather be working on my films."

"I'm so glad to hear you say that!" Julia said. "I had a feeling you were getting burned out."

"So's Greg. He's been sitting in with Mental Floss for the last few weeks, and he's thinking of bailing."

"I'm thinking of leaving, too," said Julia. "I got invited to play in the orchestra of a show at the Intersection… with a salary!"

"Soooo… the *Andrea Doria* begins to list," Erin said.

"Everyone head for the lifeboats," Steve added. "Drums and keyboards first."

"It's dark up there," Erin remarked, when they pulled up to Julia and Mark's loft on Minna Street.

"Yeah… well… it's three a.m. He doesn't always wait up for me."

"He could leave a light on, though. He hasn't been coming to your shows much, has he?"

"He can't stand Rodney."

Erin and Steve dropped Julia off, helping carry her equipment up the stairs. Then they headed up to Erin's place in Santa Rosa.

Inside the loft, snowy static from the TV shed a pale, silvery glow on the floor. Julia pulled the plastic Reagan-on-a-noose chain to turn on the lamp and saw Mark sleeping on the couch. Four empty bottles of beer surrounded the red Plexiglas bong on the coffee table. "Tch," she left out a soft sigh. *This sucks. I'm really going to talk to him tomorrow.*

"Wake up… they're baaack!" she teased, shaking him gently.

"Who?" he asked, stirring.

"The TV People."

"Wha? Oh, yeah... right..."

"Come on, get up and come to bed," Julia said.

"I'm too tired to get up. Just lemme sleep here..."

"Come on. You'll be all stiff tomorrow."

Mark rolled over and snored.

Julia took a hit from the bong on the coffee table and went into the bedroom to change out of her tight black flight suit. In spite of her exhaustion and needling disappointment, she always loved entering the bedroom that had hosted many a bawdy romp. One side was decorated with Chinese umbrellas opened and lit from behind. Mark had sawed off the handles so they looked like fairy-tale mushrooms growing out of the wall. Their bed had a canopy frame that they'd covered with sheer mosquito netting and tiny white Christmas lights. On a table in the corner, Julia had piled dozens of seashells and stones she collected from the beach, to which Mark had added a half-buried Statue of Liberty and some tiny plastic monkeys. They liked adding stuff to their informal art pieces, and always seemed to agree on each other's ideas. She reached for the rheostat that controlled the umbrella lights, turned them down to a faint glow and sighed, still hopeful that Mark would wake up and join her in bed.

The next morning, Julia awoke to the smell of hot cinnamon rolls. When she put on her kimono and came out of the bedroom, she saw that the entire living room area had been cleaned. Warm sunlight streamed through the floor to ceiling windows and Mark was over by the stove cooking.

"What do you want in your omelet, sweetie?" he asked.

Julia sighed. *Maybe I'm just overreacting.*

A few weeks later, Julia sat with Ed and Rose at Old Uncle Gaylord's Ice Cream Parlor in San Francisco, while Ed shook three pennies and dropped them into the center of the table.

"Aha. Another broken line," Julia said, drawing two lines side by side in her notepad.

"What does that mean?" asked Rose.

"We have to wait until he throws the coins six times, and then look up the hexagram in the book," answered Julia.

"Number three, Conflict, changes into number forty-six. Pushing Upward," Julia announced, reading from her *I Ching Book of Changes*.

"Sounds like what's going on now," Ed said.

"Yes, conflict," Rose nodded. "Especially since he gave up smoking."

Things hadn't been going well in San Jose, either. The clinic where Ed worked had closed its doors due to administrative problems, and he'd been struggling as a consultant for over a year without a steady income. Then a hospital in Pennsylvania offered him the job of Medical Director at a new facility. Both Ed and Rose were excited about it. Rose could be living closer to her children again, and the money was great. When they came up to San Francisco on their monthly pilgrimage for Japanese food and Uncle Gaylord's, they were still trying to decide.

"We love it out here," Ed said, "but this sounds like the deal of a lifetime."

"You can't really argue with Pushing Upward. Listen to this," she said, reading from the book. '*A blade of grass pushing up through the earth.*' It sounds just like you guys, with your new lives. Maybe you should go."

When Julia reported the outcome of the I Ching to Erin, she remarked, "Sounds like they *should* go. But I still think Confucius was a pig."

"Maybe he's just been over-interpreted. But my father and Rose have decided to make the move. They're coming up this weekend to say goodbye. Want to come down to the city and see them?" Julia asked.

"Sure. I'd love to."

"Steve too?"

"I don't know. He's about to leave for Panama. He got that grant to film down there and he's going crazy trying to get ready. I'll ask, though."

When Ed and Rose arrived, they wanted to see the Exploratorium. Julia winced, remembering that Rodney worked there, but they'd be in a large pack including Erin and Mark.

"Looks like a giant science fair," Ed remarked, when they entered the cavernous museum. "Teddy used to love that stuff!" he added, pointing to a room where the ultimate Erector set had been built, with helicopters landing and taking off from a huge industrial complex.

A few minutes later, Ed and Julia sat opposite each other at the "Everyone is You and Me" exhibit, twisting the knobs of the dimmer switches to make their faces go from bright to dark. A plate of glass stood between them.

"When I make mine brighter, I can see more of my face in yours," Julia said. As they continued to adjust the knobs, Ed and Julia's faces eventually merged into one composite image.

"Weird," Ed said.

"Yeah," Julia agreed. They both stood up.

"Warning," Mark announced. "Doofus at two-o'clock."

Rodney was walking through the hall looking very important. He was the manager of the gift shop, his "straight job" until the band took off. The meeting was unavoidable. There was no time to duck behind an exhibit, and they met face-to-face.

"Hi, Rodney," Julia said. She watched his expression as it scrambled to decide whether to grimace or act professional. "This is my father and his w-wife, Rose," she said.

Rodney opted for a business-like smile and offered his hand. "Nice to meet you. Julia and I used to play music together."

Taking the opportunity for a jab, Mark asked, "So how's the music business treating you?" He knew that *Andrea Doria* was floundering. Even after replacing Julia, Steve and Greg, they couldn't seem to get a record deal.

"Oh, we're still happening. Got a great new lineup. We're going down to L.A. again next week. Well, I gotta keep moving. Nice meeting you." He nodded to Ed and Rose and walked away. Julia and Erin stifled guffaws.

"So how's the organ playing?" Ed asked.

"I still sub sometimes at the church," Julia answered. She'd been getting strange looks from the congregation ever since showing up with pink streaks in her hair one Sunday morning after a show the night before. When the music department at San Francisco State began demanding more music history classes from her, she decided to take a break. Her rock and roll career was starting to take off anyway.

"I'd hate to see you give up that stuff," Ed said.

"I'm not. I just made a recording with a band at the church last month. Someone wanted the sound of a real pipe organ."

"What about that martial art you were taking? Karate?"

"Aikido. I had to stop. It was too hard to get to the classes with my music and everything."

Later, when they pulled up in front of the loft on Minna Street, Julia had a lump in her throat. Ed got out to give her one more hug and she stood on the curb, unable to speak.

"Don't cry," he said. "You'll be okay. Come and visit us when we get settled."

Julia went upstairs and wept on the couch for the next half hour.

"I didn't want him to see me doing this," she sobbed. "I just wanted him to feel okay about leaving for a better job."

After Erin left for Santa Rosa, Mark tried to cheer Julia up by holding a match next to his butt and farting. A three-foot flame erupted out of his crotch each time and Julia, due to an unfortunate weakness for fart jokes, bubbled over with laughter in spite of herself.

TWENTY-EIGHT

A S JULIA'S FLIGHT CROSSED THE COUNTRY, she looked out the window over the vast Midwest with a sigh of relief. It was relaxing to see so much space. After a stressful week of recording with a new wave band called Zipper Flippers and an emphatic lecture from Erin over her relationship with Mark, cruising at 30,000 feet with a Bloody Mary provided a soothing break. The jet slid across the sky toward a bank of darkness, and a spring evening on the east coast. She could practically smell the lilacs and cut grass.

Several months ago, after Ed and Rose moved to Pennsylvania, Clarisse had called Julia one day to say she was considering moving in with Don Frank.

"Mom! That's so... *progressive!*" Julia exclaimed.

"Well, your father did it. Nate and Uda aren't married, and neither are you. If there's anything I've learned, it's not to marry too quickly."

Julia eventually agreed to come east to help Clarisse move from the small cottage she'd rented in Pattituck Cove after the divorce. She could see their place and then visit her father in Pennsylvania in one trip. Plus Nate was living in New York with Uda, working with a small off-Broadway theatre company, and he'd gotten tickets to *Cats*. Mark had declined to go with her, claiming work was too busy. Julia knew he was lying. Friends from his day job at an ad agency parked themselves at a tavern on Kearny Street every night after work under the guise of brainstorming new ad campaigns. Julia was so busy she didn't notice the regularity at first. In addition to sitting in with several local bands, she was now sought after as a session keyboard player. Her nightlife with Mark had become a game of who could stay out the latest.

"You've drifted apart," Erin told her firmly. "You guys were a good couple for awhile but admit it, you've outgrown him."

"Maybe we just need counseling or something," Julia said.

"Counseling? Are you kidding? Have you even talked about long term stuff by yourselves?"

"We started to a year or so ago and then dropped the subject when neither one of us wanted kids."

"You don't need a counselor. Just sit down and talk with each other about what you both want. See where it goes. Jeez... why do people make this so difficult?" Erin snorted.

"We've been together for more than four years. I'd hate to just throw all that away because we've hit a rough patch. Besides, he still makes me laugh."

"Julia, he's staying out just to party with people from work. Do you *really* think he still has the same affection for you as he used to?"

"Well, the truth is...our sex life hasn't exactly been stellar lately. I mean, we still do it, but not very often. I even started comparing our relationship to other peoples."

"Don't go comparing! You never know what other people are hiding up their superficial asses."

Julia laughed and then said softly, "You know what? When I first moved in with him I was homesick for my apartment in the Inner Sunset for months, so I let myself get whisked away by all the romance. But lately I've noticed a craving to be in my own space. The other day I was thinking how great it would be to have a little sports car and just go wherever I wanted, without having to compete with anyone for attention. Like you and Steve. You get to be with him when he's around, and when he travels, you have your own life."

"Maybe you should take some time by yourself, then. Don't become one of those people who's so terrified of being alone they'd rather shackle themselves to someone completely unsuitable."

"Do you really think I'm like that?" Julia asked.

"No! Of course you're not like that. We've known each other since junior high. You're a free thinker. I was just being... subjective. Even I get moody when Steve's not around and I worry that something awful might happen to him down in Central America. It's always one thing or another."

"Why *am* I still with him?" Julia wondered, taking a sip from her Bloody Mary. She sighed, thinking about the loft they shared. It had grown into a comfortably sweet, eccentric sort of place, complete with a tiny music studio they'd partitioned off for her, where they'd sound-proofed the walls with egg cartons, painting tiny eyes into the cups of each one.

"You're so thin!" Clarisse exclaimed when Julia came through the airport gate.

"I walk up and down hills a lot," she answered, hugging her mother. A man in jeans and a corduroy sports jacket stepped up to shake Julia's hand.

"I'm Don," he said.

Fleeting images of The King and I and Bozo the Clown quickly passed through Julia's mind as she said, "Nice to meet you. As an adult, I mean." They both laughed.

On the way out the Long Island Expressway, Don was curious about Julia's progress in the music industry. "Do you have steady work?" he asked.

"Yes, especially since I got into the Musician's Union. Things aren't as crazy as they used to be, playing in all those art bands, but I still have a lot of fun and I get paid. I travel down to L.A. a lot, too."

Julia glanced at her mother from the back seat of Don's comfortably aging BMW. She seemed much more relaxed now, sitting next to a man Julia hadn't seen since she was six. Looming jet lag and the Bloody Mary smoothed out any awkward feelings. "So, how are things on the Pattituck Cove stage?" she asked Don. As he began describing the latest production of *Anything Goes*, Julia settled back in her seat, happy to relinquish her part of the conversation.

It was after ten o'clock when they turned off the Jericho exit and headed toward Oyster Bay. They pulled into a driveway in front of a modest house in Bayville.

"It's not the Palace of Versailles, but it's home," Don said.

Nate and Uda were already there, making cocktails and snacks.

"The rock star!" Nate exclaimed.

"The actor!" Julia cried, as they hugged.

Teddy appeared from the kitchen and Julia shrieked, "When did *you* get here?!"

"A couple days ago. It's my last chance to take a vacation before I change jobs."

"Change jobs?"

"Yeah. I finally landed one in Northern California, near Mt. Shasta."

"Yay!!!" Julia shouted, before noticing her mother's tiny, momentary look of disappointment.

"That's right, my children are beginning to migrate out to the west coast," Clarisse said.

"Not me," Nate spoke up, putting his arm around her.

After Julia unpacked her things, she tried to call Mark, but the machine picked up. She left a quick message telling him she'd arrived and then went downstairs.

"We're not too far from the beach. We can go down there tomorrow," Clarisse said.

The next morning it took Julia several minutes of lying very still, to accept waking in a house where her mother and a different man were living together. She felt empty, as if this piece of her family were staying at an outpost somewhere; a temporary refuge.

After breakfast they all walked down to the beach. As they crossed over the same parking lot Julia remembered from the sandstorm ten years ago, Nate remarked, "Wow. We sure came a long way."

"Look!" Julia exclaimed, pointing east. "You can see Matinecock Point from here!"

"And the Sandbar!" Teddy said. "Must be high tide."

The tiny shoal was barely visible, as waves lapped over the top.

"Do you think there was ever really a sea monster there?" Nate asked.

"Hard to say," Don said. "If there was, he kept a very low profile."

"Remember The Wreck?" Julia asked.

"I remember Dad going down there to spear-fish," Teddy said. "After Uncle Bill died he just stopped talking about it."

Julia, Clarisse and Uda drove over to Pattituck Cove later that day to pack up Clarisse's things while the men rented a van. They stopped at the local Rite-Aid to pick up some tape and cleaning supplies and were just rounding the corner of the paper towel aisle when they nearly ran into Ceddie.

"Oh!" everyone said at once, jumping back.

"And where have *you* been?" Ceddie asked, rubbing her chin tentatively with her index finger to expose a diamond engagement ring. She'd had her hair permed into one of those new "poodle-do's," as Mark called them.

Julia wondered if this represented an up or down movement in her social climbing efforts. "San Francisco," she answered.

"Oh? Who with?"

"I'm a musician there."

"All by yourself?"

"No. I live with a man named Mark. He's an artist for an ad agency," she added. *Dammit, I can't believe I'm stooping to take her competitive bait. Stop it right now!*

"Any plans?" Ceddie asked, using her bejeweled left hand to brush a stray cork-screw lock away from her forehead.

"Oh yes," Julia said, gearing herself up to deliver a whopper. "We're planning a trip to South America in a couple of months. I've gotten a generous grant to study the effects of concertina music on the breeding patterns of the poison dart frog."

Ceddie's mouth dropped open. "Well... that certainly sounds ambitious."

A package of bathroom tissue hit the floor behind Julia, who turned to see Uda picking it up, using it to hide her laughter.

"We've got to hurry," Clarisse said, nudging Julia. "They'll be here with the truck soon."

In the parking lot, Julia fumed. "Do you believe her? 'All by yourself?'" she mimicked in a whiny voice. "Like being in a couple is the most important thing."

"Great response," Uda said. "I almost laughed in her face."

"She really wanted us to see that ring," Clarisse added.

"I know. That's why I purposely ignored it. I just couldn't resist. Aren't you going to miss bumping into her, Mom?"

"Well, she has provided comic relief over the years, but I think I'll get over it."

Julia and Uda burst into laughter. As she watched her mother slide into the driver's seat and start the car, Julia noticed a strength in Clarisse that she hadn't remembered since junior high. Her sense of humor had resurfaced. She was wanted by someone again. *Oh my God—there's a real person in there!* She laughed to herself, mentally filing away the expression for her next conversation with Erin.

Later that week, Julia rode the train from Grand Central Station out to Pennsylvania to see her father and Rose. They picked her up in Scranton. His beard was now fully grey, a marked contrast to his wavy brown hair.

"He looks more distinguished that way, don't you think?" asked Rose.

The next day Ed gave Julia a tour of Shifting Pines; a huge estate converted into fifty-bed hospital and rehab center. As they walked the halls, it was just like Julia remembered as a child, with nurses popping their heads out of doorways to say hello to her father. He still acted glad to see them.

Downstairs in the hospital wing, Ed stopped to have a conversation with one of the nurses, and Julia glanced at a chart tacked to a bulletin board. According to the graph, several drinks per week would put a person into a category of risk. Having a drink every single day would move a person into a high-risk category that encouraged professional help. *That's what Mark and I do all the time and we're not alcoholics. I think this chart is a little extreme.*

They stepped outside and Ed directed her to a newer, more modern building. "This is the family center. People related to our clients get to stay here for a week and learn about their relationship to the problem."

"Looks like a vacation condo," Julia remarked, as they toured inside the main room with its huge stone fireplace. A small group of people relaxed on a circle of pillows, talking softly.

"You can stay here for a couple days if you like, while Rose and I are working. Not that I'm trying to get rid of you. I just think you might enjoy it. Maybe meet some kindred spirits."

"I learned a lot about myself when I did it," Rose said over take-out Chinese food that evening. "You can watch your father in action, too."

After dinner, Julia took a shower and called home. The machine picked up again and she hung up without leaving a message. She joined Ed in his den, where he'd parked himself in front of a game of Frogger. "Still like to play games, eh?" she asked.

"It's my favorite way to unwind after a day of dealing with angry drunks and drug addicts."

The next morning Ed took Julia to the family center and introduced her to the counselors.

"This is Karen, and Barbara. It won't be long before Rose joins them," he said. "She only has a year left before she finishes her degree. Well, I gotta go. Come by my office at noon and we'll have lunch together."

Julia joined the small group sitting on pillows next to the fireplace. Besides the counselors, Karen and Barbara, there was a man who looked to be in his late forties, a young woman Julia's age, and a middle-aged woman. Judging by their clothes and hair, Julia immediately assumed that they led more conservative lifestyles than she did; that it would be impossible to share anything intimate with them. *I'm not like them, really. I don't have a partner with a serious problem.* Still, she felt drawn to their stories.

"I just love him to death, but sometimes I feel like I have two kids instead of just one," the younger woman said, describing her husband.

"I'm always trying to hold the line," the man said. "So things won't blow up. I'm afraid if I don't keep a constant vigil, she'll go ballistic."

The middle-aged woman sat on her pillow and wept. "Or disappear," she choked out between sobs.

At least my father's on the other side of all that now, thought Julia. Then when it was her turn, she surprised herself by saying, "I'm lonely." It just popped right out. "Even though I'm in a couple and we like a lot of the same things, I always feel as if I'm on my own."

"We've learned to stuff our feelings deep inside," Karen said, nodding. "We're so worried about upsetting people, we shove our emotions far enough away that they won't show."

"Then they fester inside of us, creating reactive, irrational behavior," Barbara said.

Julia felt bewildered. She didn't remember having to hide her feelings when she was growing up. Not with all that music and art in her life. But she was curious about these people, and decided to meet with them again that afternoon. When the morning session was over, she walked over to the main building to see her father.

"He's doing an intake," the receptionist told her. "But you can wait in the room next to his office. Just be quiet."

Julia tip-toed into the room and sat down. The door to Ed's office was ajar, and she could see her father from behind, meeting with a man in his thirties. Sitting across from the desk, the man looked sweaty and exasperated.

"They scape-goated me," he said. "If you want my honest opinion, I think it was political."

"You're here because your company gave you the choice of either treatment or termination," Ed answered.

"Well, maybe you could sign something that says I'm actually okay, so I can skip this and get back to work. 'Cause it's a bunch of B.S."

Her father's voice cut through the muck patiently. "I'm afraid I can't do that. You're here because you messed things up. Now you have the chance to take a personal inventory and make some improvements."

"Hey, I might've partied a little too much, but I've been under a lot of stress. Someone at work just overreacted."

Julia could just imagine the look on her father's face. She'd seen it many times as a child. *I see through you. I know you're full of it, but I'm going to stand my ground and let you figure it out.*

"Take more than that," Ed remarked, as they edged their way through the treatment center cafeteria with trays. "You're too thin. Have some pie."

"Everybody keeps saying that. I'm afraid Mark won't even recognize me when I get home."

"Look at this," Ed said, pointing to the coffee urns. "No caffeine allowed. It's all decaf."

"Darn. I was hoping for a little lift, myself."

"I think they have some real coffee back at the family dorm. Ask Barbara."

"That guy in your office was really mad," Julia said, sitting down at a table.

"Yeah, most of 'em come in that way."

A few minutes later, the people from her family group showed up and Julia waved.

"Invite them over," Ed suggested. "I have to get going soon anyway."

"This is my father," Julia introduced him proudly, a lump forming in her throat. "He's the Medical Director."

David, the man in their group, said, "I've heard some great things about you from my wife."

"I was in training for a long time," Ed answered, chuckling.

It happened later that afternoon when one of the counselors was getting Julia to role-play a typical disagreement with Mark: "Everything's fine. I'm just trying to relax. *You're* the one who should learn to take it easy," Karen mimicked. "You're *always* acting like the uptight one."

Julia felt something well up inside of her that wasn't lunch. It was a hot sensation she mistook for anger. By the time it reached her throat, tears began to fall, and then she was sobbing openly. It was as if the crying were a separate entity, racking her body so hard that all she could do was rock back on forth on her pillow holding a tissue over her face. She couldn't speak for another five minutes as she cried while David and Deidre, the other young woman in the group, patted her shoulders. The middle-aged woman named Greta sat on her pillow and wept along sympathetically.

"Where did *that* come from?" Julia asked, when she found her voice.

"Storage," answered Barbara.

"Whew." Julia blew her nose. "Could we make some coffee? The regular kind?"

"Yes. Good idea. I think we need a little break," Karen said.

That night Julia stayed in the dorm of the Family Center. She was feeling emotionally filleted, and wanted to remain in this new cocoon of fellowship she'd found. It was chilly enough to build a fire in the stone fireplace, and she sat in the living room with David, Deirdre and Greta after dinner, exchanging stories about their partners. Her head still throbbed from crying.

"Have an aspirin," Deidre said, offering her a bottle. "I wore myself out crying the first day."

"This place is amazing," David added. "They even had the foresight to stock the place with extra-large tissues."

"I guess I had a little more in 'storage' about my family than I thought," Julia said. "That role-playing with Mark just triggered it. I mean, it's not like Mark's an alcoholic or anything. Sure, he likes beer, but he's really responsible. And he never drinks in the mornings," she added.

David and Greta exchanged glances.

"I used to say that about my husband," said Greta. "Then things just started to slip away from us and he became someone else."

Deidre's husband called from the main building three times, begging her to come and take him home. "Good job staying strong," David said, every time she returned from the phone.

"You sound stuffed up," Mark said, when Julia called him from the pay phone in the lobby.

"Allergies," she answered. "I forgot how bad they were back here."

"I miss you." His voice was warm and gentle. "I wish I was there."

She didn't tell him where she was staying. "I miss you, too. How're things at work?"

"The art director is leaving. Now everyone's wondering what's going to happen. All of a sudden we're eyeing each other competitively."

"Do you want the job?"

"I dunno. Not really."

"Why not?"

"It's more responsibility than I want. The money would be better, but I wouldn't be doing as much of the creating. The scary part is that they're considering Laurel, and she's a total incompetent. We think she had a 'couch interview' today."

"Ugh, Laurel?" Julia had met her a few times at the ad agency's Christmas parties. She'd ask you a question and not wait to hear the answer before either interrupting you or walking away.

"How was *Cats?*" he asked.

"I laughed, I cried, it was really excellent. But I'm getting homesick for California. A lot of people still have Big Hair and listen to Journey. It's weird."

Mark laughed. "Maybe we'll have to shave you when you get home."

"I'll see you in a couple of days. Love you."

"Me too."

The next morning the entire campus gathered in the main hall for Ed's lecture. Julia hadn't seen him speak publicly since that time in Gilroy, and she swore she would faint dead away, puke in her pocketbook or die before walking out on him this time. He bounded to the front of the large room and introduced himself. Again, tears rushed to Julia's eyes, but she took a deep breath and exhaled slowly.

Ed walked around with the microphone as he spoke, relating the history of alcohol abuse in America. "We tried making it illegal for awhile, but that didn't work," he said. He showed slides of a person trapped inside of a bottle, and a three-headed dragon. He looked so happy up there, so complete. He loved what he was doing. When he finished, the audience thundered with applause. Julia was in awe. *He used to have a job making people go to sleep. Now he helps them wake up.*

The meeting began breaking up into small, lively discussion groups, motivated by her father's lecture. One circle was forming around a middle-aged man with a flat-top crew cut. He read from a crumpled piece of paper. "I just had two cans of beer sitting on the dashboard of the locomotive cab. It's not like they were open or anything..."

"What are they doing?" she asked Ed.

"That guy in the middle is in the 'Hot Seat.' He's reading his story, and then his group will try to 'roast' him out of denial," Ed whispered.

Even though the man was gruff looking and she could sense his insincerity, Julia felt sorry for him. Ed steered her away from the circle saying, "That one's kind of private."

"That's okay. I think I'll go back to my group anyway."

"Are you having fun with them?"

"Yeah. We're helping each other uncover lots of old stuff."

"That's great. You'll feel a lot better in the long run."

Julia thought she detected a look of sorrow on Ed's face, but she was still so astonished by his lecture, she said, "I didn't know you were such a great speaker. And I didn't even run away this time."

He laughed. "Have a good time then. I'll see you later for dinner. Rose is cooking up lasagna for your last night."

"I think I was always torn between feeling weirded out by people, and afraid of being left behind at the same time," she told Ed later, after dinner.

"Watch out for 'left-outedness,'" her father warned. "You have a tendency to isolate yourself, so you have to make the extra effort to get out and be with people you can relate to."

"But it seems like I'm always around a lot of people now," Julia protested.

"It's not the same as being around a lot of people in a crowded nightclub or a recording studio." Then he drew a breath and said, "I'm sorry. I wish I could've done better back then. But this is where we are now. You have to remember that you didn't *make* me do anything. So go find a good group back there, and keep talking."

The trip back to San Francisco seemed much longer than her trip east. Julia had to take a puddle-jumper from Scranton that bounced in the wind for nearly an hour before reaching her connection in Newark. Now relaxing in the window seat of the 747, she felt as if she'd been emotionally flushed and reenergized. She'd spent the past few days crying as the family counselors helped her expose deeply buried, hurt feelings and air them out. She couldn't wait to get home and tell Mark about her experience with the family program. It would be like showing him a whole new dimension of herself, and she was sure he'd gain some insight from it.

When Mark picked up Julia at the airport, she noticed a new dent in the fender of his Toyota.

"Where did you get that?" she asked.

"In a parking lot." he answered. "In Berkeley."

"Did you call the insurance company?"

"No. I don't want my rates to go up. Hey, a bunch of us are meeting at Café Flore. Laurel didn't get hired, so we're celebrating."

"I'm kind of tired," Julia said.

"Just for a little while, okay? We can have dinner there."

Three hours and a number of beers later, they were still at the café. Julia was starting to drift to sleep when the table erupted into raucous laughter. She snapped awake, and saw that Mark was standing at the head of the table making yet another toast, and exchanging rapid-fire, droll quips with a man she recognized from the editorial department of the ad agency. She sighed and nodded to him with an urgent *I want to go home* expression.

"I'm sorry," he said, biting back a belch as they walked to the car. "Let's get you home to bed."

"Maybe I should drive," Julia said.

"No, I'm okay. Besides, you're probably all jet-lagged out. You were asleep a few minutes ago. Come on. I'll be careful." Mark gave her a quick hug and opened the passenger door for her.

The car lurched forward into Market Street. Julia assumed her position of the constant vigil until they reached their loft.

At home, dishes were piled in the sink, and a pot of week-old spaghetti sauce sat on the stove, its sides caked with crusted tomato paste. A heap of doll parts, PVC pipe and model train landscaping trees lay in one corner.

"I was on a roll," Mark said quickly, noticing her look of horror. "See?" he said pointing to his latest work in progress, a giant head with HO train tracks running all over it.

Julia pushed her mild disgust aside for a moment. "Not bad."

"I'm really glad you're home," Mark said, running his hand over her butt and kissing her. It felt sloppy. Beery. She felt as if she hadn't come home at all. After two weeks of traveling to alien spaces occupied by both of her parents, she felt like she'd arrived at yet another strange place. All the energy she'd gathered at Shifting Pines was leaving like the slow leak from a tire.

When they climbed into bed, Mark went right to work on her clit with his tongue, as if he'd been starved. She cringed slightly, then realized that she really had missed him while she was away, but had forgotten until now. She rallied for a few minutes, warming herself in the glow of his affection, as she arched her back and moaned. He kept licking her, grunting happily, until she became tired of the same repetitious movement. She tried to move his head around to get a more varied rhythm, but he acted clueless. She felt like kicking him, but nudged his shoulder with her foot instead. He brought his head up and smiled, climbing on top of her. He plunged into her and stroked her hard for several minutes before he came. Then he rolled over, panting. "Welcome home, sweetie."

TWENTY-NINE

A FEW DAYS LATER, MARK AND JULIA SAT SPELLBOUND on the living room couch watching the underwater camera of the *Jason Jr.* as it moved slowly around the *Titanic*. It panned the "rusticles" that had formed on the railings of the most luxurious ocean liner in history, and then zoomed in on small objects. A tin cup on a boiler, sitting just as if someone had momentarily set it down to run an errand. A doll's head, a champagne bottle nestled within a railing, and a pair of men's shoes resting on the sandy floor as if the poor soul had landed standing up, leaving only the position of the shoes to describe his fall, his death, his station in life.

"So it broke in half," Mark commented, sipping on a beer.

"Yeah, I remember reading that some of the crew thought they saw it breaking. I guess everyone sort of forgot."

"It's because they were hauling ass to get away from the suction."

The front half of the ship lay misshapen, settled into the sand, while the stern had landed hundreds of yards away in its two-mile fall to the ocean floor.

That night Julia dreamt she was aboard *Titanic* as it sank. Probably a lot of people did, since it was the first TV showing of the newly discovered wreck. She clung to the railing as the boat dropped down, people and objects flying away from the sides like effervescence. There was one big group scream as the mammoth liner cracked in half and plunged downward, growing lighter as each person gave up and let go.

The next day Mark went into a tizzy of art-making. He bought an entire case of cheap beer for the event, parking it in the refrigerator. When Julia returned from a recording session that evening, he was dashing around the art studio, fitting small Barbie-sized arms into the portals of a giant model steamship he'd mounted onto a pedestal. Empty beer bottles stood around the studio in every available flat space.

"Look!" he chortled. "It's my homage to *Titanic!*"

He'd attached an aquarium filter to the bow and stern of the model. When he pushed a button, the two halves of the ship began to separate as tiny pink hands waved from the windows.

"I'm going to build a Plexiglas tank and fill it with water so it can really sink!"

Julia stood back and shook her head. "It's not funny. You're making a joke out of a mass grave."

Mark looked at her, his glasses slightly askew. "Party pooper."

"The subject doesn't quite lend itself to humor or sarcasm. That's how all those people *died*."

"Jeez, what were you recording today? Funeral music or something? Lighten up."

Julia sighed and went into the kitchen. Opening the refrigerator, she saw that there were only two bottles of beer left.

"Did somebody else come over?" she called across the loft.

"No, I've been working straight through."

How is he still standing?

The phone rang. Julia picked up and Steve was on the other end.

"Hey, Steve, what's up?"

"It's Erin. We're at the hospital in Santa Rosa. She's in surgery. They think one of her kidneys is failing."

Julia sat down at the kitchen table as her heart began to pound.

"They say she'll probably be okay, but I'm staying here all night," Steve continued.

"I'm on my way." She hung up and walked over to Mark's studio. "Erin's in the hospital. I have to go up there right now."

"Wha—?" Mark stood up and swayed, pushing his glasses back up on his nose.

"She's having some kind of… kidney problem," Julia said, her voice shaking as she went into the bedroom and stuffed a few things into a knapsack.

Mark followed her. "Do you want some company?" He looked so disheveled and childlike standing there, the only expression that came to her mind was *extra baggage.*

"No. I'll be okay," she said. "It'll probably just be a lot of sitting around waiting. I'll call you when I know something."

Driving under the orange lights of the Golden Gate Bridge that night, Julia was afraid to think about Erin. Even though she knew her diabetes was a particularly bad case, she still acted stronger than lots of healthy people Julia knew, in spite of her life-threatening illness. She thought about Mark instead. They'd been together for more than five years now, and Julia realized that she was either angry or embarrassed most of the time she was with him. He drank way more than she was comfortable with, and even though she'd made a huge stink about not bringing any cocaine into the house, she was fairly sure he was tooting on the side. Every few months or so they'd have a fight about it and Mark would cut way back on drinking and become sweet and romantic again, cleverly deflecting any possible references to Julia's trip back east. It usually lasted for a couple of weeks. They both had money coming in, so they didn't fight over that, although they did tend to argue about whose time was more important. She'd never seen him drink a whole case of beer, though. *Dammit,* she thought, speeding over the hills toward Sonoma County in the barely used Honda station wagon she'd just bought. *This isn't a partnership. It's entrenchment. How did I let it happen?*

Steve looked blanched when she got there. "She's okay," he said. "They had to take out one of her kidneys. We can see her in the morning."

Julia and Steve spent the night side by side in chairs in the hospital waiting room, covered in blankets a nurse offered them when they made it clear they weren't leaving.

When Julia entered Erin's room the next morning, she burst into tears. Erin was awake, but pale. Her freckles seemed to be floating in the air over her ashen face.

"Hey, don't cry. I'm the one who's in the bed. I'm just cruising on one engine, now," she rasped cheerfully. "The hard part will be having my mother here for two weeks."

"I was too scared… to even think about it," Julia wept. Steve stood on the other side of the bed and they each held one of Erin's hands, kneading it gently with their thumbs as the machines beeped.

"Just pretend you're in the electronic music studio," Erin suggested.

When the nurse came in and kicked them out, Julia and Steve went downstairs to the cafeteria.

"I guess she's more used to this than we are, but I think she's putting on an act," Steve said. "I don't feel good about leaving, but I need to get back to Santiago soon and finish this project. Can you come up and stay for awhile?"

"Yeah, I think so," Julia said, nodding. "I think I might be able to make it look like a coincidence."

When Julia drove back down to San Francisco several days later, Mark was out. She stayed up waiting for him until almost one in the morning, and was just drifting off to sleep when she heard him trudging up the steps. A flash of white-hot anger bolted her awake again.

"You're back," he said.

"I said I was coming back today," she answered, sitting up. "Were you out with the guys from work?"

"Yeah…" He turned and went into the bathroom, where she heard him brushing his teeth. He always did that, no matter how loaded he was. When he climbed into bed he put his arms around her and spooned up behind her, falling right to sleep. He smelled like beer and Pepsodent. Julia's heart still beat angrily. She lay awake until dawn, her mind bouncing back and forth between the fear of losing Erin, and her eroding relationship with Mark.

Julia slept in the next morning and then cleaned the place while Mark was at work. Late in the afternoon, he came bounding up the stairs. "Come on!" he said. "We're meeting everybody down at the Tivoli."

"What are you wearing?" Julia asked, noticing a string of oversized plastic lavender pearls around his neck. He looked ridiculous.

"What, these?" he asked, glancing down at them. "We were goofing around at work."

"I'm not going with you if you're wearing those."

"What is your *problem?*" he snapped.

"Look, I'm kind of freaked out about Erin and I don't want to go out and attract a lot attention someplace." *Someplace where anybody in the music business might see me.*

Mark stalked out of the room and she heard him banging around in the kitchen. He came out with a beer. "Hey listen, I asked you if you wanted company that night. You went up there and hung out with Steve the whole time."

"What? Is that what you think? That we were hanging out for fun or something? My friend nearly died and all you can think about is me fooling around? This is more about your stupid wounded ego than anything else!" she shouted.

"*Yadda, yadda, yadda,*" Mark said.

"Don't give me *yadda, yadda!*" Julia shrieked. "I hate fucking *'yadda, yadda!!*'"

Mark took a swig of beer and removed his pearls, flinging them at her. "Do you want to come or not?"

She shook her head, choking back a sob. "I don't even remember what it's like to see you without a beer in your hand."

Mark leaned against the doorjamb and said, "This stopped being fun about two years ago, when you put on a fucking suit of armor so nobody could be close to you anymore!" He turned and lumbered toward the stairs. Pausing at the landing, he swayed, pointing back at Julia. "Life's too precious," he snarled, "to have to spend it with an uptight bitch like you." He pounded down the steps, slamming the door after him. Julia stared at the empty space in disbelief. *What suit of armor?*

The phone rang and she picked up, thinking it might be Steve.

"Hi, Pearlie," her father's voice bubbled from Pennsylvania. "How are things going?"

Slightly taken aback by a nickname she hadn't heard in a long time, Julia tried to draw a deep breath but it stuck midway.

"Are you all right?" he asked.

Tears ran down her face and she cried for several minutes while

Ed waited patiently on the other end. She finally croaked out, "I'm too embarrassed to tell you."

"Your buddy Mark… drinking a lot?" he ventured.

"How did you know?"

"Just an educated guess. Have you been to a meeting lately?"

"Well, I tried to go to one here in town, but it was mostly angry alcoholic lesbians, so I didn't go back."

"You have to shop around until you find the one you feel most comfortable in. I found an AA meeting that has the best cheesecake, and I like the people, too."

Julia laughed. "Okay. I'll try again."

"I have faith in you. Meanwhile, would you draw me a cartoon of the *Titanic* sinking in one of those red circles with the 'No' slash over it? We've been talking about that image a lot lately, and I'd like to add a slide of it to my lectures."

"It might take me a little while, but I think I can. Erin had a kidney removed this week, so I've been up and down to Santa Rosa. I'm thinking of staying up there for awhile to sort things out for myself."

"Poor Erin. She's a strong one though. Like you. Just keep hoping for the best. By the way, we've got a new member of our household."

"Who?"

"A little kitten named Jake. Someone at work found him on a doorstep. He's so tiny, I've been feeding him with an eyedropper."

"A kitten? You? What color is he?"

"He's orange and white. I'll send some pictures. Meanwhile, hang in there. Let me know what happens. I'm rooting for you."

After they hung up, Julia sniffled as she packed all the keyboards and clothes that would fit into her station wagon and headed back up to Santa Rosa.

THIRTY

A FEW DAYS LATER, STEVE DROVE JULIA BACK to San Francisco in his truck to pick up the rest of her things. Mark wouldn't answer her calls, so she finally left him a message that she'd be there at noon. As Steve eased his pickup truck into a space on Minna Street a few doors down from the loft, Julia spotted Michael getting out of his car across the street. He'd offered to come over and help them carry stuff down the stairs. She started to get out when the door to the loft opened and Mark appeared. A woman in a red leather jacket popped out behind him, giggling. Oblivious to Steve's truck, Mark leaned over and gave her a long, face-sucking kiss.

An electric current passed through Julia.

"Jeez... he didn't waste any time," Steve commented.

"Oh my God, it's Laurel from the ad agency," Julia whispered, slipping back into the truck. Her heart pounded as she tried to regain composure while Mark and Laurel took off down the street in the other direction, arm in arm.

"Whew," Steve said. "At least they went the other way. I'm sorry," he added touching Julia's arm.

Michael knocked on the window and Julia rolled it down. "Are you all right?" he asked.

Her voice shook. "If this day were a fish, I'd definitely throw it back."

"Think of it as a positive purging. Let's pack up your stuff and get out of here."

"At least he didn't change the locks on me," Julia said, fiddling with her key.

"Evidently he had better things to do," Michael scoffed.

"I saw all the signs," Julia told Michael later, when he called to check up on her, "and I still didn't do anything. What the hell is wrong with me?"

"Well, one theory is, people tend to choose partners with the same characteristics as a dysfunctional parent, trying to correct something that happened in childhood. All the failed mending you attempted with that parent is still drifting around inside you like an unfinished expression. So you keep finding partners with similar problems, hoping for a chance to say the one thing that will elicit a healing."

"And it never happens, right?"

"Hardly ever. People tend to be fairly resistant when their partners try to make them change."

"Yeah, I always felt an invisible wall going up when I tried to talk to Mark about my father."

"What were his parents like?"

"I only met them a few times. His mother was a servile bore and his father tried to pick fights with us about how great he thinks Reagan is, so we just avoided them."

"Big surprise. Well, remember, it's finding the expression within yourself that counts. Think of the other people as facilitators to that end."

"Yeah… right. All the world's a stage… but I still feel like going down there and throwing a cement block through his window."

"So you're human after all," Michael said. "Good thing you're fifty miles away. Plus you might hurt yourself trying to get a cement block up to the second story. Besides, maybe he'll fart too hard one night and set the loft on fire."

"I'll *never* stop loving you," Julia replied.

A few days later Julia sat in the spare bedroom at Erin's house, drawing the stern of the *Titanic* from an old photograph of the doomed ship. Ink waves lapped at a tragically upended hull with a red circle and slash over it. *How did Mark become a stranger so fast? It felt totally surreal the other day on the street. I was stupid for letting it get that bad.*

Erin appeared at the door, still pale and fragile from the surgery. "Keeping busy?" Her soft red hair was illuminated by the emerald green kimono she wore.

"Trying to. I can't stop thinking about it. I keep taking the same circular trips around the inside of my head, going from anger to guilt. I feel like I've been poisoned."

"These things take time. You've just got to find a way to stay busy. I mean, *busier*. The good news is, my mother's going to help me buy this place."

"That's great," Julia said. She loved Erin's little Arts and Crafts style bungalow on a quiet street. It had three small bedrooms and a fenced-in backyard with Santa Rosa plum trees. "But—is she moving in?"

"Heavens, no. She's just helping me with the money. She made some really smart decisions in the stock market. So stay here. It's not that far to the city anyway."

"That's true. It's not like I have to go down there every day. And Michael said I could stay at his place if I have a gig or something."

"All this time, we've never actually shared a place together. We'll have fun."

Julia felt relieved that it was Erin's idea; now she could keep an eye on her.

"Hey, that's pretty good," Erin remarked, pointing to Julia's illustration. "It would look great on a t-shirt or something."

"Or on a shirt pocket. *Hmmm....*"

Later on Julia made a miniature version of the drawing and two stencils, one for the black ship and another for the red slash, and airbrushed the design onto the pocket of a man's tailored shirt. When she sent the illustration to Ed, she packed the shirt with a little note that said, "To wear during your lectures."

"Hey, this is really something!" Ed exclaimed, when he called the next week. "Everybody wants one. Why don't you make a dozen and we'll see if we can sell them at the canteen."

She threw herself into a frenzy of shirt-painting, which helped perforate the steady stream of angry thoughts about Mark.

"I'm living in this house with some vague acquaintances," Julia said, nestled in a bean bag chair at a therapist's office outside of Santa Rosa as she described a recurring dream she'd been having. "It's a nice old neighborhood, with Victorian houses. We've accumulated a lot of furniture that's beginning to crowd the rooms. I walk into the hallway and down a flight of stairs I've always known was there, but haven't paid much attention to. On the next landing there turns out to be a whole other wing. It's like we all forgot about it or something. The rooms are empty but really inviting; they're huge and they all have great, tall windows. I start planning how I'm going to move my stuff into one of the bigger ones. As I walk around, the building grows even larger, as if the rooms are multiplying. Then I wake up."

"And how does that make you *feel?*" the therapist asked. She was fifty-ish, severe and taut in spite of her long, floral dress. Julia had picked her out from an ad in a local alternative newspaper.

"Well, this morning was the first time I woke up after the dream and stayed in a good mood for more than a minute. I mean, since Mark and I split, I usually wake up in the morning feeling happy for about thirty seconds before I realize where I am, and then everything comes rolling over me like a thick, black cloud."

"And how does *that* make you feel?" the therapist asked.

Julia looked up at her, annoyed at the woman's air of detachment. A wave of anger quickly overwhelmed her.

"HOW DO YOU THINK IT MAKES ME FEEL?!?" she blurted out, collapsing into tears.

The therapist sat quietly, watching as Julia wept. When she began to calm down, she prompted, "Use descriptive words."

Julia reached for a Kleenex and blew her nose. *Not even the man-sized kind. What was she thinking? Ha! Dad would've liked that one.* Clearing her throat, Julia decided to try and make this session worth her money. "Betrayed… sad…"

She left the therapist's office feeling empty, as if she'd gotten up from the dinner table still hungry. She headed for the Farmer's Market in Sebastopol. Picking out some zucchinis, she thought, *'How does that make you feel?' Give me a break. I could just make a recording of that and cry at home. I wish she were as cool as Michael.*

Dr. Michael. She was so proud of him. He'd worked hard to get his clinical psychologist's license and now he was practicing at a small office in the Castro district of San Francisco. *I should've just gotten a referral from him for someone in the city.* She backed away and nearly bumped into the woman standing behind her.

"Oh, I'm sorry!"

The woman turned around and they both stared at each other in faint recognition until Julia realized it was one of her old aikido teachers.

"Do you remember me?" she asked. "I used to train in San Francisco about five years ago."

The woman ruffled her brow and then nodded. "You do look familiar."

"Are you still teaching?"

"Yes. We have a little dojo near Occidental. Come by sometime," she said, reaching into her bag and handing Julia a card.

Julia showed up for a class the very next night. She'd had the presence of mind to save her old training *gi*, even though her music schedule and Mark's total disinterest in the art had kept her away for so long. The movements came back to her like a joyful dance.

Afterwards, Julia disclosed to the teacher, Robin, that she'd recently ended a long-term relationship and was still dealing with a lot of anger.

"You've got to get that out of your body. I like to wail on the tire, myself." Robin walked over to a wall rack and removed a wooden training sword, bowing it toward the front of the room at the *shomen*. Then she carried it to a tire mounted on a homemade frame, and let out a piercing yell as she whacked the tire with the sword.

"Wow…" Julia said.

"The breath exiting the body releases a lot of tension. And you get whole lot bigger when you extend your energy out through the *bokken*," she said, handing the wooden sword to Julia. "Go ahead. Try it."

The dojo was empty except for the two of them. Julia raised the wooden sword and brought it down on the tire with a soft yelp.

"You can do better than that," Robin said. "Take everything you've been feeling about your relationship, all your anger, mistrust and betrayal, and let it rip."

Julia drew a deep breath, thought about the plastic pearls, the smell of cheap beer and Laurel, and raised her sword.

"AIIIIIIIEEEEEAAAA!!!"

The wooden sword hit the tire and the walls of the renovated barn echoed. Julia felt a layer of stress lifting off her like a wet overcoat.

"Not bad," Robin remarked. "Some power, eh?"

Julia tingled with renewed energy on the drive back to Erin's house.

"You look like a different person than the one who left earlier," Erin remarked, when she got there. "A much happier one."

THIRTY-ONE

1993

"I DON'T KNOW," JULIA HESITATED. "I've heard the Renaissance Faire is really hard to get into."

"We'll just have to come up with something unique," Erin persisted. "Besides, maybe there'll be some interesting men for you. Come on—it'll be fun!"

Julia winced. In the eight years since she'd moved up to Sonoma County from San Francisco she'd left a messy trail of short-lived boyfriends—those she'd tossed off before they got too close, or those who drank too much and then dumped her when she attempted to save them.

Steve was still in love with Erin and lived at the house in Santa Rosa when he wasn't traveling around the world making documentaries. She loved him back and occasionally accompanied him on trips, but neither of them felt like getting married and starting a family. Erin joked about her health, saying that she was living on borrowed time and didn't want to burden him with a weakened wife. She was a tenured anthropology professor at Sonoma State by then, and taught a Saturday morning mask-making class for children at the Cotati Community Center.

Julia maintained a steady career as a professional musician. She'd worked on a number of film soundtracks and CDs, but had cut back on live performances. She liked living in the quiet Sonoma Valley, teaching keyboard lessons when she wasn't traveling for work. She'd even found a small Lutheran church that let her play their pipe organ in exchange for substitute availability, but still abstained from going in to practice late at night. And she'd kept up with aikido this time, finally earning a black belt in the art at the tiny dojo in Occidental. Best of all, she could keep tabs on Erin should a health emergency arise, especially when Steve was out of town—in fact, she could even be Erin's body guard if needed.

How does she stay so bubbly? Julia thought about her friend and the habitual understanding that had kept them close for so long resurfaced: *This is special. Don't squander it.*

"Okay then," Julia said the next day. "Let's go for it. Don't we have to send away for an application or something?"

"Already done," Erin answered cheerfully, drawing out a thick envelope of instructions.

"You're diabolical."

Inspired by their two cats, Joey and Bee, Julia and Erin developed an entire fantasy world of Elizabethan animals with paper mâché heads who stayed up late at night snitching fabric and fashion from the humans to create their own subculture. They made prototype dolls of Sir Hamlet the Pig, Friar Duck, and the Squirrel of Leicester. Finally, naming their prospective booth "Menagerie," they took some photographs of the costumed dolls and sent in their application.

Several weeks later, the Renaissance Faire selection committee called wanting to see the actual dolls. Julia dropped off some samples at the Faire site in Novato and a contract arrived in the mail a week later. Even though one talon of Saint George the Dragon had popped off during the jurying process revealing a 20th century plastic straw, they'd been invited to participate in the Faire.

"Did you know we had to do all this?" Julia asked, flipping through pages and pages of booth rules.

"Sort of," Erin shrugged. "We'll just ask for help if we get stuck."

"Can we run away now?" Julia whispered to Erin a few weeks later, as they sat on a straw bale on Stake-out Day listening to the Faire's department managers. They'd have to build a booth out of wood, twine and burlap. Then they were required to create or buy authentic Renaissance costumes and get them approved by the Costume Department, and attend mandatory Elizabethan speech and culture classes.

"Shhh—don't be such a wussy!" Erin whispered back.

"In order for the peasant costume to be truly authentic," the costuming teacher chirped, "you can leave it in a corner of your room during the week after you wash it so it will stay appropriately wrinkled and not smell too much like modern detergent."

Julia and Erin were assigned a space under a giant bay tree, and spent the rest of the day clearing brush and planning their booth.

Later that evening, Ed called from Teddy's home up north near Mt. Shasta. "We're here!" On their way to visit Rose's parents in Oregon, they'd flown into Redding and rented a car.

Julia was exhausted, but knew she'd have to take the time to drive up for a quick visit.

"I've got some tree-poles you can have for the booth," Teddy told her, when he got on the phone. Lowering his voice, he added, "He doesn't look too good."

During the four-hour drive up I-5 to Teddy's place, Julia thought about the last time she'd seen her father, two years before. She'd gone back to Long Island to watch Clarisse and Don get married in a quiet civil ceremony with the Justice of the Peace in Bayville, and took the opportunity to visit with Ed and Rose in Pennsylvania. Ed had cut back on work, having been diagnosed with a mild case of emphysema.

"I guess I didn't quit smoking in time," he'd told Julia, over a dinner of Asian noodles and salmon in Nanticoke. "My doctor has me riding my bike and playing golf, though. *And* I finally got a hole-in-one!" He pointed toward the fireplace mantle, where a trophy with a gold-plated golf ball sat.

Ed's two cats, Jake the orange tabby and Kinkster, a Siamese someone had gifted him after a successful stay at Shifting Pines, wandered around the table, picking their way over the dishes and bowls. Kinkster paused to take a swipe at a noodle as it headed toward Ed's mouth.

"Dad!" Julia scolded, shooing him away. "I never let Joey and Bee on the table!"

"Yeah, I kinda spoil 'em," he said. "They're good company when

Rose is working."

He'd described in great detail the way Jake nuzzled under his neck when he watched TV, and showed Julia how Kinkster could fetch a jingle-ball. *He's returning to simple pleasures,* she thought, pushing her car a little faster up I-5, trying not to dwell on mortality.

By the time Julia arrived at Teddy's they'd already started a backyard barbeque. Sparkling apple cider flowed freely while Ed entertained them with stories of some of the famous people who'd stayed at Shifting Pines. "This is in *strict confidence,*" Rose reminded them. "It's supposed to be anonymous."

Ed had a pronounced limp from a case of gout. He was still devastated over the recent loss of his cat Jake, who'd died from feline leukemia. "I would do anything," he told them, shaking his head sadly, "to have him back with me again." During the night Julia could hear the familiar cough he'd had when she was growing up.

She tried to get a bead on Rose. She could tell that her father's second wife still worshipped him as a sort of savior from her previous life. Besides that, they seemed to have a private understanding between them, something reserved for people who'd gone over the edge into alcoholism and come out the other side. Still, she was a good twenty years younger than Ed and easing comfortably into her new career as an addiction counselor. Julia wondered whether Rose would be available to take care of her father, should the need arise.

The next morning, Teddy helped Julia tie the wooden poles for the Renaissance Faire booth onto the roof rack of her car before she left.

"Come back east and visit us sometime soon," her father said, giving her a hug before she got into her car.

On the way down to Santa Rosa, she tried not to think about the prospect of her father festering away in old age. It was one thing to shrug off letting his cats wander around on the dinner table, but this time around he looked tired, weak, and a bit like a worn-out version of Colonel Sanders. *Of course Rose will take care of him,* she decided, turning up the music on her CD player.

Back at the Faire site in Novato, Julia and Erin built their booth using the poles from Teddy's property, with generous amounts of twine and nails holding them together. They hung a sign across the top with pictures of Elizabethan animals in snoods and feathered hats, amid brightly colored paw-print flags. Michael even came up one day and added a counter with shelves, plus a backstage area with straw bales for resting.

During the pre-Faire weekends, the sound of hammering and sawing mingled with the practice of Elizabethan accent and song. Red dragonflies swirled around in the sunlit areas of the dell as young men gregariously showcased their ability to bellow and belch, pirate-style. Young women were sent back to the costume department to fix their bodices so their nipples wouldn't pop out. Fiddlers drilled the folk dancers for hours as they clumped around on the wooden stages. In the middle of a 16th century country dance, they'd often slide into television theme songs, switching to "Jeopardy" or "I Dream of Jeannie" without changing the rhythm.

Across from Julia and Erin's booth, a small stage had already been built, festooned with frog flags. Over the top was a sign that read, "Mr. Toad's Belching Contest," with a pair of tipsy looking frogs clanking mugs.

"How gross is *that* going to be," Julia wondered out loud, nodding at the sign.

"I don't know," Erin answered. "But it can't be nearly as gross as Mark's fart-burning."

Julia chuckled. It had been eight years since she'd seen or talked to Mark, after a brief and shallow closure between them. "That was a timing thing. You had to be there to fully appreciate it."

"Are you sure you're not too tired?" Julia asked Erin each evening, when they drove back to Santa Rosa to have a quick dinner and make more dolls.

"I feel great. I like being too busy to think," she'd answer.

When the Faire finally opened, the air became filled with the scent of bay leaves, roasting meat, incense, beer, lavender, sweaty humans, marijuana, dust and straw. People roamed the paths gnawing on giant turkey legs, wiping the trails of grease with their ruffled sleeves. Julia and Erin had created French merchant outfits with long skirts, brocade vests and straw hats. Each weekend, the feathers in their hatbands increased, as well as the brass bells they tied onto their costumes. The Menagerie booth quickly became a pet owner magnet. "That one looks exactly like our Mitten!" tourists would exclaim, pointing to a cat dressed in Elizabethan baby's pajamas and pulling out their checkbooks. Then there were the sightseers who wandered by in t-shirts and shorts complaining about the high prices of everything, until Erin got tired of hearing it one day and quipped,

"Sir, tis a fairly brazen thing you say;
"Perhaps thee would favor Mart of K!"

"Asshole," she muttered to Julia, when the man turned and left amid raucous laughter from the other shoppers.

Beating drums and wooden flutes signaled that the Dance Macabre was coming down the dirt path. Everyone in this parade was dressed as a skeleton. Some of them ran ahead to hide, popping out from behind trees to scare Fairegoers. Condemned criminals in rags were hauled down the path in a rustic wooden cart for a staged flogging, clinging to the bars and ranting madly.

"Braaaaaaappppp!"

People were arriving for Mr. Toad's Belching Contest, which took place every hour on the hour. Both men and women gathered early to practice, milling about with mugs of beer and soda to prime themselves. Each contest drew a large crowd of spectators who cheered the contestant on. Prizes were awarded on a somewhat arbitrary basis, Julia decided, having to do with the ferocity of the belches and the cheers they received. Mr. Toad, the booth's proprietor, wore a half-toad mask over his eyes with an ostrich feather sticking out the top, and a merchant's costume. Light brown curly hair churned above his mask and down to his shoulders. At the beginning of each contest he stood on the makeshift stage ringing a large brass bell calling out, "Gather 'round, ye gaseous folk!"

Each contestant paid a dollar to come up onto the stage and deliver their finest belch. The prize was a pewter mug with a pair of toasting frogs etched onto it. Julia and Erin had heard people belch the entire alphabet, shy little burps from children, long winded belches that often caused the contestant to rapidly exit the stage with a hand-covered mouth, and one attractive teenage girl who could burp whole sentences. They did a brisk business selling "Sir Frogsly of Bogsly" dolls after each contest.

Mr. Toad turned out to be an actor named Sam from San Francisco who'd been doing both the Northern and Southern Faires for eight years. Between belching contests, Sam came over and chatted with Erin and Julia. He had a modest career as a bit actor, with an emphasis on Shakespeare. "I have the mugs mass-produced in Thailand now," he'd divulged to Julia and Erin once. "Don't tell the Faire, though. They'd have a fit if they found out." Julia was on vigilant guard duty. Even growing up in a family with two brothers, she still found the belching booth slightly disturbing.

"Sam likes you," Erin remarked one afternoon, stitching up the collar of a frog doll's nightie.

"He's cute, but... please... a guy who runs a belching contest? It would just be another addition to my Gallery of Ghouls."

"Still, you have to give him a little credit. He's a Shakespearean actor trying to make an extra buck."

"I know. I have to admit, I did feel a slight attraction in the beginning. Why can't I find a nice finance wizard, or a marine biologist? Why is it always the eccentric types who give me that buzz of excitement?"

"That scent of eccentricity?" Erin joked. "Maybe you should have your palm read at one of those fortune telling tents."

"I'm not sure I want to know if I'm totally doomed to loneliness or not," Julia answered.

"I was kidding," Erin said. "I'm going in the back to lie down for awhile. I'm feeling a little tired."

"Are you okay?"

"Yeah. It's probably the heat."

The Queen's Parade was approaching, on its afternoon trip through the Faire. Town criers announced it, ringing their bells and shouting, "Make Way, Make Way!" followed by children dancing in paper mâché horses, then the highest ranking guildspeople, the orchestra, and the Queen's guards. The royal courtesans and jesters preceded Her Majesty, as did the most notable characters such as Sir Francis Drake, the Earl of Leicester (who'd quickly snatched up the first Squirrel of Leicester doll), and William Shakespeare. "Good Queen Bess" was borne along in her Royal Progress, waving, blowing kisses and toasting the audience with her silver goblet. The combination of her pearl and gold-studded purple dress with her bright orange wig was stunning, and everyone in the booths cried, "God Save the Queen!" as she passed. A rag-tag assortment of characters followed in her wake, including jugglers, peasants, lunatics, and a chicken lady on stilts.

Sam's brass bell clanged, announcing the start of another contest. A crowd gathered around his booth, and the power-belching began again.

"Julia..." Erin's voice called from behind the burlap curtain.

Julia ducked backstage where Erin lay over several straw bales pushed together. She was pale and shivering.

"Something weird is happening..." Her words slurred together. "It feels like... a waterfall is gushing through my head."

"Do you need a candy bar? Where's your bag?" Julia asked.

"No. I don't know. I can't move my right side."

"Oh my God. We've got to get someone!" Julia ran out to front of her booth and yelled, "Help!"

"*Braaaaaaaaaaaaaaaaaaaaapppppp!*"

"Seriously—help! I need a doctor!"

A man in a ruffled white shirt and wire-rimmed glasses stepped away from the tightly packed crowd and said, "I'm a doctor. What's the problem?"

"Behind our booth. My friend... she's going into shock or something. She's a diabetic," Julia added, her voice shaking. He followed her backstage and checked Erin's pulse.

"We need to get her out of here right now," he said, pulling a mobile phone out from a leather bag on his belt. "Go get some strong arms while I call for an ambulance."

Julia ran back out to the front. "Get Sister Ruth!" she yelled to some actors nearby. "Tell her we have an emergency!"

"*Brupppp-brupppp!*"

Just then, the wooden jail-cart appeared in front of the booth, trying to press through the crowd. "Make Way!" the driver called. Incarcerated peasants waved from behind the scraggly bars, belching back at the contestants.

"We need this!" the doctor shouted, stepping out from behind the booth and gesturing toward the cart. "NOW!"

The driver stopped just as Sister Ruth, a middle-aged R.N. dressed as a nun, came running through the crowd. "What's going on?" she panted.

"I think someone's having a stroke," the doctor said, pointing behind the booth.

"Get these people out of the wagon!" Sister Ruth ordered. "We've got to get her down to the front entrance! Guards!!!" she yelled. Elizabethan guardsmen appeared from the crowd and helped the doctor carry Erin out from behind the booth, laying her down in the cart. The doctor and Sister Ruth climbed in with her, shouting at the nearby street performers to push the cart as fast as they could down to the front gates. A flank of armored knights arrived, parting the crowd for the cart to pass through.

"Wait! I need to go with her!" Julia cried.

"Follow us!" Sister Ruth called back.

Sam came running over when he saw the cart rushing off with Sister Ruth and Erin inside.

"What's going on?" he asked, touching Julia's elbow.

She burst into tears. "She's... having a stroke or something... I have to get down there... I don't know... about all my stuff..." Julia trailed off, glancing back and forth between the booth and the wooden cart.

"Don't worry. I'll pack up your stuff. Go ahead. I'll catch up with you later. I've got to get back." He gestured toward his booth.

"Braaaaaaapppppp!"

Julia rolled her eyes and grabbed her bag, making her way through the crowded Faire with tears running down her face. When she got to the front gate, they had just finished loading Erin into an ambulance.

"I'm her friend!" Julia cried breathlessly. "I have to go with her!"

"You'll have to follow us. We're taking her down to Marin General." The EMT slammed the back door of the ambulance shut and they pulled out, turning on the siren. Julia was numb with fear.

Sister Ruth appeared next to her. "Are you alright, dear? You need to calm down before you drive. Have some water," she added, handing Julia a 20th century plastic water bottle.

"Yes. I think I'm okay." Her voice shook.

Julia called Erin's mother from the hospital. "They think she had some kind of stroke. She's getting a CAT scan now."

"Oh my God..."

"Here's the doctor's phone number. He said you can call him in about thirty minutes when he knows more," Julia broke off, crying.

Sam appeared several hours later, looking dashing in his Elizabethan costume minus the toad mask. "I packed up everything and put it behind your booth, except this," he said, handing her the cash box. "How is she?"

"They say she had a mild stroke. She has to stay here for awhile."

Julia had been sitting in the waiting room with her eyes closed, sending a steady beam of light toward Erin. The nurses agreed to let her into the ICU for a couple of minutes, and Julia was happy just to see Erin breathing on her own. Her eyelids fluttered, and she'd raised the fingers on her left hand.

"How are *you?*" Sam asked, in the waiting room.

"I've been better. I have to get back to the house and straighten up before her mother gets here," Julia said absently.

"Need some help?"

"No... thanks. I'm really tired." *And I don't want to complicate things.*

"Here's my phone number," he said, handing her a business card with laughing frogs on it. "You call me right away if you need anything." He gave her a warm hug.

THIRTY-TWO

LATER THAT FALL, JULIA AND SAM SAT IN A BOOTH at The Plum & Thistle Ale House in Santa Rosa, each nursing a pint of stout.

"Boiled hamburgers and greasy potato slices they call 'chips', with everything," Sam said, describing his recent trip to London. "Thank heaven for the Indian food. The weirdest part was having the bars close at eleven. I felt so limited."

"What are 'Mushy Peas'?" Julia mused, focusing on the menu. She was picking up a date vibe from Sam when she'd only wanted to meet for a reconnaissance beer and snack, after not having seen or heard from him in several months.

"Probably some *bloody-awful* side dish," Sam quipped in his best British accent.

"I think I'll try them anyway," Julia said. "I've got to find out."

"So, how is she doing?" he asked, referring to Erin.

"Very well—she's making a full recovery. At first she was slurring her words a lot. It made her sound a little drunk, but after a month or so of speech therapy, she improved. She still limps on her right side a little, and she hates it when you say anything about it."

"Is she going back to work?"

"Maybe in the spring. Sometimes I can't decide whether she's amazingly strong or bullishly stubborn."

The waitress came by with two orders of fish and chips, and a large side dish of mashed green peas which she set in the middle of the table. After she left, Sam nodded and said, "Yep. Mushy Peas."

Julia dabbed her fork into the smooth green mound and sampled them. "They don't taste like anything."

"Not surprising." Sam broke a chip in half and embedded it in the top of the pea-heap. Julia followed suit, breaking off another piece and inserting it next to Sam's.

"Have you given any more thought to the Southern Faire in LA?" Sam asked, adding another half of a chip to the mound.

"No. I mean, I don't want to do it alone. It's too long of a haul, anyway," Julia said, considering the last weeks of the Renaissance Faire after Erin's stroke. She'd had to finish the booth contract by herself. Sam was good company, and she'd even spent the last weekend in his makeshift apartment behind the belching stage. *What the heck*, she shrugged, indulging in a few nights of frolic partly to prove to herself that she wasn't getting too old to be attractive. But then Sam had called her in Santa Rosa, wanting to meet for a drink.

Julia shaped a tail out of the mushy pea-clay. "Besides, I won't have time to make more dolls. I'll be working on the soundtrack of an independent film starting in January. Our friend Steve is producing it."

"Oh yeah? What's it about?" Sam asked, as he continued to push chips into a line on the back of the pea-creature.

Julia began forming a serpent's head on a long neck and answered, "The tidal wave that hit Nicaragua a few years ago." She squeezed little green legs from the sides of the mound and used her fingernails to form tiny webbed feet. "Do you have any acting jobs coming up?" she asked.

"I'm a street performer at the Charles Dickens Faire at Fort Mason this Christmas. I do a bit as the Ghost of Christmas Past," he said, sloshing down the rest of his beer. His nose was larger and redder than she remembered, plus the lack of a fancy merchant costume and half-frog mask left him with a ruddy complexion, a slight paunch, and a self-effacing shrug when he spoke. A nagging sense of déjà vu began to roll over Julia. *Oh, boy. Another funny guy who drinks too much.*

Sam took the leftover fan-tails of his deep fried shrimp and stuck them into the sides of the beast. "Ta-da… fins!" he announced.

The waitress began taking their plates away. "Are you done with this?" she asked, pointing to the chip-studded monster they'd created.

"Yes, *please* take it away," Julia answered.

Moments later, the chef appeared tableside, steaming and extra large in his stained white coat. Beads of sweat glistened on his forehead. "That was a totally immature thing to do! If you didn't like the dish, you should have sent it back." He turned and stalked off to the kitchen.

Julia and Sam stared after him for a few seconds and then broke into muffled laughter.

"Touchy, touchy," Sam said, as they got up to leave.

Outside, the soft fall sun was beginning to set over the unique combination of palm and pine trees in downtown Santa Rosa. Dread began to descend over Julia as she stood on the sidewalk in front of the pub.

"So, what next?" Sam asked, starting to put his arm around her. "Want to see a movie?"

"Sam... I just want to go home."

"Okay. How about we rent something?"

"I mean, I want to go home by myself... and..." she stood back, took a deep breath and centered herself. "I don't think it's going to work out with us being lovers."

Sam wavered, and then said, "But we're so good together."

"I know. It's fun and you're an adorable person," Julia said, looking him squarely in the eyes and speaking earnestly. "Please don't be insulted—I just can't right now. I'm really sorry." Julia could feel the sidewalk underneath her as if the earth were supporting her in this bold, heartfelt expression of sincerity.

"Okay, well, fine then. See you," he said, turning and walking toward his car. Then he stopped. "Wait," he called, coming back. "I need a goodbye hug." They stood together on the sidewalk in a friendly embrace before separating. Julia watched him for a few seconds and then turned, walking down Fourth Street. She could smell the salty air rolling in from the coast. *I finally did it. I resisted.*

THIRTY-THREE

THE FOLLOWING MARCH, Julia and Erin sat in a garden café in Sebastopol, nibbling on falafels and polenta fries.

"Look at all the new growth," Erin remarked, pointing to the tiny green ends of branches on the nearby trees. The rain was taking a break, leaving poached iridescent drops to shimmer in the sunlight. "I'm still *sooo* glad I moved out here," she added.

"Do you think your mother will eventually migrate here, too?" Julia asked.

"Probably not. She found it amusing that the downtown merchants sprayed fake snow in their window displays," Erin laughed, citing her mother's recent Christmas visit. "She's pretty entrenched back east anyway."

"I'm glad you moved here, too. We're so lucky, getting to hang out together for all these years. I can't imagine what my life would be like without you."

They both paused. Erin chewed on a fry while Julia indulged herself in the one thought she avoided saying out loud. *How much longer would Erin's life actually be?* It was a constant inner vigil that seemed to work well over the years.

"Sometimes I think it's just all those blue-green algae molecules holding hands," Erin remarked, referring to her latest health regimen, and reading Julia's mind.

A woman and her three young children entered the café. The two older boys immediately sprinted to the toy box, while the toddler wailed from her stroller. The mother sighed and dropped into a chair.

"God, even her hair looks tired," Erin whispered.

"Yeah, the Haggard Breeders," Julia whispered back.

"It's a dirty job. Someone has to do it," Erin added.

"And people call *us* the spinsters…yikes! That looks like a hostage situation."

"Spinsters… that's such a joke. Besides, look at all the cool single women in history: Florence Nightingale, Susan B. Anthony, Greta Garbo…"

"Willa Cather and Harper Lee," Julia added. "Sometimes I think we just got passed over when it comes to the right combination of reproductive chemicals. We like boys, but neither of us feels driven to breed. There must be a word for people like us, who fall through the cracks of everything."

"How about *'Swinks'*?" Erin laughed.

That night Julia's father called. "I wanted to let you know I'm having a little procedure done tomorrow at the hospital. They just need to *roto-rooter* a clogged artery in my neck. I've had a couple of little 'mini-strokes' and my doctor tells me that it would be a good idea."

"Mini-strokes?" Julia repeated. It didn't seem to fit with the term "little procedure." Her heart began to thump. "How long will you be in the hospital?"

"A few days. It's not a big deal. Just a normal procedure for us old guys," he said with a soft chuckle. "So not to change the subject, but how are your cats?"

"They're fine," Julia answered. "I've been trying to discourage them from bringing birds and mice in through the kitty door. Especially Joey. He likes to show them off. How about Kinkster?"

"He's a real sweetie. He still comes on walks with me."

Julia felt uncomfortable, wishing to return to the original purpose of her father's phone call. "So you'll call me as soon as you can and let me know you're okay?"

"I will. I'll be fine. I love you."

"I love you, too," Julia answered.

Rose called the following evening to report that the surgery had gone well and their father was resting. Then early the next morning the phone rang and it was Teddy. "I just talked to Rose," he said.

"Dad took a turn for the worse sometime last night."

"What? What happened? Did the surgery go bad or something?"

"He was awake, and getting the nurses to quiz him. He remembered all their names and everything. Then he started having trouble breathing. They thought he was having some kind of asthma attack. By the time they got the tracheotomy into him, he was very agitated. They've been giving him Demerol to keep him quiet."

"Shit. So... that's all they know?" Julia grabbed a tissue and dropped into the easy chair by the phone.

"He's had some kind of stroke. But every time they start to let him wake up, he gets freaked out, so they put him under again."

"Should we go back there now?"

"Let's just wait and see what happens," Teddy said.

"Okay. Keep me posted."

"Erin recovered from *her* stroke last summer. Maybe he will, too."

Julia stayed awake most of the night, imagining her father trapped in an eerie, half-lit world, unable to regain consciousness. She sat up with a candle on her night table, sending mental streams of light toward his hospital bed in Pennsylvania.

"Low oxygen for 22 minutes?!?" Julia cried into the phone at Teddy the next day. "What the hell does that mean? Did they forget to turn it on all the way? Christ, this is the 90s! How did this happen?!?"

"They said it was all the swelling in his neck from the surgery. It took a while to keep his airway clear."

"We have to go *now*," she wept.

"I spoke with his brain surgeon. He said we could use his name to get a family emergency fare with the airlines. I'll come down and pick you up on the way to San Francisco."

The next day Julia packed a few things and, deciding at the last minute to bring some comfort reading, grabbed *Jitterbug Perfume* on her way out.

"...to boldly go where no man has gone before!"

Nate turned up the volume of the small hospital TV as loud as it would go. "Wake up, Dad!" he called. *"Star Trek's* on." He rubbed his hands together and placed them over his father's forehead, then smoothed them gently over his temples and ears.

Ed lay in the ICU with tubes marking the entrance of every orifice, including a new hole in the center of his throat for the ventilator. A giant, freshly sutured scar ran down the entire length of his neck. His false teeth lay submerged in a glass on the table, leaving his lips to curl over his gums. His wavy hair was completely grey now, and he lay slightly tilted on one side, like a ship listing at sea. One eye would occasionally open, and he twitched now and then as if to try and remove the sensor on his thumb.

"He really hates that thing," Rose remarked.

Teddy and Julia stood on the other side of the bed, totally spaced out from their flight. They'd had a two-hour layover in Washington D.C. where they tried to sleep in the airport chairs, and then a bouncy ride in the puddle jumper to Scranton.

"His lips look so chapped," Julia said. Dipping a Q-tip into a glass of water, she rubbed it across his dry, flaky lips. A nurse came in and shooed them away, so they all headed down to the cafeteria. Then Julia remembered that she'd left her overnight bag in the room and went back to get it.

Alone for a few minutes with her father and an annoying cacophony of monitor beeps, she put her hand over his heart and bent down next to his ear. "I want you to know that whatever you decide to do is okay with me. I'm proud of who you are, and I promise I'll be all right if you want to let go and see what else is out there."

Ed turned his head. It seemed as if he were summoning every muscle he could find to open his eyes and pull his lips into a smile. She knew that he'd heard her.

When the CAT scan revealed one major stroke and another small one, the neurologist told them, "The best-case scenario would be limited mobility on his right side. The respirator is only doing about twenty to thirty percent of his breathing, and he's still initiating on his own. But truthfully, I'm not very optimistic. Give it another day or so. Then you'll have to make a decision."

Everyone cried in the car on the way back to Ed and Rose's.

"He put a DNR order on when he checked into the hospital," Teddy said. "He must have known something was up."

"He tried to downplay it," Rose said. "Even though the mini-strokes were making him temporarily blind in one eye, his doctor had to practically collar him into the hospital."

Julia and her brothers called Clarisse when they got back to the house. "Remember," their mother warned, "people in comas can still hear you, so be careful what you say. He has a lot of physical stamina, though. Maybe he'll pull through."

"He's an old battle ax," said Erin, in a subsequent phone call. "He'll probably wake up and last another twenty years."

They stayed at Ed and Rose's for a week, driving back and forth to the hospital every day. A large East Indian population in the greater Nanticoke area added a slightly magical flavor to the experience. Women came and went in brightly colored saris, while Nate and Julia entertained themselves by trying to pronounce the doctors' names on their office signs. In the first few days, they'd massaged their father, joked with him, told funny stories, and managed to get him to twitch and blink more. When Julia put her hands on his right leg and offered to pay back her college tuition, his entire right side jumped. Everyone saw it. Even Dr. Krishnamurti was impressed, and granted Ed another two weeks in the hospital to see if there were any further improvements.

"Hallo!" he would call into Ed's ear, shaking him. "Dr. Lloyd? Can you hear me?"

By the end of the week, he was moving both legs and opening his eyes. Some friends from AA stopped by, and it quickly became the rowdiest room on the ICU.

"You're the one who made the *Titanic* shirts!" one of them exclaimed to Julia.

Then Teddy had to get back to work, and Julia was due at a recording studio in San Francisco the following week. She hated the idea of leaving her father, but Nate and Uda would be coming up from New York to help Rose keep an eye on him.

During the six weeks Ed spent in a coma, Julia felt suspended over a chasm of bewilderment while her father lingered in the fathomless space between life and death.

"Maybe he's still deciding," her teacher Robin suggested, after an aikido class. "Sometimes people go back and forth a number of times before they make up their minds."

Julia and her brothers teetered between the panic of having their father wake up with extreme brain damage and the grim void of losing him forever. They phoned each other every night, exchanging bits of information about comas, eulogizing him and hoping for a miracle at the same time. After a few weeks, the doctors had unplugged his ventilator and he continued to breathe on his own.

"He could still have a miraculous recovery and start a religious cult where they wear white and eat raw vegetables," Julia said to Rose one evening.

"That would be nice. But there's something I have to tell you. The last day we were all together in his hospital room, even though we thought he was improving, I could feel him pleading with me to let him go."

A few days later, they unplugged the feeding tube and Ed was moved to a hospice facility closer to home.

"I don't think he's in there anymore," Nate said. "They say his movements are mostly reflexive."

"Maybe he'll be able to slip away on his own now," Julia mused.

The next morning Rose called. With Erin at work, Julia had the house to herself as she listened to Rose brief her about the phone call she was about to receive from a social worker at the hospice. "Get yourself ready. She's going to ask you whether or not they should resuscitate your father if he starts having problems."

Julia was seated on the living room couch when the woman from hospice called. "Miss Lloyd? I'm sorry to be meeting you under these circumstances. I'm going to ask you two questions. All you have to say is yes or no."

"Okay. I'm ready." Everyone else in the family had already agreed to say no, so Julia figured a one-word answer wouldn't be too difficult. Still, she stood up to center herself, as if she were about to face an attacker in aikido.

"In the event that your father starts having breathing problems, should we take him back to the hospital to be revived?"

Julia shook her head, drawing in a breath to answer the woman, but her voice caught. She had to clench her teeth to force a sticky "No" through them.

"If he stops breathing on his own, should he be artificially resuscitated?"

She opened her mouth, but nothing came out. She suddenly felt dizzy, and clung to the back of the couch with one hand. The social worker waited patiently, until Julia was finally able to croak out a softer "No."

They said goodbye and she hung up sobbing as she crumpled onto the couch.

THIRTY-FOUR

"IBELIEVE ALL BOATS HAVE SPIRITS," Julia said a few days later, from a wharf-side restaurant table in Bodega Bay. Celebrating her fortieth birthday at The Tides, her small group of friends watched fishing boats chug into the harbor, each one with a gull and pelican escort in its wake.

"Evidently the seagulls seem to think so," Michael remarked.

All Julia wanted was a quiet, non-intrusive gathering. She didn't want to mess with the cosmic order of her father's condition by pushing him one way or the other. Erin was there and Steve too, on a break from his travels. Michael and Monte had driven up from San Francisco for the occasion, and they all sat at a table on the patio in the soft, gossamer blush of a spring afternoon. Sailboat riggings clanged against masts in the gentle breeze. Julia flipped through the pages of *The Tibetan Book of Living and Dying* Michael had just given her, while Erin chattered about her upcoming summer trip to the Amazon to assist Steve's filming of indigenous South Americans.

"This one rainforest tribe, the Shintui, creates herbal healing remedies that surpass anything the pharmaceutical companies produce, so of course, the corporate world is attempting to demonize them. Steve's producing a documentary about their sustainable culture."

"We'll be in a river boat for a few days, and then stay right in the village with the tribe," Steve added. "I can't wait to show Erin the pink dolphins that live in the Amazon."

Julia felt an aching in the pit of her stomach when she thought about being alone in the house for the summer, but she wanted Erin to have a good time. She was happy just to let everyone else carry on the conversation while she sat back with a Campari and soda, basking in the warmth of her friendships.

"So Julia, what do you *really* want for your birthday?" Michael asked. His dark hair had begun to sprout tiny gray highlights over his temples, and his carefully tended Fu Manchu moustache displayed the signs of early salt and pepperism. Julia nearly chuckled out loud at the sight of her old college lover now gay, a doctor, and brilliant.

"Besides my father miraculously waking up from a coma and resuming a normal life? Let me see..." she paused. "I want to feel real love. I know it sounds like a cliché, but I don't think I've ever felt it. Of course, I've *started* to, and I've been majorly infatuated," she added quickly, hoping Michael wouldn't be insulted. "I've enjoyed a long, close partnership, and even been to the brink of baby-making a few times in the height of passionate sex. But then I feel like I'm compromising my feelings, and things invariably start to look empty after a few months... or years. Plus it would be nice if the guys who look like they're having the most fun don't always turn out to be drunkards."

That night, Julia woke to the sound of women's voices singing. At first she thought she was in a recording studio, listening to a track of back-up singers. She began drifting to sleep when she heard it again. The distinct sound of four or five voices, swirling around her bedroom ceiling. It was the purest thing she'd ever heard. Other-worldly. Not even the best sound engineer could've come up with something that perfect in a studio. It reverberated for a few seconds after she sat up. Instead of the cold, anxious sweat and pounding heartbeat that usually follows a nightmare, she felt bathed in happiness.

When the phone rang the next morning, Julia reached for it reluctantly, fully aware that her father had died.

"He passed away last night after visiting hours were over," Teddy told her, adding that the airline flights were daunting, even the bereavement ones.

"Give me a few minutes," she said, feeling a wave of choking emotion begin to roll over her.

Julia sat on her bed and cried. Erin had already left for her morning class, but Julia was quickly flanked by their cats, Joey and Bee, both curious and sympathetic. She could feel her father close to her. She'd just read a passage in *The Tibetan Book of Living and Dying* where Sogyal Rinpoche spoke of how peoples' souls are extremely sensitive and clairvoyant following death. She opened the book, lit a candle and choked her way through the Tibetan phowa[1]:

> *Through your blessing, grace and guidance,*
> *through the power of the light that streams from you:*
> *May all Edward's negative karma,*
> *destructive emotions, obscurations, and*
> *blockages be purified and removed,*
> *May he know himself forgiven for all the*
> *harm he may have thought and done,*
> *May he accomplish this profound practice of phowa,*
> *and die a good and peaceful death,*
> *And through the triumph of his death, may*
> *he be able to benefit all other beings,*
> *living or dead.*[2]

She drew her fingers through her curly hair, grabbed a box of tissues and sat down at her computer to look for airfares.

When Erin came back, she sat with Julia quietly, hugging her as she cried. Then she cooked a light meal and lit candles all over the house, while Julia spoke to Clarisse. Her mother would be staying on Long Island, and see them the day after the funeral. Steve came home with a bottle of wine, and the three of them sat on the deck in the flickering light, speculating about life after death, and where they thought the spirit might go.

"Maybe all the pets you've ever had come to escort you," Julia mused, thinking about her father's cat, Jake.

"Did he leave any instructions about how he wanted to be buried?" Steve asked.

"No. I mean, nothing besides cremation. In fact, my mother told me

---

[1] *Tibetan practice of cleansing and transference of consciousness*
[2] *The Tibetan Book of Living and Dying, by Sogyal Rinpoche, HarperCollins 1994, p. 215.*

he used to think funerals were barbaric. Rose mentioned something about spreading his ashes over Long Island Sound, though."

"When my time comes," said Erin, "I want as little trouble and expense as possible. I bet I'll have so much fun being able to fly, that I wouldn't want people crying over me. An outdoor party would be nice, though. With Chinese lanterns and Mai Tais."

THIRTY-FIVE

THE MAJESTIC TRESTLES of the Lackawanna railway loomed over Julia, Teddy, Nate and Uda, as they headed toward Nanticoke. When Ed and Rose's pastor came over to accompany them to the funeral home, Julia asked to speak at the service on behalf of the children.

"Are you sure?" he asked. "Some people say they want to, but when the time comes, they find they can't get out of their seats."

"I think I can do it. I'm used to performing. We're part of the other half of our dad's life—the one before this one," Julia said, referring to his life before the spaghetti dinners all those years ago.

"Okay then. When it's time, I'll look over at you. If you don't think you can do it, signal by shaking your head. Otherwise, we'll be glad to hear you speak."

"Time to get grounded," Nate said, as they stood on the porch of the funeral home the next morning.

Julia took a deep breath and went in. Everyone else headed for the room with the casket while she made a restroom check to clean up the mascara she'd already cried off. "Stupid idea," she thought, dabbing the black smudges under her eyes. "Stupid, stupid, stupid."

When she came out she realized she was left to enter the viewing room by herself. Standing at the doorway, the smell of flowers was overwhelming. Her father lay in the Newport Poplar among the folds of silk, surrounded by bouquets. Energy poured from Julia's heart as she walked toward the casket, as if a giant magnet were pulling her down the aisle.

The funereal mystery was over in an instant. Ed looked much better than the last time she'd seen him. He was dressed in a dark blue suit with tiny pin stripes and a paisley tie. He had his boat propeller tie-tack and the lapel camel pin, with his hands folded over his chest and his glasses on, as if he were resting between clients. They'd put a little too much rouge on his lips, so he appeared vaguely amused by the situation. She could hear Nate sobbing quietly as he sat in one of the chairs with Uda beside him.

Julia reached into a rolled-up scarf and quietly drew out her Japanese *tanto*—a small wooden knife used in aikido practice. She leaned over the casket. "Looks like we both turned out to be warriors of one kind or another. Would you hold onto this for a little while?" she whispered, setting it next to her father's right hand.

Teddy came up beside her. "What's that for?"

"It's just something I wanted to do," she answered. "My teacher's suggestion. Nobody else needs to know about it."

The afternoon was a blur of guests moving past the casket and through the receiving line.

"He was a great man," people would say. "He saved my life," or, "I wouldn't be here today if it weren't for him." They spotted Teddy right away as the oldest son. "You're a dead ringer," they'd say, offering a hand.

"Not an expression *I* would have chosen today," Julia muttered. Sometimes they would miss her entirely, partly because she was the smallest person in the line, but mostly because of Teddy's astonishing resemblance to his father. Occasionally Rose would turn to them and make discreet comments about the guests. "That one was a total mess when she first came in," or, "We didn't think he was going to come around at all." The recording of a Brahms Requiem featuring Ed with his Singer's Guild wove its way through the clustered mourners.

When there was a break, Julia and Nate leaned over their father.

"It almost looks like he's still breathing," Nate said.

Charles, the funeral director told them, "It's because your mind is accustomed to seeing him alive, and trying to fool you into believing that he still is."

Julia touched Ed's hand. "It's really hard... and cold."

Nate reached in and felt it. "Yeah... weird. My first dead guy."

Teddy abstained.

As the afternoon dragged on and people trickled in and out, Julia wished she hadn't worn her stylish Italian boots. Once the initial shock of seeing the body was over, they talked about the food they'd seen arriving back at the house.

"How can we even think of eating at a time like this?" Julia wondered out loud.

"I don't know," Teddy agreed, "But that lobster bisque looked pretty good."

"Yeah, I bet Dad misses that already," Nate said.

"He's probably hanging around to see who shows up," Rose added, glancing around the ceiling.

After the first viewing, they drove back up to the house, kicked off their shoes and snacked. Kinkster the cat wandered around, acting unaware that he'd brought a live chipmunk in through the kitty door the day before. The Have-A-Heart trap Teddy had picked up at the hardware store hadn't attracted the chipmunk-at-large, even though it was slathered with peanut butter. Squirrels milled around on the patio outside, eyeing the sliding glass door. Julia was scooping a handful of peanuts from the jar Ed kept by the door when she saw the chipmunk leap from behind the television. She shrieked, and they all jumped up and chased it into the living room, where it hid behind the baseboard heater and squeaked at them.

"I can't believe I screamed at that," she muttered to herself.

"This is going to be the big one," Rose projected, when they returned to the funeral home for the evening viewing. From seven o'clock on, a constant line of people streamed in the door past the casket, shaking hands with the family. All the doctors from the community came to pay their respects, and every single nurse from Shifting Pines was there. Hundreds of people Ed had treated came through the line; slick, achiever types, bewildered looking older people, and twenty-something recovering addicts, all brimming with gratitude. Rose looked tired. She was already burnt out from the long haul of Ed's coma, and began sneezing halfway through the viewing.

As the evening wound down and the last of the grievers trickled out, Julia went back into the room where Ed lay, selecting a perfect red rose from one of the bouquets. Placing it over Ed's heart, she kissed his cheek and said, "For good luck in your next thing." She slid her *tanto* out and wrapped it in the scarf. Rose and Charles came back into the room and Charles removed Ed's rings, placing them in a small envelope. He handed it to Rose. Julia realized that it was Rose's last private moment with Ed, and she left the room to sit on a bench in the hallway with her brothers, where she wept quietly. Then they drove back up the hill through the mist.

The next morning they got up slowly, each one carefully giving the other space to get ready and have enough hot water. Teddy and Nate helped Julia polish up her speech while they nibbled on bagels. Crocuses and daffodils bloomed on the ridge behind the patio while robins fluttered around cheerfully on the warm spring morning.

"He's supposed to *be* here. He shouldn't have to be missing this," Nate said.

A soft breeze rang the wind chimes, sending low, rhythmic pulses through the air as if it were possible to signal the dead.

Julia glanced out the front window. A long black limousine was parked outside, and the chauffeur stood next to it, smoking a cigarette. "You guys—there's a gigantic ride out there waiting for us."

They arrived at the church in the limousine, looking like a cliché of the stricken family, all in black with sunglasses. Aunt Margaret and her husband, Alan, waited at the top of the steps. Ushers handed them the service program and led them to their seats. "Edward Joseph Lloyd, Born June 20, 1923, Entered into Rest April 30, 1995," read the cover. It still felt surreal. Unbelievable.

The service began, and Julia heard the organist make a tiny mistake. Imagining that her father heard it too, they had a private laugh together. When the first hymn started, she forced herself to sing instead of cry. The pastor and a pair of acolytes wheeled the closed casket slowly up the aisle and parked it next to the pew where the family sat.

When the choir began the anthem, "Jesu, Joy of Man's Desiring," Julia thought she would die herself. She keeled over at the waist, sobbing, when she heard her father's voice calling her softly, "Julia, Julia... my sweet little pearl..." Uncle Alan put his arms around her and helped her back to an upright position.

Then Ed's AA sponsor stood up and delivered an upbeat eulogy about how much Ed loved food. He described Ed's reaction to a really good cheesecake when they first met.

"Bells went off—whistles—there may as well have been fireworks! And you know the little indentations in peoples' desks that hold paper clips? He kept M&M's in those!" The church erupted with laughter.

Afterwards, the pastor looked at Julia and she nodded. She stepped up to the lectern and thought she heard her own heart beating over the microphone.

"Years ago," she explained to the congregation, "Our father had the same sparkle you've come to know and love, except *he just had a little drinking problem.*" The whole church broke into a chuckle. She went on to describe Ed as a sportsman, a diver, a fisherman, and animal lover. "You can honor him by emulating the things you liked about him," she said. Then she asked them to join her in the Tibetan *phowa*.

"Use the image of your own deity," she told them gently. "Imagine its love pouring down toward Ed, drawing him into its light." As she glanced over the church, she was surprised to see people actually closing their eyes in meditation, as if they were trying it.

Afterward, they filed downstairs where the church ladies had prepared tables with coffee and cheesecake. People were calm, even joking about the things Ed had done that made them laugh. Several of them asked Julia where the *phowa* came from, and if they could get copies of it. She felt as if they had all done him a great favor.

There was a mountain of food back at the house, and loads of people. Julia felt slightly nauseous as she changed into jeans and a black silk shirt. *Okay, we're finished now. Why do we have to keep entertaining? Can't we just be miserable by ourselves?* But she stayed cordial, talking and feeding the squirrels that came up to the sliding glass doors. "He used to do that when he was little," Aunt Margaret remarked. "He got the squirrels to climb up the fire escape."

The neighbors from across the street stopped by to tell Julia and her brothers that they would always have an image of Ed taking his daily walk with his cats, carrying his golf putter along.

When everyone finally left, Rose took a nap while Nate, Uda, Teddy and Julia went for a walk. Julia grabbed her father's golf club on her way out. "Rose says that Dad made peace this past year with the pain he carried about his alcoholism," she said, swinging the putter back and forth absently.

"*And* he got to be Santa in the Nanticoke Thanksgiving Parade," Nate added.

As they passed the golf course, Teddy spotted a green near the road with some golf balls surrounding the hole. "Go ahead and hit one in his honor, Julia," he suggested.

"But I suck at golf," she said, glancing toward the clubhouse.

"Come on. No one's around. I double-dog dare you."

Julia scrambled over the fence and putted a ball past the hole twice, then tapped it in.

That evening there was more scuffling in the kitchen. Teddy and Nate jumped up and chased the chipmunk into Ed's bathroom. Julia heard them banging on the shower walls and the floor.

"We got him," Nate announced, as Teddy emerged with a covered bowl. They took it out to the patio and opened the lid. The chipmunk jumped out and stood on the garden wall for a few seconds to get his bearings. Then he sniffed the evening air and swaggered into the bushes.

The next morning Julia woke up at dawn. She stayed in bed trying to figure out where she was, when she began hearing the first birds of the day. More of them joined in, and the sound swelled to a dense wall of peeping and twittering outside the window. In its core, she distinctly heard Erin's voice say, "Yeah, bird world."

Dammit! Julia thought. *How can they sing so loud? Don't those stupid birds know what just happened?* She got up and slammed the window shut.

Rose's cold had leveled her by then. "Let's talk about doing something with the ashes later on," she wheezed between coughs. "But please, choose some things of your father's you really want before you go." Julia chose his brass ship's clock and the *Titanic* shirt she'd made a few years back. Charles showed up and they passed around death certificates and copies of the will. Then they hugged Rose goodbye and headed for Long Island to see Clarisse.

Julia slept most of the way until the car began bouncing over potholes on the Cross Bronx Expressway. Tired of processing the events of the last two months, everyone sat quietly and let a classic rock station fill the space. When they reached Bayville, Clarisse and Don were cooking dinner.

"Oh boy, more food," Teddy joked.

"Well, you've got to keep your stamina up," said Don. "Especially if you're flying. Keeps the immune system strong."

Julia and her brothers walked down to the beach and watched the gentle waves lapping at the sand.

"Well, we did it," Teddy said.

"Yeah, what a long haul," Julia added.

"I wish you guys didn't have to leave tomorrow," Nate said, skimming a rock over the surface of the water.

"We'll come back in the summer and do the ashes. Charter a boat and spread them over The Wreck or something," Julia suggested.

Later that evening, Julia sat on the porch with Clarisse, sipping tea. "I really *am* proud of him. He made such a great recovery." She was all cried out by then. "I just wish you didn't have to bear the brunt of his problems, Mom."

Clarisse nodded. "But remember, we had lots of good years too, with the boat and everything."

"Yeah, we did have a few adventures."

"I have something I want to give you. It's a little silly, but I thought you might want to have it." Clarisse went upstairs, and returned with a small white box, handing it to Julia. "I've been saving this for years."

Julia opened it, carefully unwrapping the crumpled tissue paper to reveal a white and gold-embellished porcelain reindeer.

"It's from a set I made once," Clarisse said. "This is the last one left."

A chill swept through Julia, carrying the faint memory of her father angrily sweeping Santa and His Eight Tiny Reindeer from the mantle with one hand. "This one's a survivor," she said softly, rubbing its shiny white back.

The next day, the customs scanner at JFK Airport revealed Ed's ship's clock in Julia's bag, sending out a stern electronic beep. The attendants made her unpack it and unravel her entire kimono bathrobe, where she'd carefully rolled it. On the verge of tears, she had just enough time to stuff it back into her bag before she bolted to the nearest restroom and cried her heart out.

Back in San Francisco, the eucalyptus trees waved Teddy and Julia through Golden Gate Park toward the bridge. Happy to be home on the west coast, they sped over the hills toward Sonoma County.

"Whew," Julia remarked, when Teddy pulled off the freeway at Santa Rosa. They wound through the quiet neighborhoods until they arrived on Julia's street, where a number of cars were parked in front of the house. "I wonder what Erin's up to?"

Teddy parked a few doors down, and helped Julia carry her bags.

"Come on in and rest for awhile before you head home," she suggested.

Steve was sitting on the front porch, rocking in the wicker chair with Joey in his lap. His face was pale and streaked with tears.

"Where's Erin?"

"She's gone."

"What do you mean she's gone? Where?"

The front door was ajar, and Julia could see Erin's mother and some other people moving around inside. A wave of shock ran through her. It started deep in her solar plexus and then burst, until she was shaking visibly.

"She died yesterday."

"What? No!"

Julia shivered on the front porch, gripping the railing for support. Erin's mother saw her through the screen and opened the door. They locked eyes and wrapped their arms around each other.

THIRTY-SIX

JULIA SAT IN THE KITCHEN, trying to decide whether to attempt grocery shopping or just return to bed, where she'd spent a great deal of the past several weeks. Joey and Bee sidled up to her and took turns brushing against her legs. Steve had stayed on for a while, and over and over again they watched the video from the church where Erin was permeated by the ghost. Then there was the letter, which Julia figured she'd read about a hundred times by now:

My Dearest Julia,

If you're reading this, you're probably still crying, so stop it. We both knew this would happen more sooner than later. When that ghost at the church walked through me, I felt myself leave the planet for a moment. I became bigger than anything I've ever known, as if my body had burst into a million particles of energy. How I continued to pursue a career involving the study of humans still puzzles me, when I should have switched to quantum physics, or paranormal psychology. But the point is, I had a strong sensation of my impending mortality that night. Curse me and call me selfish if you like, but I couldn't sabotage the spontaneity and joyfulness of our friendship by telling you. It would've wrecked everything, and I wanted to have as much fun as I could in the time I had left.

As my mother has probably told you, I'm leaving the house to you, plus this small, personal artifact to remember me by. I know you'll treat them both with utter respect.

Julia, we had the best time being humans together. Our precious friendship was more than a person could have hoped for. I'll really be pissed off if you don't keep it together after this because you're such an amazing person. Okay. That sounded like a cliché. Sorry. Anyway, if you're hanging around in bed, please get up and do something interesting today, try not to cry yourself into prunehood, and keep an open heart.

Love Always, My Wonderful Friend,
See you on the other side.

Erin

Wiping her tears, Julia folded the letter and returned to her bedroom, where she tucked it gently in her nightstand drawer next to the box that held Erin's glass eye. The last few weeks had dissolved into a blur of heartache and soggy Kleenex. She'd tried to recite the *phowa* for both her father and Erin, but usually crumpled in a weeping blob before she could finish. She resented not being able to mourn each one separately. She'd been out a few times—once early on, to the Neptune Society with Erin's family. Erin had choreographed her own funeral in advance, with specific instructions not to do anything except cremate her and have a party. She was emphatic about not having a viewing of any kind, wanting instead to be remembered as a living person.

Braced with her love for Erin, Julia carried on with the soirée in their backyard, complete with Chinese lanterns, exotic cocktails, and blown-up photos. She invited Erin's friends from Sonoma State, her own friends from aikido, and people they knew from the neighborhood. The worst part was making all the phone calls to tell people that Erin had died suddenly of a heart attack. Even Morty, now balding, made a brief, cross-country trip from New York with his wife, so there were moments of laughter as they recounted some of Erin's crazy antics at school. Clarisse and Don offered to come out and keep Julia company, but the house had been so packed with Erin's family that she politely declined.

Now she longed for peace and quiet. Yesterday she'd taken Steve to the Park n' Ride for his return to the Amazon, which Erin had ordered him to do in his own letter from her. Michael had been up and down from San Francisco a number of times, arriving an hour after Julia first called him. He sat with her on the living room couch for hours, holding her hand silently as she wept.

Grief rolled over Julia in waves. One minute, she'd be in the backyard cracking jokes in her mind with both Erin and her father, and the next she'd be overcome with sobbing. She didn't trust herself to go out to a store for fear of breaking down in public. Even more disconcerting was the huge aching hole left by Erin and her father. Sometimes she felt transparent, as if they'd led her to the very brink of life and death, giving her the opportunity to peek over the edge and see infinity, and then left her. Mostly though, she couldn't bear the thought of having to be around people who were cheerful.

"Funny," she told Michael one night. "I asked for real love on my birthday and it's never felt so real as now."

The ferry chugged slowly through thick fog. Chinese lanterns glowed from invisible strings around the deck where couples promenaded, laughing and clinking champagne glasses. Foghorns called to each other in the darkness.

Suddenly a flame burst through the forward deck, exploding in a ball of fire over the boat. There was another blast, and the captain hurried through the crowd in his white uniform. "Now it's every man for himself!" he cried, waving his arms.

"Oh come on, that's such a cliché," snorted Erin.

The front of the boat was engulfed in flames. Its funnels blew smoke and tooted helplessly as the ferry began to sink.

"I think he's coming," Erin said.

"Who?"

"Christ, dummy. Didn't you ask for a major deity during the phowa?"

"Yeah, well... I guess. Not for myself, though."

"Shhhh! He's about to walk by."

Julia glanced down the deck at the receiving line. A bustle of white robes approached, and she held her breath in anticipation. His entourage arrived in front of Julia and she reached out her hand, feeling a surge of love and compassion. Just before they touched, he morphed into a full moon which grew larger until it burst, drenching Julia in white light.

Then she was sinking, headed for the bottom in the glowing boat.

"There's the markers!" she heard her father call out, as the boat plunged downward through a curtain of seaweed and plankton, its bow still aflame.

"I always wondered what this would feel like," she mused. The boat paused, as if looking for a suitable place to land, and then dropped into the silt, rocking a few times before coming to a stop.

"So, are we supposed to be like, born again or something?" Erin asked.

"I don't know. I thought that meant you got to stay at the surface. Funny how we can still breathe, though," Julia answered.

She began to wake up, as she heard her father's voice fading in the distance:

"There's something else..."

Joey and Bee were on her bed, picking their way over the blanket, plying Julia with soft head-butts and licks until she got up to feed them. Pondering the *"something else,"* from her dream, she forced herself to ride her mountain bike over to Annadel Park. Suddenly fuming that Erin hadn't given her time to say goodbye, she pounded to the top of the Rough-Go trail and flung herself into the chilly water of Lake Ilsanjo. She imagined steam hissing from her angry body and laughed out loud.

Returning to aikido a few days later, she broke two wooden swords whacking the rubber tire after class.

"It's all right," Robin said. "They're the cheap ones. Better them than the students."

A few weeks later, Julia sat at The Cantina with Jim and Gail, a couple from her Adult Children of Alcoholics group which met in the very basement of the Lutheran church where she played the organ. Munching on a quesadilla, she attempted to describe her Jesus dream.

"That sounds pretty amazing," Jim commented.

"Yeah, it's like he became the whole universe or something," Gail added.

"What did it feel like?"

Julia suddenly felt a deep urge to be alone. The pain of shifting back and forth between despair and trying to be considerate of Ed and Erin's early stages of death was exhausting. Gail and Jim were such a sweet, clean-cut couple. A little too mainstream for Julia's taste but still, they were kindred spirits in a search for inner peace. "Kind of like a bath of light," she answered.

"Oh..." they both nodded.

"Well, I've got to get going," Julia said, pushing her chair back. "I have a recording session tomorrow in the city."

"Can we give you a ride home?"

"Thanks, but it's only a few blocks from here. I'd like to get some fresh air anyway."

On her way out, Julia had a delicious flashback of her old Walking Tours in the Spaghetti Afterlife with the Invisible Girl. *How about an encore?* She bought a pack of cigarettes from a machine in the lobby and took off down the street.

Downtown Santa Rosa was nearly deserted. The sun had already set, leaving an orgasm of pink and yellow clouds in the western sky. Pausing to light a cigarette, she inhaled and nearly choked. It tasted like a sickening combination of gas and chemicals. *Ugh! I can't believe people still do this!* Dizziness overwhelmed her, and she bent down to scrape the burning end off with the bottom of her shoe. *Stinking tar sticks...* Standing back up, she looked around for a garbage can to throw the entire pack away and quickly became nauseated. Ducking into the alley next to the furniture store, she threw up. Afterwards, she glanced around the empty alley and imagined her father chuckling, "That'll learn ya."

She continued down Third Street, obsessing about the dream. *There's something else? What else? In the water? At The Wreck?* Memories of the soft lapping of the waves against the hull during the night swirled through her mind. *That's too long ago to matter anymore.* "You have a tendency to alienate yourself when things get difficult," she recalled Ed telling her once, when he was first in recovery. *Did he mean there's something else in Adult Children of Alcoholics?* She'd gone quite a few times in the past month and cried a lot. She liked the people, but couldn't figure out why they wanted to repeat the same shortcomings about themselves at the beginning each meeting. *So I'm alienated. Big Deal. What difference does it make? Who even cares? I'm invisible anyway.* "Something else..." she snorted. *Jeez... seems like it's all just a big fucking pile of nothing else anymore.* Tears stung the edges of her eyes as Julia turned the corner onto E Street. Passing the camera store, she sensed rustling behind her, and quickly gathered herself. *Dammit, I should have been paying more attention.*

"Bitch, I'm gonna give it to you soooo good," a voice growled.

Julia whipped around to face a paunchy man in a sweatshirt and baseball cap. The smell of stale beer quickly filled her nostrils.

"The hell you are."

The man lunged at her. She stepped back, but he caught a piece of her jacket. She grabbed his sleeve underneath his elbow and yanked it down, drawing him toward her as she drove the heel of her other hand into his face.

"What the fuck *are* you?!?" he cried, reeling as blood dribbled down over his lips. He drew a knife from his pocket and took a slash at her, but she willowed back again, letting it pass. Then she sprang forward and grabbed the back of his arm, pushing him into a stucco storefront. She tried to take his knife, but he twisted his hand and cut the side of her wrist. Then she kicked him hard on the outside of his knee and he screamed, dropping to the ground. A police cruiser appeared at the curb and whooped its siren. Two officers stepped out in the flashing light.

"That crazy bitch attacked me!" the man screamed, clutching his knee.

"He—came up behind me—and—had a knife," Julia stammered, trembling. *Oh shit.* She turned away and threw up again.

"You okay?" One of the officers touched her shoulder. Julia straightened up and saw that it was a woman.

"Hold on, you're bleeding," the officer said, heading toward the squad car. She returned wearing rubber gloves and bandaged Julia's wrist while the other officer handcuffed the man and called for an ambulance.

Julia swore she felt Erin and her father sitting next to her on the gurney while the doctor stitched up her wrist.

"Good thing you got cut," said Officer McKean, the woman from the police cruiser, stepping into the emergency room.

"Huh?"

"Otherwise he could try to press assault charges."

"But I was defending myself!"

"We know. And just between you and me, that was some darn good fightin'."

THIRTY-SEVEN

O N A WARM OCTOBER MORNING MONTHS LATER, Julia sat on the edge of a Zodiac inflatable adjusting her dive mask. The sun shone brightly in the cove just south of Mendocino, causing the gentle ripples on the sea's surface to sparkle.

"We couldn't have asked for a better day," remarked Rob, her scuba instructor.

"Yeah," another diver chimed in. "Usually people take off from work when they hear about this kind of visibility. Looks like we're in for a *black tide*," he added, pointing to the increasing number of divers gathered on the shore in wetsuits.

"Is your air on?" her dive buddy Eva asked.

"Yes." Julia checked her gauge again. Ever since she'd seen a poster for the Try Scuba! class at the Y, she'd been hooked. She hovered near the bottom of the pool that first evening, watching the colors of the sunset shift from under the water as she breathed through the regulator. The weightlessness was intoxicating. She signed up for the Open Water Certification course right away, and spent the rest of the summer diving the coast of Sonoma and Mendocino until Rob talked her into taking the Advanced Class. Now, sitting on the edge of the inflatable, she got ready for her first one hundred-foot dive. She put the regulator in her mouth, her hand to her mask, and rolled off the Zodiac backwards. Landing in the water upside down in an explosion of bubbles, she waited patiently until she bobbed back up. The empty hole left by Erin and her father was beginning to fill in, but now she wished they were here. Then she shrugged. *Well, maybe they are.*

Eva popped up next to her. She took her regulator out and said, "Just go down slowly. There's no hurry. When you get past fifty feet, you'll start to sink faster, so remember to neutralize yourself with your BC vest. You'll use up your air and bottom-time more quickly, too. Ready?"

Julia nodded. She pressed the button on her buoyancy vest and the air hissed out slowly as she dipped beneath the surface. She enjoyed the state of surrender necessary to release herself to the underwater world. The visibility was spectacular for the Northern California coast. More than fifty feet. Keeping an eye on her dive computer, she descended alongside Eva, while pinnacles of rock encrusted with sea life rose around them. She pinched her nose and blew, equalizing the pressure in her ears. Nearby, the kelp forests waved and glittered in the filtered morning sun, in perfect rhythm with the movement of the ocean. Julia began to drop faster, and pushed the air button on her BC vest lightly, slowing her descent. Below, she could see the rest of the class beginning to land in a clearing surrounded by boulders, air bubbles rising in columns from their regulators. Curious sea bass wandered in between them. She brought herself to a stop just over the sandy bottom and hovered there. Eva tapped her shoulder. Her face was pure white, as she nodded and put her thumb and forefinger into the "okay" sign. Then she waved her hand back and forth, signaling, "Let's swim around," and Julia followed. Sea cucumbers were perched on the boulders around them, and when Julia looked down, she saw a white starfish with more than twenty legs. She began counting them, when Rob appeared next to her, holding a flattened tennis ball in front of her face to demonstrate the pressure at a hundred feet. She nodded. It was like being on another planet. Feeling slightly giddy, she rolled around in somersaults. *This is what it's like to be in the other world!*

Then Eva tapped her on the shoulder and pointed her thumb to the surface. They rose slowly, Julia being careful to match Eva's ascent. When they reached fifteen feet they stopped for their three-minute decompression, releasing the air that had accumulated in their BC vests. Struggling to stay neutral at fifteen feet, she blew all the air out of her lungs and kept an eye on her dive computer. Getting bent on her first deep dive would be a total embarrassment. She glanced up at the surface, where several more inflatables had gathered, surrounded by the bottom halves of divers preparing to make their descents. Only thirty seconds more. Then Eva nodded and they rose, popping up a few yards away from their inflatable.

"That was awesome!" Julia exclaimed. Other heads began appearing around them.

"Unbelievable!" someone else yelled.

They motored back to shore and took off their equipment. Eva whispered to Julia, "You were doing really well, but I thought you might be getting *narked* when you started doing those somersaults."

"Well, I felt pretty good, but not completely goofy. I used to do somersaults underwater all the time when I was a kid."

As the class spread their lunches over the blankets on the beach and sat down, Rob announced, "Everybody passes the deep water dive. As a treat, we'll do the cave this afternoon." He pointed to the rocks on the north side of the cove, with a small opening in the center.

"All *right!*" Eva exclaimed. "You'll love this," she said to Julia. "You can swim through to the other side where there's a hidden cove."

A wall of fog was moving inland when Julia awoke from her nap. It would gobble up the sun in the next hour or so. She sat up and saw the rest of the group assembling their gear. Some other people from the dive shop were gathering driftwood to start a bonfire.

They suited up and finned out to the cave in a group, submerging themselves right by the entrance. Julia switched on her underwater flashlight. The walls were covered with mussels, starfish, anemones, and the occasional abalone. There was still enough daylight coming from each end to allow light in the water, although it seemed more like a twilight dive. Soon the cave was filled with divers moving slowly around, shining their lights and picking at things on the walls with their knives. Julia moved closer to examine a *nudibranch* stuck to the wall. The tiny, translucent sea slug with orange nodules stood bravely atop a scallop shell, waving with the motion of the water. As she moved her light around, the wall revealed more purple and orange starfish. Barnacles snapped shut as she passed, like the windows of a Lilliputian village. Then Eva gave her a nudge and motioned with her flashlight into the recesses of the wall. An octopus slithered into a crevice for cover. *It looks like a giant testicle!* Julia laughed out loud, right into her regulator, sending a shower of bubbles into the cave. *Erin would've loved that.* Then they swam out to the other side and came to the surface in a tiny cove surrounded by high crags of mussel-studded rock. Several more divers popped up around them. Eva took out her mouthpiece and said, "Isn't it amazing?"

"Stunning! After a while, it looks like everything is alive, watching you." Treading water, she looked up at the sky just as a pair of pelicans flew overhead.

"Beautiful, eh?" a man behind her remarked.

"Yeah…" Julia mused, turning around in the water. A man in a green mask smiled at her. She smiled back. He seemed familiar, but with hoods and masks covering most of their faces, not to mention the giant fish lips created by their regulator mouthpieces, most divers looked alike except for body shape and the colors of their gear.

"Let's go back down," Eva said. "We can check out the wall of this cove, and then go out through the cave again. Watch out for the sea urchins."

"Okay. Ready when you are." Julia put her mouthpiece back in and they bubbled down. Long, dark needles of the sea urchins sprouted from the sides of the cave, and Julia was careful not to step on any, recalling a chilling story Rob had once told about sitting on one. They explored the inside of the rock-enclosed cove, and then returned to the cave. It was darker now, and Julia could see the rest of the divers making their way out the other end. She shined her flashlight on the wall and studied the encrusted sea life as she went, peering into the crevices. When they reached the edge of the cave, she saw a scallop attached to the wall, and loosened it with her gloved hand. It was a small one, but when she turned around to show it to Eva, she was staring right into the face of a young sea lion, who promptly snatched the scallop from her hand and darted away. She could see Eva laughing inside her mask, emitting a spray of bubbles. They lingered in the cave for as long as their air held out, and then headed back.

"Maybe he knew you didn't have a fishing license," Eva said, when they surfaced.

"Yeah, they're probably trained by the local game warden," Julia laughed.

On the beach, Rob and the other dive masters had lit the bonfire and were warming themselves as the fog settled in. Julia and Eva swam back and sat on the edge of the shore, pulling off their fins.

"Need some help?"

Julia turned her head to see a man squatting next to her in a wetsuit, his salt and pepper hair still dripping. She was never one to decline help with her air tanks. "Sure," she said, unhooking her buoyancy vest. She had a feeling of déjà vu as the man lifted her dive gear from her back. She stood up and faced him, and there was a jolt of potent recognition between them. *He's the man in the little cove. But... there's something more.* She pulled off her neoprene hood and tried to straighten her hair.

"I'm sorry if this sounds like a cliché," he said, "but I have the feeling I know you from somewhere."

"Besides the cove a few minutes ago?" Julia joked, fearful that she might have sea-snot hanging from her nose. She wiped with the sleeve of her wetsuit.

"No... something more.... ancient."

"Are you from Santa Rosa?" she asked.

"No. I live here in Mendocino." He paused. "Where did you grow up?"

"Now, that's getting personal," Julia laughed, and then drew in her breath, staring at him. The wavy dark hair and five o'clock shadow suddenly came back into focus. "Oh, my God... you were a teacher in my high school!"

He nodded slowly. "Yeah... a couple lifetimes ago."

"And then you left to travel to... the Galapagos Islands or something, right?" A wave came in and lapped the edge of her fins, threatening to carry them out to sea. She bent over to pick them up.

"That's right. I'm bad about remembering names, though," he said.

"You're..." she paused. "...*Mr. Ohlman!* I... I bet I remember a dozen things about you!"

"Uh-oh."

"I'm Julia," she said, beginning to shiver.

"Paul. Let's go warm up next to the fire."

She turned to Eva, who nodded her head in Paul's direction and winked.

"This is amazing," Julia said, drying her hair with a towel as they sat by the bonfire.

"Yeah... of all the little coves in the world..." he said.

Their eyes locked. It felt as if there were a conduit of energy connecting them. Fog had blanketed the coast now, and misty lights glowed in the hills around Mendocino.

"Can I get some help?" Rob called from the inflatable at the shore.

"It's my class. I have to..."

Paul followed Julia and they helped carry the boat up the beach and load it onto a trailer.

Julia flashed on Mr. Ohlman sliding into a convertible next to a blonde woman. *Just stay open and see where it goes.*

As the beach began to grow dark, Paul said, "Would you consider giving me your phone number? I bet we have a lot to catch up on."

"I can't stop tingling," Julia said to Eva, on the ride back to Santa Rosa. "It's so unbelievable!" A harvest moon was beginning to emerge over the water, veiled by translucent fog. Julia felt suspended over the vastness of the ocean as they wound their way down through the curves on Highway 1.

Thirty-Eight

JULIA WOKE IN A DAPPLE OF EARLY SUMMER SUN. Paul was spooned up behind her with his arm draped over her waist. He stirred, and a shiver of anticipation ran through her body as his fingers slipped down, playfully diddling between her legs. She rubbed her backside against him, feeling him harden and tickle her cheeks. Then she rolled over and he wrapped his arms around her, covering her mouth in a long, tongue-swashing kiss. They rocked together, Paul entering and stroking her with delicious intensity. After a moment, he cradled Julia's butt in his arms and sat up, carrying her along. She wrapped her legs around him and they lap-danced for another few minutes until Julia shrieked with pleasure. Paul laid her back down and amped himself up one more time until he moaned with delight.

"What a great way to wake up," Julia said, licking the tiny drip of sweat that still quivered on the end of Paul's nose.

"An auspicious start to a curious vacation," he added, kissing her and rolling back over.

Seeing their opening, Joey and Bee leapt onto the bed and began prodding Julia for breakfast. She scratched their chins and told them, "Auntie Eva will be here at supper. She'll come and take care of you for five more *darks* after that," she reminded them, holding up one hand and counting each finger. "Then we'll be back."

Hours later, flying into the fading light of the east coast, Paul and Julia snuggled in their seats, leafing through a book with color plates of sea life. Together for more than six months, they basked in the relaxed comfort they shared. Their mutual attraction had been immediate. Conversation came naturally as well as silent ebbs, where they were able to sit back and sigh, savoring their good fortune. Of course, Julia had put him through her stealth eligibility tests. How much did he really drink? Did he interrupt her? Did he have a girlfriend stashed in every town from here to the Virgin Islands? Could he accept a woman with a black belt?

On the day she'd asked, he answered, "I don't mind having a surreptitious body guard at all. More importantly though, can you accept that about yourself in a relationship?"

"I guess. I mean, it does afford the luxury of being able to be myself with greater confidence than I had before. Besides, if I count the amount of times I've been thrown onto a mat and gotten back up again, it's probably around 175,000. That's a lot of humility."

One night she'd even lit candles and incense all over the house in an attempt to communicate with Erin. *"Just go ahead and snuff one out if you think this is wrong,"* she whispered, watching the smoke from a nearby sage stick curl upward. Nothing happened. Even Michael approved.

Julia loved the way Paul listened with genuine curiosity, waiting for her to finish her stories. His body was in great condition for a fifty year-old. Not rock-solid, but well lived-in. He'd published several books on marine restoration and survived a tumultuous, childless marriage early on, though not with the blonde in the red convertible. He had the thoughtful, focused intent of someone wanting his life to make sense. One evening as they lay wrapped around each other in his bathtub in Mendocino watching the meteor showers through an open skylight, Julia quietly surrendered, letting the love surge over her like an incoming tide.

Back on the plane, Paul pointed to a picture of a puffer fish. "Maybe if we're lucky we'll see one of these."

"As long as it doesn't gobble the ashes all at once," Julia whispered.

Teddy dozed in the row in front of them, exhausted by the drive down from Mt. Shasta that morning and his date the previous evening, which apparently went very well.

Streaking into the nighttime sky, they flew eastward on their way to Long Island for the scattering of her father's ashes. More than a year after his death, Julia, her brothers and Rose had finally decided to charter a boat in Pattituck Cove and drive it over to The Wreck. Julia would descend underwater accompanied by Paul and uncap the urn, letting the ashes disperse around Ed's favorite dive spot.

"You realize this is more for you than for him," Clarisse said. Still, understanding her children's need for closure, she offered her and Don's home for a buffet afterward, even including Rose.

Paul had contacted a local dive shop on the North Shore of Long Island, learning that The Wreck was broken apart by now, mostly devoured by sea life and salt. "At least the water's a lot clearer than it was a decade ago. It'll be fun. Besides, I'm due for a trip back east anyway."

The next day in Bayville, Clarisse and Don's house buzzed, packed with people and platters of food.

"Looks like last year all over again," Teddy remarked. "Except for the squirrels."

"*And* the chipmunk," Nate added.

Rose arrived accompanied by Phil, one of Ed's closest friends from AA. Julia watched in surprise as both her mother and Rose seemed to drop shields of resentment, giving each other a quick, perfunctory hug. Moments later, Julia exclaimed to Clarisse in private, "Mom! You guys were so cool about it."

"We talked on the phone the other night," Clarisse said. "It just seemed like old business to both of us. Besides, I said goodbye to your father a long time ago."

"This place sure changed," Teddy whistled the next morning when they drove up to the entrance of the marina in Pattituck Cove, now a full-fledged yacht club. Paul held the office door open for Rose and Julia. Nate and Uda followed, until their entire group filled the room, milling around and looking at the boating pictures on the walls.

"May I help you?" a voice squawked.

At a desk on the far side of the room sat Ceddie. Her hair was cut in a bob and frosted, and she wore a crisp navy pant-suit. Julia felt Erin chuckling in the background. *"See? God really does have a sense of humor."*

"We called about the charter," Nate said. "Last name is Lloyd."

Julia hung back behind Paul, trying not to double over with laughter.

Ceddie stiffened. She looked frail, hunched over the desk with Julia's relatives all gazing down at her.

"Hi, Ceddie," Julia said, stepping out from behind Paul.

"Hello… w-what happened to your own boat?"

Julia drew a breath to tell her to mind her own business when a wave of compassion permeated her. For all Ceddie's attempts at social climbing, it looked as if she'd been left behind to perform the duties of secretary at the marina. *She's still being her weird bitchy self, like she can't help it. That's just what she does. So what. There's no need to hammer her.*

"It broke its mooring in a storm and sank," Julia answered. "We're going to try and salvage some of the things that went down with it." She waited until she saw Ceddie's brow ruffle faintly as if she were trying to remember a recent storm, then drifted back to gaze at some old black and white photos of Oyster Bay. Paul, the one with an actual pilot's license, completed the paperwork for the charter.

"You brat," Paul teased on the way down the ramp, pinching her lightly on the butt.

"I just couldn't be mean to her. She looked fragile enough as it was."

Paul drove the small cabin cruiser out of the marina, past the cattail marshes. Even though the old corrugated metal fence had been replaced by a restaurant with a patio, people still fished from the edge.

"Look!" Julia exclaimed as they chugged past the bobbing channel markers. "There's the old nun and the can!"

The Sound glittered calmly in the morning sun.

"No wonder your father liked this so much," Rose remarked, staring at the boat's wake.

"He used to talk about his boat all the time," Phil added.

Paul gave Nate the wheel and joined Julia, who was assembling her dive gear.

"It looks pretty calm today," he said, pulling his wetsuit out of a duffle bag. "Besides that, The Wreck's only thirty feet down, so we can take our time and look around."

Julia nodded. She'd drifted back to that surreal time more than a year ago, when she couldn't believe what was happening. Her stomach churned and she took a deep breath, forcing herself not to cry.

"It takes about two years to get over the initial shock," Paul had told her, shortly after they met. He'd lost both parents more than a decade before.

"You mean to stop having a Dad or an Erin 'moment'?" she'd asked, referring to those times when a song or even the faint scent of Old Spice would send her into spasms of crying.

"Uh-huh."

She took a deep breath and focused on her equipment. She just wanted to get it over with.

"There's Matinecock Point!" Nate shouted as they passed the breakwater. "Everybody hold on to something!" He pushed the throttle forward and they sped up.

A few minutes later, he slowed down again as they neared the peninsula. "Remember how to do this?" he called to Teddy.

Paul stepped over. "You just press a button now," he said, pointing to a switch on the dashboard labeled "Anchor."

After the motors had been turned off, they sat in the cockpit and listened to the waves lapping at the hull.

"Well, it's not like he hasn't already gone," Rose said. Her chin quivered as she reached into a bag and drew out an extra large Oreo cookie tin.

There was a stunned silence, and then everyone burst out laughing.

"He just loved those," she said.

Everyone took turns petting the tin.

"He might get a charge out of winding up as fish food," Phil said, chuckling.

"Bye, Dad," Nate said, starting to cry.

"See 'ya," Teddy added.

Rose held a handkerchief to her nose and wept quietly.

Paul stood ready with his gear at the side of the gunwale. When Julia was ready, she came over and leaned against him for support, slipping on her fins and mask. Teddy put the cookie tin into her collecting bag and she rolled backwards over the side, plunging underwater. Paul dropped in next to her and they righted themselves, gave each other the "okay" sign and began their descent.

A moment later The Wreck came into view. It was a tatter of old wooden planks with the barest hint of a boat, but when they swam closer Julia could see traces of the rotted side wheel dissolving in the sand. She neutralized herself, hanging in the water over The Wreck, and reached into her bag for the tin. Paul hooked his arm through hers to hold her steady. *"No crying underwater,"* she imagined Ed saying as she pried open the lid. Water rushed in and ashes flew out in a simultaneous fury of bubbles and dust. Blackfish converged instantly by the dozens, nipping at the billowing particles that were once her father. Fully aware of the irony, Julia laughed, adding more bubbles to the fray. *What a great farewell party!* They watched for a few minutes, suspended over The Wreck until the fish frenzy subsided. Then Julia noticed a faint sparkle in the filtered sunlight, dancing on one of the planks. She moved toward it, hovering over the old ferry bits. On a lone, chipped board sat the moss-covered skeleton of a long serpentine creature, curled in a spiral. In its center lay one tiny pearl.

THE AUTHOR

L.J. Zinkand lives in Southern Oregon with her husband and five cats, who often ply her with tiny head-butts and licks.

www.ingramcontent.com/pod-product-compliance
Lightning Source LLC
Chambersburg PA
CBHW070222260626
47160CB00002B/646